"WHO HE?"

"WHO HE?"

by
ALFRED BESTER

WILDSIDE PRESS

DESIGNED BY WILLIAM R. MEINHARDT
Printed in the United States of America
By The Haddon Craftsmen Inc., Scranton, Penna.

"WHO HE?"

· CHAPTER I ·

EVERY MORNING I HATE TO BE born, and every night I'm afraid to die. I live my life within these parentheses, and since I'm constantly walking a tightrope over hysteria, I'm perceptive to the dilemmas of other people as they cross their own chasms.

I'm a script-writer by trade, specializing in mystery shows. I'm married to an actress. We're both of us second-raters in the entertainment business . . . mostly anonymous to the public, fairly well-known to our colleagues. Between us we make from ten to twenty thousand dollars a year, depending on the breaks. This is only fair money in our business.

It seems like a fortune to our families, and we dazzle them with our glamour. We hate this, but we can't dispel the illusion that General Sarnoff claps me on the shoulder and calls me by my nickname. Now we've given up trying. We realize that people want their friends to be glamorous, so we've stopped trying to avoid undeserved admiration. But I can't stand deception, and if I appear to be cynical in this story, it's because I'm leaning over

3

backwards to tell you the truth. As a matter of fact I'm the reverse of cynical . . . rather naive, in love with adventure and romance, with the moral and ethical standards of an Eagle Scout. This is all I intend telling you about myself, because the story isn't about me; it's about some tightrope walkers I know, and their strange adventures in this fantastic frontier town we natives call The Rock. The Rock, of course, is Manhattan Island, the only part of Greater New York that we consider to be the genuine New York; and in our business there is a very small society of natives born and raised on The Rock. You'd be surprised at how few there are.

The Rock is the roaring frontier of the new life we are all beginning to live, a life that is a terrifying mixture of the conscious and unconscious levels of our minds. It is new and terrifying because the unconscious depths which were concealed up to now, have become exposed, and participate openly in our everyday life, turning it into a savage, merciless war.

It's like those subway rides you take on trains that tunnel deep under the city, emerge abruptly into the daylight to roar past third-storey windows, and then plunge down into the lower levels again. So, when you meet people on The Rock, you never know when some unexpected turn will carry you up for a flashing glimpse through the windows of their souls, or down into the black depths of their hatreds and formless desires.

Adventurers from all over the world crowd into our town, just as fortune-hunters went west a century ago. In the old days in Denver and Fargo you fought for your life and your fortune, but in our frontier town you fight for your sanity as well. The drives and ambitions, the deep passions and compulsions, the blind search for symbols and compensations that bring the bandits to The Rock are naked and exposed, and this is where the danger lies. A man may declare war on you because you're a threat to his job, or merely because you're the symbol of a threat to his precarious stability. When you cross a street you never know whether you're going to be sandbagged by a thief's blackjack or a neurotic's nightmare.

The Rock is so wild and wide-open that nobody ever pretends to mask the deep chasms and smouldering fires in their lives. We carry our fears and fixations like naked weapons as we walk our tightropes, and we use them as quickly and murderously as Billy The Kid used his six-gun. The result is that we fight, love and adventure on all levels and never bother to distinguish reality from illusion because both are equally living and dangerous.

I'll try to separate fact from fancy in this adventure I'm going to tell you, but in the end I think you'll agree that it's unnecessary. Like the classic bartender in the classic Western, you'll duck behind the beer kegs at the first shot, whether it comes from a real gun or the explosive ferment in a man's mind. And don't imagine for a moment that this story is a plug for psychoanalysis. Whether you believe in analysis or not, you must admit that man, like the iceberg, is nine-tenths submerged. I'm simply going to describe what life is like in our frontier town where the submerged levels float up to the surface.

The locale of this story is a show I never worked. It's a TV variety clam-bake called "Who He?" . . . one of those lunatic mish-mashes that started out as a panel quiz show and ended up as a musical. It stars Mason & Dixon, supported by Kay Hill and Oliver Stacy. It's directed by Raeburn Sachs, written by Jake Lennox, with music by Johnny Plummer. It's produced by Melvin Grabinett Associates and costs the client, Mode Shoes, $50,000 a week.

"Who He?" is not an expensive show as TV variety shows go. It's in the middle bracket. I think you might be interested in a rough break-down on the budget which will give you some idea of the stakes for which the people in this adventure were fighting. The monetary stakes, that is. The network charges $25,000 for a half-hour of coast-to-coast time. Mig Mason, the star, gets $2,000 a week. Diggy Dixon, who is co-starred with him, doesn't get a nickel because Mason's a ventriloquist and Dixon is the dummy. Stacy, Kay Hill and other talent and specialties including the dancers get $3,000.

The writers, Jake Lennox and Mason's gagmen, split $1,500 between them. Lennox also gets a small cut in the producer's take for helping create the show. Incidentally, one of the gagmen got married for the first time on his forty-third birthday. The marriage broke up after two weeks. The bride went home to Canada and the gagman went down to Washington and became a spy for the government. We're still trying to figure it out. Maybe he decided that any tight rope, even an espionage tight rope, would be safer than the one he was on.

Raeburn Sachs gets $750 a week for directing "Who He?." How Sachs got started in the business is one of the great legends, and the only explanation for his weird public and private life. He was a stencil clerk in a Chicago advertising office, and one day he drove to work in a new Cadillac. He also wore new clothes and a new look. Everybody asked Ray if he'd robbed a bank. Chicago-type joke. Ray told them proudly that he'd written a hit tune called "Lumbago" or something like that.

Nobody ever heard of the tune. The office did a little detective work and discovered that "Lumbago" did exist, had truly been written by Ray, and had been recorded as a favor to him by a cousin who led a band working for a Chicago recording company. The gimmick was that there was another side to the record, the Flip, they call it, and Sinatra was on the Flip. Sinatra made the sales, but Ray shared the money. That made him a reputation and started him as a variety expert. He's been trying to justify that wrong Flip ever since.

Here's a little more budget: Johnny Plummer, married to the most exotically beautiful noodnick in the world, is allotted $1,500 a week for orchestra, copying and his own fee. The noodnick has standing orders to keep out of the theater because she disrupts the camera men, and camera time is counted like radium. Cameras and technicians cost $2,000. Sets and props cost $3,000. Special effects like rain, snow, Acts of God and Rear-Projection cost $500. The producer, Mel Grabinett (Mr. Blinky to his enemies; he has no friends) takes $3,000 which he cuts up with Jake Lennox and Ned Bacon who developed "Who He?" with him. Jake and Ned get two and a half bills each. That's $250. Borden, Olson and Mardine, the advertising agency representing the client, adds 15% of the gross cost of the show for agency fee, and that plus prize money and incidentals comes to $50,000 a week to demonstrate the superior quality of Mode Shoes.

Some forty hard-working, variously talented people put together "Who He?" every week . . . artists, technicians and business men. Each of them is walking his own private tightrope, but all of them must walk the communal tightrope of the show on Sunday night at nine o'clock before 37 million viewers. The individual pressures added to the common tension of the show make it seem inevitable that the program will blow up during rehearsal and never get on the air. Yet "Who He?" has appeared 39 weeks in succession without mishap. Without mishap, that is, until the performance on New Year's night.

It was one of those nightmares. Everyone who saw the show knew something was wrong. Mig Mason performed so badly that you could see his mouth twitch and his neck muscles jerk during the ventriloquist routines with the dummy. Oliver Stacy handed out the wrong prizes. Johnny Plummer missed his cues. Floor managers and stagehands wandered dazedly before the cameras. The dancers went through the production numbers as though they expected the roof to collapse at any moment. *Variety* happened to catch the show that night and murdered it.

Variety was unfair. Their reviewer should have checked first. He would have learned that the show went out the window because one man fell off his private tightrope with such a disastrous jar that everyone else was shaken. He would have discovered that less than five feet of sight-line saved the theater audience and the

TV viewers from the spectacle of a dead man hanging by the neck from the iron grid above the stage.

For twenty-nine minutes and thirty seconds, stars, actors, dancers and technicians went through the motions of playing "Who He?" under a corpse with starting eyes and swollen tongue . . . a victim of the savage, merciless warfare in our frontier town, murdered by the ferment in a man's mind.

I knew the corpse. I know what killed him. I'm still friendly with most of the cut-throats who watched him die. I've spoken to them, questioned them, and heard what they couldn't say as well as what they said. I've pieced out all the strands that wove themselves into a rope around a man's neck. This is the story of what happened. . . .

· CHAPTER II ·

JAKE LENNOX HAD BEEN
fighting a losing battle with himself for ten years, and it was a
struggle he had never been aware of. The two levels of his mind
hated each other and were tearing him apart. Jake had a conscious ideal, the model of the man he wanted to be . . . austere,
kindly, infallible, sophisticated. Like many of us, he suffered from
the Mignon Complex. He was bitterly ashamed of his background. He had had a squalid childhood as the son of a drunken
Long Island clam-digger, and would have liked to awaken one
morning to discover that he was really the second son of the
Marquis of Suffolk.

But deep down inside, Jake was a hell of a rowdy guy; full of
laughter and boisterous energy, yearning for ribald friends and a
burning girl he could love and marry and riot in bed with. He
was not aware of this. He believed in the conscious image of what
he wanted to be. And while the lusty passions within him fought
to overturn and destroy the world he had made for himself, his
conscious mind was fighting desperately to hold it together.

9

Occasionally the conscious mind gave way, which is why Jake Lennox awoke on Christmas night in the role of another man. He was convinced that he was Mr. Clarence Fox from Philadelphia. I got this story from Jake and from Aimee Driscoll when I went up to her apartment to claim Jake's overcoat and precious gimmick book. Jake couldn't face Aimee again. She represented the turmoil inside him which he could not acknowledge.

Aimee (how about that name?) is a blonde with a poached face and the fattest behind and bosom in the hustling racket. If you looked at her through a gin bottle you might imagine that she was a busty Swedish acrobat, which was what betrayed Jake. There are front-men and rear-men, Aimee kindly explained to me, and she parlays both into a lovely living. Mr. Clarence Fox was an All-Around Camper.

He awoke, still drunk and still bloody from the brawl in Ye Baroque Saloon where he had acquired Aimee. He wore his underwear and was cramped into an overstuffed sofa and covered with a gritty Navajo blanket. It was dark. Lennox let out a roar that slid into a ballad which he'd composed the night before and with which he'd been injuring ears ever since.

Aimee heard the racket, ran into the living room and turned on the lights. Lennox winced, closed his eyes, and sneezed three times in stately waltz tempo.

"Less light," he muttered. "A switch on Goethe. I am excessively educated, and all by hand. Need more crud in my blood." He began to roar again.

"Stop that noise, Clarence!" Aimee called from the door. "Stop that goddam singing."

Lennox finished the ballad which included every dirty word he knew. Seventeen, by actual count.

"And stop talking dirty," Aimee told him primly. She was wearing a bra, panties and high black net stockings; not, she pointed out, in hopes of arousing the beast in Mr. Fox. It was her conventional uniform. As a matter of fact she knew he was still drunk and hoped he wouldn't start anything. She waddled to the sofa and bent over Mr. Fox solicitously. He had been very generous to her even though her professional services had not yet been requested. Mr. Fox stared up at her bursting cleavage, then suddenly thrust his heavy hand down into it.

"The All-Mother," Lennox laughed.

He hurt her. Aimee squawked and jerked back. Lennox held on to the bra and tore it away. He began to cheer: "Brah! Brah! Brah!" waving the bra like a college pennant.

"You goddam lousy bum!" Aimee screamed. "You're mean. You're mean dirty drunk. I never liked you from the beginning, you goddam lousy son of a—"

"No, no," Lennox protested. "An act of admiration. 'Fair is my love, for April's in her face, her lovely breasts September claims his part . . .' Poem by R. Greene. Speaks for C. Fox."

He lurched up from the sofa, captured Aimee and clutched her reverently. He pressed his face between her breasts. He had not shaved in a day and a half, and his beard was excruciating. Aimee fought and twisted and thrust him away. Lennox straightened and rocked like a high mast.

"'But Cold December dwelleth in her heart,'" he mumbled sorrowfully. "Where's the woman who'll give passion with the sweetness of virgins and the lunacy of whores? You give, Aimee, but you taste like money." He staggered, tripped on a mass of cardboard and wrapping paper, and fell heavily into a three-foot Christmas tree that expired with a jingle and pop.

Aimee burst out laughing. She was revenged. Lennox arose in a fury, seized the Christmas tree by the butt and beat it savagely against the wall. Aimee protested. He leaped toward her and lashed her across the high fat buttocks. Aimee screamed. Lennox slipped and bruised himself on a solid square object covered with tissue paper. He clutched it.

"You leave that alone, Clarence," Aimee yelled. She forgot all other outrages and ran across the room. She clawed at Lennox and tried to pull him off. The tissue paper tore away.

"What'r you protecting? Virginity?" Lennox growled.

"It's the Christmas present you gimme. You bought it last night. Don't you bust it!"

Lennox peeled away tissue paper to reveal a dark wood console and a twelve inch TV screen.

"The Monster!" he cried. "The One-Eyed Beast!" He hammered the top of the set with his fists. Aimee fought him helplessly, then darted away and returned with an empty quart beer bottle. She swung it with both hands and clubbed Lennox across the back of the neck. He fell forward into the rubbish like a tackle throwing a rolling block. He was the size of a tackle.

Lennox climbed to his feet, his throat working convulsively. "Bathroom," he croaked. He was sick. Aimee knew the symptoms well, and no vendetta was worth another cleaning bill. She turned Lennox around and pushed him competently through a narrow door into the small bedroom and then into the bathroom. She turned on the light, flipped up the toilet lid and with the skill of long experience, bent his head down to the bowl. Then she backed out and slammed the door.

During the preliminary moment of agony, Lennox thought: "They play Boys' Rules. Oh Virgins! Respectables! Learn from them—" Then the purge began.

When the heaving stopped, Lennox straightened painfully, flushed the toilet, then examined his face in the mirror. To him it was the face of Mr. Clarence Fox, the visiting Quaker from Philadelphia. His cropped hair was still sleek; nothing could ever muss it. But his dark eyes had heavy purple shadows around them, and his lined face was bruised.

He was purged, still drunk, but beginning to sober. He staggered to the bedroom, found his clothes neatly hung in a closet, and dressed. He went out into the living room. Aimee had straightened it. She wore a white housecoat blemished by green and scarlet petunias, and was kneeling alongside the new television set plugging it into a wall outlet.

"If you got any on the floor you better clean it up," she said icily.

"Merry Christmas," he answered. "Happy to pay for damage to life and limb."

Lennox reached into his pocket, took out his wallet and was fingering through it for money when his eye noticed the identification card.

"This isn't my wallet," he said.

"What?"

Lennox plucked at his shirt dubiously. "Not my clothes either."

"What are you talking about, Clarence? Them's your clothes."

Aimee switched on the set and fiddled with the controls.

"No. Not mine. Belong to somebody else. Character named Lennox."

"Who?"

He extended the wallet for Aimee to examine. "My name's Fox. Clarence Fox from Philadelphia. This is Jordan Lennox, says here. See? Jordan Lennox. How'd he get into the act?"

The screen ignited, herringboned, then sprang into life. The blast of Johnny Plummer's orchestra filled the room with bright expectation. A Main-Title card displayed white comedy letters against a cartoon background while the voice of Oliver Stacy read it with frenetic sell: "THE MODE SHOW . . . STARRING MIG MASON AND DIGGY DIXON . . . PLAYING—'WHO HE?'"

"Who He!" Aimee called over the burst of studio applause. "I love that program. I get every question right. I could make a fortune if I could get on." She backed up, feeling for a chair, her eyes fixed on the screen.

Jake Lennox's consciousness ignited, herringboned, then sprang into life.

" 'Who He!' " he burst out, stunned and bewildered. "That's my show."

Clarence Fox stole back to Philadelphia.

"That's my show," Lennox repeated.

"How do you mean, your show?"

"I write it. I own a piece of it."

"That's a hot one," Aimee laughed.

"Don't you understand? It's my show. I'm Jake Lennox. I write that—I— What the hell am I doing here? I'm supposed to be at the theater."

Lennox turned and stumbled out of the apartment. He clattered down the brownstone stairs and fell half a flight. It was bitter cold on the street. Snow and rain were falling, and the air was like ice-water. Lennox ran west to 3rd Avenue, the great exposed nerve of The Rock's delirium. It was empty. The bars exuded urine-colored light. The antique shops blazed with cut-glass chandeliers. Alongside him, a darkened barber-pole still revolved its red and white spiral with the sound of guillotines.

A small man in a derby, pea-jacket and white duck trousers passed him and addressed him brightly: "Hiya, Dan. Nice to see you again." The man in the derby continued up 3rd Avenue greeting empty doorways in friendly tones: "Hello, Jerry. Long time no see . . . Hiya, Pete? How's the family? Glad to see you, Ed." Lennox stared at him, then saw a cab, ran for it and leaped inside.

"Gotham four one thousand," he called to the driver. He shook his head. "No. That's the backstage number. I— Let's take it from the top. Venice Theater. 50th and Sixth. I'm in a rush, Mr. . . . ." He tried to focus on the license card above the glass partition. It would be considerate to call the man by his name instead of Mac or Bud. His eyes bleared and he gave it up.

He sat on the edge of the seat, terrified by his abrupt return to sanity, fighting to recapture the Lennox he admired and wanted to be . . . the sober Lennox, the second son of the Marquis

14

of Suffolk. He found his wristwatch in his jacket pocket and put it on. Nine-three. Mig Mason would be starting the first Mason & Dixon spot on the show. What was it this week? The football routine. Mason in moleskins. The dummy under a sheet. *What football player made ghosts famous? For five hundred dollars, Who He? Red Grange. That's ab-so-lute-ly* CORRECT! (Applause). Lennox began to shake.

"What's happened?" he muttered. "Where've I been? I'm in a panic. Why, for five hundred dollars?"

Lennox sorted through his shattered memory of the past twenty-four hours. He was afraid to unearth, uncover, reveal; yet compelled, like a man exploring the pain of an aching tooth. The fragments were incomprehensible and crumbled under the most delicate touch. A Chinese face appeared, then faded. A series of meaningless explosions sounded like a vanishing execution squad. There was a knot. A gleaming African smile. The knot again. A brass-bound staff and the brazen uproar of gongs. A knot. A target. A knot.

"And fear," Lennox said. "Fear. For God's sake, I was drunk, that's all. Nothing more. Why am I afraid? What've I done?"

He examined his wallet. Twenty three dollars left out of four hundred. How much had gone for that television set bought for the blonde . . . What was her name? Anna? Mamie? Bought for her by a Quaker. Mr. . . . Who was it? Charles something? Claude? Lennox winced and shook his head. The memory was going . . . going . . . like the streets disappearing under the sleet. Twenty four hours, and nothing but veiled patches left. A Quaker. A blonde. A knot.

"Christ," he prayed. "Dear Christ stand by me. Stand by me now."

Lennox discovered he was crying. He was outraged. An austere, kindly, infallible, sophisticated man didn't weep. It was that other character he was forgetting with sickening speed . . . a lurid, roaring, shameful savage. He pounded his fists together, then looked again at his watch. Nine-seven. Oliver Stacy and Kay Hill in the first song spot. Stacy dressed in sheik's robes singing to Kay wearing an English riding habit and making like Agnes Ayres. *For seven hundred and fifty dollars what famous actor was the first famous sheik? Who He? Rudolph Valentino. (Applause). Play-off from orchestra and segue into Intro for drama spot.*

The cab jammed in traffic at 42nd and Vanderbilt, and again at Madison. Lennox resisted the impulse to thrust his head out the window and roar at the hacks and busses. He fought for control. Nothing remained from the lost night but a Quaker, a blonde, a knot and terror. He turned his back on the fragments and the fear and clung to the framework of the world he knew. He was Jordan Lennox who owned a piece of and wrote most of "Who He?" He had never won a Pulitzer Prize but he had never been less than a contract writer in his life. He had never auditioned for a job in his life. He had never been fired from a job in his life. In ten years of brawling and knifing his way up in the business he had never lost a fight.

"No, by God!" he said suddenly. "What have I got to be afraid of? They're all afraid of me."

When he got out of the cab at the stage door he was no longer tremulous. He was again the Jake Lennox we all knew, sardonic, hostile, unyielding. He poked a dollar at the driver for the fare, and another dollar for a present. "Merry Christmas, Mac," he said, not unkindly, and walked into the theater. His feet left black prints on the sidewalk. The city too was covered with sleet.

It was 9:31-30. The show was two minutes off the air. Lennox pushed through the crowd of wives and friends that crammed the backstage corridor and reached the wings. Instantly, he halted. He smelled trouble, and the prospect recharged him with energy. He stared around with quick, guarded eyes.

The house was emptying out. The two glass control booths at the back of the orchestra were filled with gesticulating agency men who might or might not be berating Raeburn Sachs, the director, and Sol Eggleston, the network camera-director. Jake's nostrils dilated. The stage was in a turmoil. Six dancers in snow-crystal costumes dashed past him with their duck-footed gait, whispering nervously.

"Angie . . . Flo . . . Ruthanna!" Lennox called. They were his favorite pipe-lines to the backstage. They glanced at him with frightened eyes, looked away and scampered up the iron stairs to the dressing rooms on the balcony overlooking the stage. In a corner book-fold set representing Santa's workshop, Oliver Stacy was snarling at Kay Hill, a thin, attractive girl with acid eyes and a slack mouth.

The camera crews and stagehands were striking equipment and sets in silence. There was no chatter or laughter despite the fact that the Grabinett office had slushed them with Christmas graft and it smelled as though the graft had been sampled. Lennox turned and looked across the house to the right boxes where the musicians' platform was built, searching for his friend, Sam Cooper, the rehearsal pianist. The musicians were leaving. Sam was nowhere in sight. Lennox mustered himself for another fight. Carrying his naked weapons ready for quick murder, he strode to the star dressing room on stage, knocked once and entered, prepared for attack or defense.

The star stood in scarlet Santa costume with half a beard cling-ing to his lantern jaw. Mig Mason was thin, dark, young, with a good hairline and a bad nose-job. He was sobbing hysterically. His wife, Irma, in a mink coat, wearing Christmas orchids, a bad platinum dye and a good nose-job, was trying to soothe him. The producer, Mel Grabinett, blinking and jerking, was roaring at Tooky Ween, Mason's agent. Diggy Dixon, the dummy, in gnome's costume, sprawled on the dressing table alongside the door and regarded the scene with a wooden grin.

"I don't care how much you're worth," Grabinett stuttered.

17

"I don't care how much goddam billing you handle. What the hell are you trying to do? Bury my show?"

"What are you trying to do?" Ween rumbled. "Bury my property?"

"It ain't bad enough you gouge my budget for three grand. Three Almighty Grand for that special skyscraper set so he can crawl around like a cowardy cockroach and drop the dummy and turn my show into a trappisty—"

"I told you I had to have three hours' rehearsal on camera," Mason shrieked.

"He had to have three hours," Irma said.

"But then he has to bitch the telephone contestant!" The producer's face twitched hideously. "She give him the right answer. Kris Kringle, she said. My operator was monitoring that Kansas call. She heard it. The dame give the right answer."

"She did not," Mason cried. "Tell him, Tooky. The right answer was St. Nicholas."

"The right answer was St. Nicholas," Irma said.

"It was Kris Almighty Kringle, you no-talent son of a—"

"Lay off!" Ween broke in. He glared at Grabinett. "Lay off my property. You ain't just talking to talent. He's a star."

"The question," Grabinett told the star with exaggerated calm, "was: You seen me play the part of Santa Claus in our comedy sketch. Now, for five thousand dollars, can you tell us another name for Santa Claus. That was the question. And she give the right answer. Kris Kringle. But no, you said. Sorry, you said. That's not right. Thank you. Merry Christmas. And you hung up the phone and hung me up with the FCC. That dame's husband is a lawyer. He called back before we went off the air. He's so goddam mad he's suing us for fraud. He's suing the network." Grabinett's voice broke in agony. "He's suing the client. The client!"

"The answer was St. Nicholas," Mason shouted.

"It was Kris Almighty Kringle!"

18

Lennox could have backed out and disappeared unnoticed; instead he thrust the dressing room door wide. The knob struck the dummy and knocked it to the floor. Everyone twisted around and saw him. Instantly they seemed to close ranks. Even the dummy shifted its eyes malevolently. Lennox looked them over insolently, daring them to attack. They attacked.

"Ask him!" Mason cried. "Ask him! He wrote it. He's supposed to know all the answers. The Thinker!"

"It's his fault," Irma said.

"Where the hell you been?" Grabinett blurted. "You know what happened? If you'd been around tonight we wouldn't be in this jam."

"You got one hell of a nerve writing a lousy show like this for my property," Tooky Ween growled. "I want a new writer hired."

"You don't need a writer," Lennox snapped. "You need an education. And don't try to rap me for that skyscraper fiasco. F-I-A-S-C-O. I voted for Rear-Projection at the conference."

"You can't get laugh values with projection," the agent rumbled. "You got to pin-point my boy on a genuine set."

"And what happened on the genuine set?" Lennox eyed Mason coldly. "You dropped the dummy? For laugh values?"

"They never gave me a chance to rehearse the chimney," Mason wept. "When I got halfway down with the bag of presents and I say to Diggy: Hey Diggy! This ain't the right chimney. It smells wrong. And Diggy says . . ."

From the floor the dummy cackled: "Better get your paddle out, Mig. You're up the creek."

Lennox scowled. "I told your gagmen not to use that. We agreed to cut it." He enlisted Grabinett. "You backed me up, Mel. Yes?"

"Yeah," Grabinett answered. He too scowled at Mason.

"But it's the best boffola in the routine. When I did it on the Oddfellows show last year they—"

19

"Used it last year? You swore the Santa sketch was an original." Lennox attacked Tooky Ween. "You guaranteed Mason would use nothing but original material on this show. Fact?"

"Listen," Ween began to explain, "My boy is—"

"Your boy is going to lay a suit for breach of contract in your lap if you don't watch him."

"It was so strictly original," Mason protested hysterically. "Last year we did it like a chimney sweeper and his helper. We—"

"And next year it'll be a burglar and his friend. What happened tonight in the two thousand dollar chimney? Two, Mel?"

"Three!" Grabinett howled. "Three thousand bucks so he could get his pants full of nails and drop the dummy trying to ungoose hisself. It was a trappisty!"

"Who'd he drop it on, Tooky?"

"Who cares who?"

"Mel and I care. We're still trying to find a laugh in that sketch."

"I care on who." Irma raked Ween with her eyes. "Happens he dropped Diggy on me. My head."

Lennox kept his face straight. "Did it get a laugh?"

"Nobody saw. I was behind the set."

"Cuing him from the script," Grabinett sputtered. "He didn't even know his lines."

"If you don't like my boy, you know what you can do," Ween told him.

"There's co-operation for you," Lennox said bitterly. "What does he have to lose, Mel? He's got a network contract for his boy. Two thousand a week guaranteed, work or no work. What does he care about the show?" Lennox looked at Mason sympathetically. "But you ought to care, Mig. It won't do you any good to go off and lose your fans while Tooky collects his ten percent."

"Fifteen," Mason snapped.

"Oh? Three bills a week out of you? For what? Watching? Advising? Protecting? No. 'If you don't like my boy, you know what you can do.' Agents!"

"What the hell are you trying to parlay?" Ween demanded.

"I think you're looking for an excuse to get out of the show," Lennox answered. "You're trying to duck the Kansas lawsuit. Your property got Mel into this jam. Now you want out so he'll have to face it alone."

"They'll never get away with it," Grabinett shouted. "Neither of you both. You got me into this. You're stuck with it."

"St. Nicholas!" Mason cried. "St. Nicholas!"

"Yeah? Show me where it says in the contract," Ween answered. "It ain't our headache. It's yours."

"Then how would you like it if I handed you a real genuine headache, Mr. Ween? Something I had been protecting your Almighty property from." Grabinett blinked ominously. "A nice little headache waiting for your boy up at the office in a blue envelope. Number six, it is."

"What?" Lennox exclaimed. "Another one, Mel?"

"Yeah. Another one. It come special delivery this morning. What a sweet Christmas card! Wait'll you read it, Jake. It got me so scared, I— Wait'll Mig reads it."

"What's this? What's this?" Tooky Ween said angrily. "You been holding out on my property's fan mail?"

"Not any mail he wants to read. Some elegant letters in blue envelopes which—"

"Mel! Hold the phone," Lennox interrupted. "We decided we weren't going to mention those letters to anyone. Are you going to blow it?"

"It's already busted wide open. If Kansas don't take us off the air, them letters will." Grabinett shook his fist at Ween. "Threatening letters which come addressed to 'Dear Who He' and signed 'Guess Who' and they'll curl the hair off all his property, including that atom bomb shelter he built in Westchester and this no-talent dummy-dropper."

"Cut out them insults," Ween said furiously.

"Cut out them grammar," Lennox murmured. Having turned the united front back into civil war, he felt secure again; in full control of the situation, austere and infallible. But the news about the letter was alarming. It was another attack to be met . . . a vicious, anonymous onslaught, far more dangerous than the threatened lawsuit.

"I been trying to protect my show," Grabinett continued passionately to Tooky Ween. "I been trying to protect your lousy artiste so he could earn his two yards and get us a rating, but if you're gonna rat on me, then I'll—"

"Why don't you leave me alone?" Mason screamed. "What are you trying to do? Murder me? Leave me alone!"

He scooped up the dummy, thrust past Lennox and dashed out of the dressing room. The others stared in astonishment, then all four ran after the star. Mason was at the prop table. He snatched up a ski-pole and veered out on the naked stage, whirling the pole over his head, making whimpering sounds. He smashed the single work-light hanging down from the grid, and the stage was in darkness. Irma screamed. Grabinett groaned. Tearing noises came from the back wall where the struck sets were stacked. Lennox took over.

"Angie! Flo! Ruthanna!" he shouted. His favorites heard him. They opened their dressing room door and came out on the balcony. The stage was flooded with dilute light from overhead.

"What is it, Jake? What's the matter?"

"Keep that door open. We need light," Lennox answered. He called to the star: "Mig, don't be a fool! If you want to break something, your agent's right here."

Mason stopped ripping the flats apart, dropped the ski-pole, turned and ran wildly behind the master switchboard in the left wings. An instant later they heard the clatter of his feet ringing down iron steps. They pursued him down the spiral stairs to the huge dressing room under the stage where six naked ballet boys in half makeup were standing and staring in bewilderment.

"Excuse us, ladies," Lennox called. "Where's Mig?"

They pointed to a heavy bulkhead door just oozing shut.

"Jesus Almighty," Grabinett moaned. "He's down in the cellar."

"Find the electrician," Lennox told him. "Tooky, get a flashlight. Irma, you wait here."

Lennox went through the cellar door, stumbled down an endless zig-zag flight of concrete steps, clinging to the rail. He came to the bottom of the steps, lost his grasp on the rail and was lost in blackness.

"Mig!" he shouted.

There was no answer.

"Mig! Come back. It was St. Nicholas."

He fumbled in his pockets for matches, listening for the sound of footsteps. He heard faint echoes far ahead, and ran forward, meanwhile pulling a book of matches out and trying to light one. "What a Christmas," he muttered and blundered against a wall with a stunning impact. The matches flew from his hand. He clung to the wall, waiting for the crashing in his head to subside.

"Tooky! Mel!" he called. "Hurry up with the lights!"

There was no answer. There was no light.

"There must be an easier way to earn a living," he told himself and began to grope blindly.

Suddenly he lost control again. For the second time in that monstrous day he was attacked by panic. It was inexplicable and gut-chilling.

"No," he said. "No. Please."

He was blacked-out and could not withstand this second blow. He began to wilt and fight for breath. The mass of the theater overhead pressed down on him, slowly collapsing, painfully

23

crushing. He clawed at the wall and searched feebly for the stairs. He turned a corner, another, a third. He was lost forever. A hard hand thrust into his neck. Lennox cried out and jerked his arm up. He was struck savagely across the forearm by something stiff and wooden. He backed away from this menace and blundered into a jagged field of metal bones that rattled and clashed. Lennox sagged to his knees and cried shamelessly. That was how Sam Cooper found him half an hour later; kneeling in a cellar storeroom amidst overturned music stands, sobbing before an imperious wooden Indian.

Without a word, Cooper pulled Lennox to his feet, brushed him off and led him back to the cellar stairs. His flashlight played erratically on the glistening tunnels and rotting wooden doors. In the days of past glory, the Venice had been one of the big musical houses and its vaults were stuffed with the jetsam of ancient hits: Congo masks, Hessian boots, racks of tarnished costumes, ear-trumpets, Civil War muskets, an entire Merry-Go-Round with peeling poles and blind horses.

"Love to steal them and deal them out to Mig's audience some night," Cooper murmured.

"The guns?"

"The ear-trumpets."

Cooper helped Lennox up the concrete stairs. As he thrust open the bulkhead door, he said: "Easy. Gone home. The dancers."

"Get reporters," Lennox said. "I found Judge Crater."

They entered the empty dressing room which was still lit. Cooper sat Lennox down before a bulb-ringed mirror, handed him a box of cleansing tissue and a comb. Lennox cleaned himself wearily and pretended to comb his hair. Cooper lit a cigarette and thrust it between Jake's lips.

"I don't smoke," Lennox said, handing it back.

"You smoke when you're plastered."

"I'm not plastered."

24

"It says here." Cooper took a drag. "They've got an old Bechstein Grand in that cellar," he said softly. "I'm going to take your tape recorder down some night and break it up with an axe. The Bechstein. Could sell a dub to every pianist in town. Wish fulfillment."

"Do me a favor," Lennox said.

"Name it."

"Break up the wooden Indian on the Flip."

"I thought that was Judge Crater."

"I thought it was Kris Kringle," Lennox said somberly, fingering his neck. Suddenly he asked: "Where's Mason? Dead?"

"Went under the cellar. Came up the other side. Went back to his dressing room and doing very well I hear."

Lennox grunted thrice in anguish. Cooper eyed him solemnly in the mirror. His face wore a permanent expression of perplexity. He was tall, compact, with strong hands, high cheekbones and deep-set narrow eyes. He had the well-scrubbed Princeton look, and as a matter of fact had been a big wheel in Triangle shows before he broke into television. He was a mediocre song-writer and a magnificent rehearsal pianist, which is a high art unappreciated outside the business.

Cooper and Lennox had been close friends for over three years, and for the past ten months Sam had been sharing Lennox's apartment. When Lennox invited him, Sam had moved in his grand piano, seventeen copper pots, one hundred and thirteen record albums, a complete Hi-Fi sound system, two Siamese cats, and a mink-dyed skunk. He'd said: "Gosh, fellows, let's room together all through school." They were still together, despite the skunk.

"Great God on echo!" Lennox said after a long pause, "I think I'm on my way to the booby hatch."

"Oh? Why the hell did you go charging down there? For Mig?"

"I was playing the scene."

"Rover Boys to the rescue. Which were you? Fun-loving Tom?"

"No. Noodnick Jake. And then I lost hold. . . ."

"On Mig?"

"Myself. You saw me down there . . ." Lennox winced in shame. "Hysterical."

"Maybe you're afraid of the dark."

"I wish it were something nice and simple like that; but the cellar was just the pay-off on something worse. I . . . When did you see me last?"

"Yesterday. After rehearsal. You went out for a drink with Avery Borden," Cooper answered promptly.

"I remember that. I remember the drinks. Then—I didn't sleep home last night?"

"Not last night. No."

"Christ, stand by me!" Lennox muttered.

Cooper looked bewildered. "You've slept out before. Why the production? What plays?"

"I've lost a day," Lennox said slowly. "I don't know where I was or what I was doing from nine last night to nine tonight."

"Um. Loaded?"

"Looks like."

"Smells like. What were you drinking? Caveat Emptor Reserve?"

"I've got a feeling that I did something dirty . . . Something that's going to shock hell out of me if I ever find out . . . Something as dark as that cellar. Maybe that's why I blew down there."

"You're not the dirty type, Jake."

"But I'm scared. I— You know those newsreels where they dynamite a smoke-stack?"

"Yep. Always comes after the Miami water-skis. They play suspense-type music in two-four."

"I feel like that moment just before everything collapses. But what blew up, Sam? What happened?"

26

"You think something blew up between tonight and last night?"

"I know it. That must be why I blacked out. I can remember . . . I can remember a Quaker and a blonde. . . ."

"Quaker? Man from Philadelphia?"

"Yes. A Quaker and a blonde and a knot."

"Blond woman?"

"I think so."

"What kind of knot?"

"What kind could there be?"

"Dozens. The kind you tie, like hangman's knot. How fast a ship goes. A knot in wood. A knot in palmistry. A knot in—"

"You're no help. I can't remember. Just a Quaker and a blonde and a knot. It's crazy. Why'm I shaking like this?" Lennox tried to control himself. His eyes burned with tears. "Look at me. Jake Lennox, leader of men, crying like a fag."

"You know something," Cooper told him solemnly. "On you it's becoming. Makes you human."

"Human!" Lennox burst out in contempt, grinding his eyes with his knuckles.

"You need a bath and some food," Cooper said firmly. "Leave us go home. On your feet, Beaver Patrol. Watch it! You've got your hand in something."

"Robust Juvenile No. 4," Lennox muttered, peering at the makeup jar.

"Robust and juvenile men . . . Forward!"

They left the dressing room, turned out the lights and mounted the spiral staircase. A new worklight had been hung from the iron grid high above the stage. Mason's dressing room was open and an informal party was in progress. Mason had the dummy in one hand and a bottle in the other. He was going through a comedy routine while Grabinett, Ween, Irma and a dozen others shrieked with laughter.

As Cooper and Lennox passed the door, the dummy cackled:

27

"Ah! The Thinker and the poor man's Paderoosky. Merry Christmas, boys."

Lennox pulled to a stop despite Cooper's urging. "Peace on earth, good will to all men," he answered savagely. "For five thousand dollars can you tell us what it means?"

Grabinett, Ween and Mason glared at Lennox with hatred. He scowled back and then permitted Cooper to lead him to the stage door. As they plunged out into the sleet, he growled: "I'll fight."

"Who?"

"I don't know . . . but I'll fight. I'll go down fighting, and I won't go down."

· CHAPTER III ·

THE LENNOX APARTMENT
was on Knickerbocker Square which is one of scores of hidden
relics of the past concealed on The Rock. There are elongated
sycamore trees corseted with cement, a Greek cross of gravel
paths, four square patches of grass, and a black and brass fence
surrounding all. The houses facing the square are red stone
Dutch style with copper roofs, bottle windows and glass oran-
geries in the rear. The old night lanterns and polished stone carriage posts are still standing. Lennox occupied a floor and a
quarter in Number 33.

You entered from the street into the kitchen, decorated with
Cooper's cooking utensils and garish butcher charts he had
charmed out of an influential meat-packer in Grosse Pointe.
There was also a lunatic side-arm Oliver typewriter which he
had charmed out of a Brooklyn druggist. It wrote in minims and
other pharmaceutical symbols, and Cooper typed recipes on it.
He once sent me one that read like Witch's Brew. Turned out
to be Fruit Soup.

Past the kitchen, through a short hall lined with cupboards, you came into the living room. It was forty feet long with high windows looking out on a rear garden, and had evidently been enlarged from two smaller rooms because there were two fireplaces on the right wall. On the left was the door to Cooper's bedroom, the door to the bath, and a narrow flight of steps leading up to the other quarter floor Lennox had. This was a second bedroom and study where Lennox slept and worked.

The living room contained Cooper's piano, his Hi-Fi system, his records and his two Siamese which hunted in pack. The mink-dyed skunk had conceived a passion for the bathtub and only came out grudgingly when the shower was turned on. Lennox had four or five hundred books in walnut breakfront cases and a pair of butterfly wing chairs to which he was devoted and over which he waged relentless war with the Siamese who well knew how to punish him when he offended them.

There was an Italian couch before one fireplace, which was kept practical, as we say in the business, and a sawbuck table that doubled as a bar against the other which contained an aquarium of adenoidal goldfish. The walls were decorated with smouldering photographs contributed by Cooper's sister who had studied with Berenice Abbott, but had not yet recovered from the childhood influence of a Doré Bible. There was a magnificent refectory table with six captain's chairs near the windows.

It was a warm, pleasant apartment since Cooper had moved in. His easy style took the curse off Jake's stiffness. In the past we used to dread going to Jake's parties. He was such a punctilious host that he invariably chilled the guests. But Cooper, who came from fresh-water society, had lived with protocol too long to be impressed by it. He kidded Lennox into relaxing and showing us flashes of his real self . . . the Lennox that Cooper knew. I think everyone would have loved Jake if they could have seen him the way he showed himself to his friend.

But this Christmas night Lennox was not lovable; he was impossible. It was his custom to make his prayers in the shower, asking God to keep him austere, kindly, infallible and sophisticated. He never begged. He made his request as one son of the Marquis of Suffolk to another. Now, however, he was raging. He stood under the hot downpour with uplifted head, fists clenching and unclenching, furious with himself and God. "What next?" he asked the shower-nozzle. "What else? Don't pull any punches. I won't whine or beg off. Let's have it all, and I'll show You!"

He cut off the water, wrapped himself in a towel, kicked open the bathroom door and stalked out into the living room. The mink-dyed skunk galloped past him back into the bathroom and stamped its paws angrily when it discovered the tub was wet. Cooper had a fire going in the practical fireplace, and a pot of coffee tactfully exposed on an end table alongside one of the wing chairs. It was half-past ten and the Siamese were enjoying their bedtime magic hour, skittering crazily up and down the apartment with crossed eyes and flattened ears.

Lennox dried his back and rump carefully before he sat down. He poured black coffee and drank it as though it were poison hemlock. Cooper came in from the kitchen and appeared to be having a magic hour of his own, for he was wearing his chef's hat and a dinner jacket. Lennox stared at him.

"Black tie tonight, Scout Lennox," Cooper told him, removing the hat. "All out for the Christmas jamboree."

"What the hell, Sam?"

"Pull in your feet." Cooper poked at the logs with an old bayonet. "Must apologize, Sir Jasper. Only a cad would touch another man's hearth. They teach you that in Islip? Rules for Perfect Behaviour. Like passing the port to the left."

"They taught me nothing in Islip," Lennox growled. Nevertheless he filed this lesson away, until he caught the gleam in Cooper's eye. He squirmed a little. "What's this black tie routine? More Perfect Behaviour?"

"I'll tell you, son. There's no food in the house. So I thought we'd accept Alice McVeagh's invitation and free-load. She's giving a monster rally. A debutante party. Turkey, ham, chutney, kedgeree, boiled mutton, boiled guests, boiled debs—"

"Who's Alice McVeagh?"

"You'll like her. She always passes the port to the left. Gives Square parties. Strictly Square. Nobody in the business. A pleasant change."

"I'm staying home."

"Not a crust in the house, Jake."

"I'm staying home."

"Um. You want to brood, eh? In F-minor."

"Sam, I need a party like a hole in the head."

"The hole's there already. You need to fill it. Get dressed. We'll go mingle."

"Sit down."

"Get dressed."

"Sit down."

Cooper cocked an eye at Lennox, then sat down in the facing wing chair. Instantly one of the Siamese leaped on him. Cooper calmly extinguished it with the chef's hat and deposited it on the floor where it struggled ecstatically.

"Death to the invaders," Cooper murmured.

After a long pause, Lennox pointed to the frantic hat and said: "Look, Sam. That's me."

"The cat in the hat?"

"Yes."

Cooper gazed at Lennox with solemn perplexity. "You said you were like a smoke-stack."

Lennox waved his hand irritably. "I'm fighting blind, Sam. I'm in a hassle. The show's in a hassle. You know about my blackout. You know about Mason lousing the grand prize tonight?"

Cooper nodded.

32

"That's bad enough, but there's something worse. We've been getting letters. Threatening letters. The filthiest crazy letters you ever saw in your life. Five already. Blinky tells me there's a sixth up at the office . . . more dangerous than the rest. If I don't do something about those letters, we may go off; but so help me, Sam, I'm so mixed up I don't know what to do."

"Told anybody about them yet?"

"No."

"The network?"

"How can I? All they have to do is smell trouble . . . particularly dirty trouble like this. . . and they'll yank us off. They've got a dozen clients hungry for that nine to nine-thirty spot. They've got nothing to lose."

"Um. Dangerous letters?"

"Filthy dangerous."

"That means trouble if you stay on?"

"Probably."

"What kind?"

"I don't know. It's an audience show. Suppose we let a lunatic in one Sunday night. You draw the pictures. Anything could happen."

"Police?"

"I'm afraid to go to the police."

"Why?"

"That turns it from a private stink into an official stink. That's why Blinky and I've been keeping it quiet. If the story gets out we'll be cancelled."

"Not positively."

"I won't take the chance."

"Why not? So you're cancelled. Is that the end of the world?"

"I won't be cancelled," Lennox said grimly.

"No, I guess not. You won't let anything be cancelled, will you, Jake?"

"Nobody's going to end anything for me except me."

"And you won't ever end anything."

"Why should I?" Lennox exclaimed impatiently. "I like what I've got. I'm thirty-five, Sam. I've come a hell of a long way from a kid telegrapher counting words in Islip, Long Island. What kind of a chicken-gut would I be to let it fall apart?"

"This I don't follow," Cooper said plaintively. "You mean the end of 'Who He?' is the end of everything? Exit Jordan Lennox, homeless, friendless, trudging back to that clam-shack in Islip, a broken man. . . ."

"For God's sake, will you level with me! I've had a hell of a day and I don't feel like yakking it up. Who am I fighting, Sam? How am I going to fight? Jesus Christ on camera!" Lennox pointed again to the struggling hat. "I'm like that amateur tiger . . . banging my brains out against nothing."

Cooper looked at the bounding hat, then back at Lennox. "Exactly like that," he said softly. "The cat's doing it for kicks. So are you."

"For kicks!"

"Yep."

"That's a lousy thing to say."

"Why? It's a compliment. Everybody says you've got deep freeze inside you. I know better. This is proof you've got emotions, Jake. Trouble is you only let 'em out of hock once a year, so you have to turn it into a production to make up for lost time."

"Who's making a production? We've got a law suit coming. We've got a lunatic knocking on the door. I've got a blank day full of memories I don't want to remember hanging over me. I've got emotions. What do you want me to do? Whistle 'Dixie'?"

"I want you to calm down and spread it out over the rest of the year. Make a note in your gimmick book: New Year's Resolution by Jordan Lennox. I will faithfully—"

Lennox started up from his chair. "My God! Where's the notebook?"

Cooper shook his head.

34

Lennox raced up the stairs to his bedroom. He carried a famous black gimmick book in which he noted down ideas, gags, references, characters, and so on. He had carried it for ten years. He was never without it, and had developed a nervous mannerism of feeling for it every few minutes . . . a sudden sharp flexing of his right arm against his chest to see if the precious gimmick book was in place in his inside pocket.

He came down the steps a minute later. "Where's my overcoat?" he yelled.

"Which coat?"

"The one I wore tonight."

"You weren't wearing any coat."

Lennox raced to the front closet, pulled it open and tore at the racks. Then he swung around in dismay. "It's gone."

"Which? The burberry?"

"No. Yes. I must have carried it in the coat last night. I lost it in the blackout."

"Is the coat insured?"

"To hell with the coat," Lennox cried. "I'm talking about my notebook. It's gone. Lost. The gimmick book, Sam!"

"Forget it. I was hoping you'd lose it. It was beginning to fall apart."

"But I've got everything in it. A year of ideas. . . ."

"You transcribe 'em every week," Cooper said comfortably. "You've got a complete file upstairs in the office. You haven't lost anything. Calm down."

"What the hell is the matter with you? Can't you understand? I've carried that book for ten years. I've never been without it."

"Then it's time you bought another one. Start the New Year right."

Lennox paced in agitation. "I've got to remember where I was last night. I've got to remember. I've got to find that gimmick book."

"Oh come on, Jake. How long are you going to milk this

hysteria routine? Lost nights, lost books, threatening letters . . . What d'you think you're doing? Auditioning? You need a new script writer, boy."

"You lousy bastard! Maybe I need a new friend," Lennox shouted.

"Maybe you do at that. Want to start a fight? You want to end it right now?"

"I'm damned well fighting right now."

"Then let's go." Cooper leaped up and faced Lennox aggressively. He cocked his right fist and pointed to his chin. "Go ahead. Let loose. I've been waiting three years to watch you throw a punch."

Lennox looked at Cooper uncertainly. In his blind fury he could not be sure whether Cooper was grinning in anger or amusement. At that moment the Siamese burst out of the hat, leaped to Jake's rump and clawed its way up his naked back to his shoulder.

"Jesus!" All the pressure in Lennox exploded in a strangulated yell. He doubled over. Cooper snatched the cat off his shoulder and hurled it onto the couch. He shoved Lennox into the bathroom, held his neck firmly and sluiced his back with rubbing alcohol.

"My compliments to Captain Bligh," Lennox said through his teeth. He stamped his foot in agony, almost trampling the mink-dyed skunk.

"Mutiny never pays," Cooper murmured, kicking the skunk out of the way. He swabbed efficiently with iodine, then led Lennox back to the fire and sat him down on a stool to dry. The Siamese, no fools they, had disappeared. Lennox sat rigid with control until the pain faded. He remained rigid.

"Stay mad; stay human," Cooper urged. "On you it's becoming. I could kill those cats for lousing our brawl. Let's find them, Jake. I'll hold them while you beat the bejezus out of them. Then the cats can hold me while you beat the—"

36

"Shut up. Don't be a damned fool, Sam."

"Which of us is the damned fool, Jake?"

Lennox took a deep breath and relaxed. "Me," he said. "A nuisance and a noodnick. Don't tell anybody."

"On the contrary. I tell everybody. That's why you're getting popular."

Lennox stood up, took Cooper's shoulder in his big grasp and clutched hard. He looked at his friend with a secret glance of devotion and gratitude, then turned away in embarrassment.

"After we eat," Sam said casually, "we'll go look for the gimmick book. You'll start remembering. We'll find it. And don't worry . . . You won't remember anything to be ashamed of."

Lennox choked. "How's my back?" he asked. "Is there blood?"

"Nope. Just scars."

"Tsk! And me with that Hattie Carnegie backless collecting dust in the boudoir. Black tie?"

"Black tie."

Lennox went upstairs and dressed.

Myself, I don't like Square parties; neither does my wife. Squares are all right, but there's an invisible barrier between us and them. For one thing, our tempos don't match. We can throw away a dozen gags while a Square is beating a cliché to death. For another thing, Squares persist in thinking about the entertainment business the same way they did back in Victorian times. To them we're artificial, child-like and irresponsible. When Squares learn that I'm a writer, I can see that look pass over their faces . . . the look that says: He's lazy and hates to get up in the morning.

They reveal this when they invariably ask the question: "Do you work all night?" If I say yes, they gloat, and I have to restrain the angry impulse to point out that I'm forced to work at night in order to avoid the interruption of Square phone calls and luncheon invitations and all the other pleasant devices which enable them to do four hours work from nine to five.

My wife has a tougher time. Her face and voice are highly expressive, naturally, being an actress. Whenever she's with Squares they watch her with appraising eyes and constantly interrupt with: "Oh stop it. You're acting now, aren't you? Why can't you be natural?" Once my wife lost her temper and answered a solid citizen: "You want to go to bed with me, don't you? Why can't you be natural?"

There was a gratifying hush of horror. I whipped out a pencil and scribbled on my cuff. "I've been watching you all with my keen eye," I announced, "and constantly analyzing . . . dissecting. I'm going to crucify you in the *New Yorker*." We swept out, and at the door my wife turned and said: "What's more, we're not even married. He's my brother and we're living in incest."

Jake liked Square parties. He enjoyed winning respect by admitting that he worked regularly from nine to five, by wearing proper conservative clothes, by showing the outward signs of success which business men understood and approved. He spoke about his profession like an industrialist; and although he was a sensitive, gifted writer, he pooh-poohed such matters as talent and inspiration, and discussed creativity as merchandise, his stock-in-trade.

He liked Alice McVeagh's party. It was given in her penthouse on East End Avenue, a Georgian duplex with delicate curving staircases, panelled study, oval library, a ballroom and two kitchens, one for the staff alone. The buffet in the dining room glittered with silver and crystal . . . fresh caviar on crushed ice, scarlet lobsters, smoked turkeys, great oriental melons oozing thick nectar, a frosted copper cask in which peaches soaked in liqueurs, and dozens of coffee flagons bubbling over alcohol lamps.

The guests were charming. Cool young ladies and their energetic mothers. Pleasant young men Cooper had known at Loomis and Princeton, and the jolly old gentlemen they would in time become. They were all exquisitely casual about the perfection of

38

their dress and manners. They were assured. They belonged. And how badly Jake wanted to belong on their terms. How badly all of us want to belong on somebody else's terms.

He was painfully well-behaved. He stood tall and erect and moved slowly, keeping his voice quiet and his hands at his side. He had two sherrys at the bar and chatted respectfully with guests . . . a burly gentleman who owned half the cotton mills in New England and was devoted to game fishing, the goggle-eyed son of a near-East ambassador who discoursed in French and broken English on *Le Jazz Hot*, a red-headed man loading up on white Martinis who confessed he taught scene design at Yale, a pregnant young matron who had been a famous debutante . . . Jake's deep-lined face was wooden and unrecognizable to Cooper who smiled privately.

There was music in the ballroom and couples dashed in to the buffet and back; crop-haired young men and boyish girls with delicious young figures and stereotype faces framed in straight honey hair. Lennox felt awed and hostile toward them. He escorted a brisk dowager to the buffet. She took an instant liking to him (older women always adored Lennox) and favored him with a ringing denunciation of the Metropolitan Opera Management and glowing praise for Charles of the Ritz.

Cooper rescued him at last and took him to the ballroom. "Eat enough?" he whispered. Lennox nodded. "All right, boy. Leave us mingle."

There was a Candle-Dance in progress in the darkened ballroom. Ten couples were turning and circling through a simple dance figure while the orchestra played "Pop Goes The Weasel." Each dancer carried a silver saucer candlestick in which a white taper burned. When the orchestra "Popped" the dance stopped, and the dancers tried to blow out each other's flames. When a candle went out, the dancer left the floor. The spinning and weaving of yellow flames gleaming on silk and satin and jewels made an enchanting picture.

39

Cooper nudged Lennox and handed him a candlestick and a burning taper.

"No, Sam!" Lennox protested.

"Come on, gents. All out for the sack-race."

Lennox perceived that a second dance circle was forming. There were two girls alongside Cooper, holding lighted candles and waiting impatiently to join the circle.

"But I've never danced this before, Sam. We had fire laws in Islip."

"You'll pick it up." Cooper whispered introductions to the girls. "My great and good friend, Arson Lupin. Ouch! Let's go."

The four slipped into the second circle and began the dance. It was bewildering for Lennox, but he had been a schoolboy fencer and was quick and graceful for a big man. Also, he was intensely competitive. He watched sharply, learned the simple figures and protected his flame. By the time half a dozen had been eliminated from his circle, he was able to look around and enjoy himself. There was one hand-clasp in particular that had electrified him, and he was trying to identify the owner.

It was a woman's hand, warm, slender and strong. Each time he grasped it, his spine tingled and he thought of the deep carpets in the network offices that produced leaping sparks when you touched a light switch. The hand had been helpful, too, turning him left and right with friendly pressures, leading him through his first confusion. The orchestra went "Pop." Lennox stopped, held his candle high and looked around the circle.

There was Cooper, looking solemn and perplexed in the glimmering light as he blew mightily in the direction of *Le Jazz Hot*. There were two honey-haired stereotypes in thin-strapped gowns, shielding their candles with their hands. There was a horsy woman with an extinguished flame, tramping off the floor. The music started again before Lennox could examine the others. He was cynically certain that the horsy woman had owned the hand. Then, as he circled, again came that electrifying touch. He looked quickly at his partner. Lennox had a weakness for straw-colored blondes, big-boned women who looked Swedish. This was the exact opposite. She looked like a slave on a Moorish auction block; cropped jet hair in tight ringlets, deep dark almond eyes, a full mouth, strong white teeth. The head was beautifully poised on a long neck. She had wide shoulders and the deep-cut jersey bodice revealed a high full bosom. Her skin was astonishing, very clear, very dark, and as lustrous as black pearl under the candle-light. She was slender, not tall, and moved with a lazy grace that was familiar to Lennox but not yet identifiable.

The orchestra went "Pop." Lennox and the girl stopped and examined each other, unmindful of their candles. She smiled. Her smile was sudden and changing, like the unexpected dazzle of light reflected from water. The music started again and she danced on to the next partner. Lennox watched her circling and weaving and suddenly recognized what was familiar about her carriage. She moved like a slender, graceful, cow-puncher; the shoulders square, the slim hips swaying, the arms slow and relaxed.

In that moment Lennox remembered that he had written a thousand love scenes and knew that every one had been a lie. There was a thundering confusion in his head; exultation and terror pounded in his heart. His whole life seemed drawn by the burning glass of this moment into a focus on this girl. She was smiling now at Cooper and murmuring to him. Lennox could have killed Sam.

He murdered each of her partners in succession until she came around the circle to him again. As he reached eagerly for her hand, the orchestra went "Pop." The other dancers stopped. Lennox continued until he was close to her and took her hand. In the flickering light, his face was black and white with shadows and highlights and looked almost ferocious. The girl's almond eyes widened slightly, and her smile faded, but her body did not lose its easy poise.

Dancers nudged Lennox politely. The music had started. The girl released herself and continued. Lennox went through the motions and grimly defended his flame from extinction while the girl remained in the dance. *Le Jazz Hot* left. The stereotypes left. Cooper was eliminated. Six remained. Then five. Then three. Finally it was Lennox and the girl, circling and turning, hand in hand, candles fluttering no more than his own breath.

They danced for timeless moments, and Lennox, dazed and intoxicated, was not aware that he was speaking to her in silence . . . by touch, by glance, by moving expression . . . revealing the secret part of himself that had never been shown before. Then he did something extraordinary for Jordan Lennox, the man who never quit, who never conceded, who had wanted to win a victory before those awesome spectators. The music went "Pop." He held out his candle to the girl, and with his right hand extinguished the flame.

There was a burst of applause. The lights went up. The orchestra swung into a dance tune and the floor filled. Lennox lost the girl in the crush and wandered aimlessly to the side of the ballroom where an unidentified person took the candlestick from him. He went to the bar, now inhabited exclusively by the redheaded teacher from Yale and the bartender.

"Listen," Lennox began incoherently, "A dark girl. In an off-the-shoulder dress. She . . . With cropped hair and oriental eyes. She gleamed. . . ."

"Who?" the red-head inquired, weaving violently.

"A girl with black short hair. She— You heard me. Do you know her? Know who she is?"

The bartender shrugged. The red-head eyed Lennox fixedly, meanwhile shaking his head. "Never heard of her. Never-never-never. No such thing's dark girls anymore. Species extinct. Like

42

used t'be everywhere poodles. Now only boxers. Poodles extinct. Also poodle brunettes. Q.E.D.?"

Lennox returned to the ballroom. He searched for the girl. He searched for Cooper. Two steps led up to the white door of the oval library. Lennox mounted them for a better view and found himself face to face with *Le Jazz Hot*.

"Who was she?" he burst out.

"Pardon, M'sieur?" *Le Jazz Hot* goggled at him.

"The dark girl. In the dance with us."

"I am so sorry."

Lennox abandoned him, left the steps and prowled around the edge of the ballroom. He went again to the bar, regarded the redhead and the bartender without comprehension, wandered off and discovered, in a hall of Chinese teapaper, a small Christmas tree hung with corsages. A honey-haired girl in a thin-strapped evening gown was unpinning some orchids from the tree.

"I beg your pardon," Lennox mumbled.

She looked at him curiously.

"The dark girl who was dancing with us. Do you know her?"

"Dancing with us?" All her charm disappeared in the bray of her voice.

"My God!" Lennox thought in panic. "I haven't heard her speak. What if she . . ." Aloud, he said: "The Candle-Dance. The dark girl in our circle who—"

"I wasn't in the Candle-Dance," the girl informed him coldly and turned away. She was the wrong stereotype.

Lennox went back to the library steps and began searching the dance floor, couple by couple. Below him and to one side a voice called: "Psst! Hey Jake!"

He looked down. Cooper was standing there, grinning. "Three down from the drums. With a guy in hornshell glasses."

Lennox glared at Cooper, challenging derision, then stared at the dance band. He found her and murdered the man in the spectacles. Without moving his eyes he asked: "Who is she?"

43

"Don't know."

"I've got to meet her."

"Grab her after this dance."

"I've got to be introduced."

"Come on, Jake! This isn't the nineties."

"I want to be introduced. Can you swing it?"

"I can try."

Cooper departed. Lennox remained where he was, watching the girl as the man in the hornshell spectacles whirled her out to the middle of the floor. The dance ended, the couples applauded languidly and shuffled. Lennox looked around desperately for Cooper. When he turned back to the dance floor he had lost the girl again. Before he could get panicky he saw her as the music started. She was alone on the floor, walking toward him, with square shoulders and lazy arms and hips. He could not believe his eyes. She came directly to the library stairs, stepped up and held out her hand. Lennox took it and felt both of them tremble slightly.

"Why didn't you cut in?" she asked in a candid, transparent voice.

He could not believe his ears. Drawing her with him, he backed into the white and gold oval library. She was smiling uncertainly. After a tremulous pause she asked: "Is this how it happens?"

Lennox couldn't speak. There was a long silence; a long communication that seemed to dread words.

"I'm frightened," she said.

Lennox shook his head.

"At first I thought I'd help. You know, the dance? Then I thought you were being hasty. And then it happened, didn't it?"

Lennox nodded.

"If you don't let go of my hand, I'll faint . . . I think. What do we do now?"

Before he could answer, Cooper appeared in the door with a

44

magnificent white-haired woman wearing a bronze dress and a jade necklace. Both smiled.

"Ah! Just in time," Cooper said. "Our hostess, Madam Mc-Veagh. Jordan Lennox."

"So nice to have you, Mr. Lennox." Alice McVeagh shook hands magnificently. Everything about her was magnificent and overpowering. "Gabby, dear, have you met the gentlemen? Jordan Lennox . . . Sam Cooper. Gabby Valentine." She overpowered Lennox. "Sam tells me you're an author, Mr. Lennox. Do you write all night?"

Lennox pulled himself together before the Presence. "No," he answered in the voice of the second son of the Marquis of Suffolk. "I work from nine to five, Mrs. McVeagh."

"But how disappointing. Aren't you an artist?"

"No, Mrs. McVeagh, I'm a business man. I sell ideas for a living."

"Oh dear! And I had such a lovely picture of you . . . working all night and smoking opium."

"Only when he's plastered," Cooper grinned.

Lennox looked at him stonily. Poor Jake! Standing there on his best behavior, tall and erect with his hands at his side; keeping his face wooden and unrecognizable, trying to belong on Alice McVeagh's terms, and destroying himself before Gabby Valentine. To his hostess he tried to appear austere, kindly, infallible and sophisticated. To Gabby he seemed hostile and unyielding. If only Cooper had come five minutes later. When he finally departed with the hostess and Lennox turned to resume the intimacy with Gabby, it was too late.

"Gabby . . ." he began.

"No," she interrupted, bitterly disappointed. "No. It was only the candle-light." She took a deep breath. Her smile was no longer a private matter between them. "Please forget everything I said. I thought you—" She broke off.

45

"You thought I what?" Lennox asked sharply. He was deeply hurt by her abrupt change.

"It doesn't matter."

"It matters to me."

"Please don't cross-examine me," Gabby said gently. "I made a fool of myself, that's all."

"I think you're trying to make a fool of me."

"No. It's all right. I'm the idiot, not you. What do you write, Mr. Lennox?"

"I write better scenes than this, Miss Valentine. My characters don't play games."

"Neither do I."

"Then what the hell happened?"

"Nothing happened. That's why I'm an idiot."

Lennox was furious, and, consequently, icy and sardonic. He imagined that this was an impudent young society girl, willful and cavalier, who had taken it into her head to make an ass of him. He couldn't have been more wrong.

Gabrielle Valentine was a unique creature. You meet people like that occasionally, and if you're not too cynical you treasure them . . . beautiful beings who've been loved and adored from birth and have grown up unspoiled and trusting, completely honest and without guile. This is rare because beauty is more often a curse for a woman and usually sickens her unless she turns it into her profession. No plain girl will believe this, but it's true.

Gabby had received affection all her life and gave it as freely. She was not brilliant, which was just as well. No one really likes brilliant people. She was a girl of average intelligence who had grown up in a world which she was able to treat with the disarming confidence of a child. Half the world treated her with the tenderness reserved for children. The cynical half could not abide her transparent honesty.

She was twenty-eight. Her father had been an old-line Socialist and had worked with Eugene Debs. He had come from a French Colonial family which had lived in Indo-China for generations and, I suspect, probably intermarried with natives. Certainly Gabby seemed to support the legend that women of mixed French and Oriental blood are the loveliest in the world. Her mother was still living and was a very smart couturiere. Gabby didn't see much of her. She was too busy making her own affectionate way in the world.

She had trained, of all things, as an architect, and worked as a free-lance draftsman. Drafting pays well and Gabby was able to afford her own apartment in one of the better Village studio buildings. She was political-minded, an inheritance from her father no doubt, and was an invaluable asset in fund-raising campaigns. She had once gone down to Wall Street and bearded a Republican financier in his den for a contribution to the Democratic party. Or maybe it was a Democrat for the Republican party. I forget which, not being political-minded myself. The point of the story is that she got the money.

She was an artist, but she didn't understand music. She had learned to be chic, but wasn't interested in clothes. She liked good food, but had to be told when it was good. She drank very little. She liked people more than anything else . . . liked to be with them and talk to them, provided they were honest and unaffected. Everyone came to her with their troubles and she gave all her affection and help. She had never been in love.

And then had come this burst of flame in the glimmering darkness with Lennox, and there was a stranger in his body who had killed the flame with his rigid poise before Alice McVeagh and was trampling on the embers in icy fury.

"Please go away," Gabby said quietly. "You're making me hate you, and I don't like that."

"I'm sorry, Miss Valentine," Lennox answered. "I don't know the rules of your game. Is that a request or a challenge?"

"Why should it be? Do you like to fight?"

47

"I'm enjoying this fight . . . with all my heart." Lennox showed his teeth in a smile.

"That's a sign of weakness, isn't it?" Gabby looked at him with steady eyes. "Like sick dogs that bite. Please go away."

"You've done the biting."

"Oh. You're hurt. I'm sorry."

"No, I'm enjoying the game. What do you do, Miss Valentine, when you can spare the time?"

"You can't be a very good writer if you talk like that," Gabby said slowly. "You sound as though you like to hate people."

"I'm a very successful writer."

"There's a difference."

"What big teeth you have, grandma."

"I don't like to be with people who hate," Gabby nodded gracefully. "Goodbye, Mr. Lennox."

"The end of Round One?"

"No. The end. I don't think we should see each other again."

"You'll see me often," Lennox assured her. "We'll fight this to a finish."

"There's nothing to fight."

"Something happened, and then you changed your mind. I'd like to find out how your gears mesh. Professionally, of course. I can always use a comedy gimmick." Automatically he flexed his right arm against his chest and was appalled to remember that his gimmick book was lost, but he was too angry with Gabby to concentrate on it.

"Who did you hope I was in the dark?" he asked. "Aly Khan?"

"You're making it worse."

"Who did you think I was?"

"I thought you . . ." She shook her head. "How can I say? I thought I—" Suddenly her dark eyes filled with tears. "You're not very kind. I've just made a fool of myself and I'm hurt too. Are you enjoying this?"

"Passionately."

48

"Please let me go."

She broke away from him and descended the library steps to the ballroom, her shoulders square, her carriage relaxed and graceful. The bright chandelier lights gleamed on her skin. Lennox followed her doggedly around the edge of the ballroom and into the bar. He could not let go. He would not let up. Gabby bent over the red-head sleeping on the bar.

"Phil," she said. "It's time to leave." She shook him gently. The red-head snorted and slept. Gabby looked reproachfully at the bartender who instantly became apologetic, as though he had personally supervised the downfall of the teacher from Yale.

"It's not your fault," Gabby told him. "He comes down from New Haven full of undergraduate notions. He had to work his way through college. He never had a chance to be hedonistic."

Lennox stepped forward. "I'll take you home, Miss Valentine."

"It isn't me that has to be taken. It's Phil."

"To New Haven?"

"What if I said yes?"

"Bon voyage, Miss Valentine."

"Oh, why are you so hostile?"

"Because I'm a damned fool," Lennox answered furiously. "All right. I'll take him back to New Haven for you."

"Not New Haven. New York. The Harvard Club."

"A neat one-two. Next time I'll know when to duck. I'll take you both home."

"Not me. Phil."

"You and Phil both."

"That's your price?"

"It's a bargain, Miss Valentine. Snap it up."

"I think I'd better get someone else."

She left the bar. Lennox heaved the red-head up, powerfully but not unkindly, and hauled him to the door. There, an efficient man in black uniform located hats and coats without clues and helped Lennox dress the red-head. Then Lennox dressed himself. When Gabby came to the foyer with three eager admirers, Lennox looked them over and growled: "I'm taking you both home. I'm prepared to fight for it. If you don't believe me get ready for a scene."

Her eyes flashed, but she dismissed the men and got into her coat. Together they took the teacher downstairs in a burning silence and propped him in a cab between them. As the cab drove off Lennox asked: "Why the Harvard Club? He teaches at Yale."

No answer.

He contrived to peer past the red-headed barricade at her. She was impassive. The street lights flickered on her skin like lightning on jewels. He had never wanted anyone and hated anyone so badly in his life; nor known anything so inexplicably out of his grasp.

He said: "I worked my way through college too. I was a telegrapher."

No answer.

After five minutes he said: "Can you spell hedonistic?"

No answer.

They arrived at the Harvard Club and turned the teacher over to a patient doorman. Lennox did not ask permission to re-enter the cab. He got in and slammed the door. Gabby gave her address in the Village and the cab started. Lennox was startled. He had expected a number on Park Avenue. He revised his guess about her society background.

The cab crunched downtown through crusted streets. The rain and snow had stopped. There was no wind, but the air was still bitter. A few blocks from Union Square, Lennox abruptly called to the driver: "Stop here. On the right, two doors down. Don't argue with me. Stop."

The cab stopped. Lennox opened the door and got out. To Gabby he said: "Wait here for me. Understand? Wait." He turned and ran across the sidewalk to the open door of a

Salvation Army Mission in a small store. There were candles burning in the window. He ducked into the store, removed two candles from the window, dropped a five dollar bill in their place, and ran back to the cab. He got in and shut the door.

"All right, get going," he told the driver. He handed one of the burning candles to Gabby without a word.

She smiled; that sudden dazzle of light on water, then her face lost its expression when she saw the cold fury in him. She shook her head.

Lennox slid the glass partition panel aside. "Can you sing?" he asked the driver. "Sing 'Pop Goes The Weasel.' "

"Have a heart, buddy."

" 'Pop Goes The Weasel' . . . in the key of C. Take it."

"That ain't no Christmas Carol."

"And this ain't no Christmas present." Lennox poked a bill through the slit and dropped it. "Sing."

The driver began a miserable croaking. Lennox sat back and eyed Gabby. She blew out her candle and turned her head away. He dropped his candle and trampled it.

"Listen to me," he said. "My name is Jordan Lennox. I'm thirty-five years old. Unmarried. My income is thirty-five thousand a year. I have no family left, but the Islip YMCA director will provide a character reference. My blood type is O. My eyes are twenty-twenty. My I.Q. is a hundred and nineteen. I understand people, but I don't understand you. I would like permission to get to know you better. If necessary, this oral request can be followed by a formal letter from my attorney and a bond will be posted."

The cab stopped before a squat studio building with great duplex windows. Lennox had the fare ready. He thrust it over the driver's shoulder, then helped Gabby out of the cab and with a fierce secret gesture signalled the driver to get lost.

"Well?" he asked.

She shook her head. He would not give up. He took her arm,

51

escorted her the five steps to the doorway, thrust open the door and handed her through.

"Why not?" he asked.

"Goodnight."

"Why not?"

"You wouldn't understand."

"Make me understand."

"Goodnight."

His fingers gripped her arm. "Make me understand."

"What can I say? I thought you were somebody else. I thought. . . ."

"What?"

"Once," she said slowly, "I had to study chemistry. And in the stockroom there was a glass jar filled with the most beautiful candy I ever saw. Then someone told me it was poison. Crystals of poison . . . That's what happened."

"Poison!" he exclaimed. "I'm poison to you?"

"No; but you aren't what I thought you were. It's my fault. I made the mistake and I—" Gabby broke off in astonishment. The color had drained out of Lennox's face. The fury drained out of his body. He took a step into the foyer and let go of the door which swung heavily and smashed his hand resting limp on the jamb. He wrenched his hand free and took another hypnotic step toward the row of brass letter-boxes on the foyer wall. Each had a white call button underneath the name plate. In clear block letters alongside VALENTINE was FOX.

"What is it?" Gabby cried.

" 'Fair is my love, for April's in her face,' " Lennox mumbled. " 'Her lovely breasts September claims his part . . .' " He turned a wild face to her. "What made me think of that? What's terrifying about it?"

"What's the matter?"

"I don't know," he answered, swallowing hard and lifting a trembling hand to his face. It left blood smears on his cheek.

"I'm lost. Again. I . . . Christ!" He shut his eyes and pressed his fists together. "Sam," he whispered. "Sam. Come and get me. Please."

"You'd better come in," Gabby said in alarm. She took him upstairs to her apartment and through a barn-like studio to a tailored bedroom where she helped him off with his coat and sat him down on a chaise longue. He was shaking. He tried to joke. "We shouldn't be here," he said. "Very suggestive."

"It's too cold in the studio. What's the matter? What happened to you?"

"Downstairs. That name . . . Fox. It cut me off from everything. I don't know why. I'm crying again," he groaned. "Crying. There's been nothing but dirt and tears all day. I don't know what happened."

"I'll get you a drink."

"No. Thank you. I'm not sick. It's just something trying to come back and hurting like sin."

"What do you mean?"

"I can't explain. Give me a minute . . . It'll go away again, if I'm lucky. Then I'll go too."

He sat in silence, trying to control himself, looking around the room with smarting eyes. Gabby took off her coat, left the bedroom and returned a moment later with a glass and a sealed bottle of whiskey. She tried to remove the cap and failed. She handed the bottle to Lennox who took it, opened it mechanically and then put it down.

"I didn't know you lived like this," he said at last.

"How do you mean?"

"Like this. Not girly-girly. I thought . . . Park Avenue and decorators. This could be a man's place. Do you play Boys' Rules?"

"You didn't."

"I know it. I've been trying to start all over again for the last two hours." He stood up, went to the bed and touched the pillow

53

gently. "Hello, Gabby," he said. He went to the dressing table and touched it. He touched the window drapes, the lamps, the books, the pictures ... everything that was hers as though he were touching her heart.

Without looking at her he said: "You're right. I'm poisonous ... but I love you. I'm the wrong man, but I love you. It's too quick ... only a few hours, but I love you. I hate too much, I hurt too much because I'm poisonous ... And I love you. I'd better go now. Goodnight."

He searched blindly for his coat, ashamed to meet her eyes, and the real Lennox appeared, the Lennox she had seen by candle-light two hours ago.

"Oh!" Gabby exclaimed in tears. "Oh darling . . . darling! Why did you hide from me? Why?"

He caught his breath. She came to him and he took her in his arms. After a moment he managed to speak.

"Is this how it happens? Has it happened again?"

She clung to him.

"Now I'm frightened, Gabby."

"Why did you hide from me? Why did you change like that? You were so cold and hateful. . . ."

"I didn't know I was hiding. I didn't know what I was doing. I've been half crazy all day." He raised her hand and pressed it against his eyes. "I dreamed about meeting you, but not like this. I was going to be at my best. You know? Brilliant and successful. Scattering money and charm in all directions. Winning you . . . not whining my way into your heart."

"No. No. You don't understand. No one wants to be won. We want to be wanted . . . Needed."

"God knows, I need you. God knows, I—"

"Shhh." She seated him again, ran out of the room and returned with a warm moist cloth. She cleaned his hand and his cheek. Lennox seized her suddenly as she stood over him and buried his face in her body.

54

"It's all right, darling," she whispered. "Don't be afraid. You're just used to taking, that's all. Nobody ever gave you anything."

He looked up at her. "What happened to us after the dance? What did I do then? What's wrong with me? Was I mean dirty drunk? Did I—" He stopped. He stood up slowly. In a strange voice he said: "Mean dirty drunk. Clarence Fox from Philadelphia. The Quaker and the blonde. Yes. That's where the gimmick book is. . . ."

Gabby was alarmed again. She put her hands on his shoulders. "But why can't I remember the rest?" Lennox asked in terror. "The knot. What's so horrible about a knot? What is it? Why can't I remember what it is?"

She tried to press him back on the chaise longue. He was too big to be forced but he responded instantly to her pressure.

"You're in trouble," she said. "Let me help."

He tried to smile. "Yes. It's bad. I want to hide things from you, but you empty me out. Let me keep a few secrets for a little while. I can't do it unless you let me."

She nodded.

He took a breath. "I'm afraid to break this moment. I'm remembering what happened two hours ago."

She shook her head emphatically.

"But I . . . But something's got to be written down before I forget it again. Someone has to go somewhere and get something for me."

"I'll go," Gabby offered.

"No," Lennox said sharply.

She picked up a sketch-pad and pencil from the bed table and looked at him. Lennox spoke as though each syllable were acid on his lips. "Aimee Driscoll. 900 East 33rd Street." Suddenly he burst out: "There's worse. There's going to be worse to remember!"

She came to him and took his face in her hands. "This isn't a moment, is it?"

"No," he said. "Please God, darling . . . No." He pulled her down alongside him and kissed her until he plunged into a darkness which he did not fear.

· CHAPTER IV ·

Four o'clock in the morn-
ing after Christmas I was trying to see how many different ways
I could type NOW IS THE TIME FOR ALL GOOD MEN
TO COME TO THE AID OF THEIR PARTY when my
phone rang. I was indignant but I had to find out who'd be calling at that hour. I picked up the phone. Lennox was on the
other end.

"Kitten? Jake Lennox."

"What are you calling for?"

"Are you working?"

"No. I'm hung up on a script."

"Then I'm not interrupting. I want a favor." Jake was always
direct on the horn. "I'll tell you first, then you can say yes or
no."

"Shoot."

"I think I left my gimmick book in the apartment of a woman
named Aimee Driscoll, 900 East 33rd. I can't get it myself."

"Why?"

"Just listen, Kit. I need somebody I can trust to go there and pick it up for me first thing in the morning."

"Don't you trust Cooper?"

"I can't locate him."

"Isn't he home?"

"No. You ask too many questions, Kitten."

I admit I'm curious. That's how I got my nickname; but I'm always annoyed when anyone throws it up to me.

"Ask Cooper when he comes home," I said. "And that's not a question."

"I can't." Lennox sounded a little strained. "That's why I'm asking you. Yes or no."

"Do I owe you a favor?"

"No."

"Then I'll do it."

"As soon as possible, Kit."

"Nine o'clock in the morning."

"Thanks. Meet me in Grabinett's office at ten."

"Can't you wait a few hours, Jake? Ten's too early."

"Why?"

"It's like this. If I stay hung up I'll have to research in the library for an idea. I can pick up the book first thing, but then I'd like to get a few hours work done in the Reading Room."

"Right. Reasonable. Twelve o'clock?"

"Yes."

"Meet me at Sabatini's. I'll spring for a drink."

"Sabatini's at noon. What's that noise?" In the background I could hear sound. I listened hard. It was music. Delius.

"Oh. I almost forgot," Lennox said. "I left a coat too. My burberry. Will you latch on to it, Kit? Thanks. Goodnight."

He hung up hastily. I went down the hall and looked into the bedroom. My wife was still up, reading. Robin has straight straw-colored hair and is stacked like a Swede acrobat, a fact which always made me nervous where Lennox was concerned.

58

"Put on a nightgown or pull up the sheet," I told her. "You're demoralizing the neighbors." Robin grinned shamelessly. I closed the blinds and turned on the bedside radio. "Find me Delius," I said. "I've got to write down a name and address." I wrote it down, only I spelled it Amy. Robin dialed through the stations one by one. No Delius. She looked at me.

"Dig this," I said. "I happen to know Cooper hates Delius. Won't have a record in the house. But Jake just phoned and there was 'Appalachia' blasting in the background. Big romantic stuff, and not from a radio either." I told her about Jake's call. "All right, Robin, you guess first."

"Do you think he's good in bed?"

"For God's sake! Women! Haven't you got any romance in you?"

"That was romance."

"It was not. You give us complexes. Is bed everything?"

"Yes."

"What about all the rest?"

"Bed first."

"I guess you're right," I said and I was an hour late getting to Aimee Driscoll's apartment next morning.

I was lucky at that. She'd just gotten up and was in a vicious mood. She handed me the freeze reserved for Squares and I handed it right back. That gave us an understanding and put us on a basis of armed neutrality as fellow members of the entertainment profession. The blonde and I passed a few remarks about the Quaker. She called my attention to the new television set and laughed it up because she'd gotten it out of the Quaker for nothing; but I noticed that she laughed angrily. I didn't know why.

The photograph should have tipped it. It stood on the set in a silver frame, faded and vignetted, a costume piece, circa 1913. It was a portrait of a man with heavy brows and a stern face and could have been a photograph of Lennox in costume and makeup.

59

The fact that she'd placed it on the set Lennox gave her was significant, but I only realized that after the death in the Venice theater.

"Who's the grim reaper?" I asked.

"My old man," Aimee answered. She darted a look of loathing at the photograph. It was so poisonous that I wanted to ask more questions, but before I could get started, she gave me the brush-final. I left with Jake's gimmick book and burberry and didn't get to the library until eleven. . . .

Lennox marched into the Grabinett office at ten sharp. It was in a small building off Madison Avenue in the fifties. Grabinett had started there as a two-bit agent in a rat-hole, and when he hit the big money it turned out that rentals were too tight for him to move into larger quarters. He spread into stockrooms, broke through closets and halls, had it all decorated and air-conditioned, and it still looked like a blond wood rat-hole. They held daily rat-races there.

Grabinett was in his corner office eating Danish and coffee and reading Red Channels. There was a stack of mail, Nielson Reports, *Variety, Billboard,* Radio and TV Newssheets on the desk before him. Lennox tore off his coat, revealing that he was still wearing black tie. He flung the coat on a chair piled with bundles of stenciled scripts.

Grabinett eyed Lennox with lively hatred and verged on continuing the battle from the night before until his attention was distracted by the dinner jacket.

"What's this?" he blinked.

"Costume."

"You're a panel expert?" Grabinett leaped up in dismay. "Jesus Almighty! Don't tell me A&B sold another panel show to the network. What have they got on Roy Audibon? Do they know where the body's buried?"

Lennox didn't bother to answer. He pulled a sheaf of notes

60

from his inside pocket and glanced at them. "What's your schedule this morning, Mel?"

"Loaded. I ain't got a minute."

"What about Kansas?"

"That's up to the network. I got a conference scheduled with Roy Audibon for thissafter."

"Haven't you tried anything else?"

"What the hell else is there to try?"

"I've got an idea." Lennox reached across the desk and picked up Grabinett's phone. He punched buttons until Patsy Lewis, the office operator, answered him in a jaw-clenched Bennington drawl.

"Patsy? Jake Lennox. Good morning. You were monitoring that call to Kansas last night?"

"Good morning, Mr. Lennox. Yes, I was."

"Remember the number?"

"Who could forget?"

"Get 'em for me, please. Right away." Lennox hung up.

"What the Almighty are you up to?" Grabinett cried. He reached for the phone. Lennox reached for his wrist.

"Leave go. You know what a call to Kansas costs?"

"Less than a lawsuit. Let me try this, Mel. You can bill me for the call if I louse it. Where's that love letter that came yesterday? Get me the file."

"Who the hell do you think you are this morning? Jesus H. Napoleon?"

"What? Does it show?" Lennox smiled suddenly. "That's the trouble with turning over a new leaf. You do it in the old style and people don't understand."

"Are you drunk or something?"

Lennox looked at Grabinett keenly. "You're a lot more perceptive than I thought, Mel. Yes, I'm something. Something as high as a kite. And full of New Year's Resolutions." He tapped the sheaf of paper. "My list of good deeds, waiting to be crossed

61

off. Oh!" He looked closer at the list and flushed. "Says here: Section One. People. Relations to. Paragraph One. Grabinett. Attitude toward. Make it up to Blinky for being a louse last night."

"What!"

"At the theater last night," Lennox said steadily. "I was a louse. Please excuse me. I apologize."

"Who the hell are you calling Blinky?"

"Oh God!" Lennox groaned. "She's right. It takes practice."

The phone rang. He picked it up. It was the Kansas contestant with her husband counseling her on an extension. It was eight o'clock in the morning in Kansas, and bitter cold, but no colder than those two litigants.

"Good morning. This is Jordan Lennox, the writer on the 'Who He?' show," he began smoothly. Kansas sputtered. Lennox paused and then went on: "Yes, I know. It was an unfortunate mistake last night, but of course you'll get the prize. Mr. Grabinett has mailed your check out. Anyway, it isn't important because I think you'll agree it was your good luck when you hear the proposition I have for you. What?"

Lennox waited patiently while Kansas fumed. Finally he interrupted; "I'm very sorry you feel that way. You see, the accident last night was the springboard for a new TV show that we'd like to build around you. A half-hour situation comedy about a real life couple that competes for prizes."

Grabinett's jaw dropped and he blinked at Lennox. Jake winked and continued: "The idea is to combine realism and comedy. You'll appear on all the give-away shows and compete. We'll follow your adventures, show what you do with the prizes, how your friends react, and so on. We were planning on starting promotion with a publicity spread in one of the picture magazines, but if you insist on suing I'm afraid we'd better forget— What? Certainly I'm serious. I'm a writer. I know a solid idea when it hits me in the face."

Lennox clamped a hand over the mouthpiece and whispered to Grabinett: "Get that check in the mail. Airmail special." He unclamped the phone. "Of course. Of course. I understand. Naturally you were upset; but we can forget about that now. I'll arrange for a few words from Mr. Mason. You'll get your check tomorrow and we'll start preparing your new show immediately. Mr. Grabinett will send out contracts for you to sign. In the meantime . . . Happy New Year."

He hung up, reached for the list and crossed off an item.

"Cooled?" Grabinett blinked incredulously.

Lennox nodded. "As soon as they deposit that check we're safe. Have a couple of exclusive service contracts made out to them for a show called . . . Oh, let's see . . . 'The Man and Woman from—' No. 'The Couple From Missouri.' That'll keep 'em happy."

"Genius Almighty! What was that about Mason?"

"They'll settle for an apology on the show next Sunday."

"An apology from Mason? He'll never do it."

"We'll worry about that at the show conference." Lennox consulted his list. "Can I see the letter now, Mel? That's our real problem."

"Napoleon," Grabinett muttered and went to the wall safe. He twirled a dial perfunctorily and swung the door open. He withdrew a manila folder and brought it to the desk, handling it as though it were crawling with roaches.

"The top letter," he said.

"Thanks. See about the check and the contracts, will you, Mel? Let's get the minor rap all squared off. I'll get out of your way now. Where can I go read the letter?"

"Stay here!" Grabinett exclaimed. "Don't let it out of here." He left the office and slammed the door.

Lennox opened the folder. It contained six pale blue envelopes and six sheets of blue letter paper. The quality of the paper was good. The quality of the writing was bad; clumsy scrawlings, jagged, hysterical, sick. The pirates on The Rock are notorious for the freedom of their language, but there is a vast gulf separating profanity from malignity. The first five letters had been filthy gutter abuse. This last was comparatively clean, but even more sickening for the naked venom of its hatred.

> Dear Who He:
> Do you remember me yet?
> Are you feeling the pain?
> I'm going to kill you.
> I'll tear your guts out
> and rip your eyes and
> listen to you scream. Your
> bones will smash and your
> blood will run and the
> fancy filth in you will
> pour out like sewers like
> rot like ruin. I promise
> there will never be any
> Happy New Year for you!
> This is the last warning.
> Be killing you New Years.
>
> Guess Who

Lennox closed the folder. There was no need to re-read the earlier letters. He remembered them and they were more revolting, if less specifically threatening. He took a deep breath, then went to the corner sink behind a screen and washed his hands. He had been carried down into the sewers of a sick mind. It was not a new experience, but Lennox could never accustom himself to it. Grabinett came back into the office.

"Well, Napoleon? How about that one?"

"It's the pay-off." Lennox shook himself. "We can't stall, Mel. We've got to go to the police."

"No."

64

"I'll go. Get a girl in here. The letters ought to be photostated before I take them."

"Not the cops, Jake. For crank letters?"

"They aren't crank letters any more. They're threats."

"Against who?"

"Somebody on the show."

"Which?"

"One of the permanents who's on every week. Mig. Stacy. Kay Hill. . . ."

"Kay? A dame?"

"Why not? You read the letters. They could be written to a man or a woman."

"Yeah. I guess you're right."

"Then there's Johnny Plummer. Raeburn Sachs. . . ."

"Nobody sees Ray. He ain't ever on camera."

"It has to be someone who's seen every week or whose name appears every week. Ray's name is on the credit drum after every show. So is yours."

"Me!" Grabinett cried in astonishment.

Lennox nodded. "Every week. 'A Melvin Grabinett Production.'"

"That's a goddam lie. Those letters ain't to me."

"You say. How do I know? Maybe that's why you don't want to go to the police. Maybe you're covering."

"Would I show 'em to you if I was? Would I— You get a credit too. 'Written by Jordan Lennox.'"

"That's right. Let's include me too. That makes seven. Who else appears every week . . . name or face? Oh. Charlie Hansel, the dance director. That's all. A total of eight. One out of the eight is getting threatening letters and we've got to do something about it before everything blows up in our face next Sunday."

"Throw 'em off the show, goddam 'em!"

"All eight of us?"

"No. The one that's getting wrote to."

"Which?"

"Find out which."

"How?"

"I don't know how. You're The Thinker. You think it up how."

"I can't. Not off-hand. It wouldn't do any good to ask. Who'd tell the truth with something dirty as this in their past?"

"God damn!" Grabinett blinked furiously. "Why hasn't anything happened before? Why wait 'till now?"

"I don't know, Mel. They're crazy letters. Go figure a lunatic mind. Maybe the police can. We're sitting on dynamite. The fuse is lit. We know the blow-up's coming next Sunday. We've got to do something to stop it."

"How do you know for sure next Sunday?"

"You read the last letter. It's plain. 'Be killing you New Years.' What more do you want? We have to go to the police."

"I don't believe it."

"You can't run away from it, Mel. I'll draw you a picture. Look . . . it's next Sunday night. Mig's doing the drama spot, the 'Man Without A Country' question. They're working on No. 2 Camera dollied back for the full courtroom shot. Ray's in the controls calling shots to Sol Eggleston. Sol's on the Party-Line talking to the camera crews. Johnny Plummer's got the music soft. You're with the agency men in the back of the control booth . . . Yes?"

Grabinett nodded, fascinated.

"And then there's a wild yell in the house and a lunatic comes charging down the center aisle. He's got a gun. He jumps up on the stage, and he's right on camera. He's cursing and swearing. The audience realizes it isn't a gag and starts screaming. Before Master Control can pull us off the air, he starts shooting . . . Who? What difference does it make? Thirty million people see it. And when the police start asking questions you'll have to say: 'I was

66

warned. I got letters, but I didn't do anything about it.' How long would you stay in the business after that?"

Grabinett blinked for half a minute, then pressed a button on his desk. The office door opened and his secretary came in three steps and waited.

"Got something for photostat," Grabinett said faintly.

Lennox placed the folder inside a large script envelope and handed it to the girl. "This is a rush job, please. Three copies. Tell them to handle the material as little as possible, in case of fingerprints." The secretary's face brightened with interest as she took the envelope. Lennox added sharply: "Don't read any of it. You'll be sorry if you do. This isn't for little girls."

He put on his coat and buttoned it up to the neck. As he left the office, he muttered: "It isn't for little boys, either."

He went home. Cooper wasn't in the apartment, but his bed had been slept in and the animals had been fed. Monday was the one day of vacation for the entire "Who He?" staff, and there was no telling where anyone might be on this blessed day of release from the rat-race. Lennox changed, then went to the phone and dialed Houseways, Inc.

"Miss Valentine, please."

"Who's calling?"

"Frank Lloyd Wright."

There was a pause, then Gabby's voice, soft and reproachful. "You shouldn't have said that."

"I know. There's something about a phone that always makes me lie. Being invisible, I suppose. Do draftsmen come under the Women's Employment Regulations?"

"Why . . . there's no such law."

"Of course there is. You know the one I mean, sweetheart. You lectured all about it just before I spilled the coffee. Where they have to let women out for five minutes every hour to use the bathroom."

"Oh. You mean—"

"Where's your bathroom?"

"Jordan! For Heaven's sake!"

"I can't wait till tonight to see you. I borrowed full drag from Costume. Cloth coat with fur collar. Spike heels. Eugenie hat. I'll meet you in the john. I'll smuggle in brownies and coke. We'll have a spread."

Gabby began to laugh.

"What do you say?"

"Go away. I have to work."

"Chicken! How about lunch?"

"Darling, I'm sorry. You know I can't. I told you last night."

"How about Elevenses?"

"Go away."

"Tea?"

"No."

"What do you look like when you work? Smock and beret and a calabash pipe?"

"Not nearly so glamorous. More like 'Out Of The Inkwell.'"

"Who He?"

"The old movie cartoon."

"Oh. We'll have to do something about that. I can't hang up."

"Neither can I."

"Let's be strong."

"I don't know how."

"I'll count to three. Then we'll both hang up."

"Count to ten."

"No. Three. That's the way to be strong. Ready?"

"Yes."

"One . . . Two . . . What comes after two?"

"Ten," Gabby said and hung up.

Lennox nodded to himself approvingly. She knew how to tag a scene. He called Robin.

"Robin? Jake Lennox. Did Kit pick up my stuff?"

"What time is it?" Robin mumbled.

"Eleven."

"For God's sake, Jake! I'm not up yet."

"Did Kit go downtown this morning?"

"I think so. Yes. He did. Now get lost. You're stunting my growth."

"Can you write?"

"I forget."

"Well memorize this. A call for 'Who He?' next Sunday. Showtime nine to nine-thirty at the Venice Theater. Pick up your script at the office tomorrow and they'll give you the rehearsal schedule. The job pays two bills. Can you fit it into your schedule?"

"Can I!" Robin exclaimed.

"Pleasant dreams," Lennox chuckled and hung up. He knew how to pay for a favor.

He took a cab uptown, bought a beret and smock in Saks and a calabash pipe in Dunhill's, and had them delivered to Gabby Valentine at Houseways, Inc. Then he went up to the network studios and walked in on the morning rehearsal of "The People Against—" the radio show produced and directed by Ned Bacon, his partner on "Who He?"

Bacon was a short, stocky Irishman in his mid forties. He had an impudent boyish face on which he had superimposed an expression of pugnacious cynicism. He seemed to regret that he had not been a bad boy and spent his life making up for it. There is an ancient and honorable association of Fire-Buffs, amateurs who are fascinated by firemen and run after fires. Bacon was a Thief-Buff. He spent his nights on 3rd Avenue running after crooks, cops and crime.

His crime show had been an outstanding leader in radio for fifteen years, and only the advent of television which was strangling all night-time radio was now bringing it to an end. In the old days "The People Against—" had owned the network on Mondays. It was their prized show. Its studio was sacred and officiously guarded. Inside, the orchestra minded its manners, a rare thing for musicians, and the cast worked in terror of Bacon who swaggered through rehearsals with his hat cocked over one eye.

Now, all was changed. The studio doors were unprotected. No actors stood before them waiting for a chance to smile at Bacon. Inside, the full orchestra was reduced to an organ and two instruments. The studio itself was crammed with stored television sets, leaving just enough working space around a couple of microphones before the control booth. Half of Bacon's cast was in makeup and costume. They had obviously sandwiched "The People Against—" in and were earnestly memorizing lines for TV shows. But Bacon still swaggered with his hat cocked over one eye.

Lennox sat down quietly in a corner and waited. Bacon was directing an actor in the style that had made him famous.

"You don't understand it," Bacon spoke confidentially. "You don't feel it like a gimpster. Let's have the line again."

"I want my vigorish, doll!" the actor snarled.

Bacon shook his head and sidled up to the actor like a pickpocket. "Vigorish," he explained, "is thief talk for percentage. See? You're filing a beef about your cut in the caper. But it has to mean something more. Make like you're pimping for the broad when you say that. You've got your hands up her skirt. You're naked but you're not catching any colds. Think about her naked and warm up. Then we'll try it again."

He swaggered over to Lennox. "So Mason blew it last night," he said.

Lennox nodded. Bacon eyed him pugnaciously. "It's time we separated the men from the boys."

"Oh?"

"Sachs has got to go."

"Are you going to start that again?"

"Jake, that varsity cheer-leader is turning everything into a

70

clam-bake. He's so busy playing the genius routine he's tuned in on dead air. Next Sunday's his last show. I'm taking over after the first of the year."

"Directing?"

Bacon nodded. "I'm from radio," he said bitterly. "I'm not supposed to know anything about the theater. TV's one of the Mysteries, and I don't know the pass-words. That's the line these Johnny-Come-Lately fags in TV are handing out. If you haven't got talent, turn the business into a secret fraternity so real talent can't get in. Well, the old man from radio is coming out of his cave."

"Does Blinky know?"

"He'll be notified. I got the agency on the horn this morning. Avery Borden's with me. How about you?"

"What have I got to do with it?"

"Between us we own half the show. If it comes to a Mexican stand-off with Blinky, we can swing the vote with Avery in our corner."

"I'm not ready to hassle about that yet, Ned. I've got something more important to worry about."

"This is important."

"Mine's worse."

"I thought we were partners," Bacon said angrily. "Are you welshing on me?"

"No. I'm trying to keep our show from falling apart."

"So am I. Either you're with me or agin' me. Make up your mind."

"Damn it, Ned. This is no time for Civil War. We're sitting on a blast right now."

"You gutless Summer Soldier!"

"Will you listen! The show's in a jam. We're all in a jam. We're being threatened. It's going to hit the fan next Sunday. I came here to get the name of that detective friend of yours over at the Precinct Station."

Bacon's face lost its rage and kindled. "Oh? Threats? What kind? Extortion? Blackmail? Is it one of the Heavies or a Con? I know all the rackets, Jake. That's my business. Why the hell didn't you tell me?"

"I'm telling you now."

"What rumbled? Who blew the gaff?"

"We can't discuss it here. I'll see you later and let you have everything. What's the name of the detective?"

"Fink. Sergeant Robert Fink. Tell him Ned Bacon sent you. Ned Bacon from . . ." He paused for a soundless fanfare. " 'The People Against—.' "

"Right."

Bacon escorted him to the studio door. "Tell Bob to take you out on the case. Meet the people, Jake. People are your business. Get a load of life. Break out of that Ivory Tower. Rub elbows with the marketplace."

Lennox looked at him contemptuously. "You love this, don't you, Ned? Threats . . . Rackets . . . Crooks . . . The spittoon life."

"It's people, Jake. It's life. It's my business."

"I like my life just the way it is," Lennox said. "That's why I'm going to see your detective . . . for salvation, not masturbation."

Bacon flushed angrily. "You're never the genial type, Jake, but there's times when you fill me with death wishes."

"Be seeing you, Scarface." Lennox exchanged a level glance of loathing with his partner and left the studio.

"Salvation!" he repeated emphatically. "Yes, by God! Now we know where we're going."

· CHAPTER V ·

"I'VE GOT TO LOOK INTO A
butcher store," Fink said. "Drive over with me. You can tell me
about those letters."

They got into a dusty car parked in front of the Precinct Station. Fink was a small, slender man with thin blonde hair and
the harmless manner of a bank clerk. He had a soft sweet voice.
He seemed shy. His smile was hesitant and haphazard, as though
he acknowledged humor but had given up hope of ever recognizing it.

"Shopping for dinner?" Lennox asked.

"No. The Health Department had a complaint this butcher is
selling bad meat. They couldn't find anything so they handed it
to us. You can tell me about those letters."

Lennox told him. Fink drove carefully and listened without
comment. Finally he shook his head.

"Tough," he said.

"You mean dangerous?"

"Tough to locate the writer."

"Are the letters dangerous?"

"Everything's dangerous."

"That isn't much help. I'm scared."

"It's smart to be scared. You don't know who they're written to?"

"No. Like I told you, it could be a choice of eight."

"Maybe." Fink smiled. "We'll see if we can find out who's writing them. You've got all the letters in this folder?"

"Yes."

"If you're worried about next Sunday why don't you keep the public out of your theater?"

"We can't do it, Sergeant ... Mr ... Which is it?"

"Bob."

"I didn't know you people were so informal."

"We're not. It's code."

"Code! You're kidding. I don't believe it."

Fink nodded. "Say you're in my office being questioned. One of my associates walks in and he doesn't know who you are. I have to warn him to be careful what he says. Instead of calling him by his first name I call him Mister. That's the tip-off."

"I'm flattered. You make me feel like a deputy."

"If you're worried about next Sunday why don't you keep the public out of your theater?"

"How do you know I'm not a crook, Bob? Why'd you teach me your code?"

"Any friend of Ned's."

"No. Honestly."

"You know everybody in your business, don't you?"

"Practically."

"I know everybody in my business."

"But suppose I tell other people and it gets out?"

"What difference? We're protecting ourselves. We don't care who knows it. If you're worried about next Sunday why don't you keep the public out of your theater?"

74

The third repetition of the question, identically phrased, made Lennox aware of a tenacious quality in this quiet little man. He could not be diverted.

"It's a comedy show," Lennox explained. "We have to have an audience. Our star wouldn't work without one."

"He could try."

"He wouldn't want to try."

"You can ask him."

"I'll ask him, but I know the answer. I thought . . . well, that you might put some of your men in the house Sunday night."

"For eight hundred people? It wouldn't do much good." Fink smiled haphazardly. "How do you hand out the tickets?"

"Mostly through the network. They're requested by mail."

"They never keep any record. Doesn't your sponsor get tickets too?"

"I'll let you in on our code," Lennox grinned. "We never call them the sponsor. Always the client. In case you want to pass as a TV artist."

"Thanks. Doesn't your sponsor get tickets too?"

"He gets a batch. So does the agency. Also the producer, Mel Grabinett."

"How far ahead do you hand out tickets?"

"About two weeks."

"Then they're all out for next Sunday?"

"Yes."

Fink smiled. "Well . . . We'll see if we can find out who's writing them. You've got all the letters in this folder?"

"All. Oh. I had them photostated. Is that all right?"

Fink nodded and parked the car before a small butcher store in a run-down tenement. He opened the glove compartment, placed the manila folder inside, then carefully locked the compartment. They got out of the car and he locked the doors carefully.

"Need any more from me, Bob?"

"The letters are enough."

"Then I'll be going."

"What's your hurry? Come on in."

Fink led the way to the tenement doorway alongside the butcher store. Lennox had expected him to enter the store. Instead, Fink entered the house in which the store occupied the street floor front. The letter boxes were battered and unnamed. A card stuck in the glass door read DUGAN—SUPER.

"It's a condemned house," Fink said. He pushed open the door and walked past a lopsided flight of stairs. He knocked on the door of the rear apartment. Lennox held his breath. There was an incredibly foul odor in the building.

The door opened and a shriveled woman appeared.

"Mrs. Dugan?" Fink said quietly. "The Health Department had a complaint this butcher is selling bad meat. I'm Fink from the Precinct." He slipped his wallet out, flipped it open to display the blue and gold badge pinned inside, then returned it to his back pocket.

"I don't know nothing about it, I'm sure," Mrs. Dugan quavered.

"This is just routine."

Fink pushed into the apartment, followed by Lennox. They went down a hall to a tiny parlor facing a narrow court. It was dark and cluttered with dismal furniture. Fink remained standing. He caught Jake's eye, looked down at a chair, then back at Lennox and shook his head slightly. Lennox remained standing. His skin began to crawl. Mrs. Dugan slumped down in a rocker.

"The Health Department had a complaint this butcher is selling bad meat," Fink repeated. "Anybody in the building buy from him?"

"There's nobody but us," Mrs. Dugan said.

"No tenants?"

She shook her head.

"Just you and your husband?"

She nodded.

"Dugan's the super?"

"Yes."

"You buy meat from this butcher?"

Her hands twitched on her knees. Fink waited patiently for her to answer.

"You buy meat from this butcher?"

"Yes," Mrs. Dugan whispered.

"Any of it bad?"

"No."

Fink took out his notebook and scribbled. Lennox flexed his right arm against his chest, then looked around uneasily.

"Where's Dugan?" Fink inquired.

"He went up to the roof to look for leaks." The woman tapped her knee with a stained forefinger. "On account of the snow."

"Uh-huh. Snow was pretty bad last night?"

She nodded and tapped her knee again. "Awful. He been up there all morning. The roofs is shot."

Fink put away the notebook. As he turned to leave he jerked his head at a framed photograph of a man in World War I uniform.

"That Dugan?"

"Yes," she said. "He lost his eye at Shatto Theory."

"Tough," Fink murmured and departed.

Outside in the hall the odor was sickening.

"Smell that?" Fink said. "It's why the Health Department got those complaints."

"Aren't you going to check the butcher?"

"Is the old lady still in the apartment?"

"Yes."

"Uh-huh. Where's the way to the basement? Oh. Here. Come on." Fink opened a wooden door behind the flight of stairs and produced a flashlight. He started down. Lennox followed.

"Why the basement?" he asked.

"Didn't you see her give it away?"

"Give what away?"

"When she said Dugan was up on the roof. She kept pointing down with her finger."

The basement was a reeking mass of rotting crates and cartons. There was a furnace in the middle with hot-air ducts spreading up to the low ceiling like square octopus arms. Fink located a hanging light bulb and switched it on. He walked to the street end of the basement, crouching under the ducts.

"We'll try the coal bins first," he said. "That's the usual."

"Bob! What is this?"

"She was lying," Fink explained. "You have to be good to make all of you lie at the same time. Part of you always gives the truth away. That finger gave her away. Dugan's down here." He picked up a long-handled shovel and began turning over coke in the wooden bunkers.

"Dugan's down here?"

"Uh-huh. Didn't you see his war picture? The wives hate to give up the pension when the husbands die, so sometimes they don't report the death. But they have to hide the body . . ." Fink shoveled vigorously, then grunted: "Look."

A hand and arm were thrust out of the coke. It was a left hand, rotting, swarming with maggots. Lennox let out a hoarse cry and backed away. He turned and ran crouching under the ducts to the basement stairs.

"Hey! Lennox!" Fink called in surprise.

Lennox gasped out an apology and raced up the steps. He held his breath. In the hall he came face to face with Mrs. Dugan just coming out of her apartment. He averted his head and ran out into the street. He found a saloon, went in and had two quick shots of brandy, trying to forget that hideous left hand. The brandy took hold in his stomach and he was able to relax. Presently he nodded emphatically. "By God!" he muttered. "He'll find out who's writing those letters. He'll save us. I wouldn't have believed it. A bank clerk."

He was still nodding and muttering to himself when he met me in Sabatini's. I took him to the coat room, showed him the burberry and handed him the check. I took out his gimmick book and gave it to him. He patted it fondly, the way you pat a faithful dog, and slipped it into his pocket. Then he flexed his right arm against his chest and grinned at me.

"Like getting my heart back, Kit," he said. "Thanks. I had one hell of a fantastic experience this morning. What are you drinking?"

We went to the bar and gave Romo our orders and Lennox told me about his guided tour through a nightmare and the corpse in the coke. "If you didn't come up with anything in the library," he said, "I'll make you a gift of the story."

"I can't use the story, Jake. Continuity would never pass it. But I could use the gimmick."

"It's yours."

"You mean that? Thanks." I really was grateful. Lennox knew how to pay for a favor. "It's solid, Man. That finger pointing down when she's swearing the husband's up on the roof. Great sight gimmick. It's the most." I began to drift off into a plot.

"Write it down, Kitten."

"What? Oh, I don't have to. Gimmicks like this you never forget."

"Locate anything this morning?"

"Something real odd. Poison-eaters."

"Poison-eaters? You're putting me on."

"No, Jake. I'm not kidding. I'm going to use it for a switch on the tired routine about an unknown killer menacing unknown victims. You know. Who's doing what to who and why."

Lennox spilled his drink.

"What's the matter?"

"Nothing. Go on."

"Here's the gimmick. You know about the dope habit. People start hitting heroin or cocaine and can't get off the hook. Well, the same thing happens with poison."

"I don't believe it."

"Some people acquire the poison habit. They eat arsenic for their health and—"

"Their health!"

"That's right. They take it in small doses so it isn't lethal and they build up a tolerance for it."

"Why?"

"They've got an idea it's good for them. For malaria. A tonic. An aphrodisiac. But dig this. Once they start they can't stop. It's habit-forming like dope. They've got to keep on eating poison the rest of their lives."

"I'll be damned."

"And they thrive on it, Jake. That's the truth." I waited a couple of minutes and then asked: "Why'd you throw a fit before?'

He grimaced. "That line about an unknown killer and unknown victims. It was a little too close to home."

"How?"

"I'm in the same fix, Kitten."

"You're an unknown killer?"

"No. One of the victims."

"This I got to hear."

He shrugged. "Let's have another drink. I'll tell you about it if you swear to keep it quiet."

I reached out with both arms and touched the crowd surrounding the bar. "On a stack of agency men."

Jake snorted. We had another drink and he unloaded the letter story in a low voice, his eyes flashing angrily, his fists clenching and unclenching. He had a set of photostats in his pocket, but he wouldn't show them to me then . . . not in

Sabatini's with half the business leaning over our shoulders warning Romo to leave the garbage out of the old-fashioneds. When he was finished, Lennox looked at me expectantly.

"You're a mystery writer, Kitten. How would you crack this one?"

"When I plot 'em," I said, "I've got sense enough to give myself a gimmick to get out on. A left-handed man pulls matches from the left side of the book. The U. S. didn't mint any silver dollars from 1909 to 1921. All ticket punches have different designs . . . and so on. Where's your gimmick?"

"There isn't any I know of."

"Then leave it to Fink. Smart cop, Fink. He'll find the gimmick."

Lennox nodded. "But damn it, I can't sit on my credits and wait for the explosion Sunday. I've got to do something."

"You're an amateur, Jake. Stay out of the act."

"I've got a crazy feeling that everything's hanging on this one week. If I fight through the week, I'm safe. I've got to fight, Kitten."

"You fight too much. Sit tight for a change and wait."

"No. Damn it. No." He brooded, then burst out: "I've got an idea what to do."

"What?"

"While Fink's looking for the guy who's writing these letters. . . ."

"Could be a dame."

"What?"

"A dame. A doll. A tootsie. A—"

"I heard you. I never thought of that, but you're right. It could be a woman. So. While Fink's looking for the writer, I could be looking for the writee."

"Where's your gimmick?"

He waved around at the bar. "Right here in this Violent Ward."

"You better explain. Take it from the top."

"If I called in everybody on the show and just told them about the letters, they'd deny they were written to them. There wouldn't be any impact. They'd be able to cover up the secret."

"Why should they cover?"

"You don't get threatening letters unless you've got something dirty in your past."

"Why should it be secret?"

"Because the letters are anonymous. No addressee. No signature. It's got to be a secret between two people. Yes?"

"I'll buy it."

"Whoever's sending those letters knows the right man will recognize them as soon as he sees them. All right. I know how to tag the one out of the eight who's getting the threats."

"How?"

"They're all in the business. Mixed up, neurotic, sick in the head like this sunny straight-jacket crowd in here right now. You have to be sick to like this rat-race. The higher up you rise in the spiral, the more precarious your balance becomes . . . like a kid on ten-foot stilts."

"I think of them balancing like tightrope walkers."

"But balance is the gimmick, Kitten." Lennox pounded his point like a piledriver. "Balance. Balance. Balance. Suppose I pulled these letters on them in private, one after the other. Mason. Sachs. Stacy. Kay Hill. Plummer. Charlie Hansel. Took the letters out and said: 'This was sent to you. Read it.' Watched them read it. You know how precariously they're balanced. On twenty-foot stilts. Living on nerves. Wouldn't the impact knock them off? Wouldn't the right one give himself away?"

I thought that over. "The trouble with your idea," I objected, "is that if they're all precarious like you—"

"They are. You know that. The whole damned business is.

That's what I hate about it. I feel like a visitor in a booby-hatch."

"Then they'd all be knocked off balance, guilty or not guilty. They'd all fall off their tightrope."

"No, you're wrong."

"What about Blinky? You said he threw a fit."

"But not a guilty fit. That was obvious. No, by God! It'll work. I know it'll work. I'm going to try it. You want to place any bets? I'll make book."

"My money's on Sachs. He stole that song he wrote back in Chicago."

"What about Kay Hill? From Brooklyn. Trying to pass as English. She's from Canarsie where they really breed crooks. What about Charlie Hansel, the undercover queen? Trying to pass with that hoofer he married."

"She's married? That fag?"

"Yes. To a dame named Gretel. They used to be 'Hansel and Gretel, Dansomimes.'"

"Oh no! Dansomimes?"

"The queens could be catching up with Charlie. What about Oliver Stacy? He's run through every woman in town. He went through the Rehearsal Club like a plague. Forty-three ingenues in thirty-six days. And how about Johnny Plummer? He's a Commie."

"You sure?"

"Almost positive."

"God knows, you may be right about them, Jake. When the right man reads those letters there could be a blast that no one could miss. Maybe a complete confession. If—"

I broke off because Lennox wasn't listening. He was staring at Roy Audibon, the network veep, who was passing through the crowded bar on the way into the restaurant. Vice-presidents are job lot in Sabatini's and Lennox couldn't be gaping at Audibon even though he is the original charm-boat. Tall, slender, grizzled hair, hornrim glasses, a smile that could register on a Geiger Counter . . . Audibon is the veep's veep. He's Mr. Network. I noticed that he was with a dark girl in a grey flannel suit. She had cropped curly hair, oriental eyes, and a lazy carriage. She was a looker, but you get to expect that in Sabatini's. Only the lookers get taken there. It was Gabby Valentine, of course, but I didn't find that out until later.

"Roy Audibon!" Lennox exclaimed angrily.

"What's the matter?"

"I'm in pain."

"Where does it hurt?"

"I don't know. Let's find out." He waved to Heitor, the head waiter. Heitor came bustling up to the bar prepared to give us a hard time. I saw Lennox slip him two tens and lay down the law in a whisper.

"Yes, Mr. Lennox? At once, Mr. Lennox?" Heitor always made every statement a question. "If you will bring your drinks to the table, please? The table is ready now, gentlemen?"

"I'll spring for lunch," Lennox said and we went into the dining room. Heitor bustled to the side tables against the wall and pulled an empty away from the banquette. It was alongside Audibon's. Lennox, who is invariably punctilious, broke his rule and held me back with a firm nudge. He slipped in first and sat down alongside Gabby who was gazing at him with big eyes. Then I sat down and the table locked us in.

That was one of the best luncheons I never had. I got stuck with the check, too, but that didn't bother me. I knew Lennox would settle up, once he recovered his sanity . . . if he ever did. He started off ignoring Gabby. He just pressed against her as he leaned over to speak to Audibon.

"I beg your pardon, friend. I'm a stranger in town. Would you point out some celebrities, if any?"

"Hello Jake," Audibon smiled. All the Geiger Counters went clickety-click.

84

"Are you a celebrity?" Lennox inquired genially. "They say that real life vice-presidents can be seen in the flesh, or was it the Altogether?"

"Why sure, son. Got your autograph album? There's Mr. Avery Borden right across from you." Audibon smiled across the restaurant to Avery Borden who also is the original charmboat. Tall, slender, grizzled hair and hornrim glasses. Mr. Agency. Borden smiled back. Clickety-click. Clickety-click.

"But are you a vice-president?" Lennox wanted to know.

"I'll show you my tax statement," Audibon answered and turned to Gabby.

"I beg your pardon, Miss." Lennox drew back. "Was I leaning on your derriere?"

"I'd have to answer that in French."

"Are you a vice-president?" Lennox asked her. "Answer in English."

"Not altogether," Gabby said. "Haven't you accosted me before?"

"I hardly think it possible. I just got out of stir."

Gabby clapped her hands. "Of course I know you. You're famous. They wrote you up in the *Calabash Chronicle.*"

"The Calabash King." Lennox nodded modestly. He leaned across her again, his hand groping for hers. "Are you in this here theaterical game, Mister? I hear you're all pretty fly. Bohemian. Stay up all night and drink like sixty. Is it true? Speak."

"Oysters," Audibon told the waiter. Clickety-click went the smile. "We smoke too, sonny. And ride bikes no-hands."

"I'll bet my father can lick your father."

"The hell he can. My father's a cop."

"What have you got, Meccano or Erector Set?"

"Meccano."

"Yahh!" Lennox sneered.

"What have you got, Lionel or American Flyer?"

"Lionel. O-Gauge."

"Pfff! Which do you get, *Boy's Life* or *American Boy?*"

"Both," Lennox said with a superior air.

"Oh yes?" Audibon retorted with heat. "Well let me ask you one question. Just one question. Do you get *Ropeco Magazine?*"

Lennox cringed and hung his head, then he and Audibon burst out laughing. Clickety damn click all over the place. I started looking for somewhere to hide. There was a war breaking out. They were hating each other and skirmishing in the tunnels beneath the glitter. They were hating for reasons I didn't know and probably they didn't know either; but that wouldn't make any difference, not on The Rock where you killed first and went to the head-shrinker later.

"What are you going to do about that Kansas hassle?" Audibon asked with sincere concern.

"It's been taken care of," Lennox smiled. "There won't be any suit."

"Good boy. Glad to hear it." Clickety-click. "I know you wouldn't cross-ruff the network into a Donnybrook."

"We aim to please, boss."

"It's knowing how that scores. Damn it, Jake, I wish we had more like you. We could use you on our other sick shows."

"How do you mean . . . other?"

"Now, Jake, we're a couple of Pros. We know how to count without fingers. You've got a pretty sick show, boy."

"It's got a damned good rating for an invalid."

"The best!" Clickety-click. "Of course your Sunday slot is rated at ten points better than you're doing, but that's not your fault. You can't maximize variety on Sunday."

"The client doesn't think so." Lennox smiled till it hurt. "We've got 'em convinced they're going to rename it Shoeday."

"Bless their dear little souls," Audibon enthused. "Of course they're not getting dollar and cents value percentagewise.

86

Your package doesn't integrate with their product. There's a synthetic overlap but not a genuine structural mesh."

A chill ran down my spine. When network veeps start talking like that the words don't mean anything because they're just the sound of a knife being sharpened. Lennox stiffened and returned Audibon's smile doggedly.

"We welcome suggestions," he said. "Name a mesh."

"Now don't ask me to sign this, but I think they need a Frontal Lobe show with a broad base of family appeal on a week night. They need a spacious universe type show. Something more galactic, with meaning."

"With meaning," Lennox repeated in an ominous voice. He looked at Gabby. "It's awesome. How does it feel to have lunch with a frontal lobe?"

Audibon laughed. Lennox laughed.

"Steak," Audibon told the waiter. He transferred the charm back to Lennox. "Jake, why are writers so hyper-conservative? You people are the bottle-neck of the business. Every time we try to revaluate and mock-up a new concept, you come out of the garret and say no."

"And what were you thinking of slipping into our Sunday night slot?" Lennox smiled. "A galactic 'How To' show?"

Audibon had worked his way up by parlaying a series of 'How To' panels through the agencies. How To Sing. How To Dance. How To Make A Dame. Every time you turned around there he was in another agency with another How To.

He gave Lennox the clickety-click again. "How To Educate Writers," he said. "Present writers excluded."

"You're optimistic. We gave up all hope for vice-presidents years ago. Present restaurant excluded. Tell me, Miss Calabash. Would you rather be marooned on a desert island with a mink-dyed skunk or a mink-dyed vice-president?"

"Gabby," Audibon laughed. "This is Jake Lennox. I pay him to entertain at lunch."

87

"Society's Favorite Funster," Lennox grinned. "And the lady is . . .?"

"My wife."

"That's a genuine funny. Goody for you, Roy. What's your name when he isn't dreaming galactically, Miss Calabash? Are you—" Lennox stopped. He stared at Gabby, at Audibon, then back at Gabby.

"Yes?" he asked quietly.

She nodded. Jake's face turned black. He shoved our table out, knocking glasses and rolls all over the place. He stood up, grabbed a corner of Audibon's table and slewed it into the aisle. He seized Gabby's arm.

"Out!" he said.

"Jordan!"

"Out."

"Behave yourself."

"Come on. Out!"

"Lennox! What the hell is this?" Audibon demanded.

"One more word out of you and I'll kill you," Lennox growled. He pulled Gabby to her feet and went out of the restaurant with her. Heitor saw the fuss and bustled up, ready to give Lennox a hard time. He took one look at his face and backed away.

On the street, Lennox pushed through the lunch hour crowds, never relaxing his grip on Gabby's arm. Both of them were too angry to speak. Finally Lennox spat: "Married? To him?"

"We're separated."

"How long?"

"A year."

"How long were you married?"

"Eight months."

"To him! Married to that—"

"Thank God it wasn't to you."

88

"Thank Roy, dear. He's our local god."

Gabby suddenly clutched his arm and dragged him to a stop before a sidewalk pitchman demonstrating a silver-plating fluid. The pitchman lost his audience.

"You listen to me," Gabby said.

"You answer me first. Why didn't you tell me?"

"When?"

"Last night."

"When you were so charming? The way you're acting now?"

"I mean later."

"We were talking about you."

"Exclusively?" Lennox showed his teeth. "You couldn't find a moment to let me know? It wasn't important enough even for a throw-away?"

"Is it important to you?"

"It's damned important."

"Why?"

"I don't know."

"You're behaving like a fool."

"That I do know."

He started off again, plowing through the crowds, hustling Gabby along full speed. Her skirt was narrow, she was wearing high-heeled opera pumps, it was painful for her. Lennox knew it and enjoyed it. He didn't know why he was trying to punish her; but Gabby had an inkling of what chasm might be producing the rage, and she was so transparently honest that she blurted it out.

"Dog in the manger," she said.

"Is that supposed to have meaning?"

"You're not jealous."

"I never said I was."

"You want revenge."

"Revenge for what?"

"Because you weren't the first."

"What!" He stopped and backed her into the recessed show-window of a lunchroom. "What was that?"

"You want revenge," Gabby repeated angrily. "You want to punish me because you weren't the first."

"Damn you, Gabby. . . ."

"Isn't it true?"

"No."

"You didn't need me. You needed a conquest."

"Shut up."

"You thought you owned me. From the beginning. All of me. You're selfish, egotistical, self—"

"Why didn't you say your date was with Audibon?"

"It was none of your business."

"Everything about you is my business. What did Audibon want?"

"You moved in on me last night," Gabby said. "And now you'd like to move in on the rest of my life. You want to own everything."

"Yes. Everything, damn it! You own all of me."

"I don't want it. I don't want ever to own anybody, and I won't be owned. Don't interrupt, Jordan. Listen to me." Gabby was raging. "You think you've staked out a claim, but it isn't like that at all. There'll be days when we discover we need each other and then we'll be together. There'll be other days when nothing will happen. But no claims, no owner-ship, no possession, no habit. Do you understand?"

"Do you think you're lecturing a child?"

"You are a child. Selfish. Spoiled. Rude."

"You're talking about manners. What the hell does that have to do with love?"

"Everything. Do you want to love me or use me?"

"Use you? For what?"

"Your whipping boy. You were rude to Roy in the restau-rant. I don't know why you were fighting but—"

90

"He's knifing my show!"

"I don't care. You were rude. You behaved dreadfully. Then you were ashamed and you tried to take it out on me. Is that your kind of love? Hurtful? Hateful?" She began to tremble.

"Yes, it is. I'm not going to apologize. I told you last night . . . you open me up. I look at you and my guts come out. If part is poison, I can't hide it. And I don't give a damn. I earn my living in a lying rat-race. There has to be honesty between us or what's the use?"

"Not this kind. This isn't honesty. It's—"

"I'm being honest," Lennox insisted savagely. "I can fake a romance with a woman any time, but I don't want faking between us. There wasn't any last night, Gabby. Not from me. Don't hand me that revenge routine. I didn't have any illusions. You were too good for me to imagine that I was the first—"

She slapped his mouth with all her strength, and raised her hand to slap him again. Lennox caught her wrist and twisted it down.

"Bitch!" he shouted.

She burst into tears. "What are you doing to me?" she cried in desperation. "What are you making me do? Look at us . . . fighting like this. It's horrible. But you like it, don't you? You want us to hurt each other. Don't you?"

His heart constricted. "No. For God's sake. No. I—" He looked around. People were staring. Behind them, a chef at a window grill was gaping through the plate glass. There was no taxi in sight; no hiding place. There was an empty delivery truck parked at the curb. Lennox took Gabby across the sidewalk, opened the truck door and forced her into the driving cab. He got in himself and slammed the door. Gabby was crying without control. He was shamed and elated.

"Gabby. . . ."

"Go away."

"Listen. . . ."

"Be quiet. Go away."

"Not now. Not when you're like this."

"I never hit anybody in my life. I never wanted to hit anybody . . . ever. I'm cheap and. . . ."

"No."

"I'm so ashamed. My God! How you can fill me with shame."

"I know. I warned you, didn't I!"

She didn't answer. Lennox waited, then he said: "Look at it my way. I'm having a rough time this week. I don't know how I'm going to get through Sunday. That's why I'm acting like this. I said last night I wanted you to see me at my best. This is my worst."

"It can't be just this week. It—"

"Yes it is. And I thought: Thank God for Gabrielle. I'm in the worst hassle of my life, but I've found her when I needed her most. I can depend on her forever. I've got someone sane and beautiful to hold on to in this rotten war."

"Well? Well?"

"And then Audibon was sprung on me. 'My wife.' Bang."

"Which meant you couldn't depend on me. Is that it?"

"I don't know. I was scared. Maybe I'm jealous. I was afraid I was losing you."

"Jordan—"

"No. Let me finish." He took a deep breath. "I did everything wrong. But I couldn't help myself. I think I knew I was doing everything wrong. But I couldn't stop myself. You know how dangerous a drowning man is? He'll clutch at you and drown you too if you don't hit him. That's what happened. I was drowning . . . You hit me . . . I'm grateful. . . ."

Gabby turned to him, her dark eyes searching his face. He met her gaze steadily. Her expression slowly changed from anguish to compassion, and she reached out and touched his mouth gently. Lennox smiled a peace-offering, and it was answered. He pulled her to him and kissed her until the kiss was returned. Then they sat quietly, allowing the silence to speak for them and heal the quarrel.

Suddenly the truck door was wrenched open and a burly man bawled: "What the hell are you doing in there?"

"Listen," Lennox snapped. "We're from the phone company. Why the hell don't you pay your bill?"

Gabby burst out laughing. Lennox helped her out of the truck and glared at the astounded driver. "This is your last warning, cheapskate. Next time we take the truck away."

They scampered off down the street and flagged a cab. As they got in, Lennox exclaimed: "Jesus! Me mackinaws."

"Jesus, me job!" Gabby said.

"What about lunch? I loused your steak."

"I'll have something sent up."

They sat close together in comforting silence all the way to Houseways, Inc. At the office door Lennox took her shoulders in his hands for a moment, then asked: "Forgiven?"

Gabby nodded.

"See you tonight, please?"

"Tonight."

"Don't spring another husband."

She shook her head.

"You'd better divorce him. I've got serious-type intentions."

"I can't."

"Why not?"

"He won't let me. He wants to own me too."

"How can he stop you?"

"Not now, Jordan. Some other time. But . . . I've got problems too."

She ran into the office. Lennox stood watching her and grinding his teeth on Audibon's name. Then he looked up and down the street, located a restaurant, went in and bought a lunch and had it sent up to Gabby.

"This is Monday," he muttered. "Six more days. Christ, stand by me. Gabrielle, stand by me."

He returned to Sabatini's, claimed his overcoats, and went home. Cooper was in the kitchen piling canned goods on the shelves while the Siamese climbed on him and begged shamelessly for food. There was a rigid law in the house that neither man ever questioned the other about his private life, but Cooper's face wore such an expression of blank dismay that Lennox was startled into breaking the rule.

"Sam! What's the matter?"

Cooper opened his mouth, then closed it.

"Where were you last night? Has anything happened? Speak."

"I'm famous."

"What?"

Cooper nodded. "You remember last month Mason wanted a song spot with the dummy? Comedy duet."

"Sure. I couldn't come up with a suggestion and you cooked up a tune. 'We're The Most.' So?"

"They released it last week. It . . . So help me, it's turning into a hit. Suidi took me down for a disc-jockey interview last night."

"Suidi? Who he?"

"The ambassador's son."

"*Le Jazz Hot?* Goggle-eyed guy?"

"That's him. He owns a record company. They make race records mostly, but he took a chance on 'We're The Most' and it . . . You should have heard them rave last night."

"This is sensational, Sam. Man, this *is* the Most!"

"It's an outrage," Cooper said. He was angry and perplexed.

"What's burning you?"

"I spend years writing tunes. I drudge like a sincere-type

94

writer. A veritable Irving Beethoven. And what happens? Nothing. But a lousy little novelty I work up in half an hour during rehearsal . . . It's a trappisty."

"Lay there and bleed, long-hair. This is great. Can I shake the hand that shook the hand of Irving B. Cooper, author of 'We're The Most' and countless other hit tunes which their names are legion?" Lennox pumped Cooper's limp hand and dragged him into the living room. "This needs a drink. We'll all have a drink, by God. Bring out the skunk."

He filled glasses and thrust one into Cooper's fist. "We'll plug it on the show. Maybe we can get Mason to use it for his theme. Tell me about last night. Why the hell didn't you say *Le Jazz Hot* was your publish—" Lennox did a take. "Hold the phone. You mean you were supposed to meet him at Alice McVeagh's party? It was a business date?"

"Well . . ." Cooper began.

"And you were supposed to go down for the interview afterwards. Yes or no?"

"Not exactly, Jake. . . ."

"But you didn't tell me. No. You let me bellyache and offered to go looking for the gimmick book, and you would have too, you liar. You'd have given up the interview, you perjurer. Wouldn't you?"

Cooper was flustered. "How about the book? Did you locate it?"

"All taken care of. I figured out the Quaker and the blonde. I'll tell you later."

"What about the knot?"

Lennox flinched. "That's still hanging over me. I haven't remembered everything yet." He swallowed and tried to regain his enthusiasm. "To hell with it. Kit went down and rescued the book. Here it is. Now let's have your story."

He pulled out his notebook to display it. The photostats

95

came out with it and scattered on the floor. Cooper looked down at the white writing on the black background.

"What's this?"

"The letters we've been getting. To hell with them too. I want to hear about you." As Lennox picked up the photostats, Cooper took one and examined it curiously. "Forget the letters, Sam. I've worried enough today. Let me have a few jollies. How much money are you going to make? Will you hit the jukeboxes?"

"I've seen this writing before," Cooper said.

Lennox froze. "What?"

"I've seen this handwriting before."

"Sure?"

"Positive."

"Don't put me on, Sam. This is serious."

"I am serious."

"Where did you see the writing?"

"I can't remember."

"Whose is it?"

"I don't know."

"Sam. For God's sake! Everything hangs on this. You—"

"Shut up a minute."

Lennox sat down slowly and chafed while Cooper studied the photostats. Finally Cooper looked up and shook his head.

"I'm sorry, Jake. I know I've seen it before, but that's all I can remember. It's like you and the knot. We're both stuck."

"Holy Mother on Mike!" Lennox surged up from his chair and paced the room furiously. He noticed the drink in his hand and hurled it into the fireplace. As it smashed, he turned to Cooper.

"But you'll remember, won't you?" he said. "We've got six days to Sunday. You'll remember."

"I'll try."

96

"And you'll do it. We'll lick it, won't we, Sam? We'll both fight it, and we'll come out on top Sunday."

"I don't know, Jake. Fight what? Where's top? Fill me in, boy. So far I'm just a bystander."

Lennox poured it out; the whole story up to that moment. He was discreet about Gabby. He merely indicated and let Cooper figure out the details for himself. Cooper listened in silence. When it was all finished, he looked at Lennox strangely. Then he exploded.

"You God damned stupid idiot! Ass! Imbecile! Lennox, the Thinker. Why the hell can't you stop thinking? You haven't got what to think with . . . Agency Man!"

Lennox quailed before the storm.

"What the hell is the matter with you? You've been tearing around looking for the villain in the piece like a soap opera hack. You want to find the villain who's writing the letters. You want to find the villain who's getting them. You want to find the villain who's threatening your career. Damn you, you're the villain. Can't you see that, dunderhead?"

"Me!" Lennox was amazed.

"Natch, you. You're the one who's making all the trouble for yourself. You insulted Ned Bacon. You insulted Tooky Ween and Blinky and Mason. You picked a fight with Roy Audibon. With Audibon! The one man who can ruin you in this business."

"But. . . ."

"You've been fighting with this Gabby girl who sounds like one of the angel-type innocents. That's despicable. It's shooting a sitting duck. You even tried to pick a fight with me. You're so busy fighting the invisible villain you don't realize you're him . . . he . . . it . . . To hell with the grammar. You're the only villain in the piece, Lennox. Face it."

"Jesus." Lennox sat down aghast. "Me?"

"Wake up, writer! Villains are for books. Only a Square thinks you find them in real life."

"But the letters. . . ."

"Somebody sick in the head is writing them. You're in a nasty hassle right now. Admitted. But you're the villain who's making it worse. You're the one who's building it into a crisis."

"I can't help myself, Sam. You said it's nasty. And I'm scared."

"Like friend Fink said, it's smart to be scared. But don't turn Square. Squares think there are Good Guys and Bad Guys. But we know we're all Good Guys and Bad Guys inside ourselves. Half the time we build ourselves up, and the other half we're knocking ourselves down. When a Square knocks himself down he starts looking for a Bad Guy to blame. That's what you've been doing. You ought to be ashamed of yourself."

After a long pause, Lennox said: "You're right. You're always right, damn you. I'm a noodnick."

"Hear, hear!"

"But I'm going to reform."

"Don't start any reform routine. Every time you make up your mind to do something, we have to take to the hills. Just sit tight and behave."

"I can't sit tight, Sam. I've got problems to buck and I know how to do it. I'm going to do it."

"Oh God! Is there no mercy?"

"Now don't worry. I'm going to keep on fighting, but like a goddamned Galahad."

"Are we friends?" Cooper shouted.

"Yes." Lennox was startled.

"Will you listen to a friend?"

"I'm listening."

"Leave it alone. Will you do that for me?"

"I can't."

"Here's my last warning. If you go through with this . . . if you attack it and fight it, no matter how . . . you'll regret it for the rest of your life. Now, for the last time: Will you quit?"

"No."

"Then you're dead, Lennox. You're dead."

CHAPTER VI ·

W<small>HEN</small> I <small>WAS</small> A <small>KID ON THE</small>
Rock, one of my friends turned racketeer and went into the
bicycle-stealing business. He put the heist on six bikes which
he hid in the Indian Caves in Isham Park where the Hessian
deserters holed up during the Revolutionary War. We used
to dig for musket balls and flint arrow heads up there, just
a few blocks from the spot where they found a dead-type
dinosaur.

Anyway, my thief friend was too dumb or too honest to
sell the bikes, and the first time he tried to ride one around
our neighborhood he got caught with the stolen goods. He made
his getaway and hid in the caves until dark. Then he sneaked
out to make amends and return the rest of the loot to the
rightful owners. This was up at the north end of The Rock
where there were still private homes. Nobody could sleep that
night for the crash of stolen bikes being thrown over fences
into backyards.

Likewise, for the next few days nobody in the business could sleep for the crash of Lennox switching from the Bad Guys to the Good Guys. He had a formidable list of antagonists to pacify. He had his Poison Pen Test to spring without creating any additional hostility. Lennox made an exuberant try. If he was villainous at times, as Cooper suggested, he could be heroic when he tried to combat his own villainy. Here are the highlights of his fight.

He phoned Rox Records, the offices of Suidi, *Le Jazz Hot*, prepared to do battle with the aid of a French dictionary. He was saved by a Bronx speaking secretary.

"I think we ought to promote Sam Cooper's hit," Lennox explained. "My idea is a professional party for Sam. A big name party on Wednesday or Thursday. You invite your big wheels. I'll invite ours. I've got a gimmick in mind that might be a natural for publicity. Say you're celebrating the history of song hits . . . starting with someone as far back as Handy and bringing it down to Cooper. If you could get enough names there it ought to be worth a double-truck in any magazine."

Rox Records admitted that it certainly ought.

"I want to finance this myself, but don't let Sam know."

They kicked it around enthusiastically and agreed that Lennox would be permitted to finance a cocktail party for Cooper at the studios of Rox Records on West 50th Street Thursday next.

Lennox hired a network photographer and took him up to Mason's apartment on the west side, which is the unfashionable side of The Rock.

The apartment was in a building that had never had a celebrated tenant from the entertainment business. As a result, the staff was stage-struck and dying to get into the act. The doorman cultivated a Low Dutch dialect. His eager expression informed Lennox that he was ready for Discovery. The elevator man had worked up a comedy monologue in Irish, Cockney and Chinese. He also was ready. At the top floor, Lennox rang Mason's doorbell, opened the door and entered with the photographer. The apartment was never locked.

They came into a bare foyer, the size of a boxing ring. It was ankle deep in wall-to-wall blue carpeting. Lennox called: "Mig? It's Jake Lennox." No answer. They went through an archway into a bare living room the size of a tennis court. It was naked except for wall-to-wall grey carpeting. "Mig!" Lennox called again. No answer. They peeked into the dining room and two of the bedrooms, all empty and bare except for wall-to-wall carpeting.

"Must be out buying furniture," the photographer said.

Lennox shouted again, then listened. He heard the faint sound of music. They followed it and found Mason in the study. It was the size of a study with wall-to-wall green carpeting. It was empty except for a giant TV set with a thirty inch screen in the corner. A silver plate on it proclaimed that it was the gift of the network to their well-beloved Mig Mason & Diggy Dixon. Before the set was a bridge table at which Mason and his wife were seated, silently eating canned hamburgers and watching the screen.

Mason glanced up. "The Thinker," he said morosely and turned back to the screen.

"The Thinker," Irma said.

"*Bon appetit*. French for it smells good," Lennox answered cheerfully. "Mig, I haven't had a chance to congratulate you. You were great Christmas night. Sensational. It was a great show. Sensational. Your timing was great. Your gags were sensational. It's great working with you, Mig. You make any writer look sensational."

"Thanks, Jake." Mason looked modest.

"Thanks," Irma said.

"Was it St. Nicholas?" Mason asked abruptly.

"Of course it was St. Nicholas."

"Then I was right. It was that phone girl that loused me."

"Of course you were right."

"Why didn't you say so?" Mason demanded. "You're all trying to louse me."

"Did I say you were wrong?"

"You didn't say I was right."

"Because I work for Grabinett. Have a heart, Mig. You're a great star. You can tell anybody off. But I haven't got your sensational talent. I have to work for a living. Be kind to the hired help."

The scowl disappeared from Mason's face. It also disappeared from Irma's face.

"I've brought a photographer for some pictures," Lennox continued briskly. "We're nominating you for Comedian of The Year, and by God you're going to be elected."

Mason brightened.

"Not in those clothes," Irma said. "He's got to get dressed up."

"Never mind the clothes," Mason complained. "What about the background? There's no furniture in the house."

"There's no furniture in the house," Irma told Lennox. A moment later she added: "It's all being custom built."

"To hell with the furniture," Lennox said. "We don't want formal pictures. We want behind the scenes shots. What makes a talent great. Mig in his workshop with the dummy. How he builds Diggy . . . How he paints him . . . The tricks he invented . . . All that sensational stuff you showed me, Mig."

"Great! Sensational!" Mason leaped up, delighted. He was prouder of his mechanical ability than anything else. He led the way into another enormous room, carpeted from wall to wall, containing a long carpenter's bench cluttered with tools.

Various portions of Diggy Dixon were scattered on the bench; heads, legs, arms, bodies, eyes. An open closet was hung with the dummy's wardrobe. Mason's three gag writers were seated on camp chairs in a tight circle bitching their competitors.

Lennox greeted them perfunctorily. He had long ago given up all attempts to communicate with them. Gag writers are alien creatures and even a casual "Hello" can lead to complications. Their entire lives boil down to a single-minded search for jokes and it's impossible to conduct a coherent conversation with them. In thirty-nine weeks Lennox had never been introduced to the gagmen by Mason, and although he finally discovered their names, he still identified them as the Sourball, the Post-Nasal Drip and the Monk. Incidentally, it was the Sourball who later turned spy.

"Got a sweetheart of a gag, Mig baby," the Monk beamed.

"It stinks," Sourball snapped.

"Try it on him, just for size." The Drip began snuffling in anticipation: "Hnkhhh. . . ."

"It's a sweetheart, baby. Diggy says to you: 'How's your wife, Mig?'"

"I'll have you know my wife's an angel," Sourball snapped.

"You're lucky! Hnkhhh . . . My wife's still living."

Mason looked at them nervously. The truth was, he didn't know a good gag from a bad one, and was always apprehensive.

"I'm afraid of it, fellas," he said. "Diggy's a wholesome American boy. He wouldn't make fun of marriage."

He dragged the photographer to the bench. There he demonstrated the inner workings of his genius . . . the dummy's weighted eyes, the carefully fitted mouth and jaw, the regular body with right-hand controls for the head, and an extra body with left-hand controls; for dummies, like baseball gloves, must be fitted to the hand. Mason would have been in great difficulties last September, he explained, when he had rheumatism in his working hand, if he hadn't had a lefthand dummy to switch to.

"Not rheumatism. Neuritis." Sourball said.

"Wait a minute. Room. Attic. Hnkhhh . . . Diggy's a poet working in an attic. Mig's the landlord. He asks Diggy where he could work better, in a room or attic, and Diggy says: 'That's why I'm bent over my desk. Rheumatics.' "

"Switch it to neuritis," Sourball snapped. "Diggy's an editor. Mig's the poet. Mig's sore because Diggy says his poem is old fashioned."

"Right. Right. Hnkhhh . . . Mig says: 'Which is better, the old writers or the new writers?' "

"That's it, sweetheart." The Monk took up the running. "So Diggy answers: My brother's got that."

"Got what?"

"Hnkhhh . . . Neuritis!"

They beamed at their employer.

"I don't know, fellas," Mason said dubiously. "Diggy's a wholesome American boy. He wouldn't make fun of disease."

Lennox ignored all this and concentrated on the photography business. There is nothing so sunny as the twinkle of flash bulbs, and by the time the photographer departed, Mason was suffering from 3rd degree burns and smiling happily. Lennox felt the time was right for the attack. He asked for a private conference and Mason sent his writers into the study. Then he began tinkering with a new head on the bench and told Lennox to go ahead. Lennox took the photostats out of his pocket. "Hit him hard," he thought. "Knock him off balance."

"Read these letters," he said in an ominous voice.

Mason took the photostats and read them one by one. Lennox watched him intently, searching for a giveaway expression, a gesture, a sign. Mason handed the photostats back indifferently and picked up the dummy head.

"Crazy," he said. "They write like that in subway johns.

105

What do you think, Jake? Does Diggy's new face look wholesome?"

"Mig! Don't you understand? These are threatening letters. I think they're written to you. You're in danger."

"Me?" Mason was fascinated. "Me? I never . . ." He put the dummy down and stared at Lennox.

"Yes, you. Did you read that last one? There's going to be dynamite Sunday. I'm here to help you. I want to do all I can. Who's writing them to you, Mig? Do you know?"

"Sure they're to me. Sure. I should of realized." Mason nodded with growing conviction. "Stars always get anonymous letters. Like presidents." He began to get excited. "It hits the fan on the Sunday show, huh? This is sensational, Jake. Can we have a couple of reporters there?"

"Reporters!"

"Wait a minute. Wait a minute." Mason grabbed the photostats and ran through them again. "I just thought of something. Yeah. Here. You better not let the reporters see this one, Jake. Number three."

"Don't let the reporters see . . ." Lennox echoed faintly.

"Uh-huh. Keep it back. They'll know I'm not getting the letters if they see this one, but I ought to be getting them. That Spanish faker was getting blackmailed every night when he worked The Chert Room and I got twice his billing."

"You're not getting the letters?"

"Sure I'm getting the letters. Except Number three. Here's the line. 'You east-side so-and-so.' See? This one can't be to me. I live on the west side. But the reporters don't have to know. Hold that one out on them." Mason clapped Lennox on the shoulder appreciatively. "If I ever made a crack about you thinking, Jake, it was only for laughs. You got a head on you I admire. We'll get a spread out of this if we get any action Sunday. I tell you what. Let's be smart. Hire a guy. I bet you thought of that already, huh, Thinker?"

"Hire a guy? For what?"

"In case this one don't show up. Write a little script for him and we'll have him stand by in the house. If we don't get any action by the final comedy spot you can cue him in and he'll give us a production." Mason began to laugh. "I just thought of a great ad lib for Diggy when this guy starts the fuss. Diggy says—"

"Mig! For God's sake! This is serious. The letters are legitimate. The threat's legitimate too. Don't you understand?"

"Great. Sensational. Then we won't have to use the stand-in. But have him there anyway. Jake, I love ya!"

Lennox made his escape. He was thunderstruck by Mason's reaction, then indignant, finally amused.

"One down. Five to go," he muttered and continued the campaign.

He phoned Tooky Ween and made peace.

"Tooky? Jake Lennox. I've got a promotion in mind for your property that I'd like to discuss."

"Which property?" Ween rumbled in a hostile voice.

"Far as I'm concerned you've only got one hot property. The great man. Mig."

"What's the promotion, Lennox?" Ween asked, a little more affably.

"Sam Cooper's got a hit tune just breaking. That duet he wrote for Mig and the dummy."

"What duet?"

" 'We're The Most.' "

"That's a hit?"

"On the way. Here's my idea. Mason & Dixon brought the tune out. How about using their picture on the sheet music? Might be a nice promotion."

"That ain't bad, Jake. Ain't a sour note in the whole notion." Ween was back to first names again and definitely friendly.

"It's only a suggestion. I've got nothing to do with it, but I can ask Sam for you."

"Thanks, Jake. It could do Cooper a lot of good. My boy could double his sales. So 'We're The Most' is socko, huh? Who's handling Cooper?"

"Nobody."

"A boy like that needs handling, Jake."

Lennox laughed. "That's between you and Cooper. They're giving him a promotion party at Rox Studios Thursday. Come on over. There'll be names and photographers, so bring your properties too. You can talk it up with Sam between flashes."

Kay Hill received him in her east side Early American apartment, conducted him through a Colonial hall to a Federal parlor where she seated him on a Duncan Phyfe couch. Her dark green dressing gown clashed with the background, but set off her acid eyes and acid red hair.

"Men," she spat in her strange clipped accent. "Bloody lice! They only come when they're hungry. What are you after, Lennox?"

"Trouble," Lennox said.

"We'll pickle it first. What's your brew?" Before he could answer she made a couple of drinks, handed him one and finished hers.

"When was the last time you were here, Lennox?"

"This is the first."

"They keep passing through. I lose count." She opened a window, then closed the drapes with a savage flick. She blew dust off pewter tankards and opened and slammed drawers. "I've been asked for plenty in my life but they never called it trouble." She shuffled a deck of cards once. "They've had it but never asked for it."

"I'm not asking, Kay."

"No? You're here, aren't you?" She cupped his chin in her hand, smiled contemptuously, then slapped him. "We'll pickle it."

She went to the bar. "Christ, it's bloody hot. D'you want ice?"

"No thanks."

"There isn't any anyway." She pulled irritably at the dressing gown until it opened, displaying a black bra and black panties. She fretted around the room, the green gown trailing behind her.

"Are you English?" Lennox asked.

"Are you starting something?"

"I want to know."

"I'm English. Now you know."

"The dialect bothers me."

"Not dialect, Lennox." Her speech became more clipped and more English. "It's called an accent, darling. I have most unfortunately acquired a dreadful American accent. Mummy and Daddy will be terribly amused when I come home from the States." She dropped the English. "We'll pickle it."

She made another pair of drinks.

"Jesus, Kay!" Lennox protested. She finished both, came to him and sat on his lap. Lennox was startled when he noticed her eyes were terrified. She was desperate.

"Make a pass, Lennox," she said.

"Are you putting me on?"

"No. You're putting me off."

She got up. Lennox caught her wrist and pulled her down alongside him.

"Do you know why I'm here?" he asked.

"I don't give a bloody bug why you're here."

"What's eating you out?"

"You don't give a bloody bug what's eating me out. We'll pickle it."

"Not now, we won't. There's something else first."

"I've changed my mind."

"I haven't." Lennox drew out the photostats and handed them to her. "Read these."

"What?"

"Read them."

She began to shriek with laughter. "Read these, he says." She rocked around the room, neighing hysterically. Lennox went after her, took her by the shoulders and slammed her into a chair.

"You're petrified," he growled, "and I think I know why. Read those letters, damn you, and we'll find out."

She wiped her eyes with the hem of the dressing gown and read the photostats. Lennox watched her closely. Her face reflected every word she was reading. Her body reflected her face. She was savage, sick, vicious, threatening. For the length of all six letters she was the writer of those letters. She was completely identified. When she came to the end she looked at Lennox.

"Who's writing them, Kay?"

"How should I know?"

"They're to you, aren't they?"

"No."

"Don't lie, damn you. You're halfway into a strait jacket and this is what's doing it to you."

She smiled wearily. "Clever Jordan Lennox. Mummy's favorite bright boy." She got up and kissed his brow chastely. "We'll pickle it."

Lennox followed her to the bar. "They're written to you, Kay. I came up here to help you out, but you've got to level with me. Who's writing them? Who's threatening you?"

"I told you. I don't know."

110

"This isn't anything to fool with, Kay. It's loaded with dynamite and it's set to go off Sunday."

"What the hell do I care what happens Sunday," she blazed. "The whole damned show can bloody off Sunday. Give me the damned letters." She snatched the photostats from him. "They're not to me. Look at this line in Number four. 'You black-headed lying etcetera.' Is that me?" She jabbed at her red hair angrily. "That's red. It's always been red. If you don't believe me I can show you the convincer. Go look for somebody else, Lennox."

Lennox examined the line silently, then put the photostats away. When he looked at Kay again, she was smiling crookedly, her eyes still terrified.

"What d'you say, Lennox?"

"On my way."

"I've changed my mind again."

"No you haven't."

"One for the road?"

"No thanks."

"Christ, you're a bloody Square, Lennox."

"I guess everybody is, one way or another."

"Mummy's favorite model boy. That's the way out." She waved her arm indifferently. "My love to your model roommate, Sam Stacy."

"Stacy! Is that it, Kay? Oliver Stacy?" Lennox stepped to her and took her shoulders. "Is he what's eating you out?"

"It was a slip. I meant Cooper. Sam Cooper, of course. I always get his name mixed up with Oliver's. Let go of me, Lennox. Damn you, let go of me."

"Is it Stacy?"

"To hell with Stacy. It was a slip, I tell you. Slip of the tongue . . ." She began to shake and clung to him. "My God, Lennox. My God! I haven't seen him in two weeks, outside rehearsal. 'Good morning. Good night. Take it from the top. Cue, please. Take your cross after I say the line. Oh Jesus, Lennox, what's he doing to me?"

"Running up a score, Kay. Face it."

"You son of a bitch!" Kay wrenched herself out of his arms. "You're gloating too, aren't you? All of you. Counting up your scores. Get lost, Lennox. Get lost fast!"

Lennox got lost fast. Down on the street he murmured: "But she's the one who's lost. Lost in the tunnels. At least I gave her a half hour's entertainment. Balance! Two down and four to go."

It so happened that my wife was in Raeburn Sachs' office when Lennox dropped in. She had been called down unexpectedly. Sachs' wife, a discouraged creature with a sagging figure, led Robin down a twisting corridor in Grabinett's offices to the brain room where Sachs operated. He directed all Grabinett's shows.

Sachs was thin, dry-blond, with bulging blue eyes and a mid-western twang. He liked to be overworked and fatigued, and the first impression he gave was of a bone-weary man calling on genius to surmount exhaustion. Later, you imagined you had received the wrong impression, but you really hadn't. It was Sachs who changed. His thyroid began popping and everything else in addition to his eyes bulged.

He was slumped in a chair wearing a crushed pin-stripe suit and drinking chicken soup out of a carton when Robin entered. He lifted his head wearily, smiled, then called to his wife.

"The song is out. I've just remembered it isn't in the P.D."

"The legal department said it is," Mrs. Sachs answered in a discouraged voice.

"They're wrong. Oh yes. Make a note. We'll need three extra costumes and a magician. No Mind Acts. They're not television-wise. I want a different Sawing A Woman In Half. Something fresh."

Mrs. Sachs made notes.

"Also a dog act. Call the music department and see if we can get a small band arrangement of Piston's 'Incredible Flautist.' "

"Why?" Mrs. Sachs asked.

"Because it's scored for dog barks," Sachs answered as though that explained everything. Apparently it did. His wife moused out and closed the door. Sachs smiled at Robin.

"Always rushed," he said wearily. "This is last night's dinner." He finished the soup, got up and slouched around Robin, examining her sleepily. "Yes. Yes, I see. The Hedda Gabler type." Suddenly he crouched at the desk, yanked out a bottom drawer and threw his handkerchief in. " *'Now I'm burning your child, Thea! Burning it, curly-locks!'* Manuscript into the stove business." He threw in his small change and a pack of cigarettes. " *'Your child and Eilet Lövborg's. I am burning—I am burning your child!'* Slow curtain."

Robin gaped at him.

Sachs smiled and stood up. "Or Marguerite," he said, stroking her blonde hair. " *'Ich gäb was drum, wenn ich nur wüsst', Wer heut' der Herr gewesen ist!'* Comb business at the mirror. Which show are you here for?"

"You called me down," Robin said. "Don't you know?"

"I'm directing four shows." Sachs smiled patiently. "Which are you?"

" *'Who He?'* "

"Oh yes. Yes. I see. You're . . . Robin. Lennox gave you the call. It's about the costumes." Sachs hitched a hip onto the corner of the desk, smiled cheerfully, and began flicking the hem of Robin's skirt with his toe. "They were smaller in the early nineteenth century. Much smaller. Have you seen the models in the Dress Museum? We're having trouble with those Philip Nolan costumes. I think we're going to have trouble with you."

"With me? How?"

Sachs reached back and picked up a printed card. It was the

conventional file card actresses send to all offices with pictures, measurements and credits printed on it. This one happened to be Robin's.

"I checked your card," Sachs said. "It's the bust that worries me. Thirty-six. I see you weren't exaggerating. Are you married?"

"Yes."

"Any children?"

"No."

"Too bad."

"Why too bad? What's it have to do with—"

"Children make the bust sag. You're probably too firm to get into our costumes. Take 'em out."

"What!"

"Take 'em out. Let me see them. If they're not too high we won't have any problems."

"Are you kidding?"

"Come on, come on, Robin. Take 'em out."

"You're crazy."

"This is a pictorial medium," Sachs explained patiently. "You've got to audition three-dimensionally. Now don't waste my time, Robin. We've pulled the Nolan costumes already and I've got to find the women to fit them."

The phone rang. Sachs picked it up, meanwhile snapping his fingers impatiently at Robin's bust. "Yes? Not now. I'm busy." He flipped the phone and caught it neatly on the cradle. "Took three lessons from W. C. Fields," he smiled, then brayed: " *'Master Copperfield, under the impression that your peregrinations in this metropolis have not as yet been extensive, and that you might have some difficulty in penetrating the arcana of the Modern Babylon . . .'* Come on, Robin. Come on. Get 'em out."

There was a knock on the door.

"Go away," Sachs called.

The knocking was repeated.

" *'Here's a knocking indeed!'* " Sachs intoned in Shakespearean

114

diapason. He snatched up the desk lamp and began to hobble. "Lantern business. *'If a man were porter of hell-gate, he should have old turning the key. Knock, knock, knock! Who's there i'th' name of Belzebub?'*"

"Jake Lennox. I've got to see you. Won't take a minute."

"Wait," Sachs told Robin. He put down the lamp and called: "Come in. I'm starting the clock."

Lennox entered the brain room and was surprised to see Robin. He greeted her and Sachs, then said: "This won't take long, but I'm afraid it'll have to be in private. Do you mind, Robin?"

"No. It's a pleasure," Robin said through her teeth. She stalked out of the office and slammed the door.

"Something?" Lennox asked Sachs.

"Temperament," Sachs answered wearily. He picked up the phone. "Tell the actress to wait in the reception room." He hung up.

Lennox took out the photostats and thrust them at Sachs. "Read these," he said sharply.

Sachs glanced at the photostats casually, five seconds to each letter, then slouched to his desk chair and slumped into it, regarding Lennox with tired eyes.

"I said read them," Lennox snapped.

"I've read them," Sachs answered. "I have a photographic memory." He quoted random lines from the letters, then smiled patiently. "Satisfied?"

It occurred to Lennox that Sachs must have examined the letters in Blinky's safe at another time. That killed the shock value and there was no point in calling his bluff.

"They're written to you, aren't they?"

"I don't like your Sunday drama spot, Jake. The Philip Nolan. It's weak."

"Stay with the threats, will you? They're no drama spots."

"*'Damn the United States. I wish that I would never hear the*

115

name again.' Dolly in to close-up. Yes. Your scene's out of focus. There's a value missing."

"Focus on the letters. Who's threatening you?"

"What?" Recalled from his visions, Sachs gazed at Lennox with faraway eyes.

"You're faking," Lennox said savagely. "And you're not kidding me with the act. These letters were written to you. You're the one who's putting the show on a spot."

"They're not written to me."

"I don't believe you."

"Isn't it obvious?" Sachs said wearily. "What's that line from Number Two? Yes. 'You fancy college cess-pool . . .' And so on. I'm no college man. That's why I've still got my talent. *'A set o' dull conceited hashes confuse their brains in college classes!'* What are we going to do about Sunday?"

"I don't know," Lennox said in disgust, returning the photostats to his pocket. "I'm doing the best I can with what I've got. Amateur. I should have stayed out of the act. Maybe the police can do better."

"If I could whip you into coming up with something fresh, I'd throw out the Nolan. A different 'Monkey's Paw' or—That's an idea! Instead of three wishes, make it three New Year's resolutions."

"Lay off, will you. There's nothing wrong with the Philip Nolan."

"It isn't televisionwise, Jake."

"It's as televisionwise as any book can be when you compress it into five minutes."

"Don't argue with me, Jake." Sachs spoke in deadly earnest. "I have one talent in this business, and that's all. It terrifies me because it's subconscious and I can't control it. It's a quality that nobody else has . . . I'm never wrong."

Lennox was speechless. He opened his mouth, closed it and fled from the brain room. Robin was waiting for him in the outer reception office where she told him her experience with Sachs in an indignant whisper. Lennox took Robin out of the office.

"Don't go back," he told her. "And don't worry. You've got the job. If Sachs gives you a hard time just call me. I'll take care of it." Suddenly he grinned and pinched her bottom. "This is a new role for me, Robin. I've been thinking of chasing you into bed for a year and here I am protecting you. Turns me into a pimp for virtue, doesn't it?"

"Why don't you chase me a little," Robin said wickedly. "I'm curious about you."

"I'll take a rain check."

"I've got a rival?"

Lennox nodded.

"Who she?"

He shook his head.

"How're your chances?"

"It's all reversed," Lennox said in a confused voice. "We started where most chases end and now we're working our way to the beginning." .

"Like running a movie backwards?"

"Exactly. I used to wonder what happened to those people who had to marry each other before they met. Now I know. It's exciting, Robin. It's wonderful, but it scares hell out of you. Christ, love is mixed up on The Rock."

"You got that from Kit. His favorite theme: Life and Death on The Rock."

"Death," Lennox repeated. He took a breath. "No. Three down. Three to go."

He departed.

He talked treason with Ned Bacon and made peace.

"I'll back you for director, of course," Lennox said. "And I think I've got the lever you can use to pry Sachs loose." He told him about Robin's adventure. "All she has to do is report that to her union and Sachs is through. It's your ace in the hole. My contribution to the conspiracy, but don't expect anything more. I've got these letters and threats hanging over me."

"You're not alone," Bacon said. "Why didn't you holler down the rainbarrel? I know the gimpster score. Let's hear all about it."

He heard about it, then drawled with a cynical expression: "Yep. Yep. We did it last year on 'The People Against—' I know every angle. This is how we broke the case." He instructed Lennox and Jake listened patiently to little known facts about blood sugar that could turn a normal man into a sex maniac, or perhaps it was the other way around.

"I got that from a police toxicologist," Bacon confided. "We went to the theater together and he sat there and diagnosed everybody on the stage. Just called the shots. Diabetic. Cancer prone. Tubercular. Multiple Sclerotic. . . ."

"Just by looking at them from his seat? I don't believe it."

"Jake," Bacon said kindly. "Come back from the Reichenbach Falls. There's a new thing they invented called medicine. Dr. Watson'll tell you all about it."

Again Lennox submitted patiently. He permitted Bacon to instruct him on the iniquities of The Marketplace and to educate him from the bonded warehouse of Bacon's profound experience. At the end of an hour, little Bacon felt two inches taller than Lennox and their cordial relationship was once more restored.

Between twelve and twenty, most boys have a fantasy of the kind of life they would like to lead when they become independent. It's composed of equal parts of Alexander Dumas, Richard Harding Davis and Mickey Spillane. Some of us outgrow this romantic vision. The ones that don't come roving to The Rock to turn the fantasy into reality. That's why life here is half crystallized adolescence.

Oliver Stacy had a penthouse in a converted brownstone in the east sixties. He was waiting for Lennox at the top of the stairs, dark, hollow-cheeked, romantic in black slacks, black silk shirt and black cummerbund. He looked like an illustration from a historical novel. He gave Lennox the strong, silent handclasp and took him into his apartment.

Lennox looked around wistfully. He was transported back to the daydreams of his own boyhood. The floor was polished oak, the walls creamy, the ceiling beamed and lost in shadows. There was a half finished canvas on an easel before the bay window, a self-portrait of Stacy as an officer in the French Foreign Legion. Alongside it was a lay figure on which was draped a uniform cape and a kepi. Stacy thrust a finger through a hole in the shoulder of the cape.

"Nine millimeter Mauser," he murmured. "The toughest thing we had to buck in the desert."

Two Italian epees were crossed over a blood-stained plastron with masks and gloves under them. A Luger and a Colt revolver lay on the mantelpiece. There was a cannel coal fire burning in the grate. A coffee table before the fire bore a bucket of ice in which reclined a bottle of champagne. On a couch behind the table reclined an exquisite little ingenue wearing a blue velvet dinner gown trimmed with miniver. The fire and candles were the only illumination. A phonograph was playing the "Rosenkavalier" waltzes.

"Drink?" Stacy inquired lazily. He uncorked the champagne bottle deftly and filled glasses.

"No thanks."

Stacy and the girl drank, gazing into each other's eyes over the glasses.

Lennox said: "If you'll just give me a minute, Oliver. Alone?" Stacy brushed the girl's palm with his lips, then took Lennox into a fitted dressing room hung with a dozen framed watercolors. They were nudes; all signed O.S. One of them bore a faint resemblance to Kay Hill. It was convincingly red-headed.

"It's about blackmail, Oliver."

"Pay with a gun."

"What?"

"The barrel of a gun across the bridge of a nose," Stacy spread his shoulders lazily. "I learned that lesson in Morocco."

"You've had experience before?"

"I've had every experience."

"Then read these." Lennox whipped out the photostats and handed them to Stacy who read them carefully, a lazy smile curling his mouth. His expression never changed.

"Threats," he said at last. "The ones that mean business never write."

"They don't scare you?"

"Nothing scares me."

"Who's writing them, Oliver?"

"Don't you know?"

"No."

"I thought you came to borrow a gun."

"Were they written to you?"

"To me?" Stacy shook his head slightly. "I've got enemies. A man's enemies. We know each other. We don't have to be anonymous." Stacy spread his shoulders. "I'll pack a gun to the theater Sunday. I'll back your play, Jake. I can break a nose."

"I think they're to you, Oliver."

"What difference does it make? I'm making it my fight."

"I don't want a fight. We've got enough trouble as it is. I want to avoid a fight."

"You never can, Jake. As soon as you realize that you'll grow

120

up." Stacy smiled lazily. "You go around the world and you learn one thing. It's all a fight, and the only way to keep from losing is to win."

"Oliver, if you're so hot for breaking noses, will you for God's sake find him and break it before Sunday."

"No trouble at all, Jake. Tell me where he is."

"I don't know. You do."

"Not me."

"These letters are to you. You fit the description . . . Dark man. Elegant. Live on the east side. Went to college. . . ."

"But not a vestal virgin."

"What?"

"I thought it was obvious. Didn't you notice it in the letter? Right here. He's written: 'You vomit virgin with your Judas morals . . .' Is that me, Jake?" Stacy pointed to the nudes on the wall. "Would anybody who knows me call me virginal . . . moralistic?"

"Jesus Christ!" Lennox exclaimed furiously. "If it's not you, then who? Who the hell is getting these letters?"

"Look for a coward."

"Why a coward?"

"Because a coward's writing them. You go around the world, Jake, and you learn another thing. There's class distinction in everything. You love your own kind and you hate your own kind. The jackals hate the jackals. They don't dare hate a lion."

Lennox waved the photostats impatiently.

"Why worry?" Stacy smiled. "Let him come to the show Sunday. We'll be waiting. It might be interesting."

"Interesting!" Lennox snorted. "God knows what's going to happen to who. It could be anything from a gun to a bomb. Is that your idea of interesting?"

"It's the only idea, unless you play poker for matchsticks."

"I don't play poker," Lennox said, and left.

Going down the brownstone stairs, he growled: "Four down. Two to go. It's either Plummer or Hansel. The advantage of statistics. Poker for matchsticks! Are they all crazy?"

I met Lennox in a network studio where he took advantage of an unexpected opportunity to make peace with Roy Audibon. The veep had gathered the leading script writers for one of his annual exhortations on the aims, needs and ideals of the network and the position of television in the Expanding Universe. Audibon's theme that afternoon was the fact that we writers were the bottleneck in the flow of progress because we refused to think galactically.

I won't try to reproduce Audibon's lecture. He has to be seen and heard to be appreciated. He's charming and attractive and successful. He is also a unique product of American culture . . . the erudite ignoramus. He discourses entertainingly in a jargon of advertising slang, science fiction clichés and pocket book philosophy. He can mix phrases like "cross-ruff client expediency" "fourth dimensional cybernetics" and "the Hegelian dialectics of The Thirty Years War" in one sentence and hypnotize you into believing that he's making sense. It isn't until you listen that you realize he's just talking out loud.

We all sat and kept our faces straight while Audibon drew a picture of the soaring, searching minds of the top network brass seeking the uppermost cultural levels for television only to be blocked and thwarted by the conservatism and lack of imagination of the writers.

"There are new techniques, new philosophies, new infinities to explore," Audibon told us. "Reach out to the stars. Don't be afraid to experiment in your garret. We may loathe what you do. We'll probably reject nine out of every ten scripts you send us, but that doesn't mean we're opposed to new ideas. We want new ideas. We need them. It's up to you to produce them in acceptable form for the network and clients."

When he finished we gave him a friendly hand and prepared to go about our business. Unfortunately a non-professional element had slipped into the meeting and they were either too ignorant or too indignant to go along with the joke. They got up and began filing beefs. They attacked Audibon politically, philosophically, and most of all financially. What it all boiled down to was: How dast he make a speech like that when the network kept rejecting all the wonderful scripts they sent in, and took six months to reject each script?

We squirmed in embarrassment. Audibon got red in the face and his replies to the hecklers became shorter and more cutting. Then an astonishing thing happened. Jake Lennox got to his feet, turned on the hecklers and blasted them. He was sardonic and icy; he took them apart, politically, philosophically and financially. They were so stunned it broke up the meeting. I saw Audibon step down from the studio stage, go over to Lennox, smile and shake his hand emphatically. Lennox grinned back. They spoke for a moment, laughed, shook hands again and were separated by the low network brass who surrounded Audibon. Lennox caught my eye, made a drink motion, and I nodded.

In Sabatini's we belted down a couple of Gibsons before I had the courage to bring up Jake's defense of Audibon.

"We won't discuss it," he said. "I turned whore to square that lunch hassle the other day. Which reminds me. I owe you money." He forced me to take two tens.

He brooded. His expression was contemptuous.

"Don't let it eat you out, Jake," I said. "We all whore. What were we doing listening to Audibon but whoring?"

"It isn't that," Lennox answered. "It's the Poison Pen test. That was a bomb. You were right, Kitten. I'm an amateur. I should have stayed out of the act."

"What happened?"

"I showed the photostats to all of them, looking for a sign . . . a giveaway. You remember what I told you about Fink?"

"Yes. So?"

"You think those letters knocked them off balance? Hell, they loved them. They ate 'em up. It's like those arsenic eaters of yours."

"Poison eaters?"

He nodded. "Poison eaters. They're mixed up. Sick in the head. But trouble doesn't bother them. They live on trouble. They feed on it. Can't do without it. They've got to have a diet that would kill a normal man."

"All of them?"

"All of them."

"Not one knocked off balance?"

"Not one out of six. And just to show you what an amateur I am, each one found something in the letters I hadn't noticed . . . Something that proved they couldn't be getting them."

"What?"

"Oh . . . Like . . . Charlie Hansel found a line that showed the letters are being written to someone who's big. Charlie's a midget, you know that. Plummer noticed something about a loudmouth. And you know how quiet Johnny stammers. He's always whispering the latest from the Kremlin."

"Kay Hill's loud."

"But she isn't dark."

"Stacy's dark."

"But he isn't moralistic. They've all got outs. I don't know who the hell's getting the threats. I'm no better off than I was when I started." He shrugged. "It shows you, Kitten. Everybody imagines they can do anybody else's job much better. It isn't until you try that you find out. Damn it! I'm licked. All I can do is hope Fink'll pull us out of this jam before Sunday."

"Tell me what everybody said when you pulled the letters on them."

"To hell with it."

"Let's write down how each one eliminated himself. Maybe we can add them up and find something."

After some persuasion and another drink he gave me the facts. I wrote them down in a column:

Big
Dark
Loud
Moralistic
Went to college
Fancy and elegant
Lives on the East side

"Look at this," I said.

Lennox looked.

"Who does it add up to?"

"I don't know."

"I've got news for you," I said. "You may be an amateur, and it may not be as easy as we think to do another man's job, but you've done the job. You've found out who's getting the letters. The only trouble is, you're worse off than when you started."

"What the hell are you talking about?"

"You."

"What about me?"

"You're the guy who's getting the letters."

He stared at me, looked at the list, then looked up again.

"This adds up to me?" he whispered.

I nodded.

"Loud?"

"They can hear you from the Bronx to the Battery."

"Fancy? Elegant?"

"As Mike Romanoff."

"Moralistic?"

"As a Puritan."

"This is me? This is the way you see me?"

"Yes."

He got up without another word and walked out. I don't know what staggered him most . . . the realization that he was the man being threatened, or the picture of himself as other people saw him. But I was right about one thing. He was a lot worse off than when he started.

· CHAPTER VII ·

It took Lennox eleven
hours to struggle through the script for the January 15th "Who
He?" show. He consumed one ream of paper, half a pound of
coffee, two quarts of ice cream, and answered the phone a dozen
times. All of the calls were for Cooper. They were from un-
knowns who appeared to be phoning from the vicinity of juke
boxes and spoke in hoarse underground voices. They used a
jargon that was incomprehensible to Lennox and they seemed
to be torturing Cooper.

"They want material," he groaned.

"You've got a trunkful stashed away. Submit it."

"I can't. My old stuff stinks."

"Then write new material."

"I can't."

"The hell you can't. You've arrived, son. Cash in."

"Arrived? Sure, at the wrong station. I'm a fluke." Cooper
was miserable. "You heard about the party Suidi's throwing
for me?"

"I'm coming. You'll hear me cheering in your corner."

"Cheering. My God! They'll all be there . . . Looking me over. Sizing me up. Me. A nothing. Making a fool of myself."

"Stop that, Sam. You're loaded with talent."

"Not me."

"They'll size you up and their eyes'll pop. What the hell is the matter with you? You deserve success. You've earned it. Don't you want it?"

"No, I don't want it. I just want to be left alone," Cooper shouted. "Leave me alone, for God's sake. I wish to Christ this'd never happened." He flung out of the house.

Hot and uncomfortable, Lennox stacked his manuscript neatly, placed it in a manila envelope and went out for a walk to worry about Cooper's misery and his own.

The Rock has an emotional as well as physical geography, and Lennox was unconsciously drawn to the neighborhoods that reflected his moods. On this morning he went through his customary cycle from despair to exhilaration never once remembering that he had been through the identical cycle and the identical walk countless times before.

He started at low ebb. He was confused and frightened and automatically began to wander back and forth through the crosstown side streets that always reflect the slack tide in men's souls. What was happening to Sam? Why wasn't Sam happy? What was happening to himself? Could he really be receiving the threats? Was he scheduled for violence on Sunday? The side streets were a dismal prelude to disaster.

Lennox searched his memory for guilt and enemies. He went all the way back to his small town boyhood and was drawn to Lexington Avenue, the great prototype of every Main Street in America. He could remember nothing and was overcome with sorrow for himself. He was alone . . . crucified . . . and he was driven south and east to the Bowery, the boulevard of self-pity.

There he trudged despondently, identifying himself with the tattered vagrants, with poverty and failure.

From sorrow, his mood changed to anger. He was outraged with himself for whining. He was furious with the world for attacking him unfairly. Hostile and contemptuous, he found himself walking up Broadway, glaring at the crowds, declaring war on a world that revealed itself so squalidly from Times Square to Columbus Circle. In his anger he flatly rejected any possibility that he could be the person described in the letters. The ferment within him increased until he was recharged with hope, and the cycle ended in elation.

He had nothing to fear. Nothing was falling apart. He would hold everything together . . . his delicious, wonderful world. He turned east to Madison Avenue to savor his world. He admired the women, the handsomest of all time; the men, the most successful; the shops, the richest. Fifth Avenue is as rich and beautiful as Madison, but Fifth Avenue is for dreaming. Madison is the bustling culmination of Now. It has no past or future, only the immediate Present.

"Existentialist," Lennox said to himself.

To climax this explosive surge from despair to assurance which was his main strength and weakness, he turned north and walked to a particular spot that he loved in lower Central Park. It was on a slight hill overlooking the pond and the Plaza. It was his own Exhilaration Point. There were thousands like it . . . private mastheads where the pirates stood alone and exulted over the plunder before them. As Lennox walked up the path, he was annoyed to see that his very own lookout was already occupied. He resented the intruder until he looked closer and saw that it was Gabby Valentine.

When he finally let her go, he bent down to pick up her hat and purse and his script. "Have you got a jack-knife?" he asked. "I want to carve something appropriate on a tree."

"I can just see you cutting lovers' knots," Gabby laughed.

Lennox winced.

"What's the matter?" she asked quickly.

"It was the idea of lovers' knots. Mawkish. I was thinking of something really impressive, like: D. Boon cilled a Bar on this tree year 1760."

"You're the bear," Gabby said, feeling herself tenderly. "Don't come near me again. I've got a gun."

"But what were you doing here, darling?"

"You told me about your favorite spot. I had to see it."

"Go ahead and shoot," Lennox said, but this time he was gentler.

He was right when he told Robin that this love affair was backwards. Most people meet, get friendly, turn serious and become intimate. Lennox and Gabby had started intimately and were working their way back. They'd already been serious enough for a violent quarrel. Now they were getting friendly. They spent an hour together in that blissful past tense of all couples who are exploring each other . . . "Did you?" and "Were you?" and "Had you?" They agreed, they compared, they disagreed. They matched experiences, tastes, habits, friends.

Gabby asked about Cooper and Lennox tried to describe what the friendship meant to him. "Sam's a whole man," he said. "Most men are only part men . . . like sections of a tangerine. All split up. You have to put a lot together to get a whole."

"Do you mean F. Scott Fitzgerald's ideal? The entire man in the Goethe-Byron-Shaw tradition?"

"I don't think so. Fitzgerald was obsessed with the idea that a man had to explore all his potential for good and for evil. I think he was trying to justify his own evil. I won't buy that. There's never any excuse for being bad."

"There's being human."

"That's an explanation, not an excuse."

"Tell me more about Sam."

"Well . . . most men are overspecialized, only interested in one

130

thing. The friend you like to fish with is a nuisance on a date. The friend you double-date with is a noodnick about ball games. The friend you go to ball games with can't understand books. And so on and so on. You have to make a dozen one-twelfth friends."

"Maybe you demand too much."

"No. I've got a legitimate beef. Art and music, for instance. Butch-type guys stay away from them like the plague. What happens? The fags have inherited, and that puts me in a hell of a spot. If I want to go to the ballet or the opera or an exhibit, it has to be with a fag or alone. And I hate fags worse than Squares."

"Why can't you go with girls?"

"Sweetheart, I love ladies, but I like men too. Men and women think differently, and sometimes I like to be with a man's point of view."

"I'll punish you for that," Gabby said.

"What I do?"

"Not now. Sam isn't a one-twelfth friend, is he?"

"No. He's twelve-twelfths. Whole."

"How did you meet him?"

"At Princeton. We went down for a fencing meet and Sam was host for the visiting team. You should have seen him . . . the fencer's dream. All in white except for black stockings."

"Did you really work your way through college?"

"Yes Ma'am. I was a telegrapher. I was a telegrapher my last year in high school too."

"Were you friendly with Sam right from the beginning?"

"No. Not until much later." Lennox frowned. "I was jealous at first. Princeton was elegant. Society. And I was trying to climb up from a clam-shack. I hated Sam."

"That's not nice," Gabby said.

"I was a kid from the wrong side of the tracks. That's an

explanation, not an excuse. Then I met him again in the business, and we got close."

"Had he changed?"

"No. I changed. There's nothing like making money to discharge the venom in you. Sam was always the same. A whole man." Lennox smiled gently.

"I like the way you look when you talk about him," Gabby said. "It shows how much you love him."

"Love him?" Lennox was startled. "My God! Don't say that. Men aren't allowed to talk like that nowadays."

"But you do, don't you?"

Lennox nodded. "You know how I feel about you. If you were turned into a man . . . That's how I feel about Sam." He stopped suddenly and faced Gabby. "I've got you both, Gabby. Help me hold on to both."

"I'm not jealous," she said honestly.

"I know that, but don't do one thing. If he's got faults that I can't see, don't point them out to me. You and Sam can sit in a corner and make fun of me all you like. God knows, I'm a prize noodnick. You can take my noodnickery apart and I won't care. Just let me love both of you."

"Why did you flinch when I said lovers' knots?" Gabby asked.

He looked at her in awe. "Gabrielle, you're a great woman. I thought I covered perfectly."

She shook her head and smiled.

"Talking to you's like turning a corner in March. You never know what's going to blow into your face."

"What were you remembering?"

"A Quaker, a blonde, and a knot."

"I don't understand."

"I did a bad thing Christmas Eve. I got dirty drunk. I imagined I was somebody else . . . A Quaker from Philadelphia named Fox."

"Why Fox?"

132

"I don't know. I picked up a blonde named Aimee Driscoll. A-I-M-E-E."

"I don't want to hear about her."

"I don't want to talk about her."

"And the knot?"

"That's the part I still can't remember. I lost the night from Christmas Eve to Christmas Day. The knot must be part of it. I don't know what or how. All I know is that it terrifies me every time I think of it."

"Is Lennox an English name?"

"I think so. From way back. What's that have to do with it?"

"Puritans," Gabby explained. "You're so moralistic. Always feeling guilty . . . like something out of 'The Scarlet Letter.' "

"Moralistic," Lennox repeated slowly. "Am I loud?"

"Deafening."

"And fancy . . . elegant?"

"Not the phony way you say it; but you have style, Jordan. Yes, you're definitely Edwardian."

"Jesus," he muttered and was silent.

"Stop feeling guilty. I like big loud men. And elegance is charming. I'm going to make you brocade waistcoats with silver buttons."

After a long pause, he said: "Audibon isn't loud."

"Oh Jordan. . . ."

"I shouldn't bring it up, but I've got to know. What's between you?"

"Nothing."

"What was?"

"Nothing. There never was anything."

"Then why did you—?"

"Is that kind?"

"No. It's jealous. Forgive me. And I do understand. He's strictly the network dazzler."

"I wasn't dazzled. I was sorry for him. That's why I thought I loved him."

"Sorry for him? Audibon? He's got everything."

"He has nothing . . . nothing inside. He's lost."

"Is that why he won't let you go?"

"One of the reasons. Another is that he hates to lose."

"How is he stopping you?"

"I'm active . . . politically. If I try to get a divorce he says he'll ruin me."

"That Communist routine?"

"Yes."

"Christ, what a club that's become for dirty fighters. Are you a Party Member?"

"No, Jordan."

"Tell the truth, sweetheart. If you're lying you'll give yourself away anyhow."

"Suppose I said yes. Would it make a difference?"

"It would."

"Why?"

"Because most of them are the dedicated type. Lunatic fringe. They're one-sided, and I told you I like whole people. Are you a Party Member?"

"No, I'm not."

Lennox searched her face, then nodded. He was beginning to learn how transparently honest she was. "All the same, I wish you'd quit the politics, Gabby. There must be other things for you to do."

Her eyes flashed angrily. "What other things?"

"I don't know. Lady things. Take the long view. We've got a whole life to plan together. Go vote at the polls like an honest citizen and let it go at that. You and I are more important than—"

"Have you any idea how offensive you're being?" Gabby interrupted.

"Offensive?"

"I suppose you want me to quit working too, don't you?"

"You won't have to work."

"I see. You've got it all planned, haven't you? Doesn't it occur to you that I like my work? Doesn't it occur to you that I've got political beliefs? There must be other things for me to do. Lady things. Men and women think differently. You male chauvinist!"

"Listen. I want my wife home with me because writing's the loneliest work in the world. What the hell's chauvinistic about that?"

"You not only look Edwardian, you think it. A woman's place is in the home. Cross-stitched on a sampler by loving hands at home."

"All right, Susan B. Anthony, where else is it?"

"Where she wants it to be, not where it's convenient for you!" An angry outburst trembled on Gabby's lips. She controlled herself. "We're fighting again. I don't know what it is you do to me, but we're always tearing at each other."

"What I do to you!"

"Be quiet, Jordan."

"Listen, Gabby—"

"Be quiet."

They walked in uneasy silence for a few minutes. Then Gabby stopped and faced him. Her dark eyes were severe, and her body, usually so relaxed and easy, was very straight. "You're destructive," she said. "You like to destroy people."

"The hell I do."

"Yes. It didn't just happen that time at Princeton. You haven't changed. You're still that boy from the wrong side of the tracks, jealous and envious of everybody. You can't feel equal to anyone unless you've torn him down first."

"You're wrong. I'm fighting to hold everything together."

"It's what you think, but it isn't true. You tear everything apart. You attack. You destroy. You may not realize it, but you do. You must have many enemies."

A chill numbed Lennox. He fought it off. "I can't bring any to mind off-hand."

"Of course not. You don't realize what you're doing. But you're not going to do it to me, Jordan. I won't let you." The look of consternation on his face made her relent. She took his arm again and hugged it affectionately. "Don't be frightened. It's just a part of you that we've got to heal. Don't you see, darling? The danger isn't for other people; it's for yourself."

"Myself?"

"Because if you attack and destroy others, you end up destroying yourself."

He was silent until they left the park. As they parted, Gabby to return to her office, Lennox to go down to the rehearsal of "Who He?" on Broadway, he said: "I have something serious I want to ask you. There's an outside chance one of those invisible enemies is catching up with me. I want your opinion."

"What do you mean? What's happened?" Gabby was concerned.

"Later. I'll pick you up at five for Sam's party. If we can find a corner in the Rox Studios we'll talk it over. I'm hoping you'll exonerate me. I know you will, but I'd like to make sure."

"Exonerate you from what?"

"From a lunatic on Sunday. More later. Can I have a kiss now?"

"Of course you can. Why do you ask?"

"I thought I might be in disgrace."

"Disgrace or no disgrace," Gabby said firmly. "Always kiss a man when he asks. That's one of my basic political beliefs."

Lennox went down Broadway to the Joydream Ballroom where "Who He?" rehearsed. No longer a taxi-dance joint, the ballroom had been struggling along since the war as headquarters of a lonely hearts club giving dances three nights a week for its discriminating clientele (all religious faiths). Now, television's frantic search for rehearsal space had restored Joydream to solvency.

136

In the Women's Lounge, the dancers in black rehearsal leotards were lined up before a wall of mirrors, headed by Charlie Hansel who was short, ebullient and graceful. They were watching their reflections intently as they memorized Charlie's new routines, and complaining chronically as only dancers can complain. Cooper was at the piano with Johnny Plummer's score, working out the beats for Hansel.

"You're taking it in four bar sections," Cooper was saying. "And that's throwing your rhythm off."

"Lambkin, it's written in fours. That Johnny Plummer! He's a four-cornered one, he is." Hansel spoke without taking his eyes off his reflection. None of the other dancers did either. This is not vanity. Like the complaining, it's an occupational disease.

"You don't understand," Cooper explained. "The music's in phrases, not bars. Johnny's written two longs, a short and a medium. Count ten twice, then four and then eight. You'll come out right."

"Samkin, there's no arguing with the composer of 'We're The Most.' He's a genius one, he is. Ready, kidkins? And!—"

They went into the routine, counting and complaining. Cooper scowled at the compliment and began playing. Lennox backed out of the lounge.

On the main ballroom floor, the sets for the show had been chalked and Raeburn Sachs was directing Mig Mason and the rest of the cast in the "Man Without A Country." Sol Eggleston, the network camera director, was prowling around the scene, framing it in his hands and making notes on his camera plot. This is a minute by minute schedule of the placement and occupation of all three cameras for the duration of the show, including lens settings and time allowance for changes of setting and position.

When Eggleston saw Lennox, he motioned sharply and brought him over to a table covered with blueprints and light plots. Eggleston was fat, efficient and asthmatic. Lennox liked him. He liked all the technical men. They knew their business and never wasted time promoting delusions of genius.

"We're in trouble," Eggleston wheezed. "Camera trouble."

"Oh God! Don't tell me I've asked for crossed cameras again."

"No. It's Sachs. He's got an idea for a trick shot on the Nolan."

"Something fresh and different, no doubt. What?"

"He wants to fly the 3. Hang it from the grid over the stage and shoot straight down on the courtroom scene."

"Damn him! It isn't a bad idea."

"Sure, but can we shoot the rest of the show with two cameras?"

"How do you mean?"

"It'll take an hour to fly the 3. It'll take another hour to get it down."

"Why so long?"

"The grid is practically inaccessible at the Venice. You have to go up a ladder from the fly-gallery, and there's no catwalk on the grid bars."

"I see."

"So do you want to immobilize the 3 for one shot? You want to shoot the rest of the show with two?"

"We can't do it."

"Tell Sachs."

"Can we get an extra camera for the shot?"

Eggleston shook his head. "The network hasn't enough to go round as it is. Talk Sachs out of it."

"We've got the meeting for the January 22nd show this afternoon. I'll do my best, but there's no arguing with Sachs. He's got a talent nobody else has. He's never wrong."

Eggleston wheezed cryptically.

"Wait a minute, Sol. Here's a gimmick. If the network did give us an extra camera, how much would it cost the budget?"

"About a yard and a half."

"Then don't worry. Blinky'll talk Sachs out of it. Still, I have to hand it to him. It's a nice idea."

138

Avery Borden of Borden, Olson and Mardine (nicknamed Borden's Oleomargarine by the business) arrived with disastrous news. The client had decided to go institutional for the New Year's day broadcast and eliminate the product commercials. Mode Shoes would content itself with wishing a Happy New Year to the American Way of Life in a single middle break, which now threw the entire show out of kilter. It added an extra three minutes to entertainment time, necessitating the insertion of a new number, and worse, it threw out the first and last commercials. Shows are carefully framed around the commercials in terms of tempo and climax, and the break is as essential as punctuation in a sentence.

It was for emergencies of this sort that the weekly show conference was held on Thursdays. The staff was able to cope with immediate problems as well as post-mortem the previous week's show and plan the one coming up in four weeks' time. They all met in the brain room of Grabinett's office. Presiding was Raeburn Sachs, taking notes was Mrs. Sachs. Present were: The Star, his agent, the producer, his budget, the writer, his partner, the dance director and the music director.

They post-mortemed the Christmas show. The client, Grabinett reported, was pleased but with two reservations. First: When Oliver Stacy handed each contestant his or her lovely pair of Mode Shoes as a gift for appearing on the show, it was requested that he use a French accent in naming the shoe style. The client felt that Stacy's accent was not sufficiently Parisian.

Second, Grabinett continued, the matter of prizes. The difficulty over the Grand Prize on the Christmas show made the client wonder if the questions weren't too difficult.

"Too difficult!" Lennox protested. "For God's sake! We're setting those questions at the kindergarten level now. How dumb do you have to be to win a prize?"

"It's not as if we're giving away big prizes," Grabinett blinked apologetically. "Aeroplanes and trips to Europe and islands in Canada. For big prizes you got the right to ask tough questions."

"How small is five hundred dollars?" Lennox demanded. "That's what our prizes average. And it's a lot of money. We don't have to give it by forced feeding, do we?"

"A man in public is fifty percent dumber than the same man in private," Ned Bacon drawled cynically. "We did a story about that on 'The People Against—'. We—"

"What about the prize hassle from last Sunday?" Tooky Ween rumbled.

"We took the heat off," Lennox told him. "It's all over except for one little thing. Mig'll have to say something about it next Sunday."

"Say what?"

"Oh, a little apology for the mistake."

"Not me! I'm not going to apologize for anything," Mason cried. "I didn't make any mistake. Don't turn me into the fall-guy."

"You want to ruin my property's fan relations?" Ween asked.

"It was the operator who loused it," Mason said. "That girl on the phone. She got me all mixed up."

"All right," Lennox said in exasperation. "So blame it on Patsy. Next Sunday announce that the contestant gave the right answer, but the girl made a mistake. Will you buy that?"

"She's been lousing the phone call every week," Mason yelled. "Every week she's got me worried when I should be thinking about myself. The girl has got to go."

"Leave her alone, Mig. Will you make the announcement?"

"If the girl goes."

"She goes," Grabinett broke in. "She's fired."

"The hell she is!" Lennox exploded. "That's a damned dirty trick."

"She goes." Grabinett glared at Lennox. "You want a law suit?"

"Contestants can make a lot of trouble," Bacon drawled. "We had a Case on 'The People Against—' when—"

"Listen," Ween interrupted. "My boy makes the announcement if he can say that the girl loused the prize and she's been fired. That's the conditions. We got to keep faith with the public trust."

"Then let's do it another way," Lennox pleaded. "Leave the girl out of it. I'll take the rap. The writer pulled the boner. Damn it, I'll get on camera and apologize myself."

"What are you doing, representing her?" Ween rumbled. "No. It's got to be the girl."

"Be reasonable, Tooky. Patsy's a—"

"Will you shut up!" Grabinett blinked angrily. "Jesus Almighty Galahad! What do you care about a lousy telephone girl?"

"I want a fair shake for everybody. That's all."

"Then go join the boy scouts. The girl's fired. Make the announcement, Mig. We're out of the law suit. Next?"

They discussed the extra three minutes' entertainment time. Mason wanted to add it to his comedy spot. He was supported by Ween. The staff pointed out that it would overbalance the show. Furthermore, the client had expressed a desire to have Mason's spot kept to six minutes maximum. The problem was how to fake a quick novelty without disrupting the existing show. The entire cast was tightly fitted into the program with barely enough time for costume changes. It would be impossible to hire a good outside specialty act on such short notice.

"I could let you have our two leads from 'The People Against—'," Bacon suggested. No one was interested.

"We need something fresh," Sachs murmured wearily. "A different Weber & Fields."

"Here's a gimmick," Lennox said. "Sam Cooper's tune is turning into a hit. Mig brought it out on the show two months ago."

"Great! Sensational!" Mason said. "Diggy and I'll do a reprise."

"You're already doing a duet," Lennox answered. "You can't do two. Besides, you need that three minutes to change. Here's my gimmick. Let Sam do the duet with one of the dancers. We'll introduce Sam as the rehearsal pianist on the show who wrote the tune that Mig made famous. Then let 'em guess Sam's name for a hundred bucks."

"That stinks!" Mason snarled.

"Why? It's cute. It's in the family, and it's great promotion for everybody. What do you think, Tooky?"

"We'll take it under advisement," Ween answered.

Which was tantamount to an okay. Lennox nodded to Ween, then turned to Grabinett. "Mel, can you budget us for fifteen hundred extra Sunday?"

"A yard and a half extra!" Grabinett blinked in horror.

"Ray's got a sensational idea for the Nolan. Tell him about flying the 3."

Sachs told Grabinett, first demonstrating the shot from the overhead grid and then from the stage underneath. His genius was defeated by the budget and the overhead camera disposed of.

"If that finishes next Sunday, let's get on to the twenty-second," Grabinett said.

"One more thing about Sunday," Lennox said. "The most important . . . The letters."

"Jesus Almighty!"

"I want to make a last appeal. You all know about the threats for the New Year's show. I've been around to see each of you and shown you the threats."

"Y-Your police f-friend's been around t-too," Johnny Plummer stammered softly.

"Fink? The detective? What'd he ask?"

"Lambkin, it was about the stage hands and camera crews mostly," Charlie Hansel said. "Fink's a deep one, he is."

"He's the smartest shamus in plainclothes," Bacon told them. "We did his biography on 'The People Against—'."

"Well that proves this isn't for laughs," Lennox said. "I think we're in for trouble. Bad trouble. I want to appeal to all of you

142

for the last time. If you know anything about this . . . anything at all that can help us out . . . please don't cover up. We'll be discreet. We'll keep it quiet. But at least give us a fair shake. Help us protect you and protect the show."

"Discreet will we!" Grabinett shouted. "I'll fire the lousy crook. I'll kick the Judas out so fast he won't feel it on his Almighty pants. And I can do it. I got moral conduct clauses in every contract."

"Mel! Please!"

"I ain't gonna have the name of Melvin Grabinett associated with the louse who's let us in for this trouble. And I'll sue. I got indemnifying clauses in every contract."

"That's lovely. Lovely. That's the sure way to make a man admit he's in trouble and needs help."

"I don't want to help him. I'm warning him. This goes for anybody. If you're gonna make trouble for the show, out you go." Grabinett blinked passionately and then continued in the same hysterical voice. "Now let's get going on the 22nd. Just remember what I tell you every week. The client wants a family show. A sweet show that makes a family feel better after they've seen it."

Out came the portfolios, the briefcases, the pads and notes. Lennox took out his gimmick book and began turning the pages looking for the ideas underlined in red pencil, which were those earmarked for "Who He?." He had production numbers, drama spots, song spots, novelty questions and various related gimmicks neatly listed in his meticulous handwriting. At a distance one of his pages looked like a leaf from a Gothic bible.

"I've got a tentative program worked out for the 22nd," Lennox said. "It's in the envelope with the finished script for the 15th, Ray. On your desk."

Sachs handed the envelope to his wife who opened it and handed him Jake's program. Sachs read it, frowned, and shook his head.

"No," he said. "No. It's all off-trail, Jake."

"I was expecting that," Lennox growled. "And I'm just nervous enough about next Sunday to throw it in your teeth."

The others looked up, startled at Jake's anger.

"I've kept a record of our show discussions for the past thirteen weeks," he went on, flipping the pages of his gimmick book. "Ten out of those thirteen you started out rejecting every one of my suggestions and ended up suggesting them as your own idea. Why don't you relax, mastermind? Who are you auditioning for? Or do you want to think you're the only man on the show who can—"

Suddenly Lennox stopped and stared at his gimmick book. His face turned white and the deep lines on it showed up grey. He swallowed once or twice, then closed the book and returned it to his pocket.

"Excuse it, please. I've got to take five," he muttered. "I'll be in the john."

He left the brain room and locked himself in the office john. He took out the gimmick book and with trembling fingers opened it and turned the pages until he found what he had seen at the meeting. In a large space between two neat paragraphs, a stranger had written a message to him in a familiar hysterical hand. The line was:

"Be killing you New Year's. Knott."

· CHAPTER VIII ·

A HEAD-SHRINKER ONCE
explained to me that people confronted with a crisis act exactly
like a J-walker about to be run down by a car. They do one of
three things. Either they dodge back to the curb, or stand helpless, or turn on full steam and sprint ahead. Lennox was the third
type. When the evidence in his gimmick book finally convinced
him that he was next Sunday's victim, he refused to retreat or
submit. He turned on full steam and sprinted toward disaster.

He returned to the show conference and forced himself to participate until it was over. He issued blanket invitations for the
party at Rox Studios, left Grabinett's office and called Sergeant
Fink from a phone booth. Fink was not at the precinct. Lennox
said he would call again, went out and consulted the phone di-
rectory. There were a dozen Knotts in the Manhattan book.
There were many more in Brooklyn, Queens and the Bronx.
None of the names looked even faintly familiar. Lennox got back
into the booth and called one at random. A man answered the
phone.

"Is Mr. Knott there, please?"

"This is Knott. Who's calling?"

"Jordan Lennox."

"Who?"

"Jordan Lennox."

"What number are you calling?"

Lennox gave the number.

"You got the right number, Mister, but I think you got the wrong party."

"You don't know me?"

"No. Should I?"

"If you've been writing me letters, you should. You—" Lennox stopped. The man had hung up. Lennox started to dial another Knott and then quit. "Am I crazy?" he asked himself. "I can't get anywhere this way."

He left the phone booth, went out into the street and realized that he felt steady and solid as rocks. The uncertainty was ended. Lennox walked a few blocks while he examined himself in his new role of victim, then went over to Houseways, Inc. and picked up Gabby Valentine. He chattered exuberantly during the cab ride to Rox, concealing the discovery he had just made and the driving resolution it had brought about in him. He was not ready to reveal the crisis to Gabby until he had lived with it a little longer.

Rox Studios on West 50th Street occupied the top floor of an ancient loft building. It was decorated in Industrial Modern with aerial photomurals, phallic light fixtures, and blond functional furniture. There were offices, recording studios, stock rooms, and an impressive reception room which had been taken over by a catering company. Over the bar and hors-d'oeuvre tables were hung giant blow-ups of the great hit records of the past. "We're The Most" was also prominent. Cameramen were arranging celebrities in groups. Flash bulbs were flaring.

On the surface, all cocktail parties are alike. You find the con-

146

ventional percentages of pretty girls, pretty boys, big wheels, nobodies, name-droppers, and the ubiquitous scrawny woman who drinks too much, insults too much, throws up too much and has to be taken home. It's the lower levels that distinguish one party from another, but on The Rock the lower levels are exposed, and consequently the percentages turn into the deludeds, the hostiles, the compulsives, the persecuteds, the insecures and the harassed.

If your eye is trained you can see their frantic gyrations as they jostle and balance on their tightropes over their chasms. If your ear is sharp you can hear their bedevilments through the brittle glitter of the talk . . . whispering with ghost voices like a badly tuned radio.

In the midst of all this, Cooper, who was usually so casual and carefree, stood rigid with terror. He was learning the bitter lesson that is taught on The Rock . . . that ambition besets us with many dangers to be fought and survived, and one of the greatest dangers is success. It's dangerous because it focuses attention, and the successful man becomes a new target for the attacking pirates.

As a nobody on The Rock, Cooper had been living in happy obscurity, ignored by the poison eaters. Now he was spotlighted and they declared open season on him. The Ned Bacons cut him down to their size. The Mig Masons resented his claim on their exclusively owned limelight. The pretty girls took hold to climb over him to fresh heights. The pretty boys saw in him another celebrated name to drop and to bitch. The property owners marked him for future possession. And all this took place under the surface of the congratulations and compliments, like a poison ring inside a Borgia handclasp.

The first opportunity he had after the formal congratulations, Lennox whispered: "Sam, I'd never bring it up at this time, but I've got to work fast. I've found out the letters were written to me."

"Letters?" Cooper was bewildered.

"The threats. You recognized the writing. Have you remembered who it is yet?"

Cooper passed his hands over his face. "No, Jake. No. I . . . No."

"Listen. I know who's writing them. Knott. The Quaker, the blonde and the knot. Remember? Knott's the name of the writer. Does that ring a bell?"

Cooper shook his head. He didn't appear to be understanding Lennox.

"Between the name and the writing we ought to be able to find him, Sam. Not now, of course, but maybe. . . ."

"Jake. Leave me alone, will you. I can't help you. I'm in a bad way."

"Sure. I'm sorry. Enjoy yourself, boy. I'm cheering in your corner."

Cooper laughed pointlessly and a trifle hysterically. He was so completely unstrung that his first conversation with Gabby hardly made any sense at all. She had waited for a break in the ring around him and then came up to him with outstretched hand. Cooper at once took her to a corner and stared at her distractedly.

"Do you trust me?" he asked suddenly.

"Of course," Gabby answered. "I like to trust people."

He looked into her dark eyes. "Yes. You're one of the honest ones, aren't you. Inside-outside girls."

"I think you've been drinking too much, Sam."

"I like the way you say Sam. No, I'm not drunk. I'm possessed. I meant your inside and outside match. Both beautiful."

"Oh. Yes, my plumbing is the envy of all the doctors."

"Are you in love with Jake?"

"I don't know. It's too violent yet."

"He's violent." Cooper nodded emphatically. "Dangerous. Do you think it'll be love after the frenzy?"

"I want it to be. Very much."

"Can I call you Gabby?"

"Please."

"Listen to me, Gabby. Go away. Get out of Jake's life. Run like hell."

She looked at him steadily without answering.

"Maybe you can come back another time, but now, keep away from him."

"I think you'd better say more, Sam."

"I can't."

"Then you should have said less."

"Are you offended?"

"A little. You don't approve of me."

"It isn't that."

"Then you'd better explain what you mean."

"How can I? This is something that has to be between Jake and me."

"You don't like me," Gabby said with conviction. "Are you jealous? Aren't you willing to share him with me?"

"Will you share him with himself?"

"I really think you've been drinking too much, Sam. You aren't making sense."

"How can I make sense? Look at me. Somebody threw me into the water. I'm trying to learn how to swim before I drown. I've got just enough breath left to shout a warning to you. I'm shouting, Gabby."

Suidi, *Le Jazz Hot,* came up to get Cooper. As he led him away to be photographed again, Cooper called over his shoulder: "I'm shouting, Gabby. Listen to me."

"What's he shouting?" Lennox asked, appearing out of the crush with canapes.

"A long locomotive for Lennox. He admires you, Jordan."

"You talked him into it. He's just the tool of a beautiful dame."

"Yes, I am rather fatal. It's a dreadful responsibility. Who's the little man who told me he married eighteen feet of wives?"

"Ned Bacon, my partner."

"Did he really?"

"Yep. Three six foot show girls, one after the other."

"What an extensive married life. Who's the dark quiet man who stammers?"

"Johnny Plummer."

"And the bald man who sounds like a subway train? The one who's been pestering Sam."

"Tooky Ween, Mason's agent. He wants Sam to sign with him."

"They're all very nice," Gabby said. "But they all seem self-conscious. Like Roy. They live in the third person."

"Live in the third person?"

"Haven't you noticed? It was never 'I'm doing this' or 'I'd like that' with Roy. It was always 'Roy Audibon is getting an idea' or 'Roy Audibon would like a drink.' He was his own audience. What was the matter with you in the taxi, Jordan?"

She took the wind out of him. He could never accustom himself to the sudden corners in her conversation. Each time he imagined he had concealed something from her, she waited patiently and then came around a corner unexpectedly into the heart of the concealment.

"Was it anything to do with the enemies you were talking about?" she asked.

"Yes," he said. "That's it exactly."

"Do you want to talk about it now?"

"Let's find a place."

They pushed through the crowd. The party was getting high and many men laid loving hands on Gabby. When she gently disengaged herself, they persisted in following her, offering drinks, cigarettes, canapes, conversation, or any other service she required. Lennox was annoyed and reminded of the three men at the McVeagh party who had offered to take the drunken professor home for her. Gabby couldn't help acquiring a coterie of men anxious to make themselves useful.

Suidi's private office was jammed. *Le Jazz Hot* goggled at Lennox and waved to him, excitedly trying to thank him. Lennox shook his head in warning and left. He and Gabby tried the stock rooms. They were all occupied. In a wrapping room stacked with acetate blanks were Cooper and Tooky Ween. Cooper was flustered and almost incoherent. Ween was aggressive.

As Lennox was about to withdraw, he heard Ween say: "Then we got to work up some other kind of financial arrangement on our tune." Jake stopped and squeezed Gabby's elbow in warning.

"What was that line . . . 'Our tune'?" he asked.

"I just been talking sense to your friend," Ween rumbled. "Only he can't count the fingers in front of his eyes."

"I'm in no condition to sign with anybody," Cooper pleaded. "Don't be mad, Tooky. Let it go at that."

"I ain't mad, boy, but you need handling. It's handling that makes the difference between a property and a non-property."

"I don't want to be property. I don't want any part of this crazy hassle. Now leave me alone, will you Tooky? I'm wrung out."

"I'm trying to do this so nobody hollers for a lawyer letter," Ween said. "If your friend—"

"His name is Cooper. Sam Cooper."

"If your friend'll let me do some good for him, then it's all in the family and no hard feelings."

"What's in the family?"

"Our tune."

"What means 'Our tune'?"

"He says Mason collaborated with me," Cooper burst out.

"Oh. I see. You want a piece of the hit, is that it, Tooky?"

"It ain't what I want. It's what's right. My boy helped your friend write the tune. We're entitled to a piece. Now if your friend wants to come into the family, then everything's cozy."

"Sure. You cut in for your fifteen percent. What makes you think Mason collaborated on the tune?"

"I asked him about it."

151

"When you smelled money."

"He told me it was his idea from the start and he made at least a dozen contributions when they was working it up in the rehearsal. Out of a total hundred percent, at least thirty nine and a half percent was my boy's ideas."

"Your boy suffers from starmania. He thinks everything is his idea. Ask him sometime. You'll find out he thinks he invented you."

"Oh, for God's sake! Let him have his piece of the tune," Cooper exclaimed in disgust. "We did do it in rehearsal. I admit Mig made suggestions. Maybe he did contribute as much as Tooky says. I want to be honest about this and I'm sick of—"

"Shut your mouth!" Lennox interrupted violently. "Do you want to give it away to the chiselers?"

"Keep out of this, Jake. Let me handle it."

"You're not fit to handle anything. You'll sell yourself out."

"Maybe that's the best thing for me. Leave me alone."

"What are you trying to do, escape? I will like hell leave you alone." Lennox turned on Ween. "Listen to me, you shyster. 'We're The Most' is Sam's tune. One hundred out of one hundred percent. How do I know? Because I heard him compose it in our house one month before your boy rehearsed it for the show."

"That's a lie!" Ween roared. "You heard what Cooper just now admitted. That's a dirty, unethical lie, Lennox!"

"And you're stuck with it. Take us into court and see what happens."

"I don't want to go into court!" Cooper looked around frantically. "You're right, Jake. All I want is out. Give him his piece of the hit. Give him the whole damned tune. I'm not cut out for this rat race. For God's sake, let me out before I turn into a twitch like Blinky."

Lennox shut Cooper up with a wave of his hand. He scowled murderously at Ween. "Look what you're doing to him, you lousy leech. You sit on the sidelines waiting for someone to hit, and then you're right in there bloodsucking. Agents! The pimps of the business! This is my boy, understand? He worked for this. He sweated for it. He waited for it, and you're taking nothing from him. Now get the hell out of here and go shove yourself up your property."

Ween left the wrapping room like a thundercloud. Lennox ignored him and stepped to Cooper's side. "You stood by me," he growled. "Now I'm standing by you. If you sign anything away . . . If you give anything away . . . If you so much as open your mouth, I'll kill you. Stop whining. D'you think this is another varsity show? You're doing business with professional cutthroats. Get the hell out there and face them."

He pounded Cooper's slack shoulders with his fists, propelled him to the door and thrust him out. He motioned to Gabby to follow and walked behind Cooper, forcing him back into the crush. Lennox kept muttering: "Smile. Grin. Shove it down their throats. They hate your guts. They hate anybody who gets a break. Well, hate 'em back. Show 'em!"

Lennox patrolled Cooper for a few minutes, showing his teeth in the icy, cutting smile called The Agency Knife. Then he took Gabby to the bar for a drink. He was sardonic, hostile, unyielding. Gabby had never seen him look more dangerous. Once again she was repelled by that frozen exterior that the business knew so well, but now she knew that this was only a part of Lennox. She took his arm with both hands and tugged gently.

"You're frightening me," she whispered. "Stop looking like that, Jordan. You're like you were in the taxi Christmas night."

"Thieves," Lennox growled. "Killers. Poison eaters! All of them. Trying to cut Sam's throat. Mine too. I won't let 'em. We'll hold on to our sanity. All of us. Won't we?" He glared at Gabby.

"Yes, sir, Captain Hook, sir," she quavered.

"And we'll give 'em nothing. Nothing! You hear me, Gabby Valentine?"

"Yes, sir."

"That's my girl. Now let's go find a place and talk."

There were only three people in the smaller sound studio, clustered around a piano flanked by microphones on stands. A bass fiddle and two copper-bottomed kettle drums stood in a corner. Still raging, Lennox stalked in with Gabby and flashed The Agency Knife on the strangers.

"I'd like a word in private with my mother," he said. "Would you mind? Thanks very much."

The strangers scuttled out and left them alone. Lennox looked through the glass panel into the control booth where a group of people soundlessly shouted and gesticulated. He rapped the microphones with his knuckles.

"Are these live?" he asked. "Control, can you hear me?"

There was no response. He took Gabby by the waist and lifted her onto the piano, then leaned against her knees and, halfway between fury and confusion, blurted out the story of the letters. He opened his gimmick book and showed her the message scrawled in by a person named Knott.

"The Quaker, the blonde and the knot," Lennox said. "It's filled in now. The knot is a person. Mr. Knott . . . a murderous lunatic who knows me. Maybe it's like you said this morning in the park . . . an enemy for something I don't even remember doing. But he's an enemy all the same. And I was with him the night before Christmas."

"You don't remember being with him?"

"No. But we must have been together. He left a line for me in the gimmick book . . . a little love note· to let me know who to expect Sunday."

Gabby nodded.

"It's a charming situation, isn't it?" Lennox said. "There's a man named Knott. I don't know him, but he knows me. First he writes me. Then he sidles up to me Saturday night and leaves a personal message where he knows I'll find it sooner or later. He hates me. He wants my guts cut out. I don't know why, but I don't have to know. He's got his own crazy reasons. All right, I'm going to find him before Sunday."

"Find him? How?"

"I'm going to backtrack on my trail. I'm going to start at the bar where I got plastered with Avery Borden Saturday night. I'm going to start remembering and keep going until I find friend Knott. After I've had a few words with him, you can come and bail me out."

"I don't think you should. It's Sergeant Fink's job."

"I'll do it myself," Lennox said stubbornly. "If I louse it, I can always go crying to Fink, but I'm not crying yet. I've got Fink to fall back on, and Sam, if he can only remember where he saw that writing. But that comes later. Right now will you let me out of our date tonight? I want to call Borden and start backtracking now."

"No, I won't," Gabby said. "I'll go with you."

Lennox shook his head.

"I'll go with you," Gabby insisted. "I can help."

"Not in this."

"You'd be surprised the way ladies can help. Anyway I don't want to bail you out of jail. You need a keeper."

"Listen," Lennox said. "I was dirty drunk that night. God knows what I did. God knows where I went. I don't want you finding out things about me. This Knott could turn out to be something so filthy that I—"

The control booth door burst open and banged against the wall. Grabinett stood in the doorway, blinking hideously. Lennox stared at him and then into the booth. The group inside was watching the scene with intense interest. One man was bent over the control panel fiddling with the Gain knobs.

"So it was you," Grabinett sputtered. "It was you all the time, you Jesus Almighty hypocrite!"

"Turn off those mikes," Lennox roared at the controls.

"Leave 'em on," Grabinett shouted. "I want witnesses. I got a moral conduct clause in your contract, Lennox. Remember? I warned you. I warned you at the office less'n two hours ago. All right. Here it is. You're fired. You're off the show."

"Did you hear everything I told her?"

"I heard every Almighty thing you told her and you're off the show."

"You heard me say I don't know who's doing this to me and I don't know why. All I want is a fair shake. Will you stand by me, Mel?"

"I don't care who's doing what to who or for why. I got a client to consider. I got myself to consider. And I got news for you. If anything happens Sunday . . . anything at all, I'll take it out of you. If the network or the client cancels, if I suffer any damages of any kind, I'll take it out of your hide."

"The hell you will."

"The hell I won't. Go home and read your contract, Lennox. Clause eight. Then you'll make goddam sure nothing happens Sunday." Grabinett blinked triumphantly. "After you read it you can tear it up, because right now in front of witnesses I'm telling you . . . you're off the show and that's final!"

· CHAPTER IX ·

LIKE MOST AGENCIES,
Borden's Oleomargarine was born of treason. In 1940, Borden,
Olson and Mardine, the three top account men of Riley & Reeves,
mutinied and set up their own agency, taking R&R's best clients
with them. The fact that Riley & Reeves had done the same thing
to Ansel, Bates & Crown in 1922 in no way mitigated their outraged charges of piracy, sabotage and unfair practice.

By the fifties, Borden's Oleomargarine owned five floors on the
top of a Madison Avenue tower in which all the elevator opera-
tors were red-headed women. It handled thirty million dollars
worth of billing a year at fifteen percent off the top, and as
representative of six of the most powerful American industries
(among other clients) was a monolith of agencies. It had offices in
Chicago, St. Louis, New Orleans, Hollywood and San Francisco.
It employed over five hundred people, among whom were the
bright young bandits who would eventually mutiny in their own
turn.

Success did not prevent Avery Borden from having a drink

with Jake Lennox and Gabby Valentine in the saloon across the street from the Venice Theater, or from worrying about his train back to Westport where he owned one hundred acres and a twenty-room house. Our business may be cut-throat, but it's democratic. We have the highest percentage of inter-denominational ulcers anywhere.

"I've got a train to catch," Avery Borden said, "But leave us bleed the lizard again." He caught the bartender's eye. "The same all around and extra special for the lady, please. Extra special."

"Yes sir, Mr. Borden," the bartender said. "I know just how Miss V. likes it."

Lennox glanced at Gabby. "They know you here?"

"I get around," Gabby smiled. "Now, Mr. Borden. . . ."

"Call me Avery," Borden cooed. "Call me Avery and I'll miss my train." Mr. Agency was turning all his powerful charm on Gabby. He was a remarkably young fifty, tall and slender, and looked so much like Roy Audibon that Lennox glared at him.

"Please don't," Gabby said in alarm. "I get train fever. My heart's beginning to thump now."

"Show me."

"You can feel my pulse."

"With your permission, Jake?"

"I could shoot you both and no jury would convict."

"I'm pleading the unwritten law too." Borden took Gabby's wrist and held it delicately.

"What law is that?" she asked.

"Open season on chicks like you."

"You see?" Gabby said to Lennox. "I'm fatal. Have I got him hypnotized?"

"He's under your thrall all right. Thrall?"

"Thpell," Borden said.

"We want a favor from you," Gabby said. "Will you help us?"

"Anything short of missing my train."

158

"What did Jordan do when he was here with you Saturday evening?"

"He drank."

Lennox nodded gloomily. "She knows that, Avery. We're looking for something else."

"Checking up on him?" Borden asked Gabby.

"For the parole board."

"He raped the cashier, murdered the boss, kidnapped their child and sold it to Procter & Gamble," Borden said promptly. "Obviously not the man for you. But I'm noble."

"I can see the blood royal in your eyes. Did Jordan talk to anybody except you?"

"Are you kids serious?"

Gabby nodded and melted Borden with her dark, candid gaze.

"We're looking for a man named Knott," Lennox explained. "I met him somewhere Saturday night and he's been giving me a hard time with threatening letters. I've got to find him and square it off."

"Did Jordan talk to anybody except you?" Gabby repeated.

"No, Miss V. He didn't," the bartender put in. "It wasn't crowded that night. I remember."

"Thank you. You're very kind. Does anybody named Knott ever come in here?"

"Not that I know of, Miss V."

"Do you know any characters named Knott?" Lennox asked Borden.

Borden was confused. "I thought you knew him."

"I don't. I'm trying to trace him."

"Try the phone book."

"I already. There's twelve Knotts on The Rock alone. None of the names look familiar. God knows how many more there are outside."

"Maybe this Knott don't have a phone, Miss V.," the bartender suggested. "Lots of people don't."

159

"Thank you," Gabby smiled. "Can I buy you a drink?"

"Oh no, Miss V." The bartender looked at her fondly.

Lennox glared at him and then asked Borden: "Did I mention the name after I got plastered?"

"Man, you started plastered. No, you didn't mention the name."

"What happened Saturday? Take it from the top."

"Well . . . We left rehearsal around five. Came over here. Cut up the show. Had a few drinks to celebrate. Cut up the business. Had a few more. Cut up Christmas. . . ."

"I deny that."

"Who's remembering this?"

"I'm a wholesome American boy. I never said a word against Santa Claus."

"Cut up Christmas," Borden continued firmly. "Had a few more to celebrate . . . And then I caught my train."

"Didn't I ask you to have dinner with me? I've got a fuzzy recollection of that foolish, headstrong invitation. Did I mention where?"

"Have a heart, Jake. I was celebrating myself."

"Please help us, Avery," Gabby pleaded.

Borden looked at her affectionately. "What do you do, love? Come and work for me."

"First show me you're worth an office pinch."

"I will now display my giant intellect." Borden considered earnestly. "Let's see . . . We were in the cab."

"What cab?"

"To the station. I gave you a lift."

"Wait a minute. Hold the phone. To the library?"

"That was your story."

"I think I remember. I wanted to check Americana scores for a production number. John Brown's ever-lovin' Body or something. Did I say where I was going to eat?"

"Some ungodly place like Chinatown."

"At The Yellow Sea?"

"It rings a bell."

"So . . ." Lennox nodded slowly. "First the library and then The Yellow Sea. Elementary, my dear Watson. No you don't, Avery. I'll take the check, please."

"I'll take my reward," Borden said, reaching for Gabby.

"And I'll pay it," Gabby said. "This time I'll give you the lift to the station."

After they dropped Borden at Grand Central, Gabby turned to Lennox.

"Am I helping?" she asked.

"I couldn't be doing it without you."

"Are you still afraid of what you're going to find out?"

"Yes, but it doesn't make any difference any more. I'm so damned mad at Grabinett and myself that— Were you ever at a *corrida*?"

"What's that?"

"A bullfight."

"Good Heavens! No!"

"I used to wonder how the bull felt. Now I know."

They entered the library from the 42nd Street side, and as they passed through the turnstile the guard nodded fondly to Gabby who smiled back.

"What the hell . . . Do they know you here too?" Lennox asked in surprise.

"I told you. I get around. He's a nice man but a terrible reactionary."

"Looks like the hedonistic type to me."

"No, he's too eclectic."

"Sweetheart, sometimes you talk just like a pamphlet."

"I know. Isn't it awful? My father used to make me study the dictionary. But I practice slang whenever I remember."

They turned right through a short corridor lined with illuminated display cases and went into the music room. It was nearly closing time for this department. The bookboys were slamming volumes back into the shelves. There were half a dozen readers at the tables. One librarian minded the desk.

"Put him under your thpell," Lennox whispered.

Gabby at once walked up to the librarian and gazed candidly into his eyes. "Please . . . Do you have any music about John Brown's ever-lovin' Body?"

"I beg your—" The librarian was startled, then he recovered. "I'll look, Miss. Please sign the register."

Gabby signed the desk register, then followed the librarian to the file cabinets, moving with her lazy, square-shouldered carriage. Lennox turned the pages of the desk register back to December 24th. He went through the signatures and addresses one by one. He found his own, third from the end, written in his heavy Gothic hand. There was no Knott. There was no name vaguely resembling Knott. To the best of his knowledge there was no handwriting resembling the hysterical scrawl in the letters.

He motioned to Gabby who returned to the desk.

"Nothing here," Lennox murmured. "Leave us take a powder."

"Oh, that wouldn't be kind. Let's wait a moment."

The librarian came scurrying up with a list of references which he presented to Gabby gallantly. She thanked him, folded the list and handed it to Lennox.

"What for?" he asked as they left.

"You wanted a production number, didn't you? Here it is."

"That was last week. I'm off the show now. Remember?"

"You'll be on it again," Gabby said confidently.

"Who taught you to say the right thing at the right time?"

"Nobody. I just tell the truth and shame the devil— Don't you dare touch me. Ouch! Oh quick! There's a taxi."

The Yellow Sea was packed with the early dinner crowd. The waiters ran and shouted. The managers darted from table to table, scribbling orders. The swinging doors of the kitchen banged open and shut giving flashing glimpses of a giant smoky room from which came the crackle of hot oil and excited chefs.

162

"This is impossible," Lennox grunted. "I'll never get a chance to ask anything in this mad-house."

"Will it always be crowded?"

"No. They'll clear out in an hour or so."

"Then let's have dinner first. I want to show off. I know how to use chop-sticks."

Lennox looked at her. "Taught to you by an eclectic Chinaman?"

"No, by a Hawaiian. He was very nice, but terribly hasty."

"Gabrielle, I swear you're a great woman. We'll have to wait for a table. Let's go to the bar."

The Yellow Sea had expanded twice in its rise to prosperity. In the forties it had added a tourist-type dining room to the original teakwood and silk-screen restaurant which now catered exclusively to the Chinese locals. In the fifties it added a chrome and neon bar. Lennox and Gabby went up a flight of stairs, down another, and entered the bar where they were unexpectedly greeted by a stranger.

"Ah!" he cried. He spoke with the explosive Chinatown diction. "Missa Hu-li Lennox. Dissa g'eat pleasuh an' honnuh." He came forward, shook Jake's hand, and said: "Lon' time no see. Yes? Ha-ha."

He was short, very stout, and either an old young man or a young old man, as is so often the confusing appearance of the Chinese. His round, boyish face was perpetually wreathed in a sunny smile to which a wall-eye lent a distracting quality. You never could be sure whether he was beaming at you or at some faraway recollection.

"You 'membuh me, Missa Lennox? Stanley Fu, the Sh'off?"

"The Shoff?"

"No. Ha-ha. Sh'off. S.H.O.Ah.F.F. Sh'off."

"Shroff?"

"Yes. Yes. Whiskey?" The Shroff led them to the bar, snapped his fingers at the bartender, then rapidly undid his immaculate tie

163

and collar and opened his shirt. He displayed a livid bruise on his shoulder. "Las' Satuhday night," he beamed. "Me'y Kissmus p'esent f'om Hu-li."

Lennox stared at the stout gentleman in amazement. "Hu-li?" he repeated. "Who he?"

"You," the Shroff beamed.

"Did he do that to you Saturday night?" Gabby asked.

"Oh yes. Yes. Ha-ha."

"Shame on you, Jordan," Gabby said reproachfully.

"I swear I don't remember. I— Gabby, this, apparently, is my good friend, Mr. Stanley Fu, the Shroff. Mr. Fu, this, positively, is Miss Gabrielle Valentine."

"G'eat pleasuh an' honnuh," the Shroff beamed. He shook hands with Gabby, then redid his shirt.

"What's a Shroff, please?" Gabby asked. "Is it something I should know?"

"Oh no. No. Issa Chinese p'ofesshun. Bankuh. Yes? Money changuh."

"How do you mean?"

"Oh yes. Silvuh into dolluh. 'Me'ican dolluh into Chinese dolluh. Papuh dolluh into silvuh." The Shroff transferred his attention to Lennox. "You put it all down. Inna liddy ole book when I te'l you Satuhday."

"In this?" Lennox took out his gimmick book.

"Yes. Yes."

"I don't remember," Lennox said. "To tell the truth, Mr. Fu, I hardly remember Saturday night at all. That's why I'm here. It's a wonderful break meeting you again. Can you help me remember?"

"Oh-ho?" The Shroff made a drinking gesture. "Yes?"

"Yes."

"Please tell us what happened Saturday night," Gabby said. "I'm worried about your bruise."

The Shroff beamed at her. "Oh yes. Happen like this. My

164

f'iend, Hu-li, come. Stan' next to me heah." The Shroff made the drinking gesture three times. "Mahtini." He made the gesture three times again and pointed to himself. "Scotch an' soda."

"Shame on you both," Gabby said.

The Shroff patted her arm fondly.

"Wait a minute," Lennox said. "Some of it's coming back. Wasn't there a calendar up over the bar? Last year's with a fencing girl on it?"

"Yes. Yes." The Shroff nodded quickly. "We talk about pictuh of liddy young lady with fff . . ." He looked helplessly at Lennox. "Foil?"

"Yes. You te'l me you ah 'Me'ican fencuh." The Shroff pointed a finger and waggled it. "I te'l you I am Chinese fencuh." The Shroff suddenly crouched and lifted both arms as though poising a baseball bat. "We go togethuh an' fence."

"We did?"

"Yes. Like Chinese." The Shroff executed a lightning swipe with both hands, then chopped at his shoulder with the side of his palm. "You give me this. Ha-ha. You 'membuh?"

Lennox shook his head. "Did I talk to anybody else at the bar before we left? A man named Knott?"

"No. No othuh man."

"Did you see anybody write in this notebook when I wasn't looking? Did I leave it around on the bar?"

"Ah? Excuse me?"

"We're trying to find someone who wrote something bad in that book, Mr. Fu," Gabby explained. "It happened last Saturday."

"So?" The Shroff's eyes became shrewd. "Man named Knott, yes? That why you ask?"

"Exactly."

"You ah only one who use book, Missa Lennox. I know."

"Well, that's that," Lennox muttered.

"Could it have happened where you fenced?" Gabby asked.

165

"Oh no. No. Owuh 'Sociashun foh Chinese people only. I show you if you like." Suddenly the Shroff beamed again. "Owuh 'Sociashun ve'y happy to see Hu-li again."

"Why do you call me Hu-li?"

"Ah? Because how you fence. Ha-ha. Ve'y quick. Ve'y clevuh. Hu-li in Chinese issa liddy ole animal . . . Issa fox."

"Fox!" Lennox exclaimed. "So that's where the Quaker's name came from."

"Excuse me?"

"Nothing, Mr. Fu. Just the pieces crashing into place with a dull sickening thud. Show us where we fenced, please."

The Shroff led them down Mott Street, around a corner, up an alley and into a crumbling brick building from which an incredible uproar came. It sounded as though a giant were methodically beating an iron water tank to pieces. They mounted the stairs to a wooden door on which Chinese characters were painted and the Shroff ushered them into a large room.

"Dissowuh 'Sociashun," he shouted. "Foh Chinese people only. No Knott heah Satuhday night."

"What plays?" Lennox roared. "What's going on?"

"We p'epauh foh Chinese New Yeah next month."

Three saturnine Chinese in black overcoats and pearl grey hats were seated in a corner, calmly hammering a drum, a brass gong and a wooden duck. In the center of the room, an athletic young Chinese in jeans and leather jacket wielded a bamboo staff in the fantastic attitudes of the medieval Chinese warrior. Three small boys with broomsticks were following his instructions.

At the far end of the room was the giant head of a Chinese dragon to which a long accordion-pleated tail was attached. A young man in a sweat suit was doing calisthenics before the head. Then he got inside and the head came to life, jerking and swaying to the deafening percussion. The head spoke. Two boys ducked under the tail, and the entire dragon began moving across the floor.

166

Gabby had a small pad and pencil out of her purse and was sketching quickly, moistening her finger to smear the lines into broad patches of shadow. The Shroff opened a closet and took out two bamboo staves, two quilted masks and two quilted cotton aprons. He offered a brass-bound staff to Lennox.

"Yes?" he beamed.

"No thanks, Mr. Fu. I don't feel like a fox tonight. You're sure there was nobody named Knott here last Saturday?"

"Oh yes." The Shroff examined Jake's face for a moment. "Ve'y impohtant to find thissa Knott, eh?"

"Very. Where did I go from here, Mr. Fu? Do you know?"

"Oh yes. You ve'y intox'ated. I took you. I take you now."

The Shroff returned the fencing equipment to the closet, waited politely for Gabby to finish her sketching, and then conducted them downstairs. He led them to Chatham Square where three cabs were parked behind a hack sign.

"I take you to taxi," he beamed. "You ve'y intox'ated."

"My God! I can't remember that. Where the hell did I go? Hey fellas!" Lennox called. "Any of you parked here last Saturday night?"

The hack drivers poked their heads out.

"Off and on, Mac," said one.

"Hi, doll," said another.

"Oh, hello," Gabby smiled.

"Is he hedonistic or hasty?" Lennox demanded.

"Behave yourself, Jordan. I told you I get around. Did any of you gentlemen pick up my friend last Saturday night? He was drunk and disorderly."

"No Ma'am."

"Could it have been another hack?" Lennox asked.

"Could of been a dozen others, Mac."

"Happen to know a hack-driver named Knott who uses this stand?"

"Nope."

167

"Then this looks like the dead-end," Lennox grunted.

"Missa Lennox," the Shroff said. "I heah you te'l taxi man wheah to go."

"You did! Can you remember?"

The Shroff beamed in faraway recollection.

"Oh please remember, Mr. Fu," Gabby said. "It's terribly important."

The Shroff patted her arm, still immersed in memory. Finally he said: "Wassa ve'y funny place. Like a fiah."

"A fire?"

"Yes. Like . . . Hudson fiah."

"Hudson fire?" Gabby repeated, gazing at the Shroff perplexedly.

"Hold it!" Lennox said. "Could it have been the Hudson School of Firearms?"

"Yes. Yes."

"What's that?" Gabby asked.

"A shooting range over near the river. Oliver Stacy told me about it last week. I must have gone there Saturday night. Let's go."

Lennox opened the door of the lead cab. Gabby ripped a page out of her sketch book and handed it to the Shroff. It was his portrait.

"Thank you very much, Mr. Fu," she said. "You've been so helpful."

The Shroff gazed at his portrait with admiration and then at Gabby with more. "I go with you," he offered suddenly. "Be ve'y happy to help you and Missa Lennox find Missa Knott. Yes?"

"I do like you, Mr. Fu," Gabby said. "You're not inscrutable at all. Please come. We can use all the help we can get."

The Shroff entered the cab with them and they drove across town to the waterfront where a sign on a doorway between a

168

chandler's store and a window filled with broken microscopes read: Hudson School of Firearms, Dn. 2 Flights.

As the three of them trotted down the steps into the sub-cellar, they could hear the bark of guns. They came into a broad low-ceilinged vault. There was a glass cigar counter and a cash register on the right. The cigar counter was filled with revolvers and boxes of ammunition. Behind it was a high display case with heavy glass doors. Inside were more guns and six silver trophies. On the left, from wall to wall, was a line of open booths with waist-high shelves dimly lit by green shaded lamps. Through the booths was the vista of a sixty foot stretch of cellar, brilliantly illuminated. The far wall was the shooting butt, heavily pocked with bullet holes. Steel trolley wires led from each booth to the butt, and along several of these, cardboard targets were sailing out to the far wall. An intermittent barrage of shots came from the booths where men were silhouetted against the light, standing with guns raised in their right hands, their left hands resting jauntily on their hips.

A square-jawed gladiator in blue serge came around from behind the cigar counter and welcomed them. He was delighted to see Lennox.

"Hey," he said in a soft, sweet voice. "It's the Philadelphia Fox again." He shook hands. "I thought you had to go home to the wife for the holidays. She come here instead, huh?"

Lennox flushed and stammered. Suddenly he burst out: "You're the Killer. I remember now. The Killer."

"Oh, that's not nice," Gabby said.

"It's just his joke," the Killer grinned shyly. "He kept calling me that Saturday. My name's Hamburger, Mrs. Fox."

"Jordan," Gabby began. "You'd better explain that—"

"Oh no. No," the Shroff interrupted, beaming madly. "Ah nothing to explain, Missuhs Fox. Ah nothing."

There was an awkward pause, then Gabby turned to the glad-

169

iator. "Why did my— Why did he call you a killer, Mr. Hamburger?"

The Killer motioned to the silver trophies and turned red. "I won them in the Nationals, Mrs. Fox." He hung his head.

"You're modest," Gabby laughed. "I like you, Mr. Hamburger. I always thought men who used guns were savage. Do you know, I've never fired a gun in my life?"

"I'll show you," the Killer offered, without daring to look at Gabby. "Fill out a card."

"Card?" Lennox asked. "What card?"

"You know," the Killer said, leading them to the counter. "You got to register. Police regulations."

"P'lice watch gun place ve'y close," the Shroff whispered to Gabby. "Doan te'l him Missa Lennox use othuh name. Be af'aid to help him."

"I'm glad you came with us," Gabby murmured.

She filled out a police registration card and accompanied the Killer to an empty booth where he ran out a target and began instructing her on the uses and abuses of the lady-like .22 revolver he placed in her hand. Gabby waited patiently until he lost his shyness and was able to meet her eyes. Then she came around a corner abruptly and asked: "Mr. Hamburger, will you help us, please?"

The Killer looked at her uncertainly. "I don't know, Mrs. Fox. We got to be pretty careful here. What do you want?"

"We'd like to go through the cards that were filled out last Saturday. We're looking for a certain name."

"The police cards! Oh no, Ma'am. I couldn't."

"It's terribly important, Mr. Hamburger."

"I couldn't do it, Ma'am. I—" He flinched in alarm as Gabby gestured with the loaded gun. "Look out, Ma'am!"

"Let me shoot this thing and get it out of the way," Gabby said. "Then I'll explain." She raised the gun, pulled back the hammer and squinted along the sights at the target. "I've got to

170

impress him," she thought, "or he'll never listen to me." She took a deep breath, steadied the gun, and let off five shots in slow, stately succession.

A two hundred watt bulb at the side of the range was shattered. One of the trolley wires went down with a shuddering whine. A large chunk of plaster was knocked out of the ceiling. Ten inches of the wooden partition was ripped into splinters, and from the adjoining booth came an angry yell: "Get the hell off my target!"

"Oh dear," Gabby said.

The Killer choked. "Bring her in, Whitey," he said in a voice that shook. The target in the adjoining alley was run in and handed over by the indignant Whitey. The Killer glanced at it and then showed it to Gabby.

"Dead center in the black," he said. He lifted his eyes and gazed around at the destruction she had wrought and then gave her a look in which awe was mixed with dog-like devotion. "I'll do anything I can to help you, Ma'am. Just name it."

After five minutes of earnest conversation, they returned to the counter. The Killer unlocked a drawer and took out a stack of registry cards while Gabby explained to Lennox.

"You came here Saturday night. You registered but you were so drunk Mr. Hamburger wouldn't let you hire a gun. You hung around telling the best dirty jokes they ever—"

"I deny that."

"They ever heard. Mr. Hamburger invited you to go bear hunting with him in the Adirondacks. A man called The Chief wanted to take you skeet-shooting. There was a rifle club here and they asked you to join. A bank guard wanted to introduce you to his sister but you told him you were married."

"Ve'y populah man, Missa Lenn— Missa Fox," the Shroff beamed.

"I sound like the Life of the Smoker," Lennox groaned. "Was there anybody here named Knott?"

"Nope," the Killer called from the counter. "Nobody named Knott. But here's the guy you left with."

"I left with somebody? That's a break. I was afraid this would be the dead-end."

"Fella named Norman. Eugene K. Norman up on 126th Street. Says here: Care of The Midnight Sun."

"The Midnight Sun . . . whatever that is. Looks like I put in a busy Christmas Eve. God rest ye merry gentlemen. Leave us hit the road."

"You going up there now?" the Killer inquired.

"We'll have to."

"The missus?"

"Of course," Gabby said. "Why not?"

"Just a minute." The Killer disappeared into a back room and emerged wearing a hat and coat. "Hey Whitey!" he called. "Lock up for me. All right, folks. Let's be on our way."

"You're going with us, Mr. Hamburger?" Gabby asked in surprise.

"Yes, Ma'am." The Killer placed himself alongside her like a bodyguard. "It's pretty late and it gets kinda rough in Harlem. I'll drive you up. I live around there anyway."

As they left the range, the raucous voice of Whitey followed them: "Yeah. Just around the corner . . . in Brooklyn."

The Midnight Sun turned out to be a giant barn which nightly conducted a giant miscegenous barn-dance. It was on the top floor of a theater building and was apparently used for basketball games during the day. It was the sort of place to which no white woman in her right mind would ever go with her date because the competition was too strong. There is nothing more exotically beautiful than the mixtures of black, brown, white and yellow races you find on The Rock. The elite of these mixtures was on the dance floor of The Midnight Sun . . . exquisite creatures with startling faces and exciting bodies.

172

"Jesus Christ on filter!" Lennox marvelled. "Don't tell me I forgot this!"

It was beautiful, chic, queasy. There was a wild orchestra competing with its echo. There were tourists at the side tables in evening clothes and ermine. Lennox noticed a sprinkling of celebrities. There were dozens of white men prowling the edge of the dance floor like wolves, stopping dark girls, dancing with them for a moment, entering their names in address books. It had the horrid atmosphere of a black auction, and over all hung the tension of race hatred.

The manager of The Midnight Sun was making difficulties. He had a nervous, sprightly air, and his smile was almost hysterical. Admission was two dollars and a half, but The Midnight Sun dances were semi-private. The party must be guests of someone.

"Didn't you manage the old Downtown Club?" Gabby asked suddenly.

"Yes, Miss."

"Don't you remember me? You used to send out for Italian cassata for me."

The manager smote his brow. "The ice cream lady! All your guests, of course. Please sign the members' book." He produced an ancient double-entry ledger which Gabby signed in pencil. Lennox turned the pages back to December 24th and looked for the name Knott. It was not there. Neither was his own name. It was difficult to decipher anything from the smudged entries hastily scrawled in the dark.

"Does Mr. Knott come here very often?" Lennox asked.

The manager smiled hysterically and knew no one named Knott.

"Is Mr. Norman here tonight? Mr. Eugene K. Norman?"

"Somewhere on the floor," the manager told Lennox. He led the party to a small table surrounded by cases of empty beer and coke bottles, and disappeared before Lennox could ask any more questions. The waiter who descended on them for their orders was no help. At the table on their left were two magnificent blonde women with upswept hair and sequined evening gowns. On their right was an alcove filled with brooms, mops, and two sullen girls in angry conversation. Lennox got to his feet.

"Mind the store," he told the Shroff and the Killer. "I'm going to case the joint for Norman."

He went around the floor, politely inquiring after Mr. Eugene Norman. No one could help. The first girl he questioned, a Congo Venus with a bosom like pears, froze him so regally and yet with such exciting challenge that he didn't dare speak to another woman. Just alongside the dance band he came face to face with Roy Audibon.

Audibon slid his address book into his pocket and shook hands. He was a little drunk. "What? The Thinker in the fleshpots? No hunting here, Jake. This is my private jungle."

"You can have it, Roy."

"I already got it, son. What's the matter?"

"I don't like it here."

"Don't like it? Look around. Enjoy. What can't you like?"

"Myself. We're intruding. Doesn't it make you feel cheap?"

"Makes me feel one thing, son, and that doesn't come cheap. You alone? Let's bleed the lizard."

Lennox hesitated. "I'm looking for a man named Norman."

"Looking for a man? Here? Man, your loins need regrinding." Audibon left him abruptly and tapped a dark brown girl on the nape of the neck. She turned and revealed a classic Egyptian face with high cheekbones and wide deep-set eyes. Audibon spoke a few words and then swept her out onto the dance floor.

Lennox went out to the foyer to enlist the manager in his search. He was informed that the manager was in the john. He investigated, but the john was empty. As Lennox was about to leave, the door opened and one of the upswept blondes entered.

"Excuse m-me—" Lennox stammered. "You're in the—"

174

"Hello Beulah," she said in a shrill fag's falsetto.

"My God!" Lennox was appalled. "You're in drag? I never—" The fag blocked the door and regarded him seductively. "You're such a fast one," he said. "Miss Track Meet making her appointed rounds. Who were you looking for? Pretty me?"

"Listen," Lennox said, trying to be patient. "You're cruising the wrong number, girl. Would you mind getting out of the way?"

"Mary! She's in such a hurry," the fag giggled without moving. Lennox took his elbow and shoved politely. Suddenly he lost control and slammed the blonde violently against the wall. He let out a piercing, falsetto shriek. Lennox yanked open the door and ran.

As he crossed the dance floor to his table, a large ebony hand reached out and stopped him. He turned and there was Gabby dancing with a powerful bald-headed gentleman whose skin was stretched so tightly across the big bones of his head that his face looked skeletal.

"Cool, Clarence," he said in a foggy voice. "Here's yuh chick. No, honey, yuh haven't got it right. It's a one and a tuh and a zig-zag-zig!"

"Mr. Norman?"

"Eugene K. hisself."

"He's a dance teacher," Gabby said. "I'm getting a free introductory lesson."

"Got tuh educate Mrs. Clarence's rhythm," Norman said.

"He says I dance Square."

"Livin' is elation and elation's syncopation. We'll turn yuh cool, Cabbage." Still moving gently against the beat of the band, with his arm around Gabby's waist, Norman grinned at Lennox. "Where's that bull fiddle, man? Yuh welchin' on the bet? No, honey. Yuh zaggin' when you should be ziggin'."

"A one and a two and a zig-zag-zig." Gabby frowned and moved her feet.

"What bet?"

175

"You came up here with Mr. Norman," Gabby explained, "And you bet him you could get a bass violin into a taxi on the first try."

"I did? Not for even money!" Lennox protested. "You didn't sucker a drunk and disorderly man, did you?"

"They wouldn't let you use the one in the orchestra so you went out to rent a bass violin. That's the last anybody saw of you."

"So it's a dead-end, is it? What about Knott?'"

Norman shook his head. "Uh-uh. The Chick asked already, Clarence. Yuh gettin' it now, honey. We didn't rub up against any Knotts while we was togethuh. That's it! Cool, Cabbage! Livin' is elation and elation's syncopation."

He swung Gabby around deftly, chanting in off-beats. A hand pinched Jake's ear, and a falsetto voice whispered: "Want to dance, Beulah?"

"Will you leave me alone," Lennox growled at the blonde. "Get lost, for Christ's sake!"

"Oh come on girl, get gay."

The blonde entwined himself around Lennox who struggled angrily, and then stopped aghast as he saw Gabby and Norman whirl in a circle and collide with Roy Audibon and the Egyptian girl. Audibon stared at Gabby and his face turned red. He let go of his girl so sharply that she at once disappeared into the crowd.

"What the hell is this?" he said.

"Hello, Roy. This is Mr. Norman. He says that living is elation and elation's syncopation."

"Cool, pal," Norman said genially and extended his hand. Audibon ignored it.

"I'm cutting in," he said.

"Not yet," Gabby laughed. "Not until I've got the zig-zag-zig."

"I'm cutting in," Audibon repeated. Without looking at Norman he said: "Get lost."

Gabby turned pale. "Are you trying to insult my friend?"

176

"He heard me," Audibon snapped. "Let him dance with his own kind."

Lennox blew. "Look out!" he roared. "Here it comes." He shook off the blonde and belted him across the jaw. He took two steps, shouldered Norman aside and belted Audibon across the jaw. The blond shrieked and clawed at the nearest man who swung on him and knocked his wig off. Audibon got to his feet and came boring in on Lennox. Eugene Norman dropped him again with a solid chop behind the ear. The Egyptian girl appeared and kicked Audibon. The blond's friend appeared and swung on Gabby. Lennox knocked him down. In five seconds that spark of violence ignited all the violent hostilities in The Midnight Sun.

"Get her outa here!" Norman bellowed in Jake's ear. He thrust Gabby into Jake's arms, threw three vicious punches, caught a blow in the throat and reeled back. Lennox steadied him and dragged Gabby and Norman toward their table, bulling through the fighting crowd with his chin on his chest. The band began riffing the National Anthem. Nobody who could hear it paid any attention. A series of crashes commenced and the wall lights began going out. There was a wild Chinese yell and the Shroff appeared, crouched low, beating his way through the mob with a mop he wielded like a bamboo staff. Behind him Lennox saw the Killer teetering on a chair as he hurled empty coke bottles with deadly accuracy. He was methodically smashing all the lights.

"Out! Out!" Lennox roared. "Come on . . . Out!"

As they snatched their coats off their chairs, two very large men charged out of nowhere and laid violent hands on Gabby. Lennox turned with a snarl and clubbed one across the back of the neck. As he dropped to his knees, the second was felled alongside him by the Killer. Gabby bent over them.

"This is not the way to do it," she said intensely. "You must organize. Organize!"

Lennox yanked Gabby up. He wanted to kiss her and spank her. The four men formed a circle around Gabby and beat their way out to the foyer. Gabby was hurling pacifist denunciations at the riot but no one could hear her. As they started down the stairs, Norman, who was fighting a rear-guard action, whistled shrilly and stopped them.

"Cool, Clarence," he croaked. "Not that way, man. The police'll be coming."

He beckoned, slammed an anonymous assailant in the belly, and dashed around the corner to the rest rooms. As the others followed, the anonymous swung on Lennox who stiff-armed him back. The Shroff kicked him and spun him around in time for the Killer to finish him.

Norman led them into the ladies' john. Three girls were standing there, unaware of the battle outside, trying to cope with a crisis of their own. They were holding on to a fourth girl who was screaming hysterically as she trampled on her dress. She wore a string of white pearls, white satin slippers, and nothing else. The black and white contrast was beautiful and worth closer inspection, but no one had time.

"She main-linin' again?" Norman inquired. He flung open a door revealing narrow stairs leading up and squeezed himself in. The three girls began screaming too.

"Her slip's showing," Lennox said. He propelled Gabby up the stairs.

"She'll catch cold," the Killer said and followed.

"Ve'y Happy New Yeah," the Shroff beamed and slammed the door behind him.

They climbed through a skylight and emerged into the chill night air. The riot below them sounded distant and detached. Norman guided them across roofs to the dim stairs of a respectable apartment house. They descended and emerged on the street, around the corner and half a block down from The Midnight Sun. There they took stock.

178

Norman grinned at the Shroff and the Killer. They grinned back and spontaneously shook hands. "Man!" he chuckled. "That bottle-bit and that mop-mop-massacre. We're a goddam Foreign Legion. Damn if we ain't!" All the men felt better after the scrap, but Gabby was very angry.

"Shame on you," she said. "Fighting like that. Hurting people. Making fun of that poor sick girl. You're supposed to be civilized. You're worse than animals."

"Honey," Norman said reasonably. "It was self-defense."

"No it wasn't, Mr. Norman. It was bad boys on a spree."

"We were protecting you, Ma'am," the Killer said.

"No you weren't, Mr. Hamburger. You were enjoying yourselves. I thought you were all such nice men. Now I'm ashamed of you. I hate fighting. There's no excuse for fighting . . . ever!"

"Gabby," Lennox said gently. "Get off the soap-box."

She turned on him. "And you started it all, Jordan. Why did you hit that poor blond man?"

"He was a fag and he was bothering me."

"That's no excuse. He's as sick as that poor naked girl. You've got to feel sorry for homosexuals. You shouldn't hate them. But you do. You like to hate and hurt."

"Ah don't blame'm," Norman muttered. "Queens is poison. Make any man want to punch 'em."

"You be quiet, Mr. Norman."

Norman shut up.

"And what about Roy?" Gabby stormed. "I know why you hit him. You hate him. You're jealous and—"

"No. I slugged him because he passed a crack at Norman I didn't like."

"He doesn't know any better. You have to reason with prejudice, not—"

"Well he damn well ought to know better."

"Do you think you taught him anything?"

"Maybe," the Shroff said unexpectedly.

"How?" Gabby demanded.

"Chinese people ve'y ole-fashun. We have ve'y ole wise saying . . ." He paused as though making a translation from the original.

"Well?" Lennox asked after a moment. "You've left us hanging, Mr. Fu."

The Shroff beamed around. "I fohget," he said.

They burst out laughing. They hooted and groaned with laughter as they lurched down the street to the Killer's car. There they parted affectionately from Norman who presented each of them with an engraved card that read: Eugene K. Norman, The Midnight Sun, Technique of the Terpischore, Living is Elation and Elation's Syncopation.

"Come to the show Sunday," Lennox called after him. "The Venice Theater at nine o'clock. Ask for Jordan Lennox." He issued the same invitation to the Shroff and the Killer.

"What show?" the Shroff asked.

"A television show called 'Who He?'"

"Who's Jordan Lennox?" the Killer inquired.

"Him," Gabby said. "His pen name. A one and a two and a zig-zag-zig." They piled into the car. "Are we through, Jordan? Have we failed?"

"You seem pretty cheerful," Lennox laughed.

"I am. So are you."

"Must be hysteria. I'm so loused up now that I don't give a damn any more."

"That's a relief."

"Why do you say that?"

"You get so oppressive when you're filled with resolve."

"You sound like Sam. Well . . . There's one last chance. I'll give it a play after I take you home."

"The blonde?"

"Keep out of this part, Gabby."

"Aimee Driscoll with two E's?"

180

"Yes."

"Do you really live in Brooklyn, Mr. Hamburger?" Gabby asked.

"Yes, Ma'am."

"Could you drop Mr. Fu at Chatham Square before you go across the bridge?"

"Sure, Ma'am."

"And could you drop us on Third Avenue at . . . What's the name of the place, Jordan?"

"I don't want you in on this."

"Where did you pick her up?"

"I think it was Ye Baroque Saloon."

"At . . . you should excuse the expression . . . Ye Baroque Saloon, please, Mr. Hamburger. It isn't a dead-end yet."

The inside laugh on Ye Baroque Saloon is that it's named after the proprietor, Chris Barokotrones, who came to The Rock and shortened his name to Baroque before he understood enough French or English to know what he was doing. By the time he found out, he had enough money to buy a building on Third Avenue and build a saloon. He had it decorated in American Baroque . . . the exaggerated theatrical style that was the vogue in saloons before the turn of the century.

Everybody in the business goes to the Baroque for a nightcap. The joint was jumping when Gabby and Lennox entered. It was a piratic crowd, very young and very handsome. Crop-haired boys with hornshell glasses who would become the Audibons and Bordens of the next decade . . . Striking young girls who would become their wives and mistresses . . . A leavening of the older men and women whom success and good living had kept young.

Gabby and Lennox went down the bar, past the booths and into the back room. Lennox saw Aimee Driscoll sitting alone at a table behind the telephone booth. Her high fat bosom pushed out over the table. Her wide fat bottom spread over the chair. Through the smoke and haze she looked, at first glance, like a lusty Swede farm girl from Minnesota; but the second glance shamed Lennox.

"Nope," he said to Gabby. "She's not here. We'll go out the side door."

They threaded their way between tables and went out the side door. Lennox took a deep breath of the fresh air and looked around for a cab. A small man in a derby, pea-jacket and white duck trousers came around the corner. He spoke to them in a bright voice. "Hi, Joe. H'ar ya? Hi, Sally?" He continued down the street, addressing empty doorways in friendly tones.

"Ah," Gabby said compassionately. "He's lonesome, poor soul. He wants friends. Do you think he's afraid of people, Jordan?" She came around a corner abruptly. "As afraid as you are of Aimee Driscoll?"

"W-What?"

"Listen to me." Gabby backed him against the wall and pointed a finger at him. "I know she's in there. At the table behind the phone booth. You should have seen your face when you saw her. Are you afraid to speak to her?"

"Yes. I'm ashamed. Revolted."

"Why?"

"Gabby, don't be naive. Suppose you picked up a strange man and— Would you want to see him again?"

"I did," Gabby said. "Last Sunday night."

"No. No, darling. It's different with us. We . . . Did you see her? What she looks like? I could kill her."

"Have I seen you? What do you really look like? Maybe there'll come a day when I'll really see you and want to kill you."

"Gabby!"

"Don't do that to me. Don't shame me now."

"What do you want me to do?"

"Don't be angry and hateful. I want you to be honest and kind to everybody. I want you to go in there and speak to her like Jordan Lennox . . . Not like Roy Audibon."

182

"Gabrielle," he said, "You're a great woman . . . but I'm not a great man."

He kissed her, then turned and re-entered the back room of the Baroque. Gabby followed him. He walked directly to Aimee's table and smiled down at her as pleasantly as he could fake.

"Good evening, Aimee," he said. "Mind if we join you?"

"Hi, Clarence," Aimee said. "Your friend deliver that coat and book?"

"That's why I'm here. Have you got a minute?"

"Sure."

Lennox and Gabby sat down. As Lennox held Gabby's chair for her, Aimee darted her a look of hostility. "Taking it from the top," Lennox said. "My name isn't Clarence Fox. It's Lennox. Jordan Lennox."

"Naughty, naughty!" Aimee said coyly. "Say, are you really the guy which writes that TV show like you said?"

"Yes."

"How about me? Popular with the big-shots. I should've asked for your autograph." Aimee glanced at Gabby.

"This is Miss Gabrielle Valentine . . . Aimee Driscoll."

"Miss Aimee Driscoll," Aimee snapped.

"Of course. I'm sorry." Lennox hesitated and finally forced himself to meet Aimee's eyes. He saw in them an anger that startled him. He'd been too drunk to notice that photograph of Aimee's father in her apartment, and even if he had noticed it, he wouldn't have seen the connection.

No one knows what happened between Aimee Driscoll and her father. Anyone can guess, but it doesn't matter. The important result was that the particular chasm over which she walked her tight rope was an inescapable physical attraction for any man who resembled her father plus an uncontrollable hatred for him. Lennox hadn't gone to bed with Aimee that Saturday night. She was relieved, professionally, and infuriated, emotionally. She looked at him now with hatred and at Gabby with venom, completely unaware of what she was feeling or how she was showing it.

"Sweet guy you are," she said archly. "Sweet guy . . . making a sucker out of a poor working girl from the lower classes. You owe me ten bucks."

"I do? What for?" Lennox was terrified of what the answer would be.

"The doctor. I had to see him Monday on account of what you done to me. You practical jokers don't know your own strength." Aimee winked at Gabby. "Your boy friend's a funny guy with a Christmas tree, Gabrielle. We had a million laughs. He tell you?"

"No," Gabby said quietly.

"I guess he wouldn't at that."

"Do you want to tell me, Aimee?"

"Me? No." She laughed, concealing her teeth with her hand. "I'm a good kid. I can take a joke. Anyway your boyfriend don't owe me a cent, not after the gorgeous Christmas present he give me."

Lennox swallowed painfully. "It was a television set, wasn't it, Aimee?"

"Modest, ain't he? What a sweet guy. What did he give you, Gabrielle?"

"Something I've always wanted, Aimee."

"Jesus! Mink?"

Gabby shook her head and smiled.

Aimee examined the smile and tried to answer it. "Look at you. Up there on Cloud Nine, ain't you?"

"Yes."

"Well, fall easy."

"Were you hurt when you fell?"

"Me? I never was up." Aimee laughed and covered her mouth. "Strictly the subway type."

"Listen, Aimee," Lennox smiled painfully. "I'd like to sit here yakking it up, but I'm in a jam and I need help."

"You're our last hope," Gabby added.

"Me? No." Aimee looked from one to the other and the archness peeled away from her malice. "Don't tell me a big-shot which can afford two names and two girls needs help."

"I do," Lennox said. "Look, we met here Saturday night. What time was it?"

"What are you checking up on?"

"It couldn't have been too late because a store must have been open. We were able to buy you that set."

"Strictly your idea, Clarence. You kept on running off at the mouth about bull fiddles."

"Yes. I found out. So we went to a music store and ended up buying you a television set. Where?"

"Who can remember?" Aimee answered, enjoying Jake's misery.

"Please, Aimee," Gabby said. "This is very important."

"Why is it important? I had enough trouble with your boy friend Saturday night. I don't want no more."

"He's been getting threatening letters from a man he met some time Saturday night . . . A man named Knott. Dreadful letters. We're trying to find Knott."

"Did you go to the cops?" Aimee asked sharply.

"Yes, I did."

"You mention me?"

"No. I'm working this out on my own. Let's see if we can't put it together, Aimee. I left Harlem and wandered down here. We met and went to a music store and bought the set. Right?"

"It was around half past one," Aimee said grudgingly.

185

"That place on Forty-second and Third. They was closed and doing up their accounts. You banged on the door until they let us in."

"Thanks. Then what happened? We took the set up to your place?"

"You got a hack and put it in. We must of hit a dozen joints on the way. Then we ate. We didn't get home until light."

"Did we meet anybody named Knott? Did I talk to anybody named Knott? Did you see anybody write anything in this notebook of mine?" Lennox pulled the book out of his pocket and displayed it.

"You're really leveling with this, huh?" Aimee said slowly. "You're really suffering, huh?"

"Yes."

"This Knott wrote something in your book?"

"He did."

"And you got to locate him or else?"

"I do. Before Sunday."

"Why before Sunday?"

"Because that's the day he lowers the boom."

"So you're going to have a tough couple of days sweating it out, ain't you, Clarence?" Aimee stared at him with delight. "Ain't it a shame I can't help you out? Tsk-Tsk! No. We never come across nobody named Knott."

"In this place?"

"Nope."

"In the music store?"

"Nope."

"Afterwards? In the bars? Where we ate?"

"Nope."

Lennox opened his mouth to ask another question, then faltered. Gabby asked it for him. "And in your apartment, Aimee?"

"He couldn't talk to nobody," Aimee snapped. "He passed out soon as we come in. Big shot! And when he come to he ran right out." She intercepted the look of salvation and relief that passed between Lennox and Gabby and began to shake with rage.

"And afterwards?" Gabby asked.

"What about afterwards?"

"The notebook was there for twelve hours after Jordan left. Did anybody named Knott have a chance to leave a message in it?"

"The only body in that apartment is named Driscoll."

"Your friends?" Gabby persisted.

"I got no friends."

"Your . . . clients?"

"What's that crack supposed to mean?"

"Look, Aimee—" Lennox began.

"Shut up, big shot. I asked her. Leave her answer."

"It wasn't a crack," Gabby said composedly. "I wouldn't dream of insulting you, Aimee. I simply meant—"

"Not now!" Lennox interrupted in alarm. "Don't be honest now, dear."

"I meant that we know you're a prostitute," Gabby continued candidly, "And one of your clients might have been Knott."

"Suffering Jesus on echo!" Lennox groaned. "Listen, Aimee, she's just kidding. She—"

"Yeah. She's a sweet little kidder. And what price does she put on her sweet little ass that makes her so high and mighty?"

"What are you ashamed of, Aimee?" Gabby asked quietly. "I'm not ashamed of you."

Aimee turned on her in fury. "The come-on's your racket, huh? The tickle and tease. You save your ass for the big price and after you're married it turns out nothing. But nothing!"

"You're old-fashioned," Gabby smiled. "We aren't amateurs any more."

"And they come crying to me and taking it out on me, like Clarence . . . Because you save it so hard you don't know what to do with it but lay on it."

"Shut up," Lennox growled.

"You must of got him plenty hot Saturday night, sister. You're so God damned glad he never touched me. You want to see how he touched me? I'll show you." Aimee stood up so violently that her chair toppled. She yanked up her skirt and displayed her naked behind, criss-crossed with black and blue welts. Then she dropped her skirt and burst into hysterical laughter, covering her teeth with her hand. "It was like old times when my old man took a strap to me after he . . . I felt like a kid again. We had a million laughs."

Lennox grunted in anguish. Gabby looked at him, then stood up impulsively and took Aimee's hands. "He did a dreadful thing, Aimee. He's ashamed and so am I. Please let us make it up to you. We'll do anything."

"You can suffer," Aimee spat, jerking away from Gabby's touch. "You can sweat. You can fry in hell until Sunday. Because I know who Knott is. This guy you're looking for. I know him. Sure he left a message in your book. I saw him."

"Aimee! For God's sake, who is he?"

"I ain't going to tell you. Suffer, you son of a bitch! God knows you made me suffer with your God damned morals and your God damned strap. Suffer!"

"What strap? Make sense. Who is he?"

"Go on. Ask a little. Beg a little."

"What do you want?" Lennox demanded roughly. "Money? How much?"

"I want you to suffer, big shot with your comical Christmas tree. We had a million laughs. Now sweat it out, Mr. Lennox." She pushed past Lennox and Gabby and waddled across the back room of the Baroque, honking with laughter, covering her mouth with her hand. The crowd gaped at her.

At the side door she turned and screamed: "I know him and I ain't going to tell. Never. But I'll be up to the show Sunday, watching. And when Knott catches up with you . . . remember my ass!"

· CHAPTER X ·

Nine o'clock the next morning, Roy Audibon left Gracie Hospital and took a cab down to the network. His ribs were taped, his face was bruised, his teeth were clenched in a dazzling smile that was sure to hurt someone else worse than it hurt him.

He rode the exclusive executives' elevator up to the twentieth floor, strode through the three anterooms guarding the holy of holies, and entered his office. It was rather ascetic compared to the conventional top-level decor. It contained a very large English desk paneled with gold-tooled leather, three Queen Anne armchairs covered with brocade, two red leather library chairs, a walnut breakfront displaying Dresden China and a brass microscope, a French stick barometer, a framed illuminated transparency of M-31, the Andromeda Nebula, and a constrained water color of Fire Island Beach signed: Valentine.

Audibon examined the picture for a moment, then went to his desk, thrust aside the mountain of predigested mail, and picked up the phone. To his secretary he said: "Get me Grabinett and Bleutcher."

"Yes, Mr. Audibon. What Bleutcher is that, please?"

"Tom Bleutcher of Mode Shoes. Brockton, Mass. Check the 'Who He?' file." Audibon licked his lips. "Everybody on my team is expected to know the name and number of every player. This advice will be of value to you in your next job which will start at the end of this week."

The secretary gasped. "I'm sorry, Mr. Audibon. I—"

"Accounting will arrange your severance pay," Audibon interrupted and hung up. He examined the water color again, remembering a dark girl in striped clam-diggers and an old shirt knotted under her bosom, sitting cross-legged on a blazing dune . . . a drawing board before her, tilted on the bleached remains of a driftwood chair . . . the tinkle of a brush washed in a jar of water.

"Never," Audibon said.

The phone rang. He picked it up. "Yes?"

"Mr. Grabinett cannot be reached in his office," the secretary reported in a suppressed voice that soothed Audibon. "Mr. Bleutcher cannot be contacted in Brockton. I left word that you called."

"Word is too little and too late. Keep trying for both."

"Yes, Mr. Audibon. John Macro is waiting to see you."

"Macro? By appointment?"

"Yes, Mr. Audibon. You told me to—"

"Send him in."

For a man who was not in the business, John Macro was the most hated man in the business. He was a Maryland manufacturer who had taken it upon himself to cleanse radio and television of subversive artists. To this he devoted his patriotic heart and ample bank account. Once a month Mr. Macro came to The Rock and purged. He was in no way equipped for the job, intellectually or otherwise. In normal times his impertinent intrusions would have been brushed as contemptuously as Mr. Macro himself would have brushed any unqualified intruder, attempting to tell him how to do his own thinking; but these were not normal times.

Honest John came to The Rock and studied the reports of his researchers who were mostly free-lance trade journal writers playing detective. He learned that so-and-so had once signed a petition. He ferreted out the fact that a certain man was known to have supported a particular drive; that this woman had lent her name to such-and-such a cause. Mr. Macro judged and accused, and such was the hysteria of the times that mere accusation was enough to make the world draw aside the hem of its garment in terror and hound the victim out of the business.

Mr. Macro was a good man and a sincere man. Unfortunately he was also a Square. He believed he was doing his duty as a citizen. Actually, he was a child playing with a gun. He entered Audibon's office with the air of a Roman Tribune. He was very bald, very handsome, with a leaden complexion and kindly features. He carried an alligator portfolio which he unlocked ceremoniously after he shook hands with Audibon. He withdrew a short list of names.

"For these," he said melodiously, "I have proof positive." He produced a dossier of stapled sheets, handed it to Audibon and then seated himself in a Queen Anne chair and waited majestically.

Audibon read the list of names and then the proof positive. He smiled at Macro without liking.

"This isn't proof," he said, "and it isn't positive."

"Every organization cited there has been listed by the Attorney General's office, Mr. Audibon."

Audibon shook his head. "But it's not *prima facie*-type evidence."

"Straws show how the wind blows."

"God help us if we're judged by straws like this."

"Good Heavens! I'm not judging, Mr. Audibon. Far be it

from me to judge my fellow citizens. Let the evidence speak for itself. If I'm wrong, as I sincerely hope I am, these persons can easily clear themselves."

"Your frame of reference is unrealistic, Mr. Macro. It's impossible for any man to clear himself today. These things are chain-reactive." Audibon flung down the dossier and began to pace energetically. "Touch the American pulse and what do you find? The systole and diastole of paranoia. Do you know cybernetics . . . the science of minds and machines? There's a cybernetic feed-back in the American nervous system today. The average American is synaptically inhibited. He can't believe in the innocence of a man once he's been accused. He can't believe in guiltlessness even after acquittal."

Macro stared at Audibon.

"Apart from the issue of freedom of conscience," Audibon went on passionately, "there's the quanta of Popular Villainism. Literature went through an Industrial Revolution in this country and was transformed from an art-form into a story business. The political thinking was metamorphised the same way. You don't find people weighing political factors and extrapolating for valued judgements. Savanarola died in vain. No, our people turn every political issue into Cops And Robbers . . . Boy Meets Girl . . . Peter And The Wolf, you should excuse the expression."

"I'm afraid I don't follow you, Mr. Audibon."

"Peter And The Wolf. Written by a Russian composer named Tchaikovsky," Audibon explained patiently. "A musico-political joke."

"But this isn't a question of Russian aliens, Mr. Audibon. It's simply—"

"It's a question of the write-in habit," Audibon interrupted. "The basic mistake radio made. Radio tried to bring entertainment into the home. Then the problem of audience response arose and we had to encourage the write-in habit for purposes

193

of analysis on a broad consumer basis. From writing in about products, the public has taken to writing in about politics. This is one mistake television will not make. We're not going to bring the show into the home. We're going to bring the home to the show."

"About these people, Mr. Audibon...."

"I know them all, Mr. Macro. They're artists, all of them; not necessarily talentwise, but because they have magic. Talent died with Goethe. These people have theatricality and mesmerization, not intelligence. Three quarters of them probably did what they did out of *Gestalt* . . . out of emotions. How can we judge them on the cybernetic level?"

"Mr. Audibon," Macro said in exasperation. "I'm a business man. Let's get down to cases. Is your network prepared to suspend the employment of these subversives, or must I call the attention of our sponsors' organization to your—"

"This network has never approved of a blacklist, Mr. Macro, and it never will. If you've come here looking for an official blacklist, you don't know the temper of our organization. However . . . I see no reason why the artists investigated by you shouldn't be given plenty of free time to prepare their defense."

Macro looked hard at Audibon. "Then you're prepared to—"

"As good citizens, Mr. Macro, we're not prepared to endorse an official blacklist. That's final. However, I suggest you monitor our network shows. If, in the future, you see any of the people on this list associated in any capacity with any of our shows, you can start a rhubarb. But until then, as good citizens, we very politely tell you to go to hell."

Macro flushed and stared at Audibon. Then, as abruptly, he smiled and nodded. "I think I understand. You have no official blacklist, of course."

"Of course."

Macro stood up. As he closed his portfolio and was about

to lock it, he hesitated. Then he withdrew a small slip of paper and consulted it.

"Is there a person named Valentine connected with your network?" he asked.

"Valentine?" Audibon stiffened. "What Valentine?"

"A Miss Gabrielle Valentine. A note here says she might be working in your art department."

"What about Gabrielle Valentine?"

"My researchers have come across the name quite often. A suspiciously active person. If she's connected with your organization I should advise you to have her—"

"She doesn't work for us," Audibon said emphatically. "But we'd hire her at any time. I happen to know the young woman rather well."

"Oh?"

"I know for a fact that she has clean hands."

"There seems to be evidence to the contrary, Mr. Audibon." Macro waggled the slip of paper.

"You know I don't spitball off the cuff, Mr. Macro. Take my word for it. You'll be making a great mistake if you mother-hen any ideas about Gabrielle Valentine."

Macro looked dubious.

Audibon smiled dazzlingly. "The lady is my wife," he said.

"Good Heavens, Mr. Audibon! I never— The idea is ridiculous, of course." Macro crumpled the slip and tossed it into a gilt wastepaper basket.

Audibon took a breath. "But here's a replacement for the name," he said. "I suggest you touch a piece of litmus paper to a writer named Lennox. Jordan Lennox. My hunch is it'll turn a bright red."

"Jordan Lennox," Macro repeated, carefully printing the name on a small pad. He locked the portfolio, shook hands and departed. Audibon picked the crumpled wad of paper out of the basket, smoothed it and tried to decipher the symbols and abbreviations following Gabby's name. Then he placed it inside his wallet. His day was made. He picked up his phone. "You're back on the payroll, love," he told his secretary. "Keep trying for Grabinett and Bleutcher. Call Program and notify them we're cancelling 'Who He?' as of the first of the year."

On the way home from Gabby's studio, Lennox took a wide detour and stopped off at the Precinct where he found Fink in a small office that smelled of disinfectant. Fink was doing paper work at a scarred desk and looked more like a bank clerk than ever. Lennox sat down and told his story from Cooper's recognition of the handwriting to Aimee Driscoll's last words the night before. He handed over the page from his gimmick book that contained the hysterical scrawled message. Fink was neither impressed nor unimpressed. He listened carefully, smiling at the wrong times, then bobbed his head.

"I was pretty sure it was you getting the letters," he said.

"How?" Lennox blinked. "I didn't know myself."

"You make the big fuss. You must have known somewhere inside your head."

"You're quite a psychologist."

"No. Strictly statistics. I wish I had a nickel for every guy in a jam who won't admit it. They make the big fuss and claim they're worried about somebody else. Turns out they're really stewing about theirselves."

"I hate like hell to be a statistic, Bob."

"We all are. There's hundreds of laws in the statute books, but cops depend on one law most of all. The law of averages."

"Is this an average case?"

"It's tough."

"Does any of this stuff I gave you help?"

"Maybe. We'll check. I like what this Cooper said best."

"About having seen the writing before?"

196

Fink nodded and smiled.

"Why?"

"I'm pretty sure someone on your program is writing the letters. That's why I like what this Cooper said best."

"Someone on the show?"

"Yeah. Ninety-nine out of a hundred it turns out like that. Someone in the office. Someone in the factory. Someone in the department store. We've been going over payroll vouchers and check endorsements on your program."

"Law of averages again. And?"

"We'll see." Fink smiled. "This Cooper is a good friend of yours, huh?"

"We share an apartment. Why?"

"How long?"

"About a year."

"How long's he been on your program?"

"He's worked the show since it started. Over nine months. What is all this?"

"You and this Cooper ever fight?"

"Now wait a minute, Bob. I'm no fool. If you're headed in that direction, I don't buy any of it. Not Sam."

"Funny, this Cooper not remembering where he saw the writing."

"He's got troubles of his own to remember."

"Sometimes a grudge lasts a long time."

"What grudge?"

"You tell me."

"There's nothing to tell. The whole idea's for laughs."

"Tough," Fink murmured.

"Forget Sam, will you! If it has to be someone on the show, maybe it's a stagehand or a cameraman named Knott. Do we have a Knott on the payroll?"

"No," Fink said. "That's what makes it tough."

"Can you get me off the hook by Sunday?"

The office door opened and a swarthy man entered briskly. Lennox saw at once that he was carrying the blue sheets and envelopes of the threatening letters from "Guess Who." They were stained and discolored and had been sprayed with a fixative that made them shine. As Lennox straightened in excitement, Fink spoke.

"Mr. Salerno," he said, "this is Mr. Lennox. He just figured out he's getting these letters."

Salerno grinned. Lennox was about to speak when suddenly he heard what Fink had just said. "*Mister* Salerno," he repeated. "*Mister* Lennox. That's the code, isn't it? You're warning him to be careful."

"You see?" Fink said. "It doesn't make any difference if you know. We're protecting ourselves."

"From me?"

"Not necessarily." Fink stood up. "Now don't worry. We'll try to get you off the hook by Sunday." He took Lennox to the door and politely closed it in his face.

Lennox departed, not at all comfortable in his mind, and went home to change. Cooper was there, in slacks and T-shirt, working feverishly at the piano. He had a pencil in his mouth, a sheet of manuscript paper on the music rack, and dozens more scattered around the piano bench. He was working his way painfully through a chord progression while he hummed to himself in the high composer's keen that only dogs can hear.

"Fink's crazy," Lennox thought, and resolutely buried the suspicion in the deepest crevice of his mind.

He tiptoed around the apartment. After he changed, he locked the Siamese upstairs in his office where they couldn't distract Cooper. He made fresh coffee and slid a cup against the left side of the music rack so as not to interfere with Cooper's writing hand. He intercepted the cleaning woman (this day was vacuum cleaner day for the living room) and told her to work upstairs first. Exiled from his own office, he got tools from the kitchen and settled down at the table before the garden windows to repair his gimmick book.

In some primitive cultures it is believed that a man's soul can be contained in an object . . . an amulet, a bit of stone or wood, a fetish . . . which is carefully concealed by the owner and earnestly sought after by his enemies. Destruction of the object means destruction of the man. Lennox would never admit it, but he felt exactly that way about his gimmick book. That was why he had become so panicky when it was lost and quarreled so unreasonably with Cooper. He spent hours at a time sewing it, mending it with scraps of leather and metal, until it was a patchwork quilt of the original. It never occurred to him that his soul might also be a patchwork of makeshift repairs.

From tinkering with the notebook, he got to reading it, and presently a forgotten idea caught his attention. He thought about it and the idea took shape. Lennox got a yellow legal pad and soft pencils and began to block out a script, grunting and mumbling softly to himself in the low writer's grumble that only seismographs can record. Working away like that, Cooper and Lennox sounded like a duet between a peanut whistle and a cement mixer.

For the rest of the morning there was peace in the room, the old kind of peace they hadn't known in the past week. Once Cooper murmured: "Virgil, which sounds better?" He played two indistinguishable phrases and Lennox rumbled appropriately. Once Lennox grunted: "Wolfgang, which sounds better?" He read two indistinguishable phrases and Cooper keened appropriately. This was the secret of their friendship and their deep need for each other.

Creation is the loneliest work in the world, which is why most artists go stir-crazy. By some miracle of human chemistry, Cooper and Lennox were able to work together. Not only did they have companionship, a rare thing for working artists, but each was able to draw on the other's creative drive and enlarge his own. They never worked so well as when they worked together in the same room.

At 11:15, Lennox grunted and mumbled his way to the kitchen for more coffee, only to meet Cooper coming out with two cups in his hand. Lennox took one and then forgot why. With his pencil he absently shaded a moustache on Cooper's lip while Sam stood with eyes shut and hummed, unaware of his disfigurement.

"No!" Lennox exclaimed suddenly. "The whole point of the scene is that the ingenue pivots. More kissed against than kissing."

Cooper nodded to this gibberish, handed the second cup to Lennox and went back to the piano still nodding like a porcelain mandarin. Lennox returned to his yellow pad. The duet continued.

At 11:45 they met in the bathroom where Lennox added a goatee to the moustache.

At 12:30 they met in the storage closet alongside Sam's room where the cigarette cartons and stationery were stashed.

At 12:55, without a word or a sign to each other, they quit work simultaneously and became aware of themselves and the world around them. They were in the manic mood that always follows intense creative concentration.

"Good morning," Cooper said. "You're new in this ward, aren't you?"

"I was here before you," Lennox said in hot tones.

"My good man, I was here before it was built. My name is Cornerstone."

"The name is familiar," Lennox mused. "But I can't remember the face."

"Ach! So. Und vhen did dis antikinetic facial phobia virst manifesdt idself, Mr. Lennox?"

200

"I can't remember, Doctor," Lennox answered in a low voice.

"You can't remember? Tausend Teufel! Vas it at your mutter's breast?"

"I . . . I don't remember."

"You must remember, Mr. Lennox, or I send you back to dat freud, Dr. Quack."

"Will you try that line again, please."

"Oh. Sorry . . . To dat quack, Dr. Freud."

"Wouldn't 'kvack' be more authentic?"

"Maybe, but I can't feel it, Mr. Sachs. There's a value missing."

"That's because you've got your dialects mixed. I know Dr. Livingston wouldn't speak low Dutch. I have a talent for never being wrong."

"Livingston? I thought we were doing Pasteur. Cue, please."

"You see, Dr. Livingston, bosoms are my problem."

"Proceed, Mr. Stanley."

"They . . . I know this sounds silly . . . but they all look alike. And there's always two. Two! Two! Two! Why can't there ever be an odd number? Sometimes I think I'll go mad, do you hear? Mad! Mad! Mad!"

"Steady on, old man . . . (Pipe business) . . . Pity you haven't read my monograph on Trichinopoly ashes and busts. I can distinguish twenty-four varieties by their action."

"Amazing!"

"Elementary. There's the plainbeat bust, the backfall bust, the double backfall, the springer, the shaked elevation, the turn, the battery, the double relish. . . ."

"Sam!" Lennox interrupted in delight. "Where did you find those everlovin' words?"

"It's musical ornamentation," Cooper grinned. "Didn't I ever tell you? They're the old names for trills and grace notes and such, but they kind of fit the front ornamentation of ladies too, don't they?"

Lennox nodded as he jotted down the words in his gimmick book.

"Kay Hill, for instance. She's the close shake. Irma Mason's the battery. All directions. The dancers are strictly the plain-beat. One bounce to a step. Robin's the shaked elevation. Your girl's the double relish."

"Who? Gabby?" Lennox blushed.

"I noticed at the party. One of the few things I did notice, outside of that hassle with Tooky Ween. . . ."

"I'm sorry about that, Sam, but I had to protect you. You would have. . . ."

"And something Suidi let slip."

"Oh? What he let slip?"

"It was your party."

"It may have been my idea, but—"

"It was your bankroll."

"Oh. He blew it. In French or English?"

Cooper hoisted himself up on the piano and sat swinging his legs. Then he began to speak, choosing his words carefully.

"I appreciate what you tried to do, Jake . . . But let me tell you how. Last year a kid cousin of mine bought me a birthday present. He saved up his allowance and bought the best present he could think of . . . a bag of marbles."

"Immies," Lennox corrected absently.

"What?"

"They call them immies on The Rock."

"All right, immies. I appreciated that present, Jake. I was really touched. I appreciated your present the same way. It touched me the same way. You understand?"

"No."

"The kid didn't give me anything I could use. He gave me what he loved."

"You mean I'm a kid?"

"No, Jake. You gave me the thing you love most. And when

202

you found out I didn't want any part of it, you tried to make me want it. You don't understand anybody not wanting to be a big wheel in the business, do you? That's your bag of immies."

"What the hell are we working for?"

"Fun."

"Fun's not the answer. We've got to have something to show."

"Fun's enough for me."

"Why don't you grow up, Sam!" Lennox said impatiently. "You talk about immies. You're the kid. Playing games with cap pistols. Soon as somebody pulls a real gun on you, you turn chicken."

"All right. I'm a kid playing games. Leave me alone. Don't protect me. Don't sponsor me. Don't try to shove a loaded gun into my hand." Cooper jumped down off the piano. "What's that line you use on the agency kibitzers when they try to make you rewrite a script their way? What do you always say? Go ahead . . . tell me."

"If you have to hang, hang on your own rope."

"Q.E.D.," Cooper said. "You want to keep things going the way they always have?"

"You know that."

"Then lay off. Let me go to hell my own way."

Lennox turned away angrily. The hidden crevice in his mind opened and Fink's dreadful hint shot up to the surface and burst like a bubble in acid.

"Who wrote those letters?" he asked abruptly.

"What? What letters?"

"You know damned well what letters. I told you yesterday I found out they're written to me. They're written by somebody named Knott. That's the writing you recognized. Who's Knott?"

"Nobody I know."

"But you know the writing?"

"I thought so."

"Changed your mind recently?"

"What's eating you out all of a sudden?"

"I don't play games. Neither does Blinky. He found out I'm getting the letters and I'm off the show. If there's any kind of trouble, he'll murder me with a lawsuit. So it's coming up to the clutch. Two days to Sunday. I'm in so deep, if anybody makes waves I'm dead. This is fun. Yak it up."

"I'm not laughing."

"If you've got anything besides immies to contribute, now's the time. Who wrote the letters?"

"Lay off, Jake. Don't badger me."

"You can't tell or you won't tell. Which is it?"

"I don't know. I can't remember."

"I think you're lying."

"That's a hell of a thing to say."

"It hurts to say it. I think you're lying."

"Why lying all of a sudden?"

"Not all of a sudden. It's a slow take. You recognize the writing, but you don't know whose. When I tell you the name, it doesn't ring a bell. Who the hell are you kidding, Judas?"

"Jake!"

"I'm fighting to hold on to what's between us, too. I don't think it can live through a lie. Not now. Not when I'm on the cross yelling for help. Is it a lie?"

Cooper shook his head.

"All of a sudden it's sour between us. Nothing I do is right. I try to plug your tune. No good. I try to hold the chiselers off. I stink. I try to fight my way out of a jam. You object. I suppose when I tell you I've set it up for you and one of the dancers to do a duet of 'We're The Most' in next Sunday's show you'll—"

"Damn you, Jake!" Cooper gestured angrily.

"I stink again. But by God you'll do it. What's got into you?

204

What are you trying to do . . . slug me when I come around the corner? I don't think you're trying to pull out of the rat-race. I think you're trying to pull me down into the grave!"

Cooper attempted to speak, then gave it up and stormed into his room. He slammed the door so hard that half a dozen books bounced off the shelves. Lennox made no move to pick them up. The phone rang. Lennox made no move to answer it. After five peals, it stopped, and a moment later the P-lady called downstairs. Lennox picked up the living room extension.

"Yes?"

"Jake, this is Melvin Grabinett."

"How are your associates?"

"What?"

"It's a question I've been wanting to ask you for years. Who the hell are your associates anyway? Helter and Skelter?"

"Are you drunk?"

"No. Unemployed."

"Listen, I'm in Tom Bleutcher's suite at The Brompton House. Been here the whole Almighty morning. Olga wants you to have lunch with us."

"Olga? Who she?"

"His daughter. You made a big hit with her last time they was in town. Come on down."

"Get the new writer."

"I got no new writer. Anyway she yens for you. Come on down."

"Why should I help entertain the client? I'm off the show. Remember?"

"You still got a piece of the royalties. You want to keep on collecting? Help keep it on the air. Come on down."

Grabinett's relations with his client were shaky because they were based on marriage. Grabinett's wife was the daughter of Pan-American Export. Grabinett's father-in-law was the biggest single purchaser of Mode Shoes, exporting thousands of pairs each year to South American dealers. So long as Mode Shoes remained on Pan-American's catalogue, Tom Bleutcher would remain Blinky's client. But he didn't have to like it.

He was a heavy man with a red face and thick iron-grey hair; a third generation German, and the Germans are the best shoe manufacturers in the world. They are also the most pig-headed manufacturers in the world. Bleutcher had formed his opinions in Chicago during the years 1900-1910. Nothing that had taken place subsequently had served to alter them. He did not believe in advertising. He did not believe in television. He was convinced that if a man builds a better mousetrap, the world will beat a path to his door. He ran his million dollar firm like a mousetrap maker and was the despair of his advertising staff.

His daughter, Olga, youngest of a family of seven, was the Intellectual Bleutcher. She had just graduated from college, had had her year at the Sorbonne, and was the soul of the Brockton Literary, Marching & Chowder Society. She was plain, verging on ugly, with a broad saddle nose and wide clown mouth; but she had good teeth and magnificent cat's eyes. Her figure was so arresting that it had to be thought of as a body, and after sufficient contemplation of that body, most men raised their eyes above the neck and even found the face attractive.

In the grill room of The Brompton House, a tiered oval around a dance floor on which visiting Firemen shuffled to the music of a lymphatic band, the quartette drank Manhattans, ate shrimp cocktails, lobster bisque, fried oysters, French fried potatoes, French fried onions, French fried eggplant, Waldorf salad, strawberry shortcake and coffee. Mr. Bleutcher insisted on fish on Friday. He saved his beef for labor unions, manufacturing costs and the iniquities of the open-toe craze.

In addition, he disapproved of smoking for women, high wages for labor, modern dress and all modern medicine outside of chiropractic correction. Although he never once looked at Grabinett or Lennox, he demanded their complete attention. Grabinett blinked his all. Lennox gave as much as he could spare from the daughter.

Olga was very young and very intense. She put her hand on Jake's arm and discussed Sartre, Kafka and Henry James. Since she was seated on his right, this made eating difficult for Jake. She was plainly excited with him as a professional writer. "Christ in close-up," Lennox thought. "She wants to be a writer too. I'm dead." She attempted an arresting originality of conversation that was exhausting. In self-preservation, Lennox asked her to dance. This was a mistake.

Olga Bleutcher was a lovely dancer, but she didn't melt into Jake's arms. She projected her body against him and operated with alarming suggestiveness. There was no escaping the pressures of her bosom, her torso and thighs. It was obvious that Olga too was aware of her big selling point. It was also obvious that she had been under restraint while she was with her father.

"My God!" she whispered in Jake's ear. "Isn't he a reactionary old fart?"

Lennox tried to turn his grunt of amazement into a chuckle.

"Do you think they'd let us sneak a smoke on the floor?" Olga asked. "I'm dying for a cigarette."

"I don't know. We can try."

"You keep dancing," she murmured. "I'll find them."

Her hands began exploring his pockets. Lennox had to explain that he didn't carry cigarettes because he didn't smoke. "What have I got myself into?" he wondered. "Is she a nympho?"

Miss Bleutcher pressed herself against him. "It's so comforting dancing with a big man," she said. "You can spread out on him.

There was a private beach north of Cannes where I used to strip and sunbathe. You feel just like the sand."

"Careful of the shells," Lennox muttered. He glanced down at her. All he could see was the cat's eyes. He was alarmed to discover that she was getting better looking.

"Where can a *soi-disant* virgin get plastered New Year's Eve?" Miss Bleutcher inquired.

"You're going to be in town over New Year's?"

"I'm going to be on the town New Year's . . . after Four-Buckle Arctics corks off."

"Who?"

Olga Bleutcher motioned with her head toward her father. "I'm going to pour myself into a strapless and come to no good. Have you got any suggestions?"

"I've got a basic suggestion, but I also have a show to worry about tomorrow night," Lennox stalled. "I'll phone. What's the password? Metatarsal?"

She laughed. "Bunions. No, leave a message for me at the switchboard. Just say it's for Olga. They understand a gal's problems."

After five minutes more of New Year's preview, Lennox managed to detach her from his anatomy and return to the table. As they sat down, a waiter appeared and presented a telephone message to Bleutcher who read it carefully, then excused himself and lumbered toward the hotel phones. Olga at once took a cigarette from Grabinett's pack, picked up her handbag and departed for the woman's lounge. Lennox and Grabinett were left alone.

There was a long pause. Finally Grabinett lifted his eyes and blinked into Jake's hard, level gaze.

"If you don't want any trouble, don't say anything," Lennox warned.

Grabinett's mouth opened and his face twitched. Lennox

208

poured cold coffee into his cup and went through the motions of drinking it.

"Borden wants you and me down to his office for a conference with Bacon," Grabinett blinked suddenly. "Two thirty."

Lennox didn't answer.

"What's Bacon after?"

"Sachs' job," Lennox answered curtly.

"The hell he is! He ain't going to get away with it."

"He is, and I'm going to help him."

"How do you think you're going to swing it? Who's running this Almighty show anyway?"

"The three of us are going to vote Sachs out. And if you give us any trouble, I've got an ace in the hole."

"What?"

"Give Ned a hard time and find out."

Grabinett blinked uncertainly. At last he blurted: "All I'm trying to do is keep a show on the air. You're giving me the hard time. That letter scandal, and now Bacon. What are you? In business or in war? Listen. I got a contract with Sachs. He gets a flat weekly retainer and it's a gut-buster. If I keep him working all my shows I just about break even. But if I got to pay out an extra seven and a half bills to Bacon for direction — Will you guys be reasonable! Have a heart!"

Lennox stared at Grabinett incredulously. "Are you human?"

"I'm asking you to be human."

"You knifed me less than twenty-four hours ago. The moment when I needed every check I could get and all the help I could get, you kicked me off the show. And now you have the gall to ask me to have a heart! Lay there and bleed!"

"You're crazy!" Grabinett explained. "A crazy writer. What are you cuddling a grudge for? You get yourself into a jam and then you blame me for protecting the show. Didn't you tell me Monday I had to keep my nose clean? So I took your advice. What do you want from me?"

"I want the same thing from you that I want from the rest of the world!" Lennox shouted. "I want a fair shake."

"Jake! Quiet! Keep it quiet!" Grabinett blinked around in embarrassment, then focussed his twitch on Lennox. He lowered his voice. "All right. Here's a deal. I'll stick with you if you'll stick with me. Yes? You're back on the show."

"How do I stick with you?"

"No Bacon on the payroll. Sachs stays. If Bacon wants to direct TV leave him do it at somebody else's expense. Not on my budget. Okay?"

Lennox swallowed.

"Hurry up, Jake. Here comes Bleutcher. Is it a deal? For the good of the show you vote with me. We're satisfied with how the show's going. We want to keep everything exactly the way it always was. Yes?"

"Yes, by God!" Lennox said. "Yes."

Bleutcher lumbered up to the table and sat down. "Mr. Audibon has been trying to reach me at the Brockton office," he explained.

Grabinett started. "What for?"

"I have not been advised as yet. His office called four times."

"Did you call him back, Mr. Bleutcher?"

"He's been out to lunch for two hours." Bleutcher compressed his lips. "It is most inadvisable for a business man to clog his digestive system with heavy foods during the working day. My staff has standing orders to restrict the midday meal to greens and roughage. Our plant cafeteria. . . ."

Bleutcher lectured on fats, proteins and carbohydrates until Olga returned to the table. Grabinett paid the check with nervous haste and the luncheon party broke up.

"We'll see you at the show Sunday, Mr. Bleutcher?" he blinked.

Bleutcher nodded ponderously.

"Just leave word for Olga," Miss Bleutcher whispered.

Lennox nodded absently.

In the lobby of The Brompton House, Grabinett darted to a phone booth and called the network. Audibon had not yet returned from lunch. Grabinett came out of the booth, blinking anxiously.

"He's been trying to get me all morning too. What the Almighty mischief is he up to? What a business! Come on, Jake. Let's take care of Bacon first."

Avery Borden's office had the quality of a court room. His high-backed desk chair looked like a judge's bench. Against one wall was a line of mahogany armchairs that looked like a jury box. When they entered, Bacon was sprawled on two of the chairs, confiding a thief-type revelation to Borden who was leaning against a window, glasses in hand, fascinated. Lennox and Grabinett sat down quietly and waited. No matter how savage warfare may be on The Rock, there is one sacred law that is never broken. No man ever kills the point of another man's story.

When it was over and Borden had reacted satisfactorily, Bacon stood up and began to swagger back and forth across the office. He preferred to sit when other men were standing, and to stand when other men were sitting. Borden obligingly seated himself behind the desk.

"Now we're all here to read the up-state returns," Bacon drawled. "The show isn't sick yet, but when you pull out the thermometer any interne can read the temperature. It hasn't broken a hundred, but it will if we don't yank the substitutes and send in the regulars."

Borden's phone buzzed. He picked it up, murmured for a minute, put it down and apologized.

"You can't run a variety show like a girl's weeny roast," Bacon continued. "Sooner or later some eager beaver is going to get a fork in her eye and drop the marshmallows into the fire."

Borden's phone buzzed. He picked it up, murmured for a minute, put it down and apologized.

"Now I'm the last man to blow the whistle on another man's act," Bacon went on. "But we were in the fire last Sunday and if Jake hadn't cut the heart of the plate from left field, they'd still be running the bases. What we need is organization and direction. The show's got to be handled like a military operation, and Sachs isn't the man to set up the cadre."

"It isn't a question of talent," Borden said tactfully. "Nobody's attacking Sachs on the genius level. But Ned feels the show needs a man more experienced in—"

Borden's phone buzzed. He picked it up, murmured for a minute, put it down and apologized.

"More experienced in the aspects of handling talent rather than providing talent," he went on. He charmed Bacon with a tactful smile. "Editor's note: This in no way implies that you can't or won't provide talent when required."

Bacon swaggered up to Grabinett and stood over him. "Here it is, wrapped for delivery. Sachs had his turn at bat. He couldn't get on base. Now it's time for the clutch hitter to come up. Are you with me or are you going to throw the game?"

Grabinett squirmed in his chair. "God damn it! This is my Almighty show. I'm satisfied with Sachs."

"Your show?" Bacon laughed. "I'll read the fine print for you. Jake and I worked this up together. It was a smart panel show with demonstrated questions that had sell. You had Tom Bleutcher in your pocket and no show for him. Of all the crap Bleutcher saw, he liked our package best. But the network wouldn't sell the time unless they could put Mason to work in a musical. So we all joined the team and pooled the bats and gloves. Bleutcher let you shove a variety show down his throat. You let the network hang Mason onto your budget. And we let you chisel fifty percent of the package out of us. But what the hell did you contribute, talentwise, that makes you the Captain?"

"I'm satisfied with Sachs!" Grabinett shouted.

"The rest of us aren't, so Sachs goes."

"And I'm not the only Almighty one satisfied with Sachs, so he stays."

"I've got my boys with me. Who've you got?"

"I got Lennox."

"Enlighten him, Jake," Bacon drawled.

Lennox took a deep breath. "Ned, I'm sorry. I have to vote with Mel."

Bacon's face froze.

"I know what your problem is, Ned, and you know I sympathize. But I've got problems too. I've got to go along with Mel."

"You yellow scab! You're selling me out? What was the price? Don't I even get a chance to bid against his thirty pieces of silver?"

"If I'd known in time I'd have warned you."

"You didn't have the guts, you cheap—"

"I know you're burning and I don't blame you, but I want to tell you something. I'm having a rough time myself this week and I'll take just so much from you and no more. You're not the only man in this office with a boom over his head. Remember that."

Bacon turned on Grabinett. "All right, shyster, you got to one juror in the box, but the fix isn't in yet. I've got another ace to play." He gave Lennox a sour smile. "Your card, Benedict."

"Don't play it," Lennox growled. "It's a deuce."

"I can have Sachs thrown off the show for unethical conduct," Bacon persisted. "That corn-ball tried the casting couch routine with an actress named—"

"Shut up, Ned," Lennox cut in. "It isn't going to do you any good. I won't back the story and neither will she if I tell her not to. Leave her name out of it."

"Damn you!" Bacon yelled. "What are you doing to me? Cutting my heart out with a dull knife?"

"He's protecting the Almighty show, that's what he's doing!" Grabinett blurted. "Why don't you let me keep it on the air? What do you want from me? I provided the client. Ain't that enough? Maybe I got no talent, but you don't see me dragging scandal into the studio. Dirty letters and dirty cracks about my director. For Christ's sake, let's all make a buck and live in peace."

"I'm going to direct my own show," Bacon answered. "And I'm starting the first of the year whether you or my former partner like it or not. You want to make a buck, do you? Then make it on another sucker's brains; because if I don't direct my own show, I want it back. I'm taking it off the air. I'm picking up my marbles and going home."

"Talk sense, Ned!" Lennox cried.

"Shut up!" Bacon looked at him with loathing. "If you ever talk to me again I'll cut your guts out. You knew what this meant to me. You know the spot I'm in. 'The People Against—' is cancelled. The old man is through. They're retired his number. This is the one hold I've got on the future and you're stamping on my fingers. For why? What've you got to lose giving me a break?"

Borden's phone buzzed. He picked it up, murmured for a minute, put it down and said: "The show's cancelled."

They all turned incredulously.

"That was Roy Audibon. The network isn't renewing our Sunday night time. I think we'd better table this hassle and get over there right away."

Tookey Ween was in one of the red leather library chairs and Audibon stood before the illuminated nebula when the three men entered the office. Before the door was closed, a five-

214

way battle was joined, and the melee continued for fifteen minutes. The only way to describe that brawl is to name the records from the network sound library that a soundman would have to use to duplicate it. Spinning two turntables, he would blend 261B —APPLAUSE: 5th CUT; BOOS AND SLIGHT HISSES, with 259A—RIOT CROWD EFFECTS: FRENCH CROWD, LARGE GROUP OF MEN, INCITED TO RIOT BY FRENCH COMMANDS. He might also hammer on the studio walls to get the desk-pounding effect.

Through all the fury, Audibon remained adamant. The network was not renewing the time. After a quarter of an hour had elapsed, he looked at his watch and took control of the situation.

"We're discussing a half hour show," he said sharply. "I can't allocate more than the show's time to the discussion time. I have another appointment coming up. Now . . . if you've been listening to me with your inner ear, you know the network's position. The nine to nine-thirty Sunday night slot is rated at ten points better than 'Who He?' is doing."

"Roy . . ." Borden began.

Audibon held up his hand. "We're not an entertainment business. We're an institution. We have prestige to maintain. We have our honor to polish. One of my responsibilities is to see to it that every one of our shows reaches and maintains its ultimate rating. Entertainment isn't our goal . . ." Audibon reached up and rapped the nebula with his knuckles. "*This* is our goal."

"Damn it, Roy," Borden exploded. "Level with me. You and I know what's behind this decision. It's the old network-agency feud. You people can't forget that you sold out your radio time to the agencies and lost control of your own business. You're so damned scared of that happening with television that you're cancelling our show . . . not because the rating isn't high enough, but because the network doesn't own the package. You want nothing but network packages filling network time."

Audibon smiled.

"It's a seller's market today," Borden shouted. "You've got a dozen clients begging for every slot across the board. You can play snotty and get away with it. But the market'll turn. If costs don't kick you out of the saddle, then boredom will. And when that happens you'll come begging to us. You'll come begging and we'll spit in your eye."

"Incidentally," Audibon murmured. "I'm having this discussion recorded . . . for legal purposes." He pointed to a small microphone on the upper shelves of the breakfront.

"It's a sick show," Ween rumbled suddenly. He got up. "For the record I want my property out of that show and out of that spot. It's a sick show on account of him!" He pointed to Lennox dramatically. "He's the one who's made all the trouble. Him and his poison pen letters. He's been writing the whole show with a poison pen . . . and now he's put my property in danger of physical violence. If anything happens to Mig on Sunday, I'll sue!"

Ween waddled to the door and yanked it open. He glared at Lennox. "Protect your property, will you? You got nothing to protect. Nothing. Now go shove yourself up it." He exited and slammed the door.

Borden looked at Lennox. "Are you behind this?" he asked icily. "That Knott business you pestered me with yesterday. Is that what he means?"

"He's getting threats for something Almighty dirty he pulled off," Grabinett shouted.

"I'm sorry to say that's one of the important reasons for cancelling," Audibon said smoothly. "The rating was only one factor; but when Tooky told me about the difficulties that Jake's been creating . . . embarrassing the star, embarrassing the show . . . We decided that we couldn't let him embarrass the network."

Borden arose, gave Lennox one deadly cut-throat stare and marched out, followed by Bacon who was too furious even to look at Lennox. Grabinett sputtered and blinked for a moment, helpless before Audibon's smile and Jake's impassivity.

"It was that sock in the jaw last night, wasn't it, Roy?" Lennox asked quietly. "You're fighting like Tooky, aren't you?" Audibon gazed at the water color and said nothing.

"Tooky ran off at the mouth because I wouldn't let him chisel a piece out of a hit tune. That was his knife in my back. You're cancelling because you were a louse last night and I called you on it. It isn't the seller's market or the rating or the galaxy or my personal mess. It isn't anything but revenge because I pasted you in the jaw. This is your knife in my back."

"You Almighty sabotoor!" Grabinett cried. "The deal is off. You hear me? It's off."

"The show's off, Mel."

"And I'm taking it out of your hide. If it's the last thing I do, I'm taking it out of your hide, you Christ Almighty Vandal!"

Grabinett flung out of the office without bothering to slam the door. Audibon sauntered over, closed it gently, then smiled at Lennox.

"So here you are, Jake."

"I'll be on my way. Perish the thought that I should hold up your next appointment."

"You're my next appointment. Sit down. Enjoy." Audibon drifted to the breakfront, opened the lower drawers and revealed a silver-lined bar. "Drink?"

"Thanks. Brandy, please."

"Soda?"

"Straight."

Audibon filled two large shot-glasses and carried them to Lennox. As he extended one glass, his control slipped, and in a blaze of fury he slashed two ounces of dark brandy into Jake's face. Lennox laughed and stood up.

"That's all I want, Roy. Thanks for the confession."

"Look at you," Audibon said in a voice that shook. "Take a

panoramic of yourself. Where are you? You've got no show. You've got no partner. Your agency's ready to blacklist you. This network's blacklisting you. You're got no friends. You've got no business. You've got nothing. Nothing!"

"But I've got something you haven't got, Roy."

"Never."

Lennox tapped the water color. "I've got the original of this."

"Never!"

Lennox smiled.

"So you're chasing," Audibon snorted. "Go ahead and chase. You'll never catch up. Not while she remembers me. . . ."

"Who's chasing?"

"Then you're bluffing, you—"

"Who's bluffing?"

Audibon went white, then red. He turned, walked to the desk and put down the shot-glasses so violently that they clattered.

"I'm waiting for your offer," Lennox said pleasantly.

"Get out," Audibon said in a low voice.

"Tooky offered to trade. Blinky offered to trade. Why not you? Let's hear how contemptible you can get."

Audibon swung around. "I'll see you in hell first!" He came at Lennox so fast that Lennox only had time enough to grasp his arms above the elbow. They strained at each other for half a minute.

"I'll see you dead and rotting first," Audibon panted. "I'll run you out of the business. I'll run you off The Rock. If she stays with you, I'll run her off too. I'll see both of you dead first."

"Do you love her?"

"I'll kill her!"

Lennox looked deep into Audibon's drawn face. "I'm seeing you for the first time," he said. "And for the first time I'm beginning to like you."

Audibon broke out of Jake's grasp and staggered back against the desk. His hand fumbled behind him, and an instant later the office door opened and his secretary entered.

"Yes, Mr. Audibon?"

"Lennox is leaving."

"It's funny what The Rock does," Lennox said. "We ought to be friends." He turned and left.

"Get me Miss Valentine at Houseways, Inc.," Audibon told his secretary. She closed the door behind her. He went to the bar and had a shot. Then he opened his wallet and took out the slip of paper Macro had thrown into his waste basket. The phone buzzed.

"Gabby? Roy. I want to see you tonight. It's important. No, I can't tell you on the phone. I said it was important. Yes. When? All right, I'll pick you up."

He dropped the phone, went to the bar and had another shot. Then he wandered to the water color and examined the picture while his fingers mechanically smoothed Macro's slip of paper. Suddenly the dazzling smile reappeared on his lips.

"Never," he said. "Never."

· CHAPTER XI ·

AUDIBON TOOK GABBY'S HAND
and pressed it gallantly. Then he led her across the sidewalk to
the waiting cab. He helped her in, followed, and gave the network address to the driver.

"I'm sorry," he explained. "My baby's in rehearsal tonight.
'Operation Universe.' I've got to look into the studio. You don't
mind?"

Gabby was examining his bruised face with concern. "That
happened last night, Roy?"

"Yes."

"That's awful . . . Awful."

"You ought to see my ribs," he laughed. "I'll let you autograph
them."

"You mean you're in a cast."

"No, just tape."

"Let me see."

"Sightseeing on odd Mondays only."

"Let me see, Roy," Gabby repeated firmly. She reached out,

unbuttoned Audibon's shirt and opened it. His entire left side was bound with white adhesive tape from spine to chest. She was so shocked and upset that Audibon's hopes began to kindle. He let her rebutton the shirt and adjust his tie.

"Artistic, isn't it?" he said. "They're poets of the intercostals up at Gracie Hospital."

"I want to pay," Gabby said.

"Pay? What?"

"The hospital bill."

"Why?"

"It was partly my fault. Maybe it was all my fault."

"No," Audibon said. "Not your fault. Never."

"I think I should make it up to you somehow."

"Do you?" Audibon's hopes rose even higher. "We'll discuss it."

The cab dropped them at the network and they took the elevator up to the big studio. It was an enormous room, half the size of an armory, blazing with flesh-colored lights hanging in thick clusters fifty feet overhead. On the studio floor were set up a country schoolroom with a blackboard on which the solar system was chalked, a miniature space-station, the interior of a rocket ship, half an observatory including a six-inch telescope, half a laboratory with an electronic microscope. The telescope and microscope were practical.

Before a fifty-foot moonscape cyclorama, a symphony orchestra was rehearsing "The Music Of The Spheres" from Gustave Holst's "The Planets." Alongside the orchestra, a technician was sprinkling glitter on the show title: HOW TO KNOW THE UNIVERSE. There were six cameras on the floor. Six hundred yards of cable coiled around the sets.

The door from the dressing rooms opened and Galileo entered the studio. He was followed by Albert Einstein in violent dispute with Jules Verne. They were joined by Sir Isaac Newton and a striking red-headed girl who looked incongruous in a

Victorian dress and pince nez. Six children from the Professional Children's School clustered around a piano on which a man in a spacesuit and fishbowl helmet played softly. "THIS IS YOUR UNIVERSE!" a voice blasted on a loudspeaker. There were muffled commands from the control talkback and the voice tried it again with different inflections: "THIS IS YOUR UNIVERSE!"

Audibon rejoined Gabby after a lightning tour of the studio and took her to a dark corner behind stacked flats, inhabited by a soda fountain and a pot-bellied stove. It was illuminated by the twelve-inch screen of a small monitor which cut dizzily from camera to camera, picking up a fag director, a fag assistant, a fag floor-manager, a fag camera director, a fag make-up artist, and finally following the red-headed girl's interesting bottom as she strolled around the studio.

"THIS IS YOUR UNIVERSE, EXPANDING WITH THE SPEED OF LIGHT INTO NEW INFINITIES!"

"Hello, pet," Audibon said softly.

"Hello, Roy."

"I'm sorry about last night too."

"I'm glad you're sorry. I hope it's for the right reasons."

"I'm sorry I wasn't with you."

"That's not the right reason." Gabby lifted a finger to lecture. Audibon caught it and held it.

"You're a schoolmarm, pet," he said, motioning to the monitor which now showed the schoolroom. "You belong on that set." He kissed the finger gallantly. Gabby reclaimed it.

"I was looking at that water color you did out at Fire Island. You know I've got it hung in my shop?"

"I wish you didn't," Gabby said slowly. "It isn't a happy picture."

"We were happy when you painted it."

"No. Not inside, Roy. That's why it turned out so badly." She looked away.

222

"It's a happy picture. We were happy." Audibon smiled. "Do you remember . . . I had an idea for a show? Following the summer around the world. I didn't want that summer to end. I wanted it to go on and on . . . with you getting darker and darker, and that old shirt of mine you wore getting tattier and bleached . . . What made us imagine it ended?"

"You're frightening me, Roy."

"Why, pet?"

"I'm afraid to say."

"Maybe you're afraid to remember. No. Listen to me. Looking at that water color and remembering how you looked high up on that dune, I did a take. The summer never ended. There's been a little winter-type weather, but it's only a station break. I don't think our summer will ever end."

"What do you want, Roy?" Gabby asked quietly.

"I'm propositioning you," Audibon smiled. He took her arms and pulled her close. "I'm asking you to make a dishonest woman of yourself and have a fling with me. It's summer in North Africa. I'm spending February in Egypt. Fly over with me, pet. Let's spend the month together. I'll bring an old shirt. You bring your brushes. We'll live in sin and improve our minds."

"And afterwards?"

"Why worry about afterwards? Maybe it'll be cold weather when we get back; on the other hand, maybe not. Let's enjoy our summer again and see how long it lasts this time."

Gabby came around a corner abruptly. "What does this have to do with last night, Roy?"

"Last night?" Audibon was taken aback. "What do you mean?"

"This is the first time you've been romantic since we separated. Something special must have happened." Gabby examined him candidly. "It was last night, wasn't it?"

"No, pet."

"I was with Jordan Lennox and he hit you."

Audibon's fists clenched. He recovered himself and abandoned the tenderness. "All right," he said crisply. "If you insist on being cerebral . . . I'm worried about you. I hate the idea of you free-lancing around from job to job, never knowing where the next check is coming from. I want to offer a contract."

Gabby looked at him steadily.

"I want to offer security and success. Not materialistically, but Rennaissancewise. Don't waste time and talent on subsistence-type jobs to keep bread in the house. Do the creative work you're equipped to do . . . and you know how stratospheric my opinion of your talent is. It needs an oxygen mask."

"Thank you, Roy."

"Stop slumming, pet. Come back to me. You and I are top-level talent. You've got to work where the work counts. Architectural design? The network's dreaming up a new office building in Cuba. Take a dive at it from the twenty-foot board. Stage design? Come into our set department and rub up our imagination."

"You're very kind, Roy."

"Not kind. Practical. New talent is our priority headache. We know it's around, but we can't tap it. The slobs outside the network think there's a cabal to keep new talent out. There isn't. We just can't mock up an efficient screening operation to locate it. But once we bark our shins on new talent, we burn incense and work overtime building it up. Let me build you up, pet. Don't waste yourself on the outside."

"This is quite a change," Gabby murmured. "When last heard from, the picture you painted of me was a Gibson girl in mink doing public relations for you."

"I've graduated since last year," Audibon smiled. "I took a post-graduate in Women's Rights. I'll even go along with your politics . . . And think for a minute how much more you can do as the wife of the network veep."

"You really are a wonderful salesman," Gabby said with admiration. She came around a corner again. "Why are you so angry with me, Roy?"

"Me? Angry?"

She nodded and blurted out the truth. "You're furious. That's why I'm frightened. I . . . It's a secret I don't have to keep any more. You only called me 'pet' when you hated me. You're hating me now."

"No."

"You are." Gabby faced him squarely. "Don't you think I remember all your tricks? You smile. You flatter. You call me pet . . . And then you pounce. I want to know why. Why are you hunting me now?"

"I'm asking you to come back to me," Audibon said in a fury.

"Why?"

"To save your neck." Audibon whipped out his wallet, opened it and removed Macro's slip of paper. "This was left in my office by a man named Macro. Do you know him?"

"I know all about John Macro." She looked at the slip of paper, holding it up to the greenish light of the monitor. "So he's got around to me at last. Did you send him?"

"No. I talked him out of it. That's why he left this slip. I saved you, pet. I told Macro you were my wife and he dropped you. I'd like to keep on saving you . . . as long as you're my wife."

"So you are hunting me."

"Listen!" Audibon grabbed her wrist and wrenched her toward him. "Macro can hound you out of work. I can run you off The Rock. How would you like that? Network veep sues for divorce. Communism and adultery. Think how the papers would play it up. Gabby Valentine, the party girl, recruiting new members in her bed. The latest volunteer . . . script-writer Jordan Lennox. Oh yes, I know all about your roll in the hay with Lennox. We had a long talk about what a lovely piece you are."

"Roy!"

"Do you know what you've done to me?" He thrust her violently against the monitor and trapped her with his body. "Do you know why I was up at the Midnight Sun last night? Why I'm up there every week? I'm looking for substitutes. I'm trying to find a replacement for you. I've tried all kinds. They don't work. Nothing works."

Gabby caught her breath.

"You know that's always been my problem. Even when we were living together, I— You said you'd take nothing from me when you walked out, but you took my last chance. You took the one thing a man can't lose. Why shouldn't I hate you? Do you understand? Do I have to spell impotence for you?"

"No," Gabby whispered.

"I'm fighting for my self-respect. You're the only woman who can give it to me. For God's sake, come back!"

"But why me? Why only me?"

"I wish to God they could tell me. Maybe they will some day, but I'm desperate now. I'm begging. The nights I've thought of cutting my throat . . . You've got to come back. On your terms. On any terms. You can't lose. I've put the whip in your hand."

"No, Roy. No."

"Some of those bitches I tried are talking," Audibon went on savagely. "The word's getting around. You know you can't keep a secret on The Rock. You've got to come back. The talk's got to stop. It's the one thing no man can stand. You can lose an arm or a leg and they're sorry for you . . . but when you lose that, they laugh."

"Please, Roy . . ." Gabby tried to escape the trap. Audibon held her.

"I'm being honest now, pet. No romantic pitch from me. I'm not asking for old-fashioned marriage and virtue and chastity. Understand? I said on your own terms. You'll be free. Com-

226

pletely . . . so long as you're discreet." Audibon's face twisted. "I'll give everything. All I want is you in my house."

"So I'm back to public relations again."

"And you in my bed . . . once in a while, to give me a fighting chance. Just once in a while. Take time out from whoever it is and give me a break. For God's sake, is that unreasonable?"

"No. It's generous and horrible." Gabby stopped struggling and looked at him with disgust. "If you don't let me go, I'm going to scream."

He flung her from him. She stumbled against the soda fountain and one of the stools toppled with a crash.

"So help me God," Audibon said, "I'll ruin you. I'll tear you apart . . . you and Lennox. I'll run you off The Rock. I'll run you out of the country. You'll lay for him in a two-bit flea-bag remembering this. Now get out!"

He turned, stalked around the monitor and walked back onto the sets, the dazzling smile corroding his face. Gabby began to cry. She opened her purse, groping blindly in it for a handkerchief, scattering the contents of her purse over the soda fountain and the floor.

"THIS IS YOUR UNIVERSE!" the voice roared suddenly. "AN INVITATION TO EVERYMAN TO ABANDON SELFISH THOUGHT AND JOIN THE GREAT GALAXY . . . CONCEIVED AND PRODUCED BY LEROY W. AUDIBON!"

When Gabby regained control of herself, she gathered her possessions and returned them to her purse. The last thing she picked up was Macro's slip of paper. She examined it again, then followed Audibon out onto the sets. She walked with her lazy carriage, shoulders square, arms relaxed, followed by wolf-whistles from the technicians. Audibon was in the schoolroom, one foot on a bench, lashing the director and assistants with his smile and his words. Gabby went to him, apologized for interrupting and handed him the slip of paper.

227

"You forgot this, Roy," she said quietly.

"Oh? Will I need it?"

"Of course. That's why I returned it." She held out her hand. "Goodbye, Roy."

He ignored her hand and turned away. Gabby smiled and left the studio. Downstairs, she went to a telephone booth and called Jake's apartment. Cooper answered the phone and sounded cold when Gabby asked for Lennox.

"He's not home, Gabby."

"Do you expect him? I'd like to leave a message."

"No, I'm not expecting him, I'm happy to say."

"Why do you say that?"

"I'd rather not discuss Jake with you, if you don't mind."

"You still don't like me, Sam."

"What's your message, please?"

"Tell him I can't see him tonight."

"I can't guarantee he'll get it."

"Oh," Gabby said. "That's bad. I don't want to stand him up without warning."

"Why don't you try the theater? They'll still be rehearsing. He may be there."

Gabby called the Venice Theater. The stage doorman was the deaf, quaint type . . . wonderful for anecdote, impossible for messages. After two minutes of patient shouting, Gabby got Tooky Ween on the phone.

"Tooky Ween speaking," he rumbled. "Make it fast. We got headaches."

"I'm sorry, Mr. Ween. That man made a mistake. I want Jordan Lennox."

"Lennox!" Ween roared. "That lousy, chiseling son of a— He wouldn't have the crust to show his crust here. If he did he'd be dead and couldn't answer the phone anyway."

Ween hung up. Gabby considered, then called the Grabinett office. It was after hours and only the line to Grabinett's desk was open. Blinky took the call himself.

"Is Jordan Lennox there?" Gabby asked.

"No," Grabinett snarled. "I only wish he was. I'd kill him with my naked hand. I'd kill him dead and do a repeat for the west coast, that—" Grabinett caught himself. "Excuse me. Are you a relative?"

"No," Gabby said. "I wanted to leave a message."

"Not here!" Grabinett shouted. "Not with this office. I wouldn't do that Almighty vandal a favor if I was to get paid for it."

Blinky hung up. Gabby made one last try and called me. When I answered the phone, Ned Bacon was in our living room, murdering our Bourbon and Lennox. Gabby could hear him cutting Jake to pieces while she gave me the message. I wanted to ask her up. I'd seen enough of her at the Rox Record party to be interested, and I had about twenty-seven questions to ask her, but there was no way of getting Bacon out of the house and we couldn't have the two of them there together. So I promised to deliver the message, if possible, and let her hang up.

That was about seven o'clock. She wandered east to the 59th Street Bridge, cutting through some of the toughest sidestreets on The Rock. She went through those streets unmolested. Gabby had a miraculous quality of escaping the common dangers that make every woman think twice. Perhaps it was because she never thought of them once. Perhaps it was her candid, virginal manner that forced the world to give her extra special treatment . . . the way men are reluctant to swear before a child, unwilling to be the first to teach it what they know it must inevitably learn.

She went to a gloomy candle-lit restaurant under the bridge. It had *avant-garde* murals on the walls, Puccini records on a phonograph, and hectographed menus. Half the waiters were enrolled with the Art Students League and were friends of Gabby's. Half the patrons knew her too. Nevertheless, she sat alone, consumed half a plate of pasta and half a bottle of California wine. She began to cry again, and had to snuff out the candle on her table. She was so upset that she wandered out of the restaurant without paying. No one made a fuss. They tucked her check in the cash register for another day.

It was half past nine when she got home. She took the elevator up, trembling, aching, yearning for a hot bath and ten hours of sleep. As she stepped out of the elevator and glanced down the corridor, she stopped short. A man was squatting on the mat before her apartment door with crossed ankles, knees high, forearms draped on his knees. It was Lennox. He arose as she approached.

"Didn't you get my message?"

He nodded. "From Sam."

"Please go away, Jordan. I can't see you now."

"I've got to see you, Gabby."

She was so weak she dropped her key. Lennox picked it up, unlocked the door and opened it for her. He followed her into the apartment, shut the door and switched on the lights with a practiced hand. Then he pulled up the giant shade that covered the studio window. Gabby sank down on a low, quilted bench before the cold fireplace and said nothing.

"I wasn't parked here because I was jealous," Lennox said anxiously. "Please don't think that. I mean . . . I am jealous, yes; but I trust you."

Gabby didn't look at him.

"I've loused myself beautifully today. I've been tramping around the Village waiting to see you."

"I can't talk, Jordan."

"Could you listen a little?" He smiled appealingly. "Comes a time in every man's life when he knows he's done bad things and feels guilty. That's when he needs a friend to reassure him. Everybody has to have somebody who believes he's never wrong."

She shook her head. "I haven't got the strength."

"Then could I just be near you a little? Maybe we can help each other without words."

"No," she said. "Please go."

"What's the matter, darling? You're in trouble too."

"I can't talk about it now."

"Something's happened?"

"Yes. You loused me beautifully, too."

"I did?"

She nodded.

"How?"

"With Roy."

Lennox went cold. He waited for her to continue.

"Roy delivered an ultimatum. Either I go back to him, or—"

"That Communist routine?"

"And adultery."

"What!"

"Adultery," Gabby repeated. "You let something slip this afternoon . . . Or did you boast?"

"This afternoon! I— Oh my God!" Lennox sat down heavily.

"Don't sit down, Jordan. Please go."

"Sit down? I'm groveling. I'm on my knees. How in Christ's name could I have. . . ."

"Be quiet. Just go."

"We've got to discuss it. We can't let him pull off a filthy trick like that. We've got to fight him."

"No!" Gabby wailed. "No! No more fighting. I can't stand it any more. I feel filthy. You're like starving dogs, all snarling and fighting and eating each other. I won't be a part of it any more."

"You're just scared, darling. Don't. . . ."

"You can't drag me into it again. Never again. Go away, Jordan. Go away. Don't come back."

"Wait a minute," he said slowly. "You don't just mean to-night? You mean for good?"

"Yes. I do."

"What the hell's got into you?" he demanded roughly.

"And now you're fighting with me again." Gabby pounded

231

her fists on her knees in desperation. "Get away from me. Leave me in peace, for pity's sake!"

"That's a hell of a way to talk. Hello. Goodbye. I thought we were in love."

"No," she said bitterly. "It was a roll in the hay with a stranger."

"For God's sake, Gabby. . . ."

"That's what you're turning it into. You're not the man I met. You're somebody else. I'm really meeting you for the first time, and I'm ashamed. I . . . If you love me . . . whatever your idea of love is . . . for pity's sake go away!"

"My idea of love isn't running away," he answered. He put his hand on her shoulder. "It's sticking together right down the line and fighting it out together."

"Please don't touch me," Gabby said, shrugging her shoulder out of his grasp. "And stop using that horrible childish word over and over again. Fighting. Fighting. Fighting. That's all you know."

"What else is there?" Lennox glared at her. "Will you grow up! Somebody mentions fight and you start screaming. Do you know what you're screaming about? Have you ever been in a scrap?"

"Don't argue like a child."

"I'm asking a question. I want an answer. Have you ever been in a fight?"

"No."

"I thought not. You're so damned pretty and so damned sweet-tempered you've never had to fight for anything. Life's handed you everything in your lap."

"I haven't had everything."

"Only because you haven't wanted everything. Sweet God, why don't you find out what it's all about before you pass sentence on slobs like me who've had to fight every inch of the way." Lennox pounded a fist into his palm. "You're blind. You've had it too easy. A writer-type guy once made up a circle. Life is Character, he said. Character is Conflict. Conflict is Life. That's the vicious circle we're all trapped in. You too."

"No! I won't be trapped in the dirt."

"Yes, you too! And it isn't dirt. You're like the prudes who think sex is dirty. What the hell are you afraid of? Try a fight. Maybe you'll get to like it. Maybe you'll get to grow up a little and come out of your dream world."

"You're impossible!" she cried. "You're hateful!"

"You make a big pitch for peace," he growled, his face darkening. "You talk it up about feeling filthy because the dogs are fighting; but that's just cover-up, girl. That isn't the truth of what's in you."

"No?" Gabby answered steadily. "What is?"

"Jealousy. Envy."

"Of what?"

"What every man has and no woman has. You love to castrate us. That's the one burning drive in you with your career and women's rights and politics. You can't forgive us for that. You try to cut every man down to your size, your sex, your weakness. I don't know what you did to Audibon with your knife, but you're not doing it to me!"

She turned white. "You're horrible," she whispered. "You're worse than Roy. Worse! I don't want to see you again . . . ever! Go away. Don't come back . . . ever!"

"So you can go back to Audibon?"

"Is that what you think I'll do?"

"What else can I think if you won't fight and won't let me fight? How else am I supposed to take this?"

She leaped up, ran to the front door and opened it. She held it open, her dark eyes flashing furiously at Lennox. He picked up his burberry and went to the door. There he hesitated.

"Listen," he began. "We can't do this. We've got to help each oth—"

233

"Go away!" she cried. "Go away and fight. Find your Aimee Driscoll and beat her up again. Or would you rather stay and beat me? That would make you feel manly, wouldn't it? Then I could go to Aimee and show her my bruises. Would you enjoy that . . . you big, virile beast?"

"Go to hell, you God damned bitch!" he shouted and blundered out into the hall. Gabby slammed the door and locked it. She began to sob and gag painfully. She ran to the bathroom and was violently ill. One thought persisted through the sobbing and the sickness. Lennox had destroyed everything and finished with her ruin.

· CHAPTER XII ·

BY FIVE O'CLOCK SATURDAY
morning, Lennox had walked himself to exhaustion. He slipped
into the apartment in 33 Knickerbocker Square and went to bed.
At nine o'clock he was shot out of bed as by a cannon. He
dressed, went downstairs, picked up his mail and left the house.
Two envelopes were from the Grabinett office. They contained
his script fee and his royalty for the "Who He?" show of December 18th, a total of seven hundred and fifty dollars.

The banks were closed on Saturday. Lennox went to a bookie
he knew on 14th Street who also operated a check cashing office. There, he converted his checks into fifties and twenties.

"Getting set for a big New Year's Eve, hey?" the bookie
laughed.

"No," Lennox told him. "I'm going to be murdered tomorrow."

He stepped into the nearest saloon and had two brandy
Alexanders.

"Startin' early, hey?" the bartender laughed.

"No," Lennox said. "I'm having my last fling. I'm going to be murdered tomorrow."

On the way uptown he had a couple of more Alexanders and then breakfast at Androuet's on Persian melon, coffee, and Croque Monsieur Roquefort, which is a blend of Roquefort, Brie and cream, broiled on Virginia ham. It is usually taken with wine. Lennox finished a bottle of Muscadet and ordered another pot of coffee and a telephone. When the phone was plugged in at his table, he called the East River Airport and chartered a plane.

"You are celebrating the New Year en l'air, M'sieur Lennox?" his waiter inquired in astonishment.

"No," Lennox answered. "I'm taking a last trip home."

It was cold and still on the East River. A heavy grey ceiling hung low in the sky. As Lennox climbed from the dock to the pontoon of the tiny Cub and then into the cabin, the pilot looked dubious.

"There's fog coming in at Montauk," he said. "I hope we can beat it."

He swung the Cub out into the river and taxied frantically toward the 59th Street bridge. Lennox wondered whether they were going under or over the bridge when suddenly the buffeting of the chop ceased and they shuddered their way skyward. Instantly The Rock was transformed into a make-believe city . . . a toy on a table.

They flew east over Long Island City and Jamaica and then northeast from Freeport up Great South Bay, past Amityville and Babylon to the Bay Shore Harbor where the Cub landed in Great Cove and taxied in.

"I won't be an hour," Lennox told the pilot.

He went to a white clapboard fish-house on the dock, phoned for a cab and waited in the bar. There was an enormous coal fire glowing in the fireplace grate and an enormous jolly proprietor glowing behind the bar. He looked like a benevolent wrestler.

"If you were drinking your last bottle on earth," Lennox asked him, "what would it be?"

"Irish," the wrestler answered promptly.

Lennox sampled the Irish until the taxi honked its horn outside the fish-house. He got into the car and they drove through Bay Shore to Islip and then down a bleak road to the Champlin Marshes.

"There's nothing down to the end of this road," the cab driver said. "It's a dead-end."

"So am I," Lennox grunted.

The road ended in a small circle of pits and ruts. Around it was half a mile of dry brown marsh reeds rustling listlessly in the light breeze. Beyond the marsh was the steel grey of Great South Bay. A rotting boardwalk led from the circle to a large shack built at the edge of a narrow creek that wound out through the marsh to the bay. The house was weathered silver, the windows had long since been burst in, the shutters had been blown away.

Lennox got out of the cab and walked down the boardwalk to the shack. When he reached the door, his hand automatically lifted high to grasp the doorknob. His lips twisted at this memory of the childhood flesh. He lowered his hand, pushed the door open and entered. For a paralyzing moment he thought his dead father was standing inside the house. Then he looked closer and saw that it was a stranger, a tall, thin man with white hair, fussing with a camera on a tripod.

"God has answered my prayers!" the photographer exclaimed. "Can I trouble you for just a moment, sir? Look here . . ." He pointed. The seaward wall of the house had collapsed. The marsh, the sea and the sky were framed in broken, silvery timber ends.

"A perfect L composition. Verticals on the left; horizontals below. The eye is led in to the middle distance from any corner. Quintessential desolation. But there's a fundamental weakness on the right. You see it?" The photographer darted to a heavy square stud and rapped it sharply at the precise spot where Jake's slicker used to hang. "This must be broken. What I need is a shoulder. Someone outside, leaning against this post, staring out to sea. We don't see him, of course. Just the part of the back and the shoulder carrying the eye back to the center. You don't mind?"

The photographer led Lennox to the stud, positioned him, and rushed back to the camera, chuckling and twittering. Lennox stood there, staring at the marsh, the creek, the remnants of the dock where his father's clam boat had been moored. He was filled with hatred and shame.

"Thank you, sir. Thank you so much," the photographer called. "If you only knew how many weeks I've been waiting for this light. And then to have you come along just in time . . . What brought you, h'mm? Are you an angel or a photographer?"

"I was born and raised here," Lennox answered. "As a matter of fact, I think I own this place."

"My dear sir! Am I trespassing?"

"Yes," Lennox said. "We both are."

He returned to the cab and drove back to the Bay Shore docks. There he sampled the Irish again until the pilot hurried him into the plane. He had been phoning up and down Long Island and the fog was closing in rapidly. By twelve-thirty when they were over The Rock again, it had covered the river.

"We can't get in here," the pilot muttered.

"What do we do? Head for Spain?"

"I'll settle for the Coney Island station," the pilot said. "How about it?"

"Why not?" Lennox said. Suddenly he began to laugh. "Do you know, I've never been to Coney Island in all my life? Why not now?"

"It's dead now."

"I'll be dead tomorrow. Why not catch up on everything

238

I've missed? What the hell am I so damned gloomy for? I'm going to enjoy."

The Cub circled and soared over the Upper Bay and sneaked down through breaks in the heavy nacreous blanket. There was no chop on the water off Coney Island, but there was a swinging groundswell as they taxied in to the small station. It made the brandy and Irish fume pleasantly inside Lennox.

He paid off the pilot, parted from him genially, found a saloon, and requested to be served with "Dog's Nose," a drink he recollected from Dickens. He was now in the first, or literary stage of drunkenness. The bartender consulted his blue book and regretfully reported that no such drink was listed. Lennox settled for a pair of Boilermakers and wandered out to the desolate amusement park, empty, canvassed and boarded up.

Lennox beamed. He took out his gimmick book and silver pencil, turned to a clean page and wrote: "Blessed be the man who sells joy. He is humanity's benefactor." He tore the page out, folded it and slipped it under the shutter of a dormant shooting gallery. He strolled to the ticket office of the roller coaster, wrote: "Better to be happy than wise," and tucked it under the window.

To the Half Man Half Woman booth he donated "Pleasure is virtue's gayer name." To the 25 CANNIBAL BEAUTIES 25 he contributed "Life is not life at all without delight." And for the Giant Swing he wrote: "Pleasure is the sovereign bliss of humankind." As he was tucking this fond salutation under the door of the boxoffice, a thought struck him. He opened the slip, considerately wrote "Alexander Pope 1688-1744" under the quotation and replaced the message.

He left the amusement park, bought a pack of cigarettes and hailed a cab. He told the driver to take him back to The Rock, and as they sped along the Belt Parkway, he opened the pack and lit up.

239

"Look at me smoking. I'm intox'ated," he told himself, and laughed immoderately, thinking of the dear Shroff.

The fog slowed the traffic and there was a slight jam as they approached the tunnel to Manhattan Island. The car behind them lost its temper and began an exasperating horn honking.

"That's rude," Lennox muttered. He called: "Stop, driver!" The cab stopped its forward crawl. Lennox got out, went to the car behind them, bowed politely, opened the engine hood and pulled the wires off the horn. He marched back to the cab, got in, and with a grand air ordered: "Drive on, coachman. Drive on!"

At Sabatini's he had three very dry Gibsons and entered the dining room where he ordered oysters, turtle soup, Shrimps Livornese, marinated asparagus, escarole and coffee. The dining room was half empty; very few of the people in the business are around on Saturdays, and fewer still on the afternoon before New Year's Eve. Lennox consumed his oysters and soup and allowed his gaze to relax on a couple at the next table. He didn't know the man, but the young lady was familiar.

She was a blonde, with enormous blue eyes and an exquisite pouting mouth. She wore a black siren-type dress that exposed her neck, shoulders and altogether too much cleavage.

"That's a Theda Bara dress," Lennox muttered in annoyance. "No ingénue ought to be wearing it."

What annoyed him even more was the fact that the ingénue was behaving like a road-company Theda Bara. She pouted, she hooded her eyes, she undulated her shoulders and heaved her poitrine like the High Priestess of the Python.

"Now where have I seen that corn-ball playing that routine before?" Lennox asked himself. Suddenly he remembered. An ingénue in a velvet gown trimmed with miniver, batting her eyes at Oliver Stacy over a champagne glass. He began to laugh. The girl looked up, caught his eye, and gave him a slinky undulation. Lennox arose and bowed. Then he reached into his water glass, took out a lump of ice and dropped it into her cleavage.

He didn't have to pick himself up off the sidewalk, but there was no doubt he'd been thrown out of Sabatini's.

"Live dangerously," he chuckled and was afflicted with thirst. He quenched it with a bottle of stout at the saloon in the network building and then wandered upstairs to visit the studios.

He poked his head into rehearsals and waved affectionately to friends and strangers. The last studio down the corridor was on the air with some kind of radio mystery. Lennox tiptoed in, waved, and placed himself alongside the sound table where the soundman stood with a gun poised in his hand while a couple of gangster-type actors snarled at each other on mike. Lennox watched the script over the soundman's shoulder, and as the gunshot cue came up, on sudden impulse he snatched the gun out of the soundman's hand.

The director behind the glass waved frantically. The actors shook their scripts at him. The soundman struggled to get hold of the gun.

"Bang!" Lennox shouted. He beamed, put the gun down quietly and tip-toed out.

"My girl doesn't approve of violence. Guns and such," he confided to the bartender in the Greek's.

"The peaceful teep, huh, Jake?"

"A veritable dove of peace." He considered. "Chris . . . What's the difference between doves and pigeons?"

"There ain't no difference, Jake."

"There has to be. Otherwise wouldn't have two different names," Lennox said. "That's relentless logic."

"No," Chris said. "I keep 'em. I ought to know. Doves is white pigeons. You sure you want all this garbage in your old fashioned, Jake?"

Lennox nodded. "My system needs ascorbic acid. Where could I buy some doves, Chris?"

"Down to the poultry market. Just ask for white pigeons," Chris added stubbornly.

Lennox took a cab down to the poultry market which adjoined the Chambers Street Food Market. In the former he purchased twelve doves (white pigeons). In the latter he consumed six banana fritters and a quart of a dangerous brew called Still Ale. The doves in their cage refused the fritters and the ale, but they partook of breadcrumbs with joy.

He carried them up to Greenwich Village, found Gabby's apartment house and rang the downstairs bell. There was no answer. He located the superintendant, bribed him, and was escorted up to Gabby's apartment by that careful man to leave the cage within. Lennox was not permitted to enter more than three steps where he was directed to put the cage down. He did so, but opened the door. He was gratified to see the studio living room fill with doves.

"Make her happy," he chuckled. "Make 'em all happy, huh? How?"

He thought it over in a basement bar where he drank Moscow Mules not, he explained to the bartender, because he was sympathetic to the Soviet cause, but because he admired the copper mugs. How to spread joy? Three Mules led him to the light.

He went back to Sixth Avenue and entered the premises of a sign painter. To him he entrusted four sheets of notebook paper on which he had printed carefully.

"Want four signs in an hour," Lennox beamed. "Make 'em six feet by three feet in black and red. Just do 'em freehand. Yes? Rush job for very special friend of mine. Back in one hour."

He crossed Sixth Avenue to a large photographer's supply store and bought one hundred flash bulbs which were packed

242

in a large carton for him. He took a cab up to Mason's apartment house. He phoned from the corner. Irma answered.

"Irma," Lennox said urgently. "Mig wants you down at the theater right away. He wants everybody. Hurry up!"

He waited. Ten minutes later Irma, her brother and his wife emerged from the building and hurried off. This was not the first time they had been summoned to attend Mig, but it was the first time that Mig hadn't done the summoning.

"Chances are he'll be grateful I remembered for him," Lennox murmured. "That is, if he remembers he didn't call 'em himself."

He went up to the Mason apartment and entered. There was no one there. Carrying the carton with him, Lennox kindly removed all the light bulbs and jammed a flash bulb into every socket in the apartment.

"Oh, it'll be a sunny New Year for Mig all right all right," Lennox laughed. He returned to Sixth Avenue, poked his head into the sign painter's to urge him on, then went to a large hardware store where he purchased one hundred pounds of moth balls.

"What the hell do you want with so much?" the hardware man asked in amazement.

"Not for me," Lennox explained patiently. "For a friend who's all the time worrying about his property. Can't protect it enough. I'm afraid he's forgot about moths."

"Crazy! Where you want this shipped?"

"Want to take it myself. Can I hire your assistant? Pay five dollars for five minutes."

"I guess so. Alfred!"

Alfred shambled out of the back of the store and helped Lennox carry the mothballs to the building where Tooky Ween had his office. They went up on the freight elevator but were dismayed to discover that Ween's office was closed for the day and locked.

"What we gone do now?" Alfred asked.

"Never admit defeat," Lennox said. "Go back to freight elevator. Was a big piece cardboard there. Bring it."

Alfred brought the sheet of corrugated board. Lennox twisted it into a funnel and inserted the narrow end into the mail slot in Ween's office door.

"Now open the boxes," Lennox beamed.

Carefully and kindly, they funneled one hundred pounds of mothballs into Ween's office.

"Won't have to worry about his property again," Lennox said.

He accompanied Alfred back to the hardware store where he purchased a stapling gun. Then he paid for his four signs, rolled them up and carried them to Grabinett's office. He nodded to the receptionist, breezed past her and entered the twisting halls of the rat-nest. There was no traffic. Lennox stopped, measured with his eye, and stapled the first six by three sign to the wall. In garish red and black letters it read:

40 FEET 40
TO THE OFFICE OF
MELVIN GRABINETT
The Man
of
V*i*s*i*o*n*!

Lennox went ten feet down the hall and stapled the next sign to the wall:

ONLY 30 FEET MORE
TO THE OFFICE OF
MELVIN GRABINETT
The Showman's
S*h*o*w*m*a*n

At the corner of the hall he stapled:

244

NEXT RIGHT TURN
TO THE OFFICE OF

```
      G
  M   R
  E   A
  L   B
  V   I
  I   N
  N   E
      T
      T
```

Alongside Grabinett's door he affixed the last sign:

O * F * F * I * C * E
O * F
MELVIN (BLINKY) GRABINETT

"Secret acts of kindness performed by stealth," Lennox murmured and returned to the hardware store. "I need Alfred again,"
he said.

"What! More mothballs?"

"No. Got a hungry friend needs taking care of. Give me
Alfred."

"He ain't gonna eat me, is he?" Alfred inquired.

Lennox beamed, patted Alfred and gave him another five
dollars. He also gave him the stapling gun, warning him that
it was loaded. Then he took him to a grocers and bought every
package of Jello in the store. They were packed into a carton
which Alfred carried behind Lennox who conducted him to
the network building and up to the twentieth floor. It was
empty. They went into Audibon's office and put the carton down.

"They sure let you in easy," Alfred said.

Lennox nodded complacently and opened the door to Audibon's private bath. He ran the hot water in the wash basin
until it came out scalding.

245

"What flavor would my hungry friend like in his toilet, Alfred?" he asked genially.

"Strawberry?" Alfred ventured.

"And strawberry it shall be."

They plugged Audibon's toilet and filled it with strawberry gelatine. They filled the floor of his enclosed shower with lime gelatine. "The only specific for athlete's foot," Lennox insisted. They mixed a potpourri of gelatine and filled his inkstands, his Dresden china, the glasses in the bar, the hollow globe of his ceiling light, and last of all, the wash basin.

"I'm not given to boasting, Alfred," Lennox pronounced, reeling slightly, "but I will venture to predict that my very good friend will never be hungry again."

He offered to buy Alfred a malted, but Alfred had a New Year's date and was anxious to get back to the store to finish work.

"So have I got a date," Lennox said, and parted wistfully from his friend.

He walked home without incident except for a car which stopped for a traffic light directly in the path of the pedestrians' crossing. Lennox would have none of that. Refusing to detour around the car, he opened the rear door, climbed through the back, opened the opposite door and continued on his way.

He entered the apartment prepared to greet Cooper with brotherly affection, but Cooper was not home. Lennox gave the Siamese and the mink-dyed skunk a holiday meal of canned crabmeat, then bathed, changed to dinner clothes and demolished the Canadian whiskey in the bar. He stole a pack of cigarettes from Sam's cache in the storage closet, put on his burberry and decided to have dinner in The Crystal Key.

The Crystal Key is a private house in the West Fifties which caters both to Hipsters and Squares. It has a butler who looks like a magazine advertisement. It has footmen in knee-breeches, waiters, French chefs, a wine steward and even a cellar to go

246

with the steward. It has a resident book-maker. It employs a slightly known chanteuse who entertains on the second, or dining floor. It provides a dozen young hostesses who will drink, chat and dance intimately on the third or supper room floor. It has a fourth and fifth floor for personalized entertainment. Lennox entered with his mind intent on dinner. He permitted an attendant to take his coat, went into the bar on the street floor, nodded to the bookie and the neighborhood cop drinking beer in a corner, and ordered sherry. He began to laugh at himself. He recalled that no matter what he wanted to drink when he entered The Crystal Key, he always ended up ordering sherry. He gave the matter some thought, blamed the knee-breeches, and went upstairs to dine.

It was fortunate there were no menus. Lennox could not have read a menu even if there had been enough light. He was served hors-d'oeuvres, mussel soup, saddle of lamb, pommes soufflés, a still burgundy, salade fatigué, and something in a covered dish which he was too hazy to investigate. His faculties were restored by the blinding discovery that the gentleman seated two table down from him was Mr. Thomas Bleutcher of Brockton, Mass. The young lady with him was not his daughter.

"The scoundrel!" Lennox muttered. "The lecherous dog. He richly deserves a lesson."

He perceived that there was a brandy inhaler before him with a half inch of cognac in the bottom. Quite defiantly, he drank the cognac off without ceremony and devoted himself to the problem of disciplining Mr. Bleutcher's morals.

"How to chastise the heart of old Four-Buckle Arctics?" he asked himself. "Hit him in his carbohydrates? No. Where is his heart? In his boots. Very funny, Mr. Lennox. Oh, very funny indeed." He shook with laughter, slid under the table and began crawling on the floor toward Bleutcher. The maitre d'hotel rushed toward him in dismay. Before he could speak, Lennox lifted a finger to his lips and gave him an urgent look. The maitre d'hotel hesitated for a moment in perplexity. Lennox reached under Bleutcher's table and seized that unsuspecting man's feet. With a violent yank, he tried to pull Bleutcher's shoes off.

Bleutcher disappeared under the table as if dropped through a trap door. The table went over with a crash, and the hostess toppled with it. Lennox arose triumphantly from the screaming and shouting with one black kid chiropractic oxford in his hand. He still had it, concealed under his coat, when he was deposited on the street outside The Crystal Key one minute later. It was fortunate for Lennox that the policeman had returned to his beat; otherwise he might have been seriously hurt.

He weaved downtown, searching for a phone. In the forties he passed a theater, entered the lobby and politely requested to be directed to a booth. He was informed that the telephones were inside the theater. He puzzled this out and with a flash of logic that delighted him, reasoned that he needed a ticket to make the phone call. There were no tickets left but he was sold standing room admission. Lennox tip-toed into the theater, went down to the men's lounge and called The Brompton House. After some hanky-panky, Olga answered the phone.

"Your father," Lennox said, "is a rogue."

"My father," Olga replied, "is a pain in the ass."

"No longer. You are revenged." Lennox described his triumph. Olga began to scream with laughter.

"Does he know it was you?" she asked.

"Couldn't say. What are you doing up in the hotel?"

"Having dinner in the suite. I got so fed up with him I played sick. What are you going to do about it?"

Lennox hesitated and then thought: "Oh, what the hell!" He said: "I was thinking of bringing his shoe back."

"Lovely. Wait for me downstairs in the bar."

"How long?"

"I'll be able to sneak out an hour after he gets back."

"He'll be back any minute . . . Unless he's going to hop into New Year. Bunion and Over."

"Metatarsal," she said and hung up.

Lennox shook his head in disgust with himself. Then he brightened and went upstairs. There was a good broad arm-rest for standees in the back of the house. He leaned against it and tried to focus on the stage. Some kind of mood piece was in progress, filled with long, poetic pauses. Lennox napped comfortably until the applause at the end of the act woke him up.

He was thirsty. He had two stingers in the saloon alongside the theater, one with green mint and one with white to determine whether his palate had lost its famed sensitivity.

"I am happy to announce," he announced to the bartender, "that my palate has lost none of its famed sensitivity." He pointed to the glasses. "That is Spearmint '34. A very good year. That is Wintergreen '26. Its pert bouquet is unmistakable to a palate of famed sensitivity."

Lennox walked east to The Brompton House. New Year's horns were beginning to blare in the streets with the sound that boys make when they blow through blades of grass pressed between their thumbs. Lennox paced massively. He had reached the Gibraltar stage of drunkenness, a mixture of Johnsonian gravity and pathological lying.

In the bar of The Brompton House, jammed by the overflow of respectables from the grill room, he ordered a pitcher of French 75s and two glasses. Olga was nowhere in sight, but Lennox knew better than to trust to his sight. He tapped a handsome bald gentleman with leaden complexion and kindly features who was seated alongside him.

"Would you be good enough to lend me your stool, sir? Just for a moment."

The gentleman got off the stool. Lennox mounted it and teetered on top, four feet above the crowd. He whistled shrilly with

249

two fingers, waited for Olga to notice him if she were present, and then climbed down again.

"Thank you very much, sir."

"May I ask why you did that?" the gentleman inquired. He looked exactly like a Roman Tribune and had a melodious southern drawl.

"One if by land, two if by sea," Lennox answered significantly. "Our identification code. You wouldn't expect us to sing the Internationale for a signal, would you? Not here."

The leaden-faced gentleman stared. Lennox nodded darkly, drank a 75 and offered a glass to his companion. "To the *counter*-counter-revolution," he said. "This year is yours. Next year is ours."

"How do you mean?"

"This country's been living in a dream," Lennox sneered. "Communists . . . Tcha! They're our decoys. We use them for red herrings to conceal us. The real us. We are the danger."

"Who are the danger?" the man asked intently.

"Us. We . . . Us."

"Can you name names?"

"Can I not? Lennox. Mason and Dixon. Mason and Slidell. Lewis. Clark. But above all, Lennox. Lennox is the man. He pulls the strings. He controls the Eastern Cell."

"Cell!" the gentleman exclaimed.

"Indeed yes. The movement is beautifully organized . . . from here through Washington, London, Paris, Rome . . . straight up to our central headquarters—"

A pair of hands blindfolded him. "Guess who," Olga said.

"Goody Twoshoes," Lennox answered. He removed her hands from his eyes and continued. "Our headquarters on Mars. We're all Martians. We're going to—"

He stopped. The strange gentleman had already removed himself, Lennox searched dazedly and saw him in a corner, unaccountably scribbling in a notebook. He shrugged, flexed his right arm to feel for his own gimmick book, then contemplated Olga. She had, in truth, poured herself into an evening gown; or better still, someone had painted it on her body and only given it one coat. Lennox handed her a 75.

"What's this?" she asked.

"Paint remover," he said.

She drank it cautiously, finished it with appreciation and held out her glass for more. They emptied the pitcher and went over to Beekman Place to look in on a party thrown by one of Olga's friends. It was in a square apartment house, in a square apartment, and it turned out to be a Square party . . . the men in one room telling dirty jokes, the women in another room shrieking with laughter and pulling up their skirts as they loaded up on martinis.

"This is from hunger," Lennox muttered to Olga. "Leave us blow."

"We'd better," she giggled. "It's the wrong apartment."

So it was. They went downstairs to the right apartment which was identically square. The party was also identically Square.

"I liked the first one better," Lennox said.

They left and went uptown to the West side where Johnny Plummer owned a house opposite the Museum of Natural History. His party was more party-line than anything else. They were required to pay five dollars each as they entered . . . in aid of some nebulous cause. No scotch was served in order to boycott Great Britain. Everyone sat around in tweeds and dirndls and sang the songs of the People to the accompaniment of an accordion and a mandolin. Lennox tried to drink up his five dollars in straight gin, but Olga gave him the out sign within half an hour.

"My turn now," she said and took him to the East side and a cosmopolitan-type party conducted in French, Dutch, Italian, Flemish and Swedish. This one, Lennox loved. He ate lobster stewed in absinthe, drank aquavit, learned Swedish massage, how to cut diamonds, when to hear an opera entitled "Teresa's Teats," where Kafka was buried, who was whose mistress at the party, and the particular sexual foibles of each of the guests. But Olga was party-hopping and impatient. She dragged him out.

"I liked it there," he complained.

"Too respectable. Where next?"

They went to Charlie Hansel's place in the Village. It was filled with ballet dancers; fag boys doing petit point in corners, sway-backed girls waddling with duck feet like pregnant women. They all talked shop to each other. They talked to nobody else.

"Out," said Lennox, yanking open the door and marching into a closet. Olga rescued him and guided him to fresh air. He was properly grateful and offered to kiss her in the taxi. She permitted this token of gratitude and startled him with her lips and tongue. He was relieved when the cab deposited them at the front door of a red brick converted stable, now a photographer's studio.

"Do I know him or do you?" Lennox inquired as he lurched in. He stared around the giant studio and rubbed his eyes. "Must be getting bloodshot," he mumbled.

It was the reddest damned party he had ever seen. Everyone wore fireman red costumes, from Santa Claus down to a snake-like woman with tangled black hair who wore fireman red Dr. Dentons with a drop seat. She turned out to be the hostess. A small man with a guilty face whom Lennox surprised searching the pockets of the guests' coats was the host. There was an insidious brew called Fish-House Punch, composed of sugar, Jamaica rum and peach brandy in an enormous crystal bowl. Lennox had three glasses and was returning for a fourth when he saw the hostess unbutton her drop seat and bathe her bottom in the punch bowl.

"Out!" he said to Olga.

"It is out," she laughed.

"I'm r'sponsible for your moral health. *In colo parentis.* Feel strongly this's no place for you."

"No. I like it here. It's not too respectable."

"Oh?" Lennox said. "You want disrespectable party? Come on. Got jus'place fyou."

He took her to Kay Hill's apartment. Olga entertained him in the cab, and when he was able to focus on her he perceived that she was a damned beautiful girl. They took the elevator up and rang Kay's doorbell. There was so much noise inside that they had to ring three times.

The door opened. Kay stood there wearing a fringed green stole and nothing else.

"Come on in!" she screamed in honest Canarsie accents.

She pulled them in, slammed the door, turned to the foyer table on which a dozen scotch bottles stood, and picked up a black grease pencil. She wrote JAKE across one white label and handed the bottle to Lennox. She wrote OLGA on another and handed it to Olga. They both had swigs. Kay led them down an endless Early American hall, past various doors, and into a Colonial bedroom. A naked girl was seated at the dressing table feebly trying to hook on her brassiere.

"Coats there," Kay said, pointing to a black mound of clothes on the four-poster bed. She turned and left.

Lennox reeled and looked at Olga. "Out?" he asked.

She took off her coat and threw it on the bed. Lennox had no intention of losing his coat in that grab-bag. He lurched into the bathroom and carefully hung his burberry in the shower. As an afterthought, he turned the water on. When he came back to the bedroom, both girls were gone.

He had a solid drink from his private bottle and wandered down the hall, caroming from wall to wall. He peeped into rooms. A seven-man poker game was in progress in various stages of undress. Three partially draped girls were decorating an oil painting with their lipsticks. Two couples in underwear and aprons were cooking something in the kitchen. Lennox investigated the pot. It contained onions, potatoes and a cookbook.

The living room was insane. Some guests were dressed, some were naked, the rest were any stage between. Everyone carried an individual scotch bottle. Lennox searched for his charge. He spoke to three different women before he finally realized he was speaking to Olga. Then he realized he was having difficulty speaking. He was pleased to see that she had not undressed. He was relieved to see that her companion also was dressed.

"What?" Lennox asked.

"I said," Oliver Stacy repeated, "You're holding that bottle upsidedown."

"Am I? Scout's Honor?" Lennox peered. "It's empty," he said with delight. He flung the bottle from him. "Who's that talking to Olga Bunion?"

"I'm right here," Olga said.

"I'm talking to her," Stacy said.

"Could you excusr minute? Most say something utmust p'ortance. Utmust!" Lennox took Olga's arm and tacked up the corridor. She stopped him in a corner and pressed the body against him.

"What did you want to say?" she asked.

"Wanted warn you."

"You wanted to warn me?"

He nodded. "Men'll temptyr chastity t'night. Mustnt succumb whilem your chaperone. Your honors my honor. See?"

She laughed and explored his mouth with her mouth. "You big old bear you," she said.

"Listen," he said. "Listen. I'm rsponsible fyou but you maket pretty tough fme. . . ."

Lennox staggered around a door-jamb and fell backwards into a room, carrying Olga with him. They landed on a soft hooked rug. It was some kind of sewing room with a dress form, blanket chest and cutting table. It was empty. Lennox tried to get up.

"Why do you keep running?" Olga asked. "Are you afraid of me?" She kissed him again. For the first time he returned the

254

kiss. His hands got busy with the tight sheath of the dress, trying to expose the body.

"Stop it," Olga said.

Lennox grinned and continued his attempt to extract her body from the dress. She pulled his hands away.

"I said stop it," Olga repeated. "Don't spoil it."

"Don't worry. Won't hurt th'dress. Zit'zip or hook?"

"You're making everything nasty. Stop!"

"Oh no. Make everything lovely."

"Stop pawing me like that. What do you think you're going to do?"

"What comes natal to a fella." He kissed her again and slid his hands along her legs. She struggled violently, bruising his lips against his teeth. She was breathing heavily. Lennox pinned her arms back with his left arm while he gently slid her dress bodice down to her waist. She screamed and bit his hand savagely. He let her go and sat up in bewilderment.

"Why allv sudden?" he asked faintly.

She scrambled to her feet and backed away, hastily pulling the dress bodice up into place. He squinted at her. She was shocked and terrified, and gooseflesh showed on her arms. Suddenly he realized what she was and the mistake he'd made.

"Oh. My. God." Lennox whispered. "You're justa baby. A tease. Virgin tease, yes? Noodnick, not nympho. Throw your body 'round. Don' know whatyr doing. Use dirty words. Don' know what they mean. A baby makin'like a woman. Yes?"

"You're disgusting!" she spat.

"No. Decoyed. Mowss-trapped. Shoulda known. You smell like babies."

"Let me out of here!" she hissed. She edged past him. He burst out laughing and flipped his hands up under her skirt. She screamed again and ran, slamming the door behind her. Lennox sat on the floor and laughed. Then he wept. He climbed to the edge of the blanket chest and sat with his arm around the dress form.

"Love on'y you, Gabby. On'y wantbe with you. On'y you, sweetheart."

The door of the sewing room burst open. A nude woman in a green stole berated him blurrily. Something about a bitch girl pulling a crying jag on some anonymous named Stacy and sneaking out to alley cat with him. The woman in the stole considered herself robbed. She blamed Lennox. He arose with dignity.

"Bringum backal ive," he said. He tottered to the foyer, picked up a bottle of scotch and wondered about his coat. He went back up the Early American hall to the Colonial bedroom and peered into the mound of clothes on the four-poster. He pulled coats, hats and trousers off the top. A left hand was revealed, thrusting up stiffly out of the coke-black mass. Lennox let out a hoarse cry and backed away. He turned and ran blindly out of the apartment, trying to erase the memory of maggots.

Yorkville was blazing with holiday lights. Festoons of red, white and green bulbs arched over the streets. Lennox blinked and blundered into a Hofbrau on Third Avenue which was aswarm with *gemütlich*-type celebration. A sign of burnt leather hung over the bar between moose antlers. It read: *Wein-Weib-Gesang!* Underneath it hung its translation: Whiskey. Women. Swing.

"No. No. No." Lennox said indignantly. "Should be wine-women'n song. Yes?" He gazed up and down the bar trying to count the customers. "Want t'buy set-ups f'the house."

"Drinks?" the bartender inquired in a genuine low Dutch dialect.

"Set-ups." Lennox displayed his bottle. He lurched playfully up and down the bar, pouring drinks for his friends into their beer, their rye, their cognacs, their wine glasses. He was quelled with difficulty. Accord was restored when he planked fifty dollars down on the bar and requested demon rum for his playmates.

256

"What happened to your hand?" someone inquired.

Lennox lifted both hands. The left was encrusted with blood. "My pitching hand!" he wailed. "My bread'n'butter hand. Don't anybody rec'nize me? Lefty Jordan, the Big Train?"

Nobody recognized him. He left the Hofbrau in a state of high dudgeon and staggered down Third Avenue until he reached the Irish bars in the sixties. He entered The Poplin crying: "Hoch Der Kaiser!" The clients of The Poplin were equally exuberant and traded drinks with Lennox generously.

"Lissen," he kept repeating. "Lissen. Lissen. Lissen."

Nobody listened and he was content. Somebody asked him his name.

"Lefty," he said. "Jus' call me Lefty. Om inna shoe business. Make shoes f'left foot only."

He vacated The Poplin and continued down Third Avenue until he reached the fag bars in the fifties. He entered The Fantasy and elbowed his way through the buzzing and the hissing and the sibilation to the bar where he fell into easy conversation with the languid boys around him. He informed them that he was Leftwich, a wealthy shoe manufacturer from Brockton, Mass. They were not impressed. They went on gossiping and name-dropping and Lennox fancied he heard something familiar.

"Anybody here jus' mention 'Who He?' " he asked.

"Oh *that* thing," a voice drawled. "The original Rigor Mortis, from the picture of the same name."

"You're so right so right so right," Lennox agreed. "I watch it up in Brockton. Come'ome fr'm hard day inna factry. See nothin' but puke. That show's vomit. That show's . . . Alla fault of a lousy stinkin' louse who writes it. Lousy phoney. Name of Lennox. Anybody here know'm?"

Somebody said they knew him intimately and he was a big queen.

"No-no-no," Lennox said. "He'sa whore. Thinksee writes clever with his fancy filth from's stinkin' sewer mind. People like

257

me don't think hesso clever. Plain people like Lefty Leftwich witha feet onna ground. Want heart and soul and meaning. Y'unnastan? Heart. And. Soul. And. Meaning . . . not garbage outa fancy barrel. Faker sells hisself out f'ra buck and sells us out too. Y'unnastan?"

No one was paying any attention. Lennox went on raging to the bored backs. "I know'm. Me. Plain old Lefty Leftwich from Brockton, Mass. Know allabout'm from way back. He could write from's guts ifee wasn't so busy pimpin' f'pennies." Lennox began to shake his fists in fury. "Lousy sewer Lennox! Fancy filthy fraud! Sells hisself downa river soee can live fancy'n'elegant like a duke or a marquiss. Betrayal. Why don't somebody honest tell'at corpse where to get off? Why don't someone kill'm an' make room frhonest writers?"

He elbowed his way from the bar, left The Fantasy and continued down Third Avenue. Below 42nd Street he made up his mind and turned east. He came to a dim stationery and candy store with K N O T T spread across the window in an arc of brass letters. He entered and staggered against the marble soda fountain, peering blearily at the faded woman who was just closing up.

"Wanna write a letter," he said. "Spehshul d'liv'ry letter. Wanna best paper'n'envelope inna house. Pen too. Teach'm a lesson."

The faded woman looked at Lennox, recognized him, and without a word produced a sheet of blue paper, a blue envelope and a cheap fountain pen which she filled. She took a three cent stamp and a special delivery stamp out of a cash box and affixed them to the envelope. Lennox picked up the pen, paper and envelope, placed five dollars on the counter and staggered out.

He entered the Baroque through the side door, stared around wildly and located an empty chair at the table behind the telephone booth. He swam to the chair through the smoke and the noise and sat down. With his breast pocket handkerchief he

258

mopped the table dry. He looked up. Seated across the table from him was a blonde who appeared to be a Swede farm girl. She was looking at him.

"Hiya Goldilocks," he said.

"Hiya," she said. "Long time no see."

"Jus' got in from Brockton."

"Where?"

"Brockton, Mass."

"Since when?"

"Since always," he said. "Live'air all my life. Inna shoe business. Permit me innaduce myself. Lefty Leftwich."

"What the hell!" she exclaimed. "You got three names?"

"Lefty. Leftwich." Lennox counted on his fingers. "Is on'y two."

"Skip it, Lefty." She laughed and covered her teeth with her hand.

"Scuse me, Goldilocks. Gotta 'portant letter to write."

She watched with increasing interest as he placed the paper and envelope on the table, unscrewed the pen, took it in his left hand and began to write in a sick, hysterical scrawl: Dear Who He . . . This is your last warning. I'm going to kill you, you fancy filth, you penny pimp, you garbage from a fancy barrel. . . .

· CHAPTER XIII ·

GABBY HAD GONE TO BED
early Saturday night. The work of catching twelve white pigeons
and cleaning up their droppings had exasperated and exhausted
her. By five o'clock Sunday morning she was half awake and positive that she heard thumpings at her door. She got up, put on a
pyjama top and padded out to the studio room. The pigeons
rustled and cooed in their cage. The thumpings continued. She
put the chain on the door, opened it an inch and peeped out into
the corridor. A large man was squirming restlessly on her door
mat trying to get comfortable. It was Lennox.

She bit her lip, debated with herself, and finally unchained the
door and pulled him in. He was semi-conscious, incoherent, rank
with alcohol, sweat and vomit. Gabby locked the door and tried
to get Lennox on his feet. He got to his hands and knees and no
further.

"Make a bes'damn oxfords inna worl'," he muttered.

"On your feet," she said.

"Name's Lefty Leftwich an' Icn lick any man inna—" He
expired.

260

She pushed and prodded him down the foyer, through the living room and into the bath. He crawled on hands and knees, whimpering dolorously. In the bathroom, she tugged and tussled until she got his clothes off. She threw the clothes into a corner and worried the hulk until it climbed into the tub. Gabby turned the shower on hot. Lennox lay under the deluge, crooning. She took off her pyjama top, got a wash rag and soap and cleansed him thoroughly. Then she turned off the water, placed a giant bath towel on the floor and got him out of the tub and sprawling on the towel. She dried his back, kicked him over and dried his front. Then Gabby harried him to her bed where he lay, prone and catercorner, snoring raucously.

She took Jake's clothes to the kitchen and placed them in a carton for the cleaners, first emptying out the pockets. On the table she placed his pocket watch, chain, keys, gimmick book, silver pencil, three dollars in change, one hundred and five dollars in bills, and last of all, a blue envelope stamped special delivery and addressed to "Who He?" in a familiar hysterical handwriting. She stared at that envelope for five ghastly minutes.

It was half-past seven. Gabby made coffee, drank it, put on a dressing gown and wandered fearfully around the living room for two hours. At last she went back to the bedroom. Lennox hadn't moved. She picked up the phone and dialed the number of Jake's apartment. She let the phone ring until Cooper answered in an inhuman voice.

"Sam," she whispered. "This is Gabby. I've got to see you right away. Can I come up, please?"

"Now?" Cooper croaked.

"It's very important, Sam. Please. Can I come up?"

"What time is it?"

"Nine-thirty."

"Oh God!" There was a pause. "Got to be at rehearsal by eleven anyway. Come up."

Gabby dressed, left a note for Lennox, and went downstairs.

On this New Year's Sunday morning The Rock was dead. She found a taxi, still littered with confetti, and was driven north to Knickerbocker Square. Cooper was dressed in slacks and jacket, waiting for her. He offered coffee which she refused and they sat down in the wing chairs in the living room eyeing each other. Gabby was frightened. Cooper looked drawn and twitchy.

"Well?" he asked.

"Do you know where Jordan keeps the photostats of those letters?"

"Why?"

"I want to compare them."

"With what?"

Gabby took the blue envelope out of her purse and showed it to Cooper.

"Another one!" he exclaimed. "Where did you find it?"

"In his pocket. It hasn't been mailed yet."

"But how did he—? Oh. He must have run up against that Knott again. Last night."

"Yes?"

"He gave it to Jake personally."

"Stamped? Marked special delivery?"

"Maybe he wanted him to mail it for him. Irony." Cooper stood up and crossed to the piano where he fidgeted with manuscript paper.

"I don't think there's any Knott, Sam. Neither do you."

"What makes you think that?"

"The way you're behaving now."

Cooper turned around. The corner of his mouth was ticking. "Hell!" he burst out. "What's the sense of pussy-footing? He's writing those letters, Gabby. I know that."

"How long have you known?"

"Since last week when he showed me the photostats." Cooper loped into his bedroom and came out a moment later with three paper slips from a telephone pad. He handed them to Gabby.

They were covered with the same hysterical scrawl, matching the writing on the latest letter.

"He has an unconscious habit," Cooper explained. "He scribbles with his left hand when he's extra nervous. While he's talking on the phone. When he's reading. It's almost like automatic writing. He doesn't do it all the time . . . just occasionally, but you can't miss it. The minute I saw those photostats, I knew."

"Does he know?" Gabby asked.

"No. That's what makes it hell."

"We can't let him find out, Sam."

"Maybe he ought to know."

"Maybe later, but not now. It would be disastrous for him. We've got to protect him."

Cooper jammed the phone slips into his jacket pocket and fretted around the room. "I tried to warn you. At that crazy cocktail party Thursday. If I hadn't been so paralyzed myself I might have— Christ! What a mess!"

"What are we going to do?"

"I don't know. He had to call in the police, yet."

"Will they find out?"

"I don't know."

"What would they do if they did?"

"Send him down to City Hospital for observation. Maybe worse. I— Jesus! What a mess!"

"You mean an asylum?"

"Yes."

"Then we'll have to keep it from the police too. We'd better destroy this letter."

"It's against the law. That letter's evidence."

"Then we'll be accessories?"

"Yes."

"Burn it," Gabby said.

She spoke with such decision that Cooper took the envelope, placed it in the practical fireplace and touched a match to the

263

corner. The flame ran along the edge and then curled slowly across the face. The letter crackled and gaped.

"Put it out!" Gabby cried so abruptly that Cooper started. She ran past him and beat the flame out with her hands and purse. Then she picked up the charred envelope and opened it. It was empty.

"What happened to the letter?" Gabby asked.

Cooper made a feeble gesture. "I can't keep up with this. I— Maybe he didn't write the letter. Just the envelope. Maybe he— Was it last night? He was probably plastered. For God's sake, who can figure anything Jake does sober, let alone drunk? I tell you, I'm lost in this. I'm nowhere."

"Isn't there anything we can do?"

"Get him off The Rock. Send him somewhere. Get him out of here."

"Is that the only answer?"

"It's the only one I can come up with."

"Did you try?"

"Try? What?"

"To make him go away last week? You tried to make me go away."

"No, I couldn't. I—"

"Why couldn't you?"

"I don't know. Quit hounding me, Gabby. I've got troubles of my own."

Gabby's face darkened. "He's your friend, Sam."

"I can't do anything for Jake."

"That's a shocking thing to say."

"Do you think I enjoy saying it? For God's sake, don't you be angry with me too. I tell you, I've got my own problems to handle."

Gabby watched Cooper while he prowled around the room as if pursued by demons. Finally she made up her mind to be frank. "I think I know what they are, Sam."

264

"Do you?" He laughed without humor. "That's more than I can say for myself."

"I wouldn't tell you if it wasn't necessary for Jordan's sake," Gabby said gravely. She came around a corner. "You don't want to be Jordan's friend. You want to be his wife."

Cooper turned white.

"You've been acting like a woman," Gabby blurted. "Jealous, possessive, hysterical. That's why you made such a fuss when he tried to protect you at the party. It was like a man protecting a woman. You enjoyed it so much you felt guilty."

"You're kidding, of course."

"No," Gabby said honestly. "I'm trying to help you so you'll help Jordan. It isn't wrong to be a homosexual, Sam. You mustn't feel ashamed. You have to face it. You haven't been able to face it and that's why you made so much trouble for Jordan."

"Are you calling me a fag?"

Gabby nodded. "You knew about the letters a week ago, and you did nothing. You let it come to a crisis when you could have stopped it. And I think I know why. You've been living on his strength and you feel guilty deep down inside because you know it's the way a woman lives on a man's strength."

"This has gone just about far enough, Gabby! I think—"

"You couldn't admit that to yourself," Gabby went on firmly. "But you had to do something to wipe out the guilt. So you let Jordan destroy his own strength. That's the way you're going to prove to yourself that you're not dependent on him . . . that you don't love him like a woman . . . that you're as much of a man as he is."

"This is insane!" Cooper shouted.

"You keep house for him. You wait on him. You watch over him like a . . . like a jealous woman. Because deep down inside you want to go to bed with him. That's why you resent me. Isn't it the truth?"

"No."

265

"And that's what makes you dangerous," Gabby said. "If you could see the truth, you wouldn't be helping Jordan destroy himself."

"I told you!" Cooper cried, shaking so hard he could barely speak. "I told you! I had problems of my own. I—"

"They're just your excuse for standing by and watching him fall." Gabby leaned forward intensely. "I can't let you do that, Sam. It isn't fair to yourself and it isn't fair to Jordan. You'll be horribly ashamed of yourself. We've got to come to an understanding and work together."

"Understanding!"

"Yes. He wants you for a friend. I promised him I'd keep you friends . . . And I'm going to keep that promise," Gabby added grimly. "But not until you understand that you're going to be his friend, not his wife."

There was an agonizing pause. The phone rang. Cooper looked around in bewilderment, then jumped up and took the call.

"What? No. He's not in. I don't know where you can get in touch with him. . . ."

"He's at my place," Gabby said.

"Wait a minute. I do know where he is. He—"

"Who's calling?" Gabby asked.

"Who is this? What? Driscoll? Aimee Driscoll?"

"I'll take it," Gabby said with determination. She seized the phone. "This is Gabby Valentine, Aimee. What do you want?"

"I want to talk to your boyfriend, sister."

"What about?"

"A man named Knott."

"You're wasting your time. That was a lie you told us Thursday night . . . a cruel malicious lie."

"Sure." Aimee laughed and Gabby could picture the hand covering the teeth. "Only now it happens I know what plays. I know who this Knott really is."

"That's another lie."

266

"Not this time, doll. I seen him write the letter. In front of my eyes. And what's more, I got the letter. So if Mr. Three-names wants to get it squared off, tell him he better come down and see me this morning. And tell him I ain't settlin' for no lousy TV set neither!"

Gabby hung up and looked at Sam. "She's got the letter."

Cooper shook his head. He was dazed.

"We've got to get it from her, Sam."

"Yes, I—" He looked at his watch. "I have to go to the theater."

"Sam!" She took his arm and shook him. "We've got to get that letter."

He stood perplexed, the corner of his mouth twitching, then without another word, he walked out of the apartment. Gabby ran after him. From the door she saw him cross the square and disappear around the corner.

Gabby went up to Jake's room, found an overnight bag and packed it with Jake's clothes. She came downstairs with the bag, took an overcoat from the closet and let herself out of the apartment. At Third Avenue she got a cab.

"Nine hundred East Thirty-third, please," she told the driver.

The cab dropped her before a brownstone apartment house. She rang Aimee Driscoll's bell and the door-release buzzed promptly. Gabby entered the house and climbed two flights with the bag and overcoat. To Aimee, who was standing at the door of her apartment wearing the green and scarlet petuniaed dressing gown, she said: "Good morning, Aimee. I dropped in on my way home."

"Spent the night out, huh?" Aimee answered, looking at the bag. "Naughty-naughty. Come in."

She closed the door behind Gabby who put the bag and coat in a corner and waited.

"Too high class to take a load off in my dump, huh?"

"I was waiting to be asked," Gabby said quietly.

"So I'm asking. Park your high-priced ass."

Gabby sat down on the sofa and looked around. She saw the television set with the framed photograph on top, and her eyes widened at the resemblance of the picture to Lennox. Then she noticed that Aimee was watching her closely.

"Pretty crappy, huh?" Aimee asked. "Not what your kind is used to."

"The trouble with you is you're old-fashioned," Gabby said directly.

"That chair's brand new modernistic. And what about the TV set? Nothing old-fashioned about that."

"I don't mean your furniture. I mean your attitude toward people . . . talking about my kind and your kind. It's Victorian." Gabby smiled. "We're both of us people. Don't let's quarrel."

"No? I thought you come up here looking for a fight."

"I don't believe in fighting. What is there to fight about?"

"Your boy friend's letter." Aimee lit a cigarette. "I won't kid you, doll. I seen him write it last night. He was so dirty drunk he forget to put it in the envelope when he sealed it. I got it right here."

"May I see it, please?"

"Wouldn't you like to?" Aimee smiled without parting her lips. "Old three-names is in a bad jam, ain't he? I ought to take that letter to the cops. It's against the law writing dirty letters like that and sending 'em through the mail."

"You misunderstand, Aimee. It was a joke."

"Yeah? Ha. Ha. A gag got you up here so fast, did it? Try something else, doll."

"I came up because I'm afraid other people will misunderstand . . . like you."

"Don't hand me that. I seen the fuss you and him made Thursday. I figured it out. That guy's off his rocker. He ought to be put away. He ain't fit to hang out with sane people. He's dangerous." Aimee crushed out the cigarette violently. "No wonder he beat hell outa me last week. I'm lucky I didn't get killed."

"Then are you going to the police?"

268

"So help me, I ought to. But I'm willing to be a right guy if he'll keep away from me . . . and make it worth while. He can afford it, being a big-shot writer."

"How much?" Gabby asked.

Aimee gave her a poker face. "Ten grand."

Gabby mustered herself and began her first lie. She burst out laughing.

"What's so funny?" Aimee demanded.

"Your price. You'll have to be a little more realistic."

"He ain't got ten grand to keep outa trouble?"

"Of course not." Gabby blushed, being unused to the sensation of flagrant lying. She inched her way further into falsehood. "How much do you think he gets for writing that show?"

"At least three-four hundred bucks a week."

"Half that."

"You're crazy."

"Half that," Gabby repeated. "One hundred and fifty dollars a week."

"I don't believe it."

"It's the truth."

"He had a couple hundred bucks on him last Saturday."

"It took him two months to save two hundred dollars." Gabby was discovering it was no problem at all to lie. She pointed to the television set. "It took him two months to save up enough to buy that present for you, Aimee. The money was supposed to be for me. I think you owe me a favor."

"All right. Here's your favor. Five grand."

Gabby shrugged. "He can't do it."

"One grand. He's got to have a thousand bucks stashed somewhere. Everybody's got a thousand bucks."

"I don't. Do you?"

"I will if three-names don't want his letter to go to the cops."

"All right," Gabby said. She held out her hand. "Now may I have the letter, please?"

"Are you kidding, sister?"

"I can't pay you until tomorrow. Won't you trust me?"

"No."

"But you want me to trust you."

"You'll have to."

"All right. I will." Gabby arose. "I'll bring the money tomorrow afternoon."

"Not you. Him."

"He may not be able to come. I'll bring the money. That won't make any difference, will it?"

"Either he brings it himself or it's no deal." Aimee insisted. She looked at Gabby malevolently.

"Why?"

"Never mind why. He brings it himself. He hands it to me like a gentleman, and he asks me extra polite like a gentleman to do him a favor and give him back the letter. Extra polite or it's no deal."

"Then I can't trust you."

"You can trust me if he behaves himself."

Gabby hesitated. At last she said: "He can't do that, Aimee. We can't let him find out he's been writing those letters . . . not now. Please understand."

Aimee's eyes lit up. "So it'll hurt him a little. It's time he found out how it feels to get hurt."

"What are you trying to do? Punish him?"

"That's between me and him."

"No. I think it's between you and somebody else." Gabby examined Aimee. "You're using him to punish somebody else."

"It's between him and my ass!" Aimee shouted.

"Don't show me your bruise again," Gabby said. "Please listen to me. He's in trouble. Don't make it worse for him. You must have been in trouble yourself. You must know what it means to need help."

"And who got me in trouble?" Aimee spat. "The nice respectable safe ones like you."

270

"Why are you so hostile to me? You think I look down on you, don't you. Why are you so class conscious?"

"Class my ass! What the hell do I care about class? They all gimme a lousy time . . . all of them. So now it's my turn to hand out a little grief."

"Stop whining, Aimee. You're just feeling sorry for yourself. I'm doing the same thing you are, but I'm not whining. Half the women in the world are too, and they don't whine either."

"Do what?"

"Sleep with men the law doesn't approve of." Gabby tried to smile. "Let's be honest, Aimee. As far as the law's concerned we're both whores. Let's stick together and help each other."

"Get outa here," Aimee raged.

"Not without the letter."

"I already told you. Let him bring the dough and beg, and he'll get the letter. Now beat it."

Gabby shook her head. "I'm sorry. It's a dreadful thing to say, but you're not even an honest whore, Aimee. You'll have to trust me for the money. Give me the letter."

"I'll give you a kick in your high-class ass," Aimee cried. She darted at Gabby, seized her by the shoulders and pushed her toward the door. "You get the hell outa my house."

Gabby tore her hands away. "How dare you!" she exclaimed.

"Yeah. Now it comes! The high-tone how dare you!" Aimee screeched. "How dare anybody like me touch somebody like you, you goddam high-assed duchess!" She leaped at Gabby in a burst of fury, kicking and clutching at her hair. Gabby staggered, then swung her purse and knocked Aimee back against the wall.

"I'll bring you down," Aimee spat.

"You aren't bad," Gabby answered grimly. "You're spoiled. You're a spoiled, selfish, lazy slut."

As Aimee advanced, she backed away, kicking off her shoes and stripping off her jacket to clear for action. Aimee clawed like an alley cat. Gabby threw up her left arm to defend herself from the tearing nails and cracked Aimee across the face with her right.

Aimee began to scream. She clinched, biting and kicking, and they staggered against the window. Gabby's blouse was torn off. Both women lost their balance and clutched at the drapes. The curtains came down on top of Aimee, pole and all. When she struggled free, she had lost the dressing gown.

She ran into the kitchen. There was a crash and she came charging back, left arm shielding her bosom, the neck of a broken beer bottle in her right fist. Gabby gave ground in terror, dodged a vicious swipe and stumbled back against the window where Aimee cornered her. In desperation she snatched up the five foot curtain pole that had fallen. She delivered a frantic chop that caught Aimee between neck and shoulder and dropped her to her knees. The beer bottle slipped out of her hand and clattered across the floor.

Aimee clawed at Gabby's legs, ripped off her skirt and brought her down to the floor. They rolled across the room, pummeling each other with knees, elbows and hands. When they jammed against the television set, Gabby twisted on top of Aimee, took her blonde hair in both hands and hammered her head against the cabinet. After three punishing blows, she stopped.

"Where's the letter?" she gasped.

Aimee screeched and swore. Gabby pounded her head three times again, and Aimee went limp.

"Where's the letter?"

"Bedroom," Aimee answered faintly.

"Show me."

She got up and pulled Aimee up by the hair. Never releasing her hold, she dragged Aimee into the bedroom. Both women were gasping and gleaming with perspiration. In the bedroom Aimee fumbled at a dresser drawer. Gabby opened it for her. Under a pile of black net nylons was a sheet of blue writing paper.

Gabby glanced at it and then released Aimee who dropped on the bed. Gabby went back to the living room, folded the sheet twice and placed it in an ash tray. She lit a match and burned the letter. She crushed the ashes with her fingers until they were dust. Suddenly she shivered.

She took off the shreds of her stockings and put on her shoes. The blouse was hopeless. She opened Jake's bag, took out his clean shirt and put it on. Over that she put her jacket and skirt. The zipper of the skirt was wrecked. She went to the bedroom and searched the dresser until she found a couple of safety pins. While she pinned her skirt she watched Aimee who hadn't moved.

"I'm sorry for you," Gabby said at last. "You should have had this lesson when you were a child. Maybe it isn't too late now."

"I'm going to the cops anyway," Aimee moaned. "I'll have him put away. I'll fix both of you for this."

"If you make any more trouble," Gabby answered in a hard voice, "I promise you'll regret it for the rest of your life."

She went back to the living room, hoping that her threat would silence Aimee for good. She picked up Jake's coat and bag and left the apartment. Her knees gave as she went down the stairs and she was trembling; but her eyes sparkled and her face wore a triumphant smile. And when, on the street, she tasted blood from a cut inside her mouth, she spat into the gutter with the cocky assurance of a kid who has won his first fight.

· CHAPTER XIV ·

LENNOX AWOKE IN THE ROLE
of Mr. Lefty Leftwich from Brockton, Mass. He turned over in
bed like a ship launched sideways and immediately began bellow-
ing the ballad about feet, feet, marching up and down again,
with which he had annoyed the patrons of the Baroque until
Chris Barakatrones had been forced to throw him out.

Gabby heard the racket and ran into the bedroom and turned
on the lights. Lennox winced, closed his eyes, and sneezed three
times in stately waltz tempo. "Less light," he muttered. "A switch
on Goethe. I am excessively educated. Need more crud in my
blood." He began to roar again.

"Stop that noise, Lefty," Gabby called from the door. She came
to the bed and sat down beside Lennox. She was wearing a grey
skirt and a slate blue sweater. Lennox immediately reached up
and seized her breasts with his heavy hands.

"The All-Mother," he laughed.

He hurt her. She eased his hands and said: "Yes, that's how
they're tattooed, Lefty."

274

He began to wrestle with her, trying to tear off the sweater.

"Take it easy," she said. "Or do you want to hurt me?"

"No, no, lady," Lennox apologized. "Act of homage. 'Pillow'd upon my fair love's ripening breast, To feel forever its soft fall and swell . . .' Etcetera. Etcetera. Sonnet by J. Keats. Theme song of L. Leftwich." He hauled her down on the bed. She kissed him once and then bit his ear until he roared with pain.

"Jesus!" he complained.

"Did I hurt you?" she inquired.

"Christ, yes!"

"I'm sorry, Lefty." She kissed the injured ear and bit the other until he roared again.

"Listen, lady," he said, half annoyed, half ecstatic, "No fair. You play Boys' Rules. I'm the fella. You're supposed to be the girl."

"Male Supremacy," Gabby said. "I am so the girl. Feel your fair love's ripening breast." She pulled his face down into her bosom and banged the back of his head with her fists. She rolled him over in bed and bit his mouth. He struggled up, protesting. She caught him and huffed and puffed against his bulk until he collapsed again.

"Fins," he said.

"You give up?"

"I give up. Fins."

She braced herself on her arms and looked down at him. He looked up and grinned. "You're the first one that played Boy's Rules with me. Why aren't there more like you, lady?"

"All girls want to, Lefty."

"Why don't they?"

"Because men won't let them."

"Why not?"

"They want girls to be girly-girly."

"Why?"

"Because it makes them feel manly."

"Crazy." He tapped the tips of her breasts. "Double-relish," he said.

"What's that mean, Lefty?"

"It's musical ornamentation," he explained after a moment's earnest concentration. "Friend of mine, Sam Cooper, said—" He collapsed and stared at her with his mouth open.

"Yes, Lefty? What did Sam Cooper say?"

"Gabby?" he faltered.

"Right here."

"But I thought you— I thought I—"

Lefty Leftwich fled back to Brockton.

"W-Where've I been?"

"Right here."

"Gabby. . . ."

"Yes, darling?"

"I think I'm going to be sick."

She smacked her palm against his nose and thrust back determinedly. He grunted in pain.

"Still want to be sick?" she asked after a minute.

"No," he answered in patient agony.

She released his nose. "Hello, Jake," she said.

He began to cry. She soothed him. "It's all right, baby. Don't cry. What's the matter, darling? You don't have to cry."

"It's the first time you ever called me Jake," he said in a muffled voice.

"Is that why you're crying, sweetheart?"

"It's like we're finally meeting for the first time . . . No . . . I— I'm mixed up again. Like last week. What's today?"

"Sunday. New Year's day."

"What time is it?"

"Six o'clock."

"Morning?"

"Evening."

He digested that information, thought intensely and groaned.

276

"I've lost the whole damned New Year's Eve. I'm blacked out again from ten o'clock last night. What filth am I going to start remembering now?"

"Don't be frightened," Gabby said briskly. "I was with you from midnight on."

"You were?"

She nodded.

"Did I do anything bad?"

She shook her head.

"Where did we meet?"

"You called for me here."

"And you went out with me? After that fight? After the lousy things I said to—"

She put her hand over his mouth. "Don't talk about that. We both apologized and made up."

"Honest?"

"You know I never lie."

"Did . . . Did we run into Knott?"

"No."

"I could swear something about Knott is flitting around in the blackout. I—"

"Your imagination," Gabby said. "On your feet, Jake. Time to get dressed and have something to eat. We've got to catch the nine o'clock plane."

"What plane?"

"Don't you remember anything from last night? We made up our minds to fly down to Mexico today."

"Mexico? What for?"

"My divorce. Your wedding." Gabby looked at him sternly. "If you're pretending amnesia to get out of it, Jake, it won't work. I've got witnesses."

"I think," he said feebly, "I'd better have some coffee."

He stood up, still dizzy and blurry. Gabby tossed him clean shorts. He put them on and followed her to the kitchen where he drank coffee humbly and in a hushed voice reported what he remembered of his New Year's Eve . . . the trip to Islip, his insane practical jokes . . . he even blurted out all he remembered of his date with Olga Bleutcher, the body incarnate. Gabby was annoyed, the more so because his memory died at the point where the date with Olga began. She covered her chagrin with a laugh.

"The pigeons were a nuisance," she said, "But after the mothballs and the gelatine I got off lucky. You're a Monte Cristo, Jake."

"No," he insisted. "It wasn't revenge. I swear I was trying to spread sweetness and light." He looked at her for the first time with something like focus. "What happened to your right eye? It's all red."

"Caught cold in it last night," Gabby said briefly. "How did you manage to get rid of fatal Olga Bleutcher?"

"I don't know. We must have gone to parties. Probably I lost her somewhere."

"And before you lost her did you—" Gabby stopped.

"Did I what?"

"Nothing."

After a moment Lennox asked: "What time did I pick you up here?"

"Around midnight."

"That's two hours not accounted for."

"We won't try to account for them. We won't even ask Olga."

"No. I mean, do you think I ran into Knott while I—"

"Forget Knott," Gabby said. "You never ran into him and I don't think you ever will. The whole thing will blow over while we're in Mexico."

"What'll Roy do to you if you divorce him?"

"To hell with Roy. Now come on, Lefty. It's time to get dressed."

"Who's Lefty?"

"You."

"Since when?"

278

"Since last night. All of a sudden you turned to me and announced you were Lefty Leftwich from Brockton."

Lennox grunted. "A comic, that's what I am. A New Year's comic. If you tell me I put on women's hats, I'll hang myself."

"You didn't while you were with me. You can check with Olga some other time."

"You aren't jealous about Olga?" Lennox asked timidly.

"Yes," Gabby said. "I am. I could knock her block off."

"But we had that fight, and she pestered me until—"

"You listen to me, Jordan Lennox. We'll probably have a lot of fights in the future, but never for a minute imagine they'll give you any excuse to chase other women." She rapped him under the chin with her knuckles. "If I ever catch you, I'll knock your block off too."

"All of a sudden you're such a fighter, all of a sudden," he said in awe. "What happened?"

"Something."

"What?"

"I don't fight and tell. Now get dressed."

He dressed and admired her for bringing him his clothes. He admired her most for preserving his sacred gimmick book from loss, theft and other catastrophe. As he placed it in his inside pocket and flexed his right arm, Gabby handed him a long white envelope.

"This is our expense money," she said. "You had a hundred and eight dollars left from last night. I borrowed another two hundred. We can make bank arrangements in Mexico. Somebody I know at the airport—"

"An eclectic Chinaman?"

"No." She laughed.

"Hasty Hawaiian?"

"No. It's a woman I met at a WVL meeting. She got me the tickets on some kind of credit. We can settle up when we get back."

"You're leveling about Mexico?"

279

"Of course I am. Now, it's seven o'clock. We have two hours to pick up our tickets and get weighed in. I packed your fort-nighter and brought it down. It's out in the foyer. . . ."

"By God, you were busy today."

"By God, you don't know how busy. All I have to do is finish packing myself. Then we'll start. Wash the dishes, Jake. Oh, and give those pigeons their freedom or something."

He swallowed. "I can't do it, Gabby."

"Don't be silly. Just take the cage to the window and open it. Nature'll do the rest."

"I mean I can't go to Mexico tonight."

"Don't be obstinate, darling. Just clean up the kitchen and keep out of my way."

"I can't go tonight, Gabby." He took her shoulders and held her. "And don't think I'm playing noble on account of Roy. I love you so much I'll marry you even if it ruins us. I'll marry you any time or any place you say . . . but I can't go tonight."

"I want to go tonight, Jordan."

"I'm sorry. I can't. I can't run out on the show."

"You can so run out on the show. They fired you."

"That isn't what I mean. I can't run out on those threats. I've got to stay and face Knott."

"Jordan, believe me, there isn't any Knott."

"How do you know?"

"I just know it."

"You mean you just hope it. Who's writing the letters? Who's threatening me?"

"No one. It's some kind of silly joke."

"A joke! That filth?"

"So it's a filthy joke; but we can't take it seriously."

"I'm taking it seriously. I want to meet the joker who's picked me out for his filthy humor. I'm going to meet him tonight."

"Jordan, please! I want to go to Mexico tonight."

"If he doesn't show up," Lennox continued grimly, "I'll drag

Aimee Driscoll down to the precinct and we'll beat the truth out of her. We'll pry it out of Sam, too. There's got to be a pay-off tonight."

"Jordan!" Gabby shook his arms frantically. "I want to leave tonight. I want it more than anything else. Will you do this for me?"

"I can't, sweetheart. I've got too much to settle up first."

"And you'll find another excuse tomorrow and the day after and the day after that. . . ."

"You know that's not true."

"Remember what you said about politics? To hell with politics because we're more important. I agree, Jordan. That's the truth. And to hell with Knott and his letters too."

"No."

"Oh, why are you so stubborn?"

"I have to do what has to be done," Lennox said patiently. "You go ahead and finish packing. We'll leave as soon as I've called the lunatic who's been crucifying me. I'm going up to the theater now. I'll phone you when we're off the air."

"No," Gabby said quietly. "The packing can wait. I'll go with you."

It was seven-thirty when they arrived at the Venice Theater. More than a hundred ticket-holders were already queued up before the main lobby, waiting for the nine o'clock show. When the doors opened at eight-thirty, there would be at least five hundred more. As Lennox took Gabby around to the stage door he passed down the length of that line, staring into each strange face, searching for his hidden enemy.

To the deaf doorman he spoke in a low flat drone that was more effective than any shouting. He was expecting a Mr. Fu, a Mr. Hamburger, and a Mr. Eugene K. Norman. If they came to the stage door they were to be admitted and given seats. If anyone else asked for him . . . A Mr. Knott, say . . . Lennox was to be called at once. He repeated these instructions three times. Gabby bit her lip.

The stage door opened into a small square foyer. To the left was the narrow corridor which led down the left hand side of the theater to the green room and thence to the right wings of the stage. There is no paradox in this reversal of left and right. Since the actor faces the audience, right and left are reversed as you cross from the theater to the stage.

A broad curtained arch led from the stage door foyer directly into the theater orchestra, opening out into the left aisle. The curtain was not drawn now. Through the arch, Lennox could see little islands of people scattered through the orchestra . . . a clump of dancers in costume, four cameramen drinking coffee from cartons, Oliver Stacy with Olga Bleutcher, Ween and Grabinett with Mason's gag writers, Avery Borden and Ned Bacon en rapport with the client.

Lennox took Gabby's arm and marched into the orchestra. He refused to be inconspicuous. It was like running the gauntlet but he made a full circuit of the house, meeting every hostile glance with an arrogant smile. He threw the smile in their faces, daring them to accept the challenge. Every hackle in the theater arose, but before the battle could be joined, Raeburn Sachs started a muffled uproar on the P.A.:

"Dress, please. Dress. Everybody on stage for dress."

The dancers and Stacy returned to the stage. The cameramen returned to their cameras. Johnny Plummer put on his ear-phones and stammered to the orchestra on the low platform at the foot of the right aisle. The gag writers assembled in the center aisle, just behind the dolly-track of the No. 2 camera, to simulate contestants for the dress rehearsal. Lennox seated Gabby and excused himself to go backstage. He did not slip around through the green room. As the orchestra began its opening fanfare, he went down to the edge of the old orchestra pit, climbed up on the rail and leaped to the stage in full view.

He turned and grinned into the lights. "Poison eaters!" he said contemptuously and walked toward the prop table in the right wings. Mason passed him on the way from his dressing room to open the dress.

"You lousy burglar!" Mason shouted in a whisper. Even feuds must be conducted sotto voce during rehearsal.

Irma was a step behind Mason. "You lousy burglar," she whispered. "We'll fix you for those lights."

"What's the matter?" Lennox inquired. "Didn't you have cameras?"

From out front came the echo of Mason's voice, the cackle of the dummy, the brassy punctuation of the orchestra. The empty house put every sound on echo. Kay Hill, in a 1920 evening gown, passed Lennox on her way to take her place on the Clara Bow "Charleston" set.

"So you helped him add another one to his score," she hissed, her acid eyes raking Lennox.

"Who?" he asked, bewildered.

"The Bleutcher."

"Maybe she added him to her score."

The ballet girls came down the stairs from their balcony dressing room in geisha costumes, and clustered around the rosin box, shuffling their feet. Across, in the left wings, the ballet boys assembled, dressed in Lt. Pinkerton whites. Stacy ran off stage, stripping off his dinner jacket to change for his second spot.

"Thanks, pal!" he whispered bitterly.

"For what?"

"For Typhoid Olga. Ask me a favor some time."

"I'll tell Kay."

Grabinett shot out from behind a drop, arguing furiously and soundlessly with the uniformed theater fireman. He stopped long enough to blink at Lennox.

"And you'll pay for them Almighty signs too," he whispered. "Defacing my office!"

283

"I'll tell the painter."

Bacon swaggered in from the green room with the client and the client's daughter. He was explaining the workings of the theater like an old showman from way back. As they drifted around behind the drops, he gave Lennox one venomous glance that disemboweled him. Olga stopped long enough to confront Jake.

"You filthy pig!" she said in a clear voice.

"Shhh! Rehearsal! All insults in a whisper, please."

She slapped his face and followed her father.

"I'll tell mother," Lennox said.

Tooky Ween waddled across the temporary bridge from the orchestra to the stage with the notes he had made for Mason's opening spot. He shook his fist at Lennox. Lennox blew him kisses. The hatreds and the hostilities were recharging him. He felt alert and stimulated. He lounged against the prop table, looking sardonic and unyielding, carrying his naked weapons ready for quick murder.

Mason came off the stage, followed by Irma. Lennox applauded soundlessly and asked for his autograph. Mason lifted the dummy to hit him, thought better of it, and continued to his dressing room, shrugging out of his tuxedo. The orchestra blared. Irma kicked Lennox in the leg.

"That's the wooden one," he smiled.

Stacy rushed out in a scarlet Grenadier's uniform.

"Olga went that way," Lennox said.

Kay Hill came back from the Clara Bow.

"Oliver went that way," Lennox said.

The orchestra blared and segued into dance tempo. The geishas and Lt. Pinkertons took position before the No. 2 camera. Raeburn Sachs tore down the center aisle from the control booth and leaped up on stage. He came back into the wings.

"Wardrobe!" he hissed. "Where's the wardrobe mistress? I told her Household Guards, not Grenadier."

"Same thing," Lennox said.

Sachs looked at him.

"Don't argue with me," Lennox said mildly. "You have a talent that terrifies me. It always puts me in the wrong."

Sachs turned, leaped across the pit and ran back to the controls.

The orchestra fanfared. The dancers came off and ran up to the balcony. Mason charged out of his dressing room, buttoning up his Philip Nolan uniform. Across the stage a group of actors were assembling on a courtroom set before the No. 3 camera. Lennox waved to Robin, picked a bunch of artificial flowers off the prop table and threw it to her. The flowers were intercepted by Oliver Stacy's face.

Stacy spread his shoulders and telegraphed the punch. Lennox stepped inside and hooked his right to Stacy's heart. Then he caught him before he could fall and disrupt the dress. They clinched.

"Rehearsal! Rehearsal!" Lennox whispered.

Stacy broke away and ran into his dressing room. Lennox massaged his fist happily. The stage manager appeared and returned the flowers to the prop table in a marked manner. Kay Hill came out in black lace court dress, ruff and cap to take position before the No. 1 camera with an Extra dressed in leather and carrying an axe. The wardrobe mistress appeared.

"Not Grenadier. Household," Lennox told her severely.

"I'm having trouble with Cooper."

"What's the matter?"

"He won't get into costume."

"Where's he dressing?"

"Up in Nine."

Lennox ran up the iron steps to the balcony, three at a time. He passed the dancers' dressing room and had a flashing glimpse of naked flat-chested girls juggling into can-can costumes. He knocked once on the door of Nine and burst in. It was the size of a privy. Cooper sat on a stool before the bulb-ringed mirror staring at a red and white blazer and a scarlet banded straw hat. His face bore a ghastly expression.

"What the hell, Sam?"

Cooper looked at him without changing expression.

"Your spot comes up in five minutes."

Cooper shook his head.

"What's the matter? Speak."

"I'm sick."

"Stage-fright, hey? Don't worry, I'll see you through." Lennox picked up the blazer. "Come on. Change."

Cooper made no move. Lennox took his shoulder and shook him. "Wake up, boy. You're on in five minutes. Take off your coat."

"Leave me alone!" Cooper knocked Jake's hand away.

"Take it easy, Wolfgang. Don't get panicky. I told you I'd see you through."

"See me through what? More hell?"

"It may be hell, but it's worth it. We're promoting you, son."

"Promoting me?" Cooper laughed hysterically. "You're an expert, aren't you? You've promoted yourself to hell."

"Maybe I have, but I'm not quitting on the way down. Don't you quit on the way up." Lennox glared at him. "For Christ's sake, Sam! Do I have to fight for both of us? Don't you have any strength of your own?"

Cooper started to his feet in horror.

"Get that coat off." Lennox jerked the coat off, spun Cooper around and put him into the red and white blazer. He cocked the straw hat on his head, tapped it into a rakish tilt and shoved him out of the dressing room. Cooper trudged to the stairs like a sleepwalker. The stage manager below beckoned frantically and he increased his pace going down the stairs.

Lennox nodded and picked Cooper's jacket up to hang it away. Three slips of paper had fallen out of the pocket in the tussle. He was about to return them; then he stopped short as his eye caught the familiar hysterical writing. He smoothed the slips out and examined them fearfully. His heart began to pound. There were fragments, phrases, names, numbers; all scrawled in that sick hand: SUIDI . . . $$$ . . . MOST . . . MERRY XMAS . . . AMPMAMPM . . . ROX . . . §§§3 . . . ¶7 . . . MY HEART & . . . BLOOD. SWEAT. TEARS . . . WHO WHO WHO WHO HE?

Lennox went black with rage. He placed the slips in his pocket and burst out of the dressing room. Down on the main floor he left the stage, leaped down the short flight of steps to the empty green room and called Sergeant Fink on the pay phone.

"Bob? Jake Lennox."

"Yeah. Hello. We'll be over in time for the program."

"Get over now. I've found out who's writing the letters."

"You don't say?"

"I do say. And I've got proof."

Lennox hung up. He glanced at the green room monitor. Cooper and one of the dancers had started their duet. Lennox turned up the speaker volume and watched, his face drawn and savage. The spot started badly. Cooper and the dancer missed their cue, the orchestra had to wait for them, they came in off beat. Their singing was inaudible and ragged. Cooper moved like a St. Vitus dancer. Even on the monitor his shaking was obvious.

"Varsity show talent," Lennox snarled.

After two agonizing minutes, the voice of Avery Borden cut through the orchestra and singing with the clarity of exasperation: "No! No! No! This is impossible."

Cooper and the dancer stopped and peered out into the theater.

"Get them out of here!" Borden shouted. "What is this? Amateur Night?"

"So they stink," Grabinett's voice came faintly from another part of the theater. "What can we do? We got three Almighty minutes to fill."

"I'd rather fill three minutes with dead air than that no-talent. Sweep 'em off the stage."

"This is a dress rehearsal!" Sachs roared on the P.A.

"This is a goddam trappisty!" Grabinett answered.

The dancer began to weep. Cooper left her and staggered off camera. Lennox ran up the steps from the green room to the stage and met him as he came into the wings. There was a confused uproar in the theater punctuated by Raeburn Sachs' repeated commands to the staff to stop their clocks. Lennox took Cooper by the scruff of the neck and dragged him back to the green room. He flung him into a chair and stood over him. Cooper shook and gasped for air.

"You son of a bitch!" Lennox shouted.

"Stand by me, Jake. I'm in a bad way."

"You're going to be in a worse way, you bastard."

"Please, Jake. . . ."

Lennox pulled the telephone slips out of his pocket and shook them in Cooper's face. "Look at these. Look at them, you filthy Judas."

"Jake . . . I need a drink. I'm in a bad way."

Cooper tried to get out of the chair. Lennox backhanded him across the jaw. Then, in his fury, he yanked him up and cuffed his face. When he let him go, Cooper collapsed.

"So it was you writing them," Lennox shouted. "What's inside you? What in God's name did you have against me? Why couldn't you come out into the open instead of sticking a knife in my back and twisting it?"

"The . . . letters?"

"Yes, the letters. The threats. The filth." Lennox thrust the slips before Cooper's face again. "I found these in your pocket. It's the same writing. Your disguised hand, yes? What are they, practice sheets?"

288

"No," Cooper said faintly. "I . . . Jake, I've got to tell you. You're writing them. You're writing those letters yourself. Not me. You."

Lennox burst out laughing.

"It's true, Jake. Those times when you get drunk and black out . . . That's when you write yourself those letters. So help me, Jake. I've been trying to keep it from you, but—"

"I thought we were friends," Lennox broke in fiercely. "I thought we were working together . . . standing by each other . . . backing each other up. I thought we were two sane men bucking the rat-race and beating them at their own game. I believed in us. I'd have killed myself to keep it from being destroyed. I should have killed you before you destroyed it. You're not sane. You're like all the rest of them . . . sick, vicious, living on hate and poison."

"For God's sake, Jake! Will you listen to me?" Cooper struggled up out of the chair and put his arm around Jake's shoulders. "You're the sick one. You're the one who's destroying everything. You—"

Lennox twisted away from Cooper and looked at him with hatred. "You can think of more vicious ways to knife a man in the back than a fag. Why didn't you dress under the stage with the other queens? That's where you belong!"

"Mr. Lennox," the doorman called in his deaf voice. "Man here for you. Mr. Fink or such."

"Be right out," Lennox answered. He showed his teeth to Cooper. "Wait here. I've got a surprise for you."

He ran out to the stagedoor foyer. Fink was standing there with his swarthy colleague, Salerno.

"He's in the green room," Lennox said. "This way."

"Just a minute," Fink smiled. "Who's in this green room?"

"Guy who was writing the letters. You were right, Bob. It was Cooper. Sam Cooper who lives with me. Look at this." Lennox waved the telephone slips. "I found them in his pocket.

289

It's the same writing. You see? You see, Mr. Salerno? Come on."

"Oh Jesus," Salerno grunted.

"Come out to the car a minute," Fink said.

"What for?"

"To talk."

"What about?"

"Tell you when we get there. Come on."

"What the hell is this?" Lennox looked from Fink to Salerno. "I tell you who's writing the letters and you want to talk. Go talk to him."

Salerno slipped behind Lennox and caught his arm in a paralyzing grasp. "Come on out to the car," he said softly.

"I will like hell come out to the car. What's the matter with you two?"

"You want it tough?" Fink asked.

Lennox was bewildered. In the background, the orchestra echoed brilliantly.

"Tell him," Salerno said.

"Now don't blow your top." Fink smiled. "We want to drive you down to City Hospital for a check-up."

"Me? City Hospital?"

"Just for a couple of days. Won't cost you a cent."

"What are you talking about?"

"Come on, Lennox. Don't make it tough."

"I asked you what the hell you're talking about. City Hospital! Is this your idea of a funny?"

"Tell him," Salerno repeated.

"We know you're writing these letters," Fink said.

"You know I'm writing—" Lennox was staggered. "You know I'm writing the letters? To myself?"

Fink nodded.

"You always smile at the wrong time," Lennox said slowly. "This is a joke-type joke at the wrong time. Yes?"

"We'll talk it over down at the hospital."

"What makes you think I'm writing the letters?"

"Tell him," Salerno said impatiently. "Maybe he'll listen to reason."

"Will you behave yourself if I show you?" Fink asked.

Lennox nodded. There was a last fanfare off and then dead silence as the dress ended. Fink took a manila envelope out of his pocket and produced the poison pen letters. He unfolded one and pointed to the hysterical scrawl.

"See? Five words to a line. In every letter. Five words to a line, no more, no less. That's an old telegrapher's habit, from counting ten word messages. We checked this program. You're the only ex-telegrapher working it. You're a professional telegrapher from twenty years back, when you were a kid in this town on Long Island."

"Islip," Lennox croaked. "Yes."

"And we found your prints in the envelopes."

"I handled the envelopes," Lennox said desperately. "When Grabinett showed me the letters."

"I didn't say on the envelopes. I said in the envelopes. We found your prints inside, under the flap, but the envelopes were slit open at the end. The only one who could leave prints inside there is the one that put the letter in the envelope and sealed it. Now come on, Lennox. Don't make it tough."

"For God's sake, Bob! How could I write them and not know about it? I was scared. I was out of my mind trying to find who it was. How could it be me?"

"They'll tell you down at the hospital. Come on."

"The lunatic ward?"

"Don't get jumpy. You won't be in a strait jacket."

"Yeah," Salerno said. "Nice down there. Pretty nurses."

"But—"

"Come on," Fink said, and for the first time a terrifying hardness manifested itself under the surface of his mildness.

Lennox whirled and wrenched himself out of Salerno's grasp. He didn't so much hit him as catapult him back into Fink with a bull thrust. He ran through the arch into the orchestra, whipping the heavy curtain across the arch behind him for cover. He squirmed through an empty row of seats to the center aisle and yelled: "Gabby!"

She turned. Everybody turned and stared through the gloom.

"Out!" Lennox roared. "Out!"

Behind him, Fink called sharply: "Lennox! You'll be sorry!"

Lennox sprinted up the center aisle, knocking aside the vague figures that blundered into his path. He cut around the glass corner of the control booth and headed for the bronze doors that led out to the theater lobby. At that moment, the doors opened and the studio audience poured into the theater in a solid mass, fighting and elbowing for the best seats.

Lennox was slammed back against the control booth. He lowered his head and tried to charge through that unyielding wave. He could hear Fink and Salerno struggling near him and shouting orders to the network pages, the house manager, the theater fireman. Lennox was carried back again and shunted to the right where the broad stairs led up to the balcony. He started up the stairs. The fireman appeared above him and came down after him. Lennox turned and ran around the foot of the stairs to the right aisle, searching for fire exits.

He went down the steep slope of the aisle toward the stage. There were no exits he could reach through the crowd. Fink and Salerno were calling to each other. The studio audience was in an uproar. Lennox leaped up on the orchestra platform at the foot of the aisle, battered his way through musicians, stands and chairs, and vaulted onto the stage. Gabby began screaming.

Lennox started across the stage to the right wings. He tripped on the No. 3 Camera cables, fell, rolled over and was on his feet again. Salerno appeared in the right wings. Lennox stopped short and turned downstage. Fink was coming at him up the No.

2 Camera dolly-track. Lennox turned to the left wings. The fireman was advancing on him from that side. He backed up, panting, trapped. As Fink came onto the stage, the curtains swept in from either side, narrowly missing him.

Lennox looked around wildly, searching the stage for a loophole . . . left, right, back, up. Suddenly he was transfixed. Still staring up into the flies, he screamed: "Sam! Sam!"

Every eye on the stage looked up. Fifty feet overhead, a figure in a red and white blazer balanced precariously on the crisscross bars of the iron grid. Cooper teetered and sat down on a bar, his feet dangling through the opening of the three foot square. Then he thrust himself off and came plummeting down, feet first, arms outstretched. There was a sharp crack and his body was jerked up in mid-flight. His shoes flew off and clattered down. The arms flailed, the body shuddered once as though the bones were trying to burst out of the skin; and then it was still, swinging gently, the feet just a yard above the edge of the teaser that masked the top of the stage from the audience.

Lennox sank to his knees and began to sob. The appalled silence was jarred by a fanfare from the orchestra on the other side of the curtain. Oliver Stacy, in dinner jacket, paused long enough to vomit in the wings, then slipped through the curtain, white-faced and smiling. There was a burst of applause. His voice rang out in cheerful greeting, and the warm-up for the New Year's Day "Who He?" show began.

· CHAPTER XV ·

THE BODY CAME
DOWN AND JERKED THE BODY CAME DOWN AND
JERKED THE BODY CAME down and jerked the body came
down and jerked thebodycamedownandjerkedthebodycamedown
andjerked THE. BODY. CAME. DOWN. AND. JERKED.
Lennox rolled out of the bed and knelt on the floor. He leaned
his elbows against the iron bedstead, pressed his palms together
and pressed his lips against his hands.

Alongside him, No. 17 slept open-mouthed and filled the
ward with the fetor of decay. No. 8 laughed in a baby voice. No.
20 scratched methodically with a monotonous rasp. No. 5 chanted:
"The Lord is my hospital, I shall not want. He marries me to
green Packards. He leadeth me leadeth me leadeth me. . . ."

"No. No. No. Not a hospital. It's a jail, that's what it is," No.
9 told him. "It's a jail run by the lousy Catholics and Masons
where they can pull off their crooked political deals. Nuns and
Priests letting on they're nurses and doctors. Spying me out. Re-
porting. Giving me blue looks and electric sparks out of the

294

walls. They know I won't let 'em run the country. I'll tell the papers. I'll tell everybody!"

"Did I ever tell you about paper?" No. 10 chattered with manic brightness. "Did I ever tell you? A sheet of paper is an inclined plane. A sheet of paper with lines on it is an ink-lined plane. An inclined plane is a slope up and a slow pup is a lazy dog."

There were steps behind Lennox, and a heavy voice said: "Jesus! Will you look at him? He's prayin' again."

Before the attendants could throw him back into bed, Lennox got up and climbed in. They laughed . . . two impervious men in identical white uniforms wearing the identical expression of indifference. The only way they could be distinguished was by their hair; one black, one red.

"Got you trained, huh buster?" the red-head said. "Not this time, though. Come on."

Lennox put on the blue bathrobe and the straw slippers and meekly followed the attendant down the ward.

"What day is today?" he asked.

"Wednesday."

The ward doors were unlocked and they passed out into a white corridor. Barred windows looked west across The Rock and halfway into New Jersey on this crisp, clear afternoon.

"More tests?" Lennox asked.

"Nope. You're all finished, buster."

"What now?"

No answer. Lennox shuffled in silence and terror.

"Are they going to lock me up for good?"

The red-head thrust open a door and led him into a tiled bathroom. Alongside the shower was a white table on which was neatly folded the clothing Lennox had worn the previous Sunday.

"Extra special for you," he said. "Why didn't you tell us you was a big wheel, buster? Wash up and get dressed."

In a daze, Lennox bathed and dressed. He looked at himself

in the wash mirror. He was completely unchanged . . . except for the three-day beard on his face.

"Why should I be changed?" he thought. "Nothing's changed inside me. I'm like all the rest. Sick. Feeding on what happened to Sam. Living on poison. Loving the poison. It's only the innocents like Sam who suffer. Our diet kills them."

Outside in the corridor, the red-head was waiting for him, sneaking a smoke like a convict. He pinched out the end of the cigarette, put it in his pocket, and took Lennox downstairs. There was a blurry business in an office of unlocking a file and restoring his possessions . . . money, watch, keys, and the gimmick book which he slid into his jacket. He flexed his right arm against it repeatedly. It was his one hold on his life.

There was further confusion in other offices; papers to be signed by a hand that could hardly bring itself to touch the pen, warnings and official counsel to be heard, a brisk lawyer whom Lennox vaguely recalled meeting before somewhere in the network. And most incredible of all, there was Ned Bacon waiting for him in the hospital lobby, leaning against a pillar like a Private Eye with his hat cocked over his brow. Bacon shook hands warmly and took him out to his car. Lennox was confused.

"Yeah," Bacon said as he drove uptown, "We kicked it around and figured the best thing would be to hand Cooper the rap. He was cooled anyway and there was no percentage letting you sit in the penalty box."

"You told them Sam wrote the letters?" Lennox faltered.

"Sure. That's how we sprung you. That lawyer could be a Federal judge if he was willing to lose money."

"But Fink and Salerno. . . ."

"Bob's a buddy," Bacon drawled. "We gave him the sign and he listened to reason."

"So everybody thinks Sam . . . ?"

"Yeah."

Lennox lay back in the seat, limp and helpless, too exhausted after three days of horror and remorse even to ask questions. He flexed his right arm against the gimmick book and let the arm drop into his lap. Bacon glanced at him and smiled knowingly.

"Been rubbing elbows in the marketplace, huh Jake?"

"I'm thinking of Sam."

"Hell, he's dead. Think about the Quick."

"I killed him, Ned."

"A rope killed him, Jake."

"I tied the rope for him."

"He was an amateur," Bacon said. "He was out of his class. Nobody killed him. He killed himself trying to mix with the pros."

"Trying to mix with the poison eaters."

"What?"

"Nothing."

"Did you write those damn fool letters, Jake?"

"Yes, I guess I did."

"What the hell for?"

"I don't know for sure yet. I think because I was sore."

"What at?"

"Myself."

"What for?"

"I don't know," Lennox said wearily. "It's like there were two of me . . . and one didn't like the other. You know how every man's got a voice inside him that talks to him like a stranger. Mine didn't talk. It wrote letters."

"You aren't thinking about taking from a head-shrinker, are you?"

"I don't believe in them."

"Stay away from those guys, Jake. I wouldn't trust a talent that wasn't crazy a little. It's the crazy that makes you the writer. Stay with it and enjoy."

"Enjoy what? I've lost everything. God knows I made it a fight . . . but I've lost everything. I've got nothing left."

297

Bacon laughed.

"If it wasn't for you, I'd still be in there doing word associations and ink-blot tests and— This is a big favor, Ned, but why? I thought you hated my guts after I sold you out to Blinky."

"Just the Irish temper," Bacon said. "I'm directing 'Who He?' starting February."

"It's going off."

"No it's not."

"But—"

"Sachs is moving over to our new show."

"Our new . . . ?"

" 'The Couple from Missouri.' "

"What's that?"

"Wake up, Jake. You remember that show we faked to cool the Kansas beef last week."

"The couple competing on give-away shows?"

"Uh-huh. The network bought it. We've had to change it around a little. Blinky'll tell you while we're signing the contracts." Bacon parked the car in the low Forties. As he got out he said: "And remember, this time we split three ways. No fifty percent for Grabinett."

They walked up Madison toward Grabinett's office. Lennox was even more dazed. A moment ago his world had been in ruins. Now it was apparently back in business and doing better than ever. He flexed his arm against his gimmick book. Then he phoned Gabby from a drugstore. There was no answer.

As they passed Borden's office building, Avery came bouncing out and saw them. Lennox flinched. Borden ran over and shook hands.

"Only got a minute," he said, glancing at his watch. "Have to grab an early train. What was it like in the hatch, Jake? They put you in a strait jacket? Do they really have padded cells? I tell you, let's have lunch tomorrow. I've got to hear all about it.

298

Give me a call, not too early." He waved buoyantly and darted into a cab.

Lennox watched him go. His jaw hung. He looked at Bacon with so much astonishment that Bacon laughed. "Wake up, Jake. You've got enough new material to eat free for a month."

"Material?" Lennox echoed.

"What else? You're lucky."

They continued up Madison Avenue. Everybody in the business was on the street and everybody greeted Lennox as though nothing had happened. Oliver Stacy hailed them and shook hands. "I'll give you a little advice, Jake. Next time you have to handle three in a hassle, don't fight high. Work low . . . from the gut down. And use your knees. Forget about fouls when the chips are down."

"Thank you, Oliver," Lennox said humbly.

Stacy spread his shoulders and massaged his ribs. "I can't figure how Cooper ever got up there. It took me twenty minutes to get across that grid and cut him down . . . and I know how to climb." He turned to Bacon. "How'd you do with her?"

"I'm going up to Brockton next week."

"She can't be that good." Stacy tilted his fingers at them lazily and departed.

Bacon led Lennox up to Grabinett's office. The signs had been removed from the corridor. Tooky Ween was in the main office with Grabinett and both greeted Lennox warmly.

"What a Christ Almighty thing!" Grabinett blinked. "That crazy Cooper jeopardizing a show like that. Tsk. Tsk. You get any good ideas down there, Jake? Ray was saying how we ought to do the mad scene from 'The Count of Monte Cristo' on the 29th. Jesus, you need a shave." He picked up the phone and ordered a barber.

"He helped my boy write a great tune," Ween rumbled. "I don't care what anybody says about him." He looked at Lennox. "Don't worry, Jake. I'm takin' good care of that property. His

299

sister's gettin' her fifty percent regular, and it ain't a bad check."

Lennox was too weary to argue. He phoned Gabby and there was still no answer. The barber arrived and shaved him while Bacon swaggered up and down the office with his hat tilted over one eye and organized the cadre of the show. It was to be a panel format on the insult level. Mr. and Mrs. Missouri would interview guest stars, challenge their right to celebrity and stardom, and demand to be shown. The stars would entertain to prove their merit. Ween would provide the stars from his stable. Grabinett would provide production and direction, Lennox would provide script.

They argued budget for half an hour and then signed the agreement. Jake's hand hardly trembled when he picked up the pen and signed his name. He was beginning to feel solid again. The three days were disappearing.

As he left the office, Grabinett called after him: "Regular show conference tomorrow at two. Don't forget. Have the script ready."

"Mel! Have a heart. I've been in the hospital since Sunday."

"So you had a nice rest. Get to work."

Downstairs, he met Kay Hill, very slim and English in tweeds and a fisher scarf, dashing into Sabatini's for a drink. She dragged him with her. Lennox went back to the phone booth and tried for Gabby at Houseways, Inc. She was not there either. He returned to Kay at the bar.

"So they let you out of the hatch, darling," she said. "Happy, happy day. We'll pickle it."

"My God," Lennox said. "Nothing's changed."

"Nothing ever does change. What's your brew?"

"Soda."

"Scotch and soda? Bourbon and soda? What and soda?"

"Soda and soda."

"Lent's a little early this year," she told the bartender. "Soda for my father. Listen, darling, there's no earthly reason why— Hello darling!" She waved to someone who kissed her cheek and clapped Lennox genially on the back. "Why you have to hire a pair of bloody squares from— Hello darling!" Another kiss and another clap on the back. "From Missouri to expert your new show. I'm your girl for the job and— Hello darling!—I'll sleep for it."

"Listen," he said abruptly. "What happened at your place Saturday night?"

"Oh that? I was bloody plastered. You pulled in around midnight with that Bleutcher bitch and—"

"Midnight? You're sure?"

"Of course— Hello darling!—and when Oliver ran out with her I thought the usual had happened." She finished her drink and snapped her fingers to the bartender. "Poor dear, he went out like something after a hot bitch. He came back like something after a cold shower; and I wouldn't turn my electric blanket on for him. What about that job? It's a cozy— Hello darling!— blanket."

Sabatini's was filling with the regular cocktail crowd, the men in the same grey flannel suits with white oxford shirts and large expensive ties, escorting the same pretty girls, exchanging the same dangerous dialogue that flashed sparks like steel knives scraping together. It was familiar and steadying. Sick, it might be, but it was the only life that Lennox knew. He actually was able to grin at Kay.

"I could use your body, love," he said, "but I wouldn't dare touch your dialogue."

"Don't be a bloody bug, Jake. You know I'm discreet on camera. I'd never say— Hello darling!" Another kiss and another clap on the back from somebody who paused to chat.

"What's with Cooper?" he inquired. "I hear he got into some crazy jam and hung himself in the middle of the first commercial."

Lennox looked at him. "It was an accident," he said slowly.

"Darling," Kay began. "Everybody knows poor Sam—"

301

"It was an accident." He turned to Kay and for a searing moment his eyes were more acid than hers. "Never forget that for a moment. Pass the word around."

"Yes, Jake," she whispered.

"He was a wonderful guy . . . too good for this business. I wrote those crazy letters. Not Sam. He died in an accident."

Lennox left the bar and walked south on Madison, the highway of his business, the highway of his life, the quintessence of Now. And the Now was the same Now of last week, last month, last year. Nothing had changed; nothing was lost, except Cooper. The life he had fought so bitterly to hold together still stood firm, better than ever . . . except for Cooper.

"I don't know how I'll ever make it up to you, Sam," he thought. "I don't know what I'm going to do. I can make the business jump through the hoop, but that's not enough of an answer."

He turned east in the Twenties, threading through the dismal sidestreets until he came at last to the little square with its sycamore trees, its Greek cross of gravel paths, its black and brass fence. He unlocked the street door of No. 33 and entered the kitchen. His heart constricted. There were the Siamese making love to what appeared to be Cooper kneeling on the kitchen floor filling their dinner plate. The figure arose. It was Gabby in blue jeans and a shirt, wearing dark glasses.

The plate was empty by the time he forced himself to release her. He looked at her, still without a word. He had knocked the glasses off in the first fierce embrace. She had a lurid black eye.

"Can you go inside?" Gabby asked. "Is it all right? We can go down to my place."

"It's all right, I think. . . ."

They went through the pantry hall into the living room. It was exactly the same, even to the pile of manuscript paper on the piano.

"Why shouldn't it be?" Lennox muttered.

"I had to give the skunk away," Gabby said. "I didn't know what she ate."

"He," Lennox said mechanically. "Raw chicken."

"Was it . . . all right in the hospital? Did they hurt you?"

"No. I'll tell you about it . . . Some other time."

With his arm around her waist, he paced up and down the long living room slowly, letting his eyes wander, not daring to think. At last he said: "A week's a long time on The Rock."

"Sometimes it's a lifetime."

"Usually it is. That's why we burn out so fast. Do you remember what you said to me the Sunday we ended this affair?"

"You mean began it."

"No. That was the end. It's been backwards all along. Here we are at the beginning. Let it be the real beginning."

"All right, Jordan."

He stopped pacing, took her hand and smiled artificially. "Good afternoon. May I introduce myself? Jordan Lennox."

"I'm Gabby Valentine."

"What does Gabby stand for?"

"Gabrielle."

"Jordan stands for Junky. That's a hophead . . . a lunatic."

"Oh Jord—"

"Shh! I'm introducing myself. I'm a crazy man, Miss Valentine. Unbalanced. That's what makes me a successful writer, they say. Some people don't believe talent is talent unless it's crazy. Do you think so?"

"No," she answered gravely.

"Now while I'm introducing myself, Miss Valentine, I should tell you what I write. You know the dirty words you see written on subway station walls? I write them. That's my job. I also compose poems in public toilets and do dirty drawings. . . ."

"Please, Jordan. . . ."

"Recently I was graduated to de luxe work . . . dirty letters. But I was so crazy I wrote them to—" He began to shake. "Remember what you said? That I was poison. I am. I am. Be kind to me. Kill me."

"You know the truth now?"

"Yes."

"Then don't waste it. Remember it. Don't throw it away. Use it."

"How long have you known?"

"Since Sunday."

"And you're still around? Why aren't you running from me?"

"I've known since Sunday morning, not Sunday night. I wasn't running Sunday, was I?"

"No. You were lying like an account man to save me." Lennox turned away. "How long did Sam know?"

"A week."

"And he tried to save me, too."

"Yes, Jordan. He tried very hard. He tried to protect both of us."

"Do you know why he did it, Gabby?"

"Yes," she said. She was about to blurt the truth of her last meeting with Cooper when she caught herself. "But you'd better tell me."

"I let him down," Lennox said bitterly. "He was a sweet guy, a whole man, the only normal in the business. He had sense enough to want to stay out of the rat-race and I shoved him into it. And then I let him down."

"How?"

"I don't like to remember."

"It'll be best for you to remember. You won't be free of it until you confess it. How did you let him down?"

"When he loused the song spot. He was shaky with stagefright. You saw him. Sure he loused it. Why shouldn't he? He wasn't a performer; he was a composer. He came offstage licked. And instead of standing by him I blew my crazy stack about the letters."

"What did you say to him?"

"Christ! What lousy things didn't I say! I called him a fag and a Judas and tried to get the cops to arrest him . . ." Lennox grunted in agony. "How can a man do a thing like that to a friend? He was half my life."

"He still is."

"He's gone."

"No, you still have him."

"I destroyed him."

"You can't destroy remembering him. Never. Always remember Sam Cooper, the whole man, your friend."

"It hurts," Lennox groaned.

"You're lucky. You can punish yourself for what you did. It's the people who can't confess who suffer."

"Is that why you think he did it?" Lennox asked.

"Yes," Gabby answered steadily.

"Why didn't he hold on? Just a few more days. I licked 'em. I beat 'em at their own game . . . maybe because I'm their own kind . . . but I came out on top. I've still got the old show. I've got a new one. I've got everything I was fighting for. Why couldn't he wait a little?"

"I put you on top," Gabby said.

"That goes without saying. I couldn't have done anything without you. I—"

"You didn't do anything. I did it for you. Roy did it for you."

"Roy! Audibon?"

She nodded. "I made a bargain with Roy. I told him I'd go back to him."

"You told him you'd . . ." Lennox slumped on a chair. "So that's why the show was renewed. That's why the network bought the new one. It was a deal. Yes?"

"Yes. So here it is," Gabby said. "The life you love . . . the life you've been fighting for so desperately . . . the life you want more than anything else in the world. Here it is wrapped in ribbon, and cheap at the price."

"Cheap!"

"Cheap. You won't even have to give me up. That's part of the bargain too. I can have a lover if I'll be discreet."

"You're kidding," Lennox said faintly. "Please don't, darling."

"No, I'm serious." Gabby watched him closely with solemn dark eyes. "You're two people in one. Everybody is, more or less, and it doesn't matter. But it does to me because I'm in love with one of you and not the other. I hate the one who built this life for you. I love the one who's trying to knock it down. He's the real Jake."

"You've got it backwards, haven't you?"

"You've got it backwards. You admire the wrong one. You're trying to protect the wrong one. I hate the one that's your favorite."

"But the letters? The crazy filth . . . ?"

"I don't care. He's the one I love. He's filthy because he's never had a chance, but he's the real Jake . . . the honest Jake. He's a man to be proud of; not the arrogant, hostile Jordan Lennox who hides him."

Lennox shook his head in bewilderment.

"Sometimes people fight to keep something alive when they should let it be destroyed," Gabby said. "That's what you've been doing. You taught me there are times when it's right to fight." She touched her eye. "I'll tell you about this some day. Now I want to teach you that there are times when it's right to surrender."

"What do you want me to do?" Lennox asked.

"Make a choice. All this and me for a mistress, or none of this and me for a wife." She backed against the piano, still watching him intently. "I won't cheat. I'll love my Jake just as hard as I can . . . as long as I can find him in you. But the rest is up to you. You can have your shows and your victories and your money, and take your chance of losing the real Jake forever. . . ."

"And you too?"

"And me too. Or you can let this life come down in ruins ... you know what Roy can do to both of us ... and start building the real Jake out of the rubble."

"Maybe you're wrong about the real Jake."

"Maybe I am. That's a chance you'll have to take. But it's a fighting chance, and you're a fighter, aren't you?"

"I used to think so."

"And there's one more thing. You know you're sick."

"I said I was."

"But you don't mean it. You're upset now, and ashamed. Later on you'll forget. You've got to go to a doctor."

"A talk-doctor?"

"Yes. It won't be easy."

"I don't believe in analysts."

"That's why it won't be easy. But you need one, badly. You'll have to promise to start and go through with it." Gabby took a breath. "All right, Jordan. There's your choice. Keep on fighting the old way, or tear it down and start fighting for something new. Make up your mind now."

Lennox stood up slowly. He looked once around the room and then was caught again by Gabby's intent gaze. For a long moment they stared at each other while a voice within Lennox cried: "Run! Run! Run!" Suddenly he reached into his jacket and pulled out the gimmick book. With one powerful swing of his arm, he hurled it through the garden window into oblivion. As the glass came tinkling down, he swung Gabby up in his arms and carried her upstairs to his bed.

"I cheated," she murmured honestly. "I dressed for the part."

"Sweetheart?"

"Ned Bacon told me you'd be home today and I know you're a sucker for girls in pants."

· CHAPTER XVI ·

THIS FRIDAY, ROBIN AND I
packed a bag, bought groceries and liquor, got into the car and
got off The Rock. We drove out toward Trenton, and ten miles
this side of Princeton Junction we turned off the express highway onto Gun Hill Road, went through the fat Jersey farmland
and finally reached Stokewold, a village of one church, one super-
market, one bank, one— Oh, one of each. You take the right
fork out of Stokewold around the pond and it's two miles to
Gabby and Jake's house which they've named Cooper Union.

By the time we reached Stokewold we were halfway into a
laughing jag. We always start laughing on the way to visit the
Lennoxes. You think about their accidents and adventures
building their house and you can't stop . . . The three sec-
ond-hand cars Gabby bargained for and bought which, one after
the other, broke down as soon as she got them home, turning the
place into a Used Car lot. The time Jake got arrested for trucking
their nine-foot plate glass picture window on the express highway. The big July Fourth party weekend when the water system

308

went haywire and Gabby tried to empty out a hundred gallon tank with a teacup. Privately, Robin and I call the house Hysteria Cottage.

Outside of Ned Bacon, Robin and I are the only people from the business who like to see the Lennoxes. The Rock's turned its back on them. But we love to come down to Cooper Union and help Gabby and Jake build their house. We hammer and saw and paint while Gabby lectures to us from Builder's Guides. Robin plants, mostly, and I'm the king of the concrete. I have a touch with a trowel that astonishes people . . . including myself.

The reason the house is still building is that they blew all their money on the property. They have about a hundred acres of farmland, meadow, timber, and whatever else they call rural-type land. The house (what there is of it) is on a small hill shaded by elms. A hundred yards behind the house is a tiny extinct quarry which was flooded out by natural springs years ago. We swim there in summer and the water's glacial.

Gabby's pregnant. Gabby's the cute type. Her figure's exactly the same except she looks like she swallowed the head of a torpedo. Ned Bacon, who lets on to be a shingling expert, spends all his time finding out if it's going to be a boy or a girl. He makes her lie down, borrows a wedding ring (Gabby doesn't have one yet), and dangles it on a string over her stomach. The theory is, if it swings in circles it'll be a girl and if it swings back and forth in a straight line it'll be a boy. So far the odds are seven to three on a boy.

Gabby hasn't changed a bit. Robin and I were there in April when they held a town meeting and we drove in with them. There were about a hundred people sitting on camp chairs in the church basement, and half of them were glowering at the Lennoxes because of the way the unfinished house looks. They're all rich Squares who write stinging letters to the Stokewold Star Times beefing about the gutter-bred Lennoxes who are turning their township into a slum.

309

This didn't make any difference to Gabby. She was on her feet a dozen times, lecturing and admonishing the township on ethics, fair play and civic corruption. Lennox sat solemnly alongside her and nodded his head emphatically to her points. Once he caught my eye and winked, but the laugh was on him because Gabby got him elected chairman of the Garbage Committee.

Jake does a few scripts now and then, most of them under a pen name now that Macro and Audibon have had him blacklisted (not officially) for Communism, which is a laugh. He sells a few stories. They struggle along. It isn't easy with those two trips a week to the talk-doctor to pay for, but they don't complain. Gabby tells me that Jake is having a rough time getting straightened out, but he doesn't bleat. Both of them are so grateful for their fighting chance that they act as though they've won already. That's why we like to visit them.

We never bring our troubles out to Gabby and Jake. You can always find someone on The Rock who'll enjoy listening to your headaches. In fact most people get sore at you if you don't complain a little. Happiness is the problem. You have to share it with someone to get full enjoyment out of it, but there's no one you can do this with on The Rock. If you tell one of the tight rope walkers you've had a lucky break, he's so jealous he's ready to kill you. So we save the good luck stories for the Lennoxes.

Gabby and Jake are glad if anyone else gets a break. They beam and shake your hand and she delivers a ringing lecture on how creative you are and how much you've deserved success. And they write you follow-up letters to ask how your success is doing and they make you forget that they've got problems too. The result is, you can't wait to be invited down to break your back building their house.

So we drove up the little hill this Friday afternoon and honked the horn. Gabby and Jake came pouring out of the house followed by the Siamese who looked like amateur tigers. Gabby kissed me. Jake kissed Robin. I wasn't too jealous because I've got a kind of yen for Gabby.

We yakked all that Friday night and didn't get to bed until three. Eight o'clock Saturday morning we were awakened by Gabby who was making weird noises in the unfinished study. When we investigated, she explained that she was trying to hammer quietly. We began to laugh, got into our work clothes, had breakfast with Jake and didn't stop laughing all day.

Sunday, the volunteer slaves started arriving to spend the day. Bacon pulled in with Olga Bleutcher. Then came the friends of exile ... the odd people who live on The Rock and never let it bother them. Eugene K. Norman brought a man with a guitar. Two of the prettiest girls I ever saw in my life drove up with a man wearing a red beard. In their car was a wicker picnic basket the size of a steamer trunk. They were artist friends of Gabby and spent the afternoon painting L*E*N*N*O*X on the RFD mail box.

After lunch, Lennox and I strolled down the hill, across the little valley and up into the rise where his stand of timber was. I looked back at the house and was suddenly struck by a resemblance.

"Jake," I said.

"Yes, Kit?"

"Look at the house from here, will you?"

He looked.

"What does it remind you of?"

"Should it remind me of anything?"

"Yes. That place you showed me out in Islip. Where you were a kid."

For a moment his face lost its calm and I had a glimpse of the agonizing road he was climbing toward adjustment. It shocked me and I was ashamed of my slip. I tried to change the subject. He stopped me.

"It's all right, Kitten," he smiled. "You haven't done anything wrong. These things have to be faced. The house does look like the old place in Islip."

"You see it?"

"I feel it." He was silent for a moment. "It's a funny thing. I spent half my life running away from that clam-shack, and here I am right back in it again."

"Any idea when you'll get this place finished?" I asked, still trying to change the subject. This time I succeeded.

"Who knows?" Jake said. "There's no rush."

"Don't those letters in the paper bother you?"

"Hell no!" He laughed. "You've seen Gabby's plans. You know how beautiful the house'll be when we're finished. What's the hurry?"

"Your neighbors'd like you to hurry."

"Squares!" he grunted. "They're just like the noodnicks on The Rock, Kitten. You find them everywhere. Rush. Rush. Rush. Nobody wants to work for the work's sake. They want it done overnight so they can have the result quick. But it's the work that's the fun. I finally found that out. Nobody's going to hustle me into rushing through the best part."

"How long do you expect to take?"

"There you go thinking like The Rock again. You mean three months or six months or a year, don't you?"

"It couldn't take longer, could it?"

"I hope it takes three generations," he said.

I didn't have any answer.

Sunday night we were the last to leave. It's a point of pride with us to show that we're the Lennoxes' favorite friends. We kissed them goodbye, drove down the hill and started back toward The Rock. We looked up and saw them, silhouetted against the lights of the house, arms around each other, waving madly. We started to laugh again.

"Crazy kids," I said.

"They're pure gypsy," Robin said.

312

"When the baby comes he'll have to get to work again."

"Gabby says they're going to name it Sam if it's a boy."

"What if it's a girl?"

"She says they'll name her Ned to teach Bacon a lesson."

We chuckled and rehashed the weekend and the glow lasted all the way to the George Washington bridge. There The Rock loomed up before us like a vast purple volcano, lights flaring over it sulphurously, the sky above reflecting the burning craters below. Robin began to cry.

"What's the matter, Robin?"

"Somehow I can't help feeling sorry for them."

As we drove across the chasm of the river back to the private chasms of our lives, we both knew she was lying. The weak never weep for the strong; they weep only for themselves.

Made in the USA
Monee, IL
15 February 2023